DISCIPLE

A NOVEL OF MARY MAGDALENE

SUSAN LITTLE

ISBN: 1451582102
ISBN-13: 9781451582109
Library of Congress Control Number: 2010904771

FOR KATHY,
WITHOUT WHOM, NOTHING.

AUTHOR'S NOTE

A woman searching for God in a man's world is often lonely in her work. Everywhere she looks, she finds men's ideas, men's experiences, men's rules. So it has been for me; so it was for Mary Magdalene. As a life-long student of the Bible, I had accepted the early church fathers' portrait of Mary as a repentant prostitute. But the light of recent scholarship reveals a different Mary, a woman of spiritual power and authority, a woman prominent among Jesus' followers. With Mary Magdalene thus illuminated, I began to imagine what her life might have been like, to create a picture consistent with my own spiritual journey. This book is the result of that imagining.

Disciple is a story of desire—the soul's longing for redemption in the divine. The characters in this story are flawed, as we are flawed. They live in a world, like ours, riddled with fear of those who are "other." And they face the timeless question: How can we embrace differences and live with each other without violence?

— Susan Little

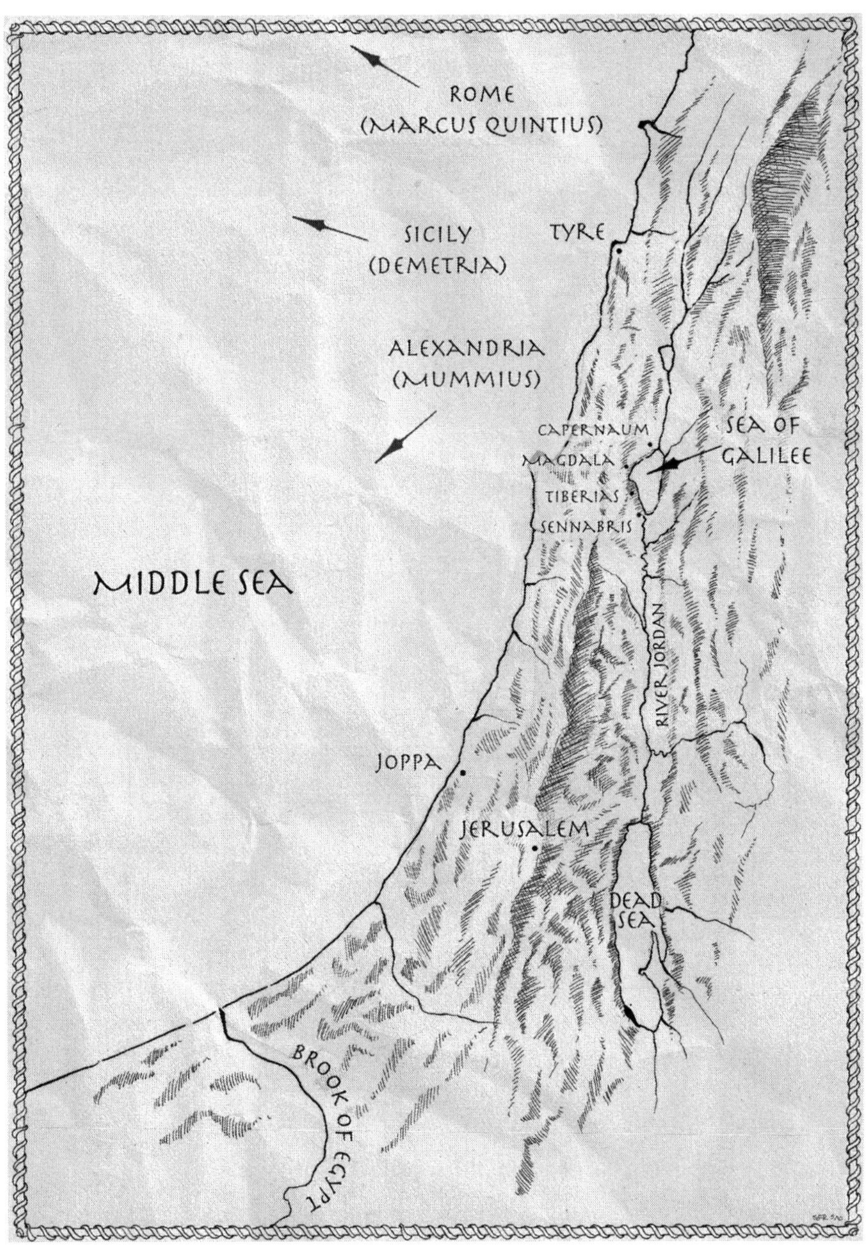
ROME
(MARCUS QUINTIUS)
SICILY
(DEMETRIA)
TYRE
ALEXANDRIA
(MUMMIUS)
CAPERNAUM
SEA OF
GALILEE
MAGDALA
TIBERIAS
SENNABRIS
MIDDLE SEA
RIVER JORDAN
JOPPA
JERUSALEM
DEAD
SEA
BROOK OF EGYPT

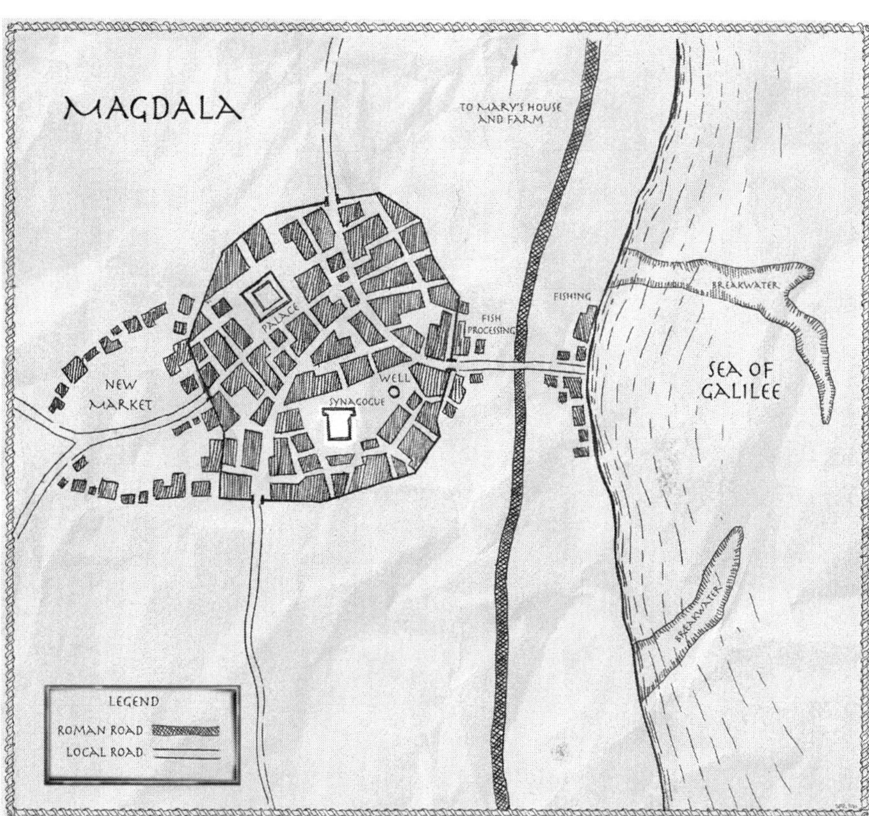
MAGDALA
TO MARY'S HOUSE
AND FARM
PALACE
FISHING
FISH
PROCESSING
BREAKWATER
NEW
MARKET
WELL
SYNAGOGUE
SEA OF
GALILEE
BREAKWATER
LEGEND
ROMAN ROAD
LOCAL ROAD

MARY'S HOUSE

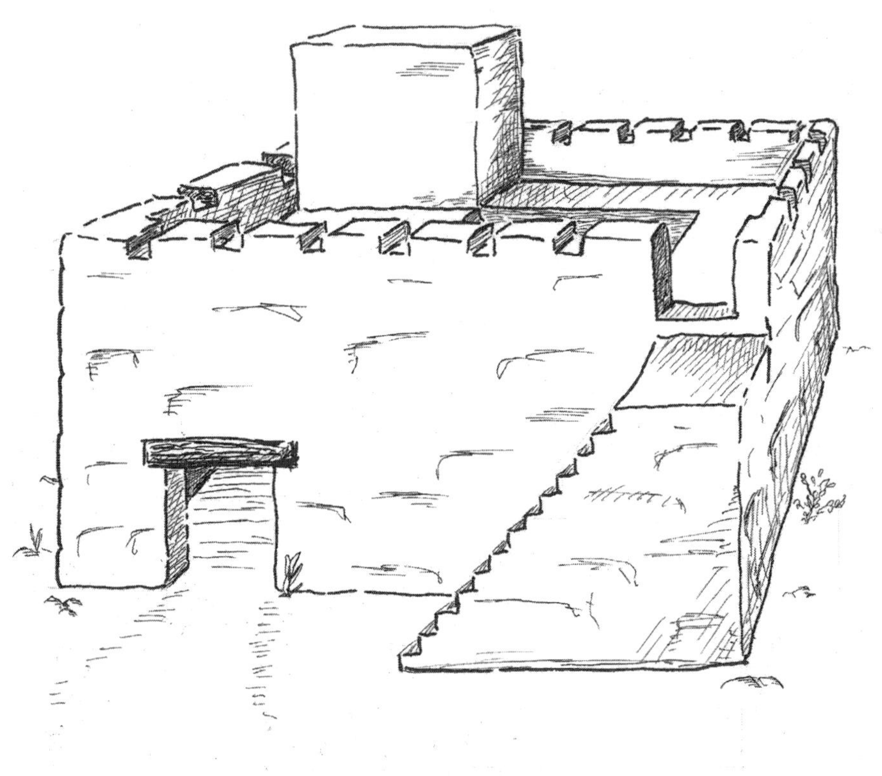

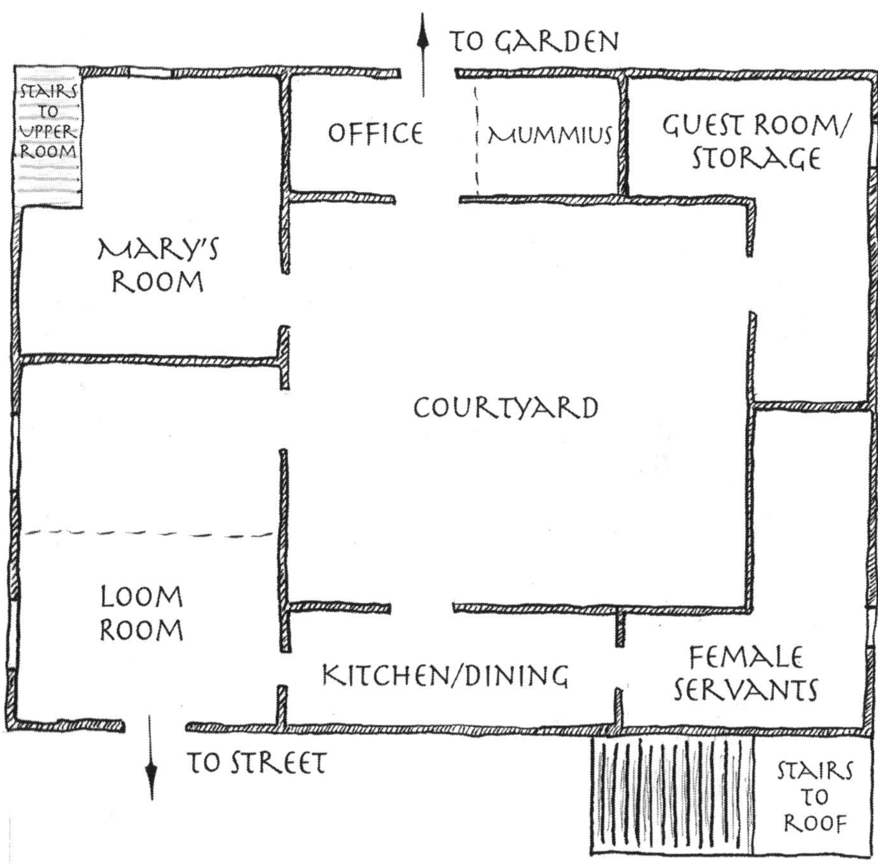
TO GARDEN
STAIRS TO UPPER ROOM
OFFICE
MUMMIUS
GUEST ROOM/ STORAGE
MARY'S ROOM
COURTYARD
LOOM ROOM
KITCHEN/DINING
FEMALE SERVANTS
TO STREET
STAIRS TO ROOF

×

SLAVE HOUSE NEAR ORCHARDS

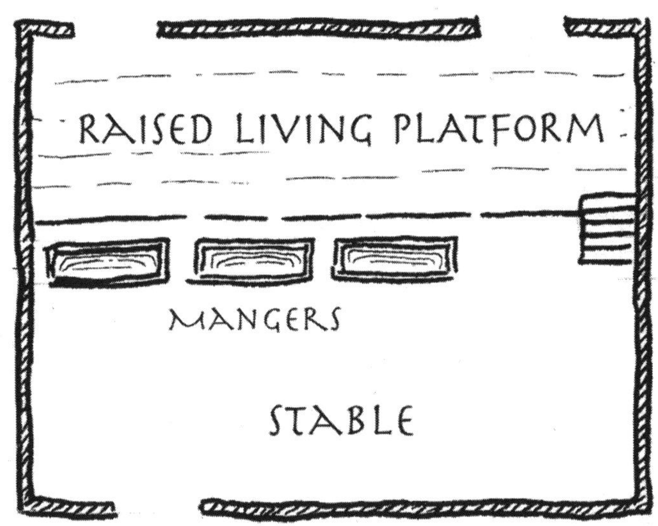

CHAPTER 1

"Demetria, why are you still in bed? It is time to go."

The Greek slave child groaned, turned over, and covered her head, leaving long blonde curls sticking out from underneath a smooth silk pillow. "Just a few minutes more," she muttered.

The woman, the strict one with the face of a cow, the one she had come to think of as the Handler, was persistent. "Get up this instant!"

Her command was followed by a shaking that told Demetria to comply immediately or she would be pulled from bed. It was then that she remembered the awful truth. She had been sold. Today she would leave Tiberias.

"Here, put this on," ordered the Handler, holding out a garment which Demetria recognized as one of her own ordinary tunics. "Quickly now!"

Prodded by the detestable woman, eleven-year-old Demetria was soon standing in the foyer of the townhouse, a great Roman domus, staring down at her sandaled feet and, next to them on the polished marble floor, a bag containing her possessions, such as they were. Her stomach growled, protesting that, because of her dawdling, there had been no breakfast.

"Pay attention, girl. This is your new mistress' steward, come to fetch you. His name is Mummius."

Turning her translucent, blue-grey eyes up to see what manner of escort this might be, Demetria found herself staring at a heavy belt clasp, hammered into an exotic artifact. She tilted her head back to take in a personage of monumental proportions.

He was a towering column of immaculate linen with a thousand vertical pleats in his long skirt and a sweep of white draping his torso and shoulders. There was a wide golden bracelet on his wrist and a collar set with rows of matching blue, red, and clear glass beads, all held together at the center by some winged Egyptian god, lying on his massive chest.

Atop it all, upon a dark and slender neck, sat his head and, on top of that, a black wig that flared out at both sides like dark sails. But it was his eyes—hooded, kohl-rimmed, cold-staring eyes—that set her shivering, as though he were palpating her spine with his stare. Demetria clutched the Handler's skirt and leaned into her.

"Good luck with this one," the woman said, peeling Demetria's hand off her dress.

"Thank you for your assistance," replied Mummius as he turned and swirled toward the doorway arch.

The Handler nodded at the bag on the floor, and Demetria understood that she was to follow him out, carrying her own bag. She lifted it with a little groan and slipped the strap over her shoulder. Mummius had disappeared; the Handler had retreated into the house. Dragging her feet across the marble floor, Demetria passed a row of marble plinths topped by statues of Roman gods. Demetria liked Mercury best of all, god of trade and travel, luck and gifts, with his winged feet and eager gaze, anticipating important adventures ahead. Perhaps Mercury would guide her on her journey. But why would he?

It seemed a lifetime ago that Demetria had been loaded onto a ship bound from Rome to Galilee where she had been robbed of her innocence and all she had ever known. Fair-haired and blue-eyed—as often happened among Greeks in Sicily—soft-skinned and tanned, she soon became the master's favored pleasure. But even as she was undressed and stroked, even as she was made to stroke and kiss other children, even as she was violated again and again, Demetria found within her misfortune a remarkable, salvific transcendence. When she was not with the master, she was largely left alone. She made little dolls of fabric scraps and painted faces on them with the cosmetics she had been taught to apply to her own face. She made up stories of being returned to her homeland by means of magical rescues and divine interventions. She giggled, sometimes, secretly, for slaves must not be overheard at play. Now she was being moved again, where and to what she knew not.

Demetria and Mummius walked along the western shore of the blue Galilean Sea. At times the diminutive girl ran a few steps to keep up with the Egyptian who strode ahead, one pace to her two, making their way from Tiberias to Magdala, a five-mile journey. After an hour, the strap tied around her bundle of belongings, not much more than a rope, really, was cutting into her shoulder.

"Is it much farther? The bag is very heavy."

Mummius responded to neither her question nor her discomfort.

Demetria turned her attention to the fascinating sparkle of the sea, or, more accurately, the lake, its surface glinting in the early summer sun. She could see a few fishing boats here and there and, beyond them in the distance, mountains the color of pinkish-grey limestone, rising up from the shore. The soothing sound of the sea lapping at the nearby water's edge was a consolation to Demetria. She had learned to take comfort when and where she could.

Demetria looked again at Mummius. *How old is he?* she wondered. *Perhaps in his fourth decade, but it is hard to know with all that paint. And where is he taking me?* The Handler had told her that she had been sold to an unmarried Jewess named Mary who lived in a town called Magdala and who needed a handmaiden. Demetria assumed that "handmaiden" was another word for bed-slave, for that was all she had known since being stolen away from her family in Sicily. She knew nothing of pleasuring women. *Who will teach me what to do?* she worried, sniffling, and causing Mummius to turn and glare. *Great Goddess, what if I must lie with him?* she thought, weeping all the more.

"Cease crying," said Mummius, holding out a handkerchief.

Demetria continued to sniffle and blow her nose as she walked, the weight of the bag becoming unbearable on her shoulder bone. When Mummius turned off the good Roman road onto a dirt path, her mind wailed, *How much longer?* She did not have to wait long for an answer. Only a few steps farther and she was standing at the door of her new home and her new life.

Compared to the well-appointed Roman townhouse she had just left, this was a hut. The walls were of mountain stone, four feet thick, dressed with plaster to make them smooth. The entrance was a simple archway built into the wall. Mummius ducked his head and went through. Demetria followed.

Standing just inside, she was surprised by how very large the room was, spacious enough to contain several looms of different sizes and construction, without crowding. Around the perimeter were crude tables laden with yards of folded fabric, mostly linen and wool, and something sheer, perhaps an exotic cotton. Before she could take in more, Mummius led her into a smaller adjoining room, obviously the kitchen. From the large table and sideboard she guessed that it served as the family dining area as well. Her escort led her quickly through another door into an L-shaped room. Demetria peered around the corner of the L and saw three cots. The one in the middle would be hers, she supposed, with neither the privacy against the far wall nor the convenience near the door. A few shelves completed the furnishings, not much else. At least it was clean.

Not surprisingly, Mummius said, "Your bed is in the middle. Put your things there."

Demetria lowered the burden of her small roll of belongings onto her bed and looked to Mummius for further instructions. Here in the rustic environment of northern Galilee, the Egyptian seemed out of place with his wig that resembled a close-fitting hat with a wide flap hanging down to his shoulders. And his outlandish, kohl-rimmed eyes. She wondered how he had acquired that unusual Roman name.

"Come with me," Mummius commanded.

They passed back into the kitchen. Across Demetria's mind flickered an image of the grand hall in Tiberias with its damask-covered couches where diners reclined to gorge themselves on roast meats and succulent vegetables, and where she had danced almost naked in front of drunken, leering guests.

Pushing the remembrance from her mind, she said under her breath, "Nothing special about this house."

"Don't be impertinent," said Mummius and cuffed her on the back of her head.

So this is how it will be. Demetria lowered her gaze, not daring to rub her head where it stung. Mummius took up a regal stance in front of her and strode outside into the courtyard. Demetria kept her distance, several steps behind.

For all the modesty of the house, the courtyard was a marvel. An expertly laid and meticulously swept limestone floor covered it. The rooms she had passed through and three others faced onto the courtyard forming a hollow square. That accounted for the L-shaped bedroom where she would sleep. In the center of the courtyard floor was a mosaic, an intricate work of art unrivaled by any the child had seen in the homes of even the important Romans. The mosaic pictured a lake teeming with fish and a flowing river. Around its perimeter were representations of the delicate pale blue flowers of a flax plant, a loom with half-woven fabric of brilliant stripes, and a fruit-laden fig tree. In a semi-circle at the bottom, as though holding the entire picture like a boat, were letters. They were all in gold tiles, and they looked like M-A-G-D-A-L-E-N-A. Demetria couldn't read, but she knew enough to recognize them as Latin, not Greek or Aramaic. She itched to inquire about the mosaic, but fearing another cuffing, kept her questions to herself.

Around the courtyard were pottery and glazed ceramic containers of every size and description, their variety exceeded only by that of the uncommon plants that flourished there. Demetria noticed a small, tile half pipe that connected the pots one with another, and water trickling through it. She had never seen an irrigation system before; in the house in Tiberias, slaves watered plants by hand. Around the courtyard, interspersed amongst the foliage, or out in the open center, were benches, some plain, some richly carved of Galilean oak. Demetria imagined the mistress of the house and her guests seated there in the evening, taking refreshments and talking or listening to music.

"Sit," said Mummius pointing to one of the benches.

She did not understand why she, a minor slave, was being invited to sit upon a bench in the central court. This house was strange. She would have to be vigilant.

Mummius swirled again and crossed the pavement soundlessly so that the effect of his movement seemed otherworldly. Demetria shivered. He was met by a stout, waddling woman, Jewish by Demetria's appraisal of her appearance. *And old!* thought Demetria. *Sixty years at least.* The woman was dressed in a tunic of rough wool, a heavy brown shawl draped in a large loop circling from one shoulder to the hem of her dress and back up again. *I hope they won't make me wear one of those ugly scarves,* thought Demetria, noting that the woman's head was covered with the kind of drab scarf common to Galilean women.

Demetria strained to hear their conversation.

"How is the mistress now?" he whispered.

"Just coming out of it. Her head still throbs when she tries to rise. What an awful night she had. I really don't think...."

And Demetria lost the gist of what came next. Mummius pushed past the woman and into the room across the courtyard. The waddler came toward Demetria, trying to hurry but only increasing the painful awkwardness of her gait.

"Demetria, is it? After one of those gods of yours. Pah!"

"Yes, Lady. Demetria."

"Don't 'lady' me! Only one lady in this house. 'Shoshanna' will do." At that, Shoshanna turned her ample rear end to Demetria and said, "Come on. Work to do."

In the kitchen Shoshanna set the child to grinding wheat with a small hand mill while she took what Demetria guessed to be dinner dishes from the shelves and set them on the table.

"You are small. How old, eight, nine?"

"Eleven years, Lady. Excuse me. Shoshanna."

"Pah! Too small," groused Shoshanna, more to herself than to Demetria. "What happened to you down there in Tiberias?"

The woman certainly was blunt, thought Demetria as she tried to decide how much to reveal. Stick to the main facts, not too many details, but no lies either.

"My mistress wanted a more experienced maid, I suppose. She is Roman and likes everything just so."

"All Romans want things just their way. Pah! Life was better all up and down the coast before that monument to Tiberius Caesar was built on our sea. The City of Tiberias, not five miles from Magdala—ridiculous! As soon as that mongrel Herod Antipas finished building it, they all had to live there, of course, like it was Rome of the East on the Sea of Galilee. They've even taken to calling our lake the Sea of Tiberias. Send them all packing, I say!"

Shoshanna looked around furtively as though to check for imperial spies who might report her indiscretion.

"You keep your mouth shut, girl. And that goes for everything you hear in this house. Especially anything about the mistress. Understand?"

Demetria nodded yes. She was very abrasive, this Jew. And that Egyptian, so arrogant. They were worse than the boorish Romans. As far as she could tell, no other youngsters were in the household. At the townhouse in Tiberias the master kept many girls, boys too. Here, it appeared she was to be alone among a handful of rude and uncaring people. She hated it already. Demetria's lower lip began to quiver, so she adjusted her position at the hand mill, turning her back to ensure that Shoshanna could not see. There she squatted, working carefully, pressing her tears down and trying to control herself.

Throughout the day Demetria was given household tasks. When she went to the roof to hang out laundry, the child could not reach over the line, so Shoshanna brought a crate for her to stand on, which had to be moved every few feet as the line filled with garments. "More trouble than you're worth!" came additional grousing from Shoshanna. And more stifling of tears by Demetria.

As she was moved from post to post, trying her best to perform her small jobs well, Demetria was aware of secret conversations between

Mummius and Shoshanna. She began to form the impression that there was something terribly wrong with the mistress. Demetria heard references to various medications and reports on whether she was resting or not and how she might be made to eat. *Maybe I am to be a nurse,* she thought, imagining herself emptying toilet pails and cleaning up after a sick old woman and wondering how this was better than being a pampered bed slave to a rich Roman.

At the end of the day, Demetria was told to wash up and come in to the evening meal. *So, I will not see her today,* she thought, since mistresses never took meals with servants. When she entered the dining room, Mummius and Shoshanna were seated at the table. Another woman was filling dishes with food.

"Hello, Demetria. My name is Rachel. I am the cook. Take a seat, there, next to me."

At last, a kind face and considerate voice. "Thank you," she said.

Rachel finished her serving, and they were just bowing their heads for the blessing when Demetria heard Shoshanna speak in a voice she barely recognized. Gone was the stridency and, in its place, love.

"Mary, my dear, what are you doing? You should be in bed."

Demetria looked up to see her entering, a woman of indeterminate age, thin yet muscular, not tall, and quite dark. Her long, black lashes were a thick fringe that framed big, glistening eyes the color of burnt umber, like the dye so prized by Romans. Her head was uncovered, and her black hair flowed down her back, a river of living ebony wood. 'Mary,' Shoshanna had called her. The mistress. The most beautiful woman Demetria had ever laid eyes on.

"It's all right, Shoshanna. I'm well enough now, and I wanted to greet our new little one. Come here, child."

Demetria scrambled from her place at the table to stand before Mary, too awed to speak.

Mary placed her palms on either side of the stunned girl's upturned face and welcomed her with the ancient Hebrew greeting, "Peace be unto you, Demetria."

"Mary!" gasped Shoshanna.

Mary kept her hands and her eyes on Demetria. "Child, what do you know of Jewish law?"

And in the barest of whispers, Demetria said, "Nothing, Lady."

"Well, our dear Shoshanna here tries to keep a very Jewish home for us. Some of our teachers say that touching a gentile is not something we are supposed to do. But you and I are going to be friends. You will get used to Shoshanna's rules, and Shoshanna will get used to you," said Mary smiling, first at Demetria and then at Shoshanna. It was in that moment that Demetria noticed the weariness around Mary's eyes and a bandage on her forearm, moist and dark from a wound underneath.

Arms akimbo, Shoshanna glared. She would not like it, a pagan minx here in their midst, but she would tolerate it. Bad enough that she had to put up with Mummius and his nonsense. Why did her darling insist on bringing these idolatrous strays into their home?

"Pah!" she grumbled and turned back to the dinner table.

And Demetria was utterly astonished to see the lady of the house take her seat at the head of the board and pronounce the blessing over their common meal.

That night Demetria lay on the middle cot with Shoshanna and Rachel snoring contentedly on either side. She had learned that there were many rules about food and dishes, preparation and cleansing. How did they keep track of it all? And yet, at dinner they all ate together, Mummius and the women, Jews and gentiles, slaves and the mistress at table together. No Roman would tolerate something like that. Demetria could scarcely swallow her bites of food for staring at the mixture of faces around the table. That and her burgeoning worship of the lady of the house.

Demetria couldn't sleep, thinking about Mary, the moment they had met, and Mary's caress that had set her cheeks on fire. Demetria's face grew warm even now remembering it. Shoshanna had kept her busy right up until mealtime, so Demetria had to rush to apply makeup to her eyes and lips and tie a ribbon in her hair, all the ways she had been taught to make herself attractive. Throughout the meal she stole glances at Mary and imagined herself being led hand in hand by the lady to her bedchamber.

It was understandable. Ever since little Demetria had been taken from her father's home and shipped to Tiberias, her one role in life was to do whatever the master wanted. She remembered the first time. The other girls had told her what to expect. They rubbed ointments on her tender parts to numb and lubricate, but it still hurt. She had been told not to scream on any account, but if she did scream, they had told her how to make it sound like a cry of pleasure.

Demetria had never before felt the lure of attraction, the way some of the girls did. Nor had she ever been sent to lie with a woman. But she would learn what Mary liked. She was good at learning. That was why the Roman mistress in Tiberias had determined to be rid of her. The master was overly fond of Demetria, and his wife was furious about it.

Demetria did not know how Mary knew of her plight, nor did she care. With that first greeting she thought she understood why Mary had brought her to Magdala. But after dinner, when Mary stood up from her place at table, bade everyone a good night, and went alone to her room, Demetria was confused.

Now from her own bed, Demetria saw the moon through the window opening that permitted a light wind to freshen and cool the room. The child turned her face dreamily into the breeze, and shut her eyes, taking in the scented night air. *She will call for me soon enough,* she thought, beginning to drift into sleep. *And it will be soft and sweet, not rough, like with men.*

CHAPTER 2

The next morning Demetria could tell by the slant of the sunlight at the window that she had been allowed to sleep late. Anxious questioning began: Was the mistress displeased with her? Was she to be thrown out? Where would she go?

Never was a sound so welcome as Rachel's voice summoning her to breakfast. Demetria hurried to the kitchen where it appeared that the rest of the household had finished eating and gone in pursuit of whatever their daily business might be. Demetria sat down on one of the wooden benches at the dining table, which had been set with a pitcher of fresh goat's milk, a bowl of figs and the remnants of last night's wheat loaves. Even as her mouth began to water, Demetria hesitated.

"Go on," invited Rachel, "help yourself."

Ravenous as a desert wolf, Demetria filled a plate with food and fell upon it as though she would not eat again for many days.

"The appetites of the young," observed Rachel with a grin.

"These figs are delicious," said Demetria with her mouth full and fig juice spurting out one side. "Excuse me," she said, wiping her mouth with the back of her hand.

"Mistress grows some of the best figs in the region," offered Rachel. "We ship them as far as Rome."

"Rome?" exclaimed the astonished Demetria. This place seemed far distant from anything Roman.

"Why, yes. She has a friend in Rome who conducts her business there. He was her father's colleague for many years. He makes a journey here every year or two. You most certainly will meet Marcus Quintius one day."

There was no end to the surprises in this house. During her time in Palestine, Demetria had developed the idea that the local Jewish inhabitants and the small but powerful population of Romans who had subjugated them were strictly divided. She had never observed any Romans mixing with Jews. But her new owner apparently had different ideas.

"If you are finished, Demetria, will you clear the table and help me with the dishes, please?"

Hardly anyone ever said "please" to Demetria and the courtesy caused her to look at Rachel more carefully. Perhaps they could be friends. She was no more than ten years older than Demetria. She wondered why she wasn't married; she was pretty enough.

Rachel showed Demetria the kitchen routines of washing, rinsing and drying dishes, how they were to be stacked, on which shelves, what food was to be discarded and what to be stored. Demetria worked in silence with the soap and scrubbing brushes she had been given. She was pleased when Rachel started to talk.

"We grow much of our own food here. We have figs, which you have already sampled. Date palms and pomegranates. Olive trees, of course. We grow wheat and barley. Nobody likes crude barley cakes, but Shoshanna insists that I make them for her. Doesn't want to get lost in the luxury of soft wheat loaves, she says. What she doesn't eat of the barley is given to the animals for fodder," Rachel teased, and they both laughed, sharing a joke at Shoshanna's expense.

"In addition to fresh milk, our goats bless us with delicious cheese and curds. Whatever else we need we buy from others or barter our produce for theirs. We certainly do not want for adequate food sources, praise to God."

"May I ask, Rachel, why you, a slave, say 'we'?"

"That would seem strange to you, wouldn't it? First of all, Shoshanna and I are not bondswomen. Jews do not often hold other Jews as slaves. Secondly, the mistress treats all of us like family, Demetria—slave and free. She does not draw social distinctions within the house. She has to keep up certain appearances in town and in her business, but here, we are family. She values our contributions and lets us know that she needs us, for the crops, the house and garden, and, most of all, for the cloth."

"The cloth?"

"Have you not seen the weaving room? Of course you have. You entered there."

"I didn't know what it was. I saw the looms, though."

"Mary is an expert weaver and she hires many others. Shoshanna is excellent, too. I am learning. The cloth produced here is quite well known throughout Palestine. Our most demanding market, though, is in Rome."

"Rome again."

"Yes, they send us lucrative orders for our cloth every year. Thanks be to God. And to Marcus Quintius Severus, too!" They laughed again. "I'm sure Mary will want you to weave. Have you ever been taught how?"

Demetria shook her head no, but with eager eyes, imagining Mary's arms around her, guiding the horizontal weft thread through the vertical threads of the warp, back and forth in a pleasing rhythm, intricate patterns emerging as they worked.

"Shoshanna is a splendid teacher, but very demanding. She can instruct you."

Demetria's daydream shattered as Shoshanna's meaty arms replaced Mary's in her imagination. She could hear the shrill voice in her ear, barking out instructions and criticism. At least Shoshanna wouldn't want to touch her. That was something to be thankful for.

"You have received a true blessing from the LORD in this home, Demetria. You will be safe and appreciated by everyone here."

Not by Mummius, she thought, remembering his whack on the head, and deciding not to reveal it to Rachel.

When the dishes were done and the table wiped clean, Rachel nodded to the sideboard that held a vase of wild tulips so red they seemed to shimmer.

"They bloomed this morning. Put them there," said Rachel.

Demetria placed the flowers in the middle of the table. The two of them stood for a moment admiring their work, the cleanliness of the kitchen, the order of the utensils and the final touch of beauty created by the tulips' flame.

"Well, now I must hurry to get the marketing done. Someone slept in quite late this morning and put me behind my schedule," Rachel said with a false pout. "Would you like to come to town with me?"

"Oh, yes! But, Rachel, I'm sorry I inconvenienced you."

"Never mind. Mary wanted you to have a good rest after your busy day. She knows what it is to need extra sleep."

What mistress concerns herself with whether a slave had a good night's rest? Demetria wondered.

Rachel went to a high shelf and took coins from a jar. She shouldered an earthenware jug and handed Demetria a basket and some woven bags.

"We can stop at the well, since I have you along to help carry the produce."

When they had walked awhile and there still was no sign of the town, Demetria asked hesitantly, "How far to Magdala?"

"A little more than a mile altogether. Our house is distant enough from the city to have access to all the conveniences, but without the disturbances. Magdala is not like Tiberias, Demetria. It has been a caravan stop on the trade route from Damascus to Alexandria for generations. It is loud and dirty. Camel drivers are all over the place. Unclean women troll in the streets."

Demetria did not react to Rachel's comment. Although she had lived a licentious life among Romans, Demetria had no thought that she might be in the category with common whores. But it was all the same under the Law, and no decent Jewish woman would be involved in such matters. Here, though, on the road to Magdala, Demetria was not thinking of her prior life. She only walked along like an innocent, taking in the activity around her.

At Magdala's center was its bustling market. The women passed a potter at a wheel in an open shop where his bowls and jars hung from hooks overhead. At the cobbler shop, sandals, goatskin water jugs, and other small leather items were stacked all around. Demetria saw a carpenter using a chisel to put ornate finishing touches on a table. He was surrounded by furniture, which might have been waiting to be picked up by its new owners. Another booth had heavy carpets from Arabia; still another, heady spices from the East. Local fruits and vegetables were displayed on long tables along with honeyed sweets from Damascus.

"Now let me see," said Rachel. "Almond oil and lentils. We are almost out of soap. And, what about a small roast of lamb? Would you like that?"

The two of them went from shop to shop making their purchases. Demetria watched as Rachel bargained good-naturedly with shop owners. She seemed to know everyone.

"Peace be unto you, Rachel."

"The LORD be with you, Nathaniel."

"Peace be unto you, Rachel."

"The LORD be with you, Esther."

By the time they got to the well, no one was there. The well was simple, a circle of stones about five feet in diameter and two feet high. Its rough wooden cover had been removed and was leaning against the stones. Demetria sat on the edge of the well and watched as Rachel prepared for her task.

"Early morning is the best time to draw water. It is too heavy a load to carry in the heat of the day. But since we are here and I brought the small jar, I will take some. Much of our supply comes from the cistern, but the water from this well is especially pure and sweet."

Rachel lowered the bucket by a rope, hand over hand, until she heard the splash far below. She allowed time for the bucket to fill and then pulled, this time with her back into it, until the bucket reached the top of the well. She carefully poured the water into her jar and set it aside.

"Here, help me replace the cover."

With effort the two of them moved the wooden circle over the opening of the well. Rachel prepared to heft the filled jar onto her head.

"Let me try," said Demetria.

Rachel laughed heartily. "Have you ever carried water on your head, girl?"

Demetria saw that it was nonsense, petite as she was, and shook her head no.

"We will save it for another time, then, Little Bit," said Rachel, giving the child a nickname that would stick.

Within a few days Demetria knew that her life had changed dramatically. She spent most of her time with Mary, learning the duties of handmaiden, like taking care of the mistress' wardrobe, refilling toiletries, and running short errands. She had not yet been asked for sexual favors of any kind. Demetria was still waiting for that, but it seemed less likely with each passing night.

One morning, early, Mary said, "Go, child, and ask Mummius to come to me. I wish to dictate a letter."

So far, Demetria had successfully avoided Mummius' quarters. When she needed to go to the garden behind the house, she took care to go out the front door and around the side rather than through the back door which led directly into the garden through his office.

"Go on," said Mary. "I'm sure he is at his desk just now."

Feeling small and skittish as a mouse sent to summon the cat, she approached the room that served as Mummius' office. She peeked around the doorway and, seeing him at his desk, took one step in.

"Excuse me, Mummius, the mistress would like you to come to her room for dictation of a letter." Then, in her unceasing effort to temper the unpleasant effect her presence seemed always to have on the steward, she added, "She sent me to ask for you."

Mummius did not raise his head from his work, but only scowled at her from under hooded eyes and grunted. Demetria knew that he would follow instantly. It had taken only these few days for her to understand that his irritation was for her alone and was in no way directed at Mary or the request for dictation. She turned and scampered back to the safety of Mary's room, leaving the Egyptian to his devices.

Early in his life as a eunuch Mummius had made a decision. He would not be the kind of eunuch who gave in to his emasculation, becoming almost like a woman and allowing himself to grow flabby of body and mind. No, Mummius was careful with his looks as well as his intellect, continually exercising both. He was angular, hard and sharp as a sword blade, working in the fields long after he could have given all labor over to others. He honed his mind with the rigors of his medicinal practice, which he had kept up strenuously, and was now of inestimable value to the mistress.

From his chest of scribal implements Mummius took out three pens of his own making and an inkhorn, which, upon inspection, he found filled with the thick, sticky substance that could be carried safely while walking. He tucked the utensils into his belt, picked up several papyrus sheets and headed for Mary's room.

He betrayed no emotion when he saw that Mary was reclining on her couch, the willowy Demetria moving around the bed cushions on her knees, gently combing her mistress' hair.

"Mummius, good morning! Do come in," said Mary to her chief steward.

"Lady," he said. And if an observer had known to listen for it, there could be heard in his tone, not only deference, but guarded affection.

Mummius positioned himself cross-legged on a small raised platform and removed the pens and inkpot from his belt and placed them beside him. He diluted the sticky ink substance with a bit of water, took up a pen, and waited for the sound of her voice. This was his moment. Mummius was fluent in many languages including the Greek, Latin, and Aramaic that Mary used, and he was vain about his script. It flowed from his pen effortlessly, and she never had to slow her speech while he wrote.

For thousands of years in Egypt scribes like Mummius had been members of a respected class, relied on by nobles and royalty to keep their treasured records. Distinguished scribes were endowed with the responsibility of making copies of the *Book of the Dead*, magical texts on papyrus scrolls that were buried with the deceased to guide them on their journey to the afterworld. This was Mummius' proud heritage. And this was his shame, that he had fallen to such a low estate, a slave in wretched Galilee, trapped in a cultureless town of the northern hinterlands surrounded by vulgar tribes and nomads. He longed for the Nile Delta of his birth. He longed for Bubastis, the city where he had learned his skills in inscription and music. He longed for his past.

Mummius' reverie was interrupted by Mary's dictation, and instantaneously square, serifed letters appeared on the paper. She was speaking Latin.

"To M. Quintius Severus from Mary of Magdala, Greeting. It was indeed a joy to hear from you again so soon after your last letter."

Mummius felt the texture of the paper through the nib of his pen. His paper. In Egypt Mummius had been taught how to harvest the giant sedge plant, form strips of its pith, lay out the strips in a vertical layer, then a horizontal layer on top and fasten them together with pressure and glue. Here, on the western shore of the Sea of Galilee, where papyrus grew in abundance, it was an easy matter for Mummius to acquire the needed materials and teach workmen how to produce excellent sheets and scrolls for his use in Mary's record keeping and correspondence.

"I note with pleasure your enthusiasm for summer in the country," Mary continued, "having been, as you were, eagerly gone from Rome with its politics and other noise. In truth, I do not know how you endure it, though it is my good fortune that you cope with its pressures easily. You were born to it, after all, and so are able to thrive there. How grateful I am that I can rely on you to handle my affairs so expeditiously. My dear, faithful Marcus Quintius, what would I do without you who have sheltered me all these years from the details of the business upon which I am completely dependent for my livelihood?"

At this there came a clatter from the platform and a slight crash upon the tile floor. Demetria laid down her lady's comb and rushed over to help Mummius retrieve whatever had been broken.

With a glare he pushed the girl aside and then knelt reverently to pick up the remains of a small onyx figurine of a cat. Sleek it was and polished to a sheen, a tiny thing that Mummius carried everywhere, a kind of talisman that he secreted within the sleeve of his robe and then arranged upon the platform or table near him as he wrote or played the lute and sang.

"Forgive me, Lady!" Mummius said, humiliated. And no one could know that in his heart he was also begging to another, *Forgive me, Maret.*

Looking at the broken statue in his hand, he remembered the day Maret first laid it there, a lifetime ago, in Egypt. Playfully, she had tied a strip of cotton cloth over his eyes and commanded, "Hold out your hand!"

He felt the cool weight of the cat in his palm and rubbed it gently. "Hmm, let me guess," he said, teasing her.

Impatient with the excitement of the surprise, Maret untied the blindfold. She bounced up and down on miniature brown feet, straight black hair swinging with the tempo. Long bangs brushed the tops of the graceful arch of her eyebrows, drawing attention to the intense, coal black of her eyes.

"The goddess Bast, for you, my love," she said, climbing into his lap and covering his face and neck with kisses. The cat goddess had a tranquil expression, and was adorned with a scarab breastplate and a golden necklace. "You see, I have had the base inscribed with her prayer: 'Hail, Bast! Coming forth from the secret place, may there be given to me splendor in the place of incense, herbs, and love-joys, peace of heart in the place of bread and beer.'" In their youth and innocence they were certain that Bast, whose purview included music, healing and fertility, would protect and bless them as they made their way through this life and the next, married for all eternity, beginning tomorrow morning, the morning which had never dawned.

"Why, Mummius, you're trembling. Let me help you," said Mary.

Demetria watched her lady climb down from the couch, glide over to Mummius, and kneel beside him. Demetria thought how Mary walked like a goddess, serene and unhurried. She liked to think of Mary as the incarnation of Demeter, the Greek goddess of agriculture, for whom she herself had been named. But Mary would undoubtedly be horrified by that sacrilege, devout Jew that she was. These Jews were so jealous of their god who, she had heard, even called himself a jealous god.

"I'm sorry, Mummius," Mary said as she laid her hand upon his shoulder, too considerate to mention the tears in the steward's eyes, or to ridicule the mourning of a cat statue.

Demetria noticed that Mummius, far from resenting Mary's interference, seemed to welcome her help. She saw him close his eyes and breathe in the lavender fragrance of her hair as he accepted her touch. *Strange*, thought Demetria, *the mistress of the house on her knees comforting a slave who has broken his silly toy and I standing here looking down on them unable to help.*

"Perhaps we can find another at the bazaar, or from a caravan sometime soon."

"No, there is no other. Please, don't concern yourself with such a trifle," whispered Mummius. Then, regaining his senses, the steward exclaimed, "Oh, my lady, what are you doing here on the floor? Let me help you up!"

Within moments order was restored, and they were back in position, Mary reclining on her couch, Demetria combing her mistress' long black hair, carefully bending curls around her fingers as she went, and Mummius upon the platform, pen poised, ready for dictation. Demetria noticed that his fingers brushed the place in his sleeve where the pieces were hidden of what had been a small onyx cat.

"Where was I, Mummius?"

"You were at '…I am completely dependent for my livelihood,' Lady," replied the shaken Egyptian, and Demetria thought she heard a choke in his usually smooth voice.

"Ah, yes. Well." She paused, collecting her thoughts. "We had quite a remarkable flax harvest this spring, under Mummius' skilled hand, and will soon be busy with our linen production. If I add one or two weavers this summer we will easily satisfy all our orders and be ready for wool when the sheep are sheared in November.

"Of late, a caravan came through carrying the most extraordinary silk from China, and thanks to Mummius' persuasive bargaining, we acquired it at a very good price. It takes dye quite beautifully, and we have been experimenting with different colors. I know you have clients who are always interested in purchasing silks. You can leave it to me to make and ship what I think those Roman ladies of yours would like, or you could send custom orders. It is truly remarkable fabric, Marcus Quintius. How your reputation as an importer will be enhanced by acquiring it! I eagerly await your instructions by return correspondence. Your devoted partner, Mary."

Mummius finished writing almost at the instant that Mary stopped speaking and began to put away his utensils and prepare to roll and seal the scroll.

"Just leave it for now, Mummius. I may add a line or two later. I will bring it to you when it is ready to go."

Mummius stiffened. "Yes, Lady," he said and swept silently away.

"You, too, Demetria. Off with you. I am sure Rachel has work for you in the kitchen."

When she was alone, Mary gazed out the window onto the garden below. It was in full summer flower, and its fragrances wafted up to her bedroom window on the warm air of midday. Normally the perfume of the garden would bring her joy. But right now, the imaginary band inside her skull started to tighten, and she had to fight off the instinct to panic, knowing that any strong odor might set off one of her headaches. Mary turned from the window. She heard the whisper of voices begin to call from within. Battling to govern her mind, she held her hands to her temples and forced her eyelids to close.

"O LORD, God, let this pass from me," she pleaded, trying desperately to banish the danger, struggling to command the unbidden.

This time, the threat subsided. After a few moments she had collected herself sufficiently to turn to the unfinished scroll and pick up a pen.

"It is with mixed feelings that I make this addendum to my letter, dear Severus. You can see that I am writing in my own hand, as I wish to keep this part of our correspondence confidential between us. I know it irritates Mummius when I do this. I grant him the benefit of my judgment that he esteems his own pure script as compared to mine and not that he harbors any desire to spy upon me in my private matters. In any case, I write to tell you that little Demetria has arrived safely but four days ago. You are right, she is indeed lovely, a bright child who will, as you suggested, respond easily to tutoring. I have not told her of my plan to teach her to read and write. I am saving that exciting bit for later when she has become more accustomed to her surroundings.

"She is adapting quite well. Rachel has taken her under her wing, though it is difficult for Shoshanna to accept yet another gentile in the house. You know how she is. Still, I am certain that Demetria will, in the end, have the old woman wrapped around her pinky finger. Mummius, however, is quite another matter. He so zealously guards his position in the household, as you are well aware. Demetria is, of course, no threat whatsoever to his influence, but if she and I are to be intimate as maid and mistress, I think he might become resentful and uncompromising toward her.

"Which brings me to my second point. Marcus Quintius, the child imagines, I think, that I am to take her to bed! This impression rests upon our first meeting during which I held her face in my hands and gave her a welcome of peace. Such was the intensity of her gaze upon me, Marcus, that I think she was quite smitten and probably mistook my gesture to have some carnal meaning. Then at dinner, she scarce took her eyes from me, though she tried to be surreptitious in her incessant glancing. I am sure Shoshanna and Mummius noticed it, too, though I have not spoken of it to them. I imagine that the child has never been the recipient of a chaste embrace from an adult, having been trained for whatever sexual pleasures were dictated by her master. Poor thing! She is fortunate, indeed, that you have been her savior.

"What was it you told me of her parents? Never mind. I shall ask her myself the circumstances of her birth. I am resolved, Marcus, to love her like a daughter, a child with whom the LORD himself has blessed me, if not in my dotage, at least in the maturity of years. I hear you disputing that you, not God, have sent her to me, but who is to say that Marcus Quintius Severus is not God's instrument, after all? The God of Israel has been known to use lesser gentiles than you in his service! In any case, when next you come to our humble Galilee, you will see quite a different Demetria and me a clucking mother. I hope that occasion will be very soon. As always, in deep affection, Magdalena."

Mary rolled the scroll, tied it with string and pressed a ball of soft clay over the knot. She ran her index finger across the top of her personal seal, an oval of lapis lazuli, dark blue, with brush strokes of gold and white near the edge, and polished like a mirror. Engraved upon the seal was an exact, tiny image of the mosaic in the courtyard. The pair had been a gift from Marcus Quintius on the occasion of her father's death when she inherited his property. Except for Shoshanna, who had been her nurse from childhood, Mary was alone in the world then, a woman of twenty years with a business to run. She had understood the gift exactly as her father's partner intended it—a vote of confidence in her abilities, as well as a pledge of his personal support. It was then that Mary of Magdala flung herself gratefully into the safety net of Marcus Quintius Severus, Roman noble.

As she had done hundreds of times, Mary turned the seal upside down and pressed it firmly into the waiting clay.

The next morning, Mary and Demetria sat together on a small bench in the center of the courtyard, so near the mosaic that their feet touched its edge.

"Where is your family from, child?" Mary asked.

"I was born in Sicily, Lady."

"Ah, Rome's breadbasket."

"What do you mean, Lady?"

"Well, it is so easy to grow things there. Sicily produces wheat and corn, fruit, wine, honey, sheep and cattle, timber and fish—the list is endless—faster than the island could ever use them. Your native land is more productive even than our farm here, bountiful as it is. Did you know that Sicily was once an important Greek state led by the City of Syracuse?"

"No, Lady, I did not."

"Well, at that time, it grew quite rich from agriculture. The Romans took it by force over two hundred years ago, and ever since, they have used it as a source of supply for their citizens and their armies. Sadly, most of Sicily's farmers were enslaved in the service of Rome's food requirements."

"My father was a slave on Sicily. Is still I suppose."

"A farmer?"

"Yes."

"Is that why you are called 'Demetria'?"

"Yes," the child said, brightening. "Demeter is a very strong and important goddess," and then fearing she had transgressed, Demetria apologized. "I'm sorry, Lady. I do not mean to offend."

Mary smiled. "Don't worry. We won't tell Shoshanna."

"Oh, good."

"Did you know that Demeter's most sacred shrine was at Eleusis on the Greek mainland? Not too far from Athens."

Demetria shook her head no.

"And did you know that from the beginning of her worship there she was subordinate to no male god? A rare thing among Greeks. Only Hera at Argos and Athena at Athens had such elevated status."

Demetria was staring now, still shaking her head.

"There is a story that Demeter was actually born on Sicily and that is why its land is so prolific. I'll tell you a secret, Demetria. Pigs are sacred to Demeter. We must not tell *that* to Shoshanna."

"But why, Lady?"

"Swine are forbidden to Jews."

Demetria drew out a long conspiratorial, "Ooohhh," as though she understood.

Mary continued, "I must say that what intrigues me most about Demeter are the Mysteries. You know?"

"I think I have heard about them."

"Mysteries are secret ceremonies that commemorate the suffering, death and resurrection of a god. They promise personal immortality for their initiates. Today, even some of our Jewish thinkers put forward the idea of a personal resurrection of the dead, though others are adamantly against it."

And Mary spoke to Demetria of the legacy of the mystic rites which were celebrated all over Greece, captivating the girl with the story. "No other god's rites could rival those of Demeter. They had begun as a simple festival of plowing and sowing but eventually grew quite elaborate. Just imagine it, Demetria, a line of initiates, called *mystai*, making a pilgrimage of fourteen miles along the Sacred Way to the temple at Eleusis. There they danced and sang songs and, after several days of fasting and prayer, were taken into the Hall of Initiation where a secret ceremony was performed. When it was completed, the *mystai* broke their fast with a communion in memory of Demeter. They drank a holy mixture of meal and water and ate sacred cakes. The rest was told to no one under pain of death," Mary said in a dramatic whisper, and the fascinated Demetria drew in a quick breath and said, "Oh, no."

Mary was able to tell no more because the secret of the ritual was successfully kept throughout antiquity. Most certainly there would have been a drama about a marriage of a priest and priestess representing Zeus and Demeter. Being very fertile, the divine couple would have a speedy pregnancy. The birth of the baby would be followed by a solemn announcement that 'Our Lady has borne a holy boy,' after which the worshippers would be led on a journey to an underground chamber representing Hades and then to a light-filled upper chamber representing the home of the blessed. There the most sacred objects would be disclosed to them, and, in a great ecstasy, they would throw off the delusion of individuality, and enter into the peace of unity with God.

Over the centuries the forms of the mysteries changed many times, but the underlying concept survived: just as the seed is reborn, so may the dead have a new life of joy and peace. Ultimately, that Greek hope would unite in Alexandria with the Egyptian belief in immortality and give rise to a force that would move over the known world. If anyone had told Mary now of that future and her role in it, she would have laughed.

Mary paused in her account, noticing that the girl's attention was fading. "Are you listening, Demetria?"

"I am listening, Lady, but my head is spinning. How is it that you know these things?"

Mary dropped her eyes and stared at the fanciful mosaic at her feet.

"I had a tutor. Or, rather, my twin brother Reuben had a tutor. Like all Jewish boys, Reuben started religious education at the synagogue school when he was six, but my father was determined that he have a broad education. Father's dream for Reuben was that he head a great trading family built on the work of our father's lifetime. He wanted his son to know the world through reading and through travel. He hired a tutor from Alexandria. It took almost the whole of that first year, but I finally cajoled my abba into permitting me to study, too. By then I was almost nine, and

I proved to be very quick. Also, I studied hard. I wanted to astonish my father, so he would not regret his decision to educate me. In truth, the tutor preferred me to my brother, who was less interested in his studies."

"Where is your brother now, Lady?"

A shroud of sadness covered Mary's face. "He's dead." After a moment of painful silence, she changed the subject. "Come, my dear. Let's go to the loom room."

The room was large by Galilean standards, perhaps six by eight paces. It was divided into two parts, the front half with a dirt floor, well packed, and the back half with a raised wooden platform. Several women were talking and laughing as they worked at looms large and small. Some were folding cloth to be added to the stacks of fabric already piled on tables around the room. And there were children, an infant sleeping in what looked like an animal manger and two toddlers playing with wooden toys on a blanket spread in one corner.

On the few occasions that Demetria had passed through this room, it was empty, save for the looms themselves. She thought little of it, only that the looms appeared somewhat ghostly, scattered still and quiet around the vacant room with no one to make them come alive. Now, they seemed to be singing. And, Demetria noticed, some of the women were, too.

Mary clapped her hands to get their attention. "Women, good morning."

They showered her with greetings. "Good morning, Mary." "God bless you, Mary." "You look well today, Mary."

"I have a surprise," she said, putting a slender arm on the young girl's shoulders. "This is Demetria, who has come to live here."

In unison they greeted her: "Peace be unto you, Demetria." The child managed a crooked little smile, caught off guard as she was by their unexpected welcome.

"Go on with your work. I will bring Demetria around to meet each of you."

Immediately to the left of where they stood, tucked into a corner by the front door, was a table piled high with wool. The fabric was three feet wide and might have been several miles long for all Demetria's inexperienced eye could tell.

"This is an order from a household in Magdala, ready to be picked up. You see it is a plain lightweight woolen. Adah will probably use it for new tunics for her children. She has five rambunctious boys whom she can hardly keep clothed, so prone are they to roughhousing. And, my goodness, they never slow their growing! Even though this is simple cloth for everyday use, we pride ourselves on good workmanship," Mary explained as she ran her palm over the wool and rubbed a piece between her thumb and fingertips as though inspecting its quality. She seemed satisfied.

"Our humblest clients are as important as the grandest. Something elegant, a scarf in silk for example, that goes to a Roman noblewoman might be used only once by her and then discarded, a meaningless trifle. On the other hand, Adah and her husband work very hard to pay for these goods. So, we are careful to be worthy in all that we do."

Mary continued around the perimeter of the room to the long table that Demetria had noticed on her arrival. "So many different kinds!" she exclaimed.

"I confess that I am proud of my modest textile factory," Mary said.

Mary guided the admiring girl down the row of piled fabrics. First came the woolens and then cottons from fibers cultivated along the Nile, some of pure white, others in a range of pale colors. Next were light colored linens.

"Mummius does an excellent job of overseeing our flax production. In the time he has been here he has almost doubled what we grow on our own property, making us less dependent on outside suppliers. The wool we buy from others."

Demetria observed that as she talked Mary was continually inspecting the cloth. Occasionally she would remove a section and hang it over her arm. Demetria tried to imagine what it would be like for a weaver to watch as Mary rejected a piece of cloth that she had woven. She would be humiliated if it happened to her.

As they moved down the row, the fabrics grew finer, more delicate or more deeply tinted. There was a medium weight silk blue as the sky with a smooth, shimmering finish and a heavy, nubbly linen the color of a ripe pomegranate. At the end of the table was a narrow bolt of cloth that drew Demetria like a magnet.

"What is this purple one, Lady?"

"Ah, you have exquisite taste, I see," replied Mary.

Mary remembered her first experience of the celebrated Tyrian purple. Her father had taken her to the renowned Mediterranean port of Tyre on one of his business trips to the coast. He hired a boatman to ferry them to the island where she saw ships that dwarfed those that sailed the Sea of Galilee. On the shore her father showed her lines of buckets containing crushed murex shellfish curing in the sun. The process of extracting the dye was laborious and costly. After harvesting, the shellfish had to be

"I enjoy making them. I can teach you, if you like," offered Jamileh. "On second thought, you would have to grow a bit, first. Put some meat on those tiny bones," Jamileh teased and added, "Welcome, Demetria."

Mary continued her tour, pointing out one more floor loom, somewhat smaller, where a woman named Hannah was making a group of bags with striking designs. Then she led the way up five stairs to the wooden platform at the back of the room. Demetria counted a total of six weavers on the platform, five of them working at vertical looms of about four feet by three feet.

"I am Sahadia," said one. "This is my daughter, also Sahadia, called Sudi. She is thirteen and just betrothed. See how she blushes! We are making her bridal veil. We are grateful to Mary for giving us this fine white wool for Sudi's wedding."

"I share your joy, Sahadia," said Mary, stroking Sudi's cheek, causing the girl to lower her head and smile at her lap.

Demetria was introduced to Judith and Leah and finally Avireina, who was making seamless robes of a kind worn by priests. "We do some of our own spinning here, but most of it is contracted out to other workrooms. Avireina's mother and grandmother are our best and most reliable spinners. We certainly keep them busy, do we not, Avireina?"

In the corner at the back of the platform was a girl whom Demetria judged to be about sixteen. She sat cross-legged on the floor leaning against the wall and working at something she held in her lap. It looked to be a decorative sash that might even have had a few gold threads woven in. "This is Chloe."

"Are you Greek?" Demetria blurted out so loudly that Chloe jumped and the others looked up from their work. "Excuse me, Lady. I just..."

"It's all right. Chloe is indeed Greek, but she cannot speak to you. She is mute," said Mary, laying her hand on Chloe's head. Mary pointed to the piece on which Chloe was working and explained, "This is twining. See how she twists the weft yarn over and under the warps simultaneously at two ends? I think she likes the feel of the fabric in her fingers as she works. Is that right, Chloe?"

The mute girl nodded vigorously. Demetria wondered what circumstances could have brought the speechless Chloe to this place.

The introductions completed, Mary stood at the back of the raised platform surveying her workroom. She looked out at the product of her labors. She looked out at eight women who were hired workers and much more. She looked out at the baby sleeping in the manger. She looked out at the best part of her life.

"You know, Demetria, this room was my parents' home when they married. They were a typical young Galilean couple, and the house was a typical one-room house. The front part with the earthen floor was where the animals were kept, their mangers lined up right where you see them. When I first opened the workroom, one of the weavers had the idea to convert them into baby cribs. The wooden platform where we are standing was our family living area, sleeping cots on one side and cooking and eating facilities on the other. I can remember as a small child, when we had overnight guests, Reuben and I would give up our beds to the visitors and take blankets down to sleep near the animals. I loved snuggling up to a warm lamb at night. It was a happy time for our small family."

Mary fell silent, and, after a while, when she didn't continue speaking, Demetria turned and saw her mistress frowning and gripping the wall behind her. "Lady, are you not well?"

Mary's tone was tense and urgent. "Get Shoshanna for me."

And as Demetria ran in search of the old woman, she caught a glimpse of her mistress' back disappearing at a run toward her bedroom.

CHAPTER 3

Demetria sprinted and found Shoshanna on the roof. When the woman heard the brief account, she dropped what she was doing and hurried to the staircase, knocking over an urn of barley flour in her haste. The stout woman's sudden agility alarmed Demetria, aware that any uncertainty concerning Mary was an uncertainty concerning herself. Demetria cleaned up the spilled flour and went back downstairs, hoping to learn something. It was a vain hope. For the rest of the day and through the evening, an air of nervous agitation stirred within the house, but no one spoke of Mary. Demetria went to bed without seeing the mistress again after the incident in the loom room. She slept fitfully until she was awakened by music, floating across the courtyard.

It was faint, but in the twilight of the early morning hours, when all the world was sleeping, it came on the still, fresh air like the soft sweep of wings. Demetria hushed her breathing, her ears trying to point to catch the melody—an alto lute, gently played, the timbre of the plucked strings deep and sensual, the sound of a caress.

The child slipped out of bed and, not bothering to reach for a shawl to cover her nightshift, tiptoed around the sleeping Rachel, through the door of their room and out the kitchen. The cold limestone floor of the courtyard stung Demetria's bare feet, but she didn't notice. Nor did she notice that the silken hair on her arms stood up in goose bumps. She was aware of nothing other than the insistent allure of the music, moving her across the courtyard.

Before she knew it, she was standing at the doorway of Mary's bedroom, pulling back an edge of the woven covering, at once knowing she should not, yet unable to resist. The room was black as the River Styx, and at first Demetria could discern nothing. But as her pupils dilated she began to make out shapes. She strained to pick out the familiar: the table with a water pitcher and bowl in the corner and Mary's bed against the wall. She could only assume that the mistress was even now sleeping beneath the piled up covers. Then something out of the ordinary. A human form sitting on the floor beside the bed. It was the source of the heavenly lute, it was—Mummius!

Demetria drew in a sharp breath and prayed to all the gods that he hadn't seen her. She lowered the curtain, still clutched in her hand, and stepped back against the outside wall, attempting to push her small body into the very plaster. Were they lovers, then, Mummius and the mistress? Demetria's pulse pounded in her ear like a drum announcing her presence. Her breath came in gasps, which she tried to muffle but which seemed louder even than Shoshanna's snoring.

Desperately, Demetria dashed for the nearest doorway. Collapsing into the corner of the room, she gripped her knees close to her chest, and waited. Her panic subsided and her respiration along with it, and again she strained to hear the music. Now, gliding above the sound of the strings was the unmistakable resonance of a human voice. The clear, high tenor held the lute in thrall, like a delicate spider web, weaving back and forth, sotto voce, largo. Demetria closed her eyes and swayed almost imperceptibly, yielding to the hypnotic sound. She seemed to be floating on the surface of water, no longer able to distinguish between her skin and the water itself, not knowing whether she breathed air or water, not caring.

With the shred of consciousness left to her, Demetria wondered how a creature like Mummius could possess such a voice. She did not recognize the language of the song, but it must be Egyptian, and this added to the enchantment. She heard the sounds, repeated languidly over and over. From the wistful melody she imagined it to be a love song, and if she had been able to understand Egyptian, the words themselves would have reinforced the thought. "Thou dost fill every land with thy beauty. Thou dost fill every land with thy beauty."

Demetria could not know, nor could the mistress herself have known, that the line was from a hymn, a prayer to Aton, Solar Disk, worshipped in the Eighteenth Dynasty as the only god, creator of everything.

"Fair is thine appearance on the horizon of heaven,
Thou living Aton, who first lived!
When thou dost rise on the eastern horizon
Thou dost fill every land with thy beauty."

Then the sound of the lute was no more. But the song continued and seemed to grow louder. Mummius must be leaving Mary's room. Demetria had taken refuge in the nearest room, a semi-public office where Mummius had his work area. There was one of Jamileh's large room dividers that separated the office from Mummius' sleeping cubicle. He would soon come right through here.

Muscles tensed, like a trapped animal, Demetria used her eyes to probe the darkness for a way out. It was too late. Mummius entered the room where she sat trembling in the corner. Demetria squeezed her eyes shut and covered her head with her arms ready for his assault.

It did not come. The song wafted past her as though she were not there. She stole a look from under the protection of her arms to see Mummius' tall form float, enchanted, across the room and around the desk. He seemed to evaporate through the heavy woven partition, like a ghost carrying a lute under its left arm.

Demetria did not hesitate. Adrenalin pumping, she jumped from her hiding place and ran for the courtyard door, around the corner to safety, and directly into Shoshanna's arms.

"Aiee!" Shoshanna exclaimed, as much surprised as the runner. "What were you doing there?"

Demetria felt her fear flow down the inside of her legs in a stream of warm urine.

"Into the kitchen!" ordered Shoshanna in a vicious stage whisper.

Demetria stumbled across the courtyard, Shoshanna following in her fast waddle. Inside the kitchen Shoshanna lit an olive oil lamp, which cast eerie shadows all around. She loomed over Demetria like a rumbling volcano in the moments before eruption. Demetria was quaking, too, from mortification and from fear of what Shoshanna would do to her. The thought of banishment back to the domus in Tiberias caused a cry to escape from her throat.

"Look at me!" Shoshanna commanded.

Demetria's eyes had been tethered to the floor, and it was with great effort that she raised them to look at Shoshanna's livid face. She stood there wretched, with salt water and mucus dripping from her eyes and nose and running in thin rivulets into the corners around her mouth. Little sobs made her chest and shoulders heave in a broken rhythm. A drop of blood was forming on her lower lip where she was biting it. She was shivering in her wet nightshift and bare feet.

"Pah!" said Shoshanna with what might have been the slightest trace of compassion. "Go change your clothes."

Shoshanna watched the miserable child drag herself to the bedroom. Much as she hated to admit it, this little Greek reminded her for all the world of Mary. She remembered Mary on the night her brother Reuben had died, flinging himself from a craggy peak at the north edge of the Sea of Galilee. She remembered Mary's parents, Rebecca and Aaron, as they watched their only son brought from the tragic scene by fishermen who had seen it. His body was carried home swinging in a crude sling and laid on the wooden platform in the servants' room. When Mary rushed in following the commotion and saw her grandparents and her parents weeping, and heard the women wailing, she knew what must have happened, though everyone circled around her, trying to spare her. Shoshanna remembered the sight of Mary, in a short tunic and barefoot, pushing free of their clutches to kneel beside her broken brother. She, too, had a face like Demetria's was now, a face distorted by grief and fear, every orifice draining into the total, wailing lament of her body.

At moments like this Shoshanna reflected on what it must be like to have the person most beloved torn away. She was older by far than Mary, had cared for her most of her life and loved her like a daughter. This love had only deepened in the years since Aaron and Rebecca died, leaving Shoshanna to protect Mary from the growing fury inside her. Shoshanna begged God to spare her Mary's death, begged to be taken first, and, in the next breath begged that Mary not be left alone in this world without her.

In the bedroom, the sleeping Rachel was roused by the noise of Demetria's fumbling for a clean tunic.

"Little Bit?" she asked, half conscious.

"Oh, Rachel, I did a terrible thing, and now I will surely be sent away from here."

"It can't be as bad as all that. Come, climb in," said Rachel holding up the blanket.

Demetria curled up beside Rachel and began sobbing again. Rachel forced herself awake.

"What is it? Tell me."

The story poured out, Demetria's anguish rising with every detail.

"Shh, shh," Rachel comforted.

"Do you think I will be sent away, Rachel?"

"I don't know, child. Let me see what I can do."

"Don't tell Mummius. And don't tell the mistress! I will never do anything like that again. Help me, Rachel."

"I will talk to Shoshanna. Say no more about it now."

Later that morning, the household gathered in the kitchen for the first meal of the day. Rachel was placing food in serving dishes and handing them to Demetria, who draggled back and forth to the table, setting them down. When Shoshanna came in, she had lost her waddle. She was on her guard, vigilant as a field commander surveying battle wreckage and making strategic decisions.

Mummius strolled in, humming. He was tall and fresh, looking as though he had slept deeply all through the night. As he took his accustomed place at one end of the table, he greeted the women with uncommonly good humor, calling each one by name, even permitting a nascent smile to crease the edges of his tight lips. Soon it became apparent that something was amiss. A lifetime of watchfulness alerted the Egyptian like a clarion. None of the women met his gaze. They spoke but little. Demetria fled from the room.

"I don't feel well," was all she said.

When she was gone, Mummius fixed Shoshanna with kohl-rimmed eyes.

"Well?"

"Last night she heard you singing."

"How?" asked Mummius, sure that there was more to it than Shoshanna would reveal.

"On her way out to relieve herself, I think," Shoshanna lied. Rachel had told her the truth: Demetria had been spying.

"What did you tell her?"

"Nothing yet."

And to Rachel, "You?"

"Nothing, Mummius, but we must explain."

Mummius and Shoshanna agreed that the time had come, sooner than they planned, for Demetria to learn the secret of the household. Shoshanna insisted on being the one to tell her.

She found Demetria standing against the low wall that ringed the roof deck looking out toward the Sea of Galilee, tendrils of blonde hair floating lightly on the occasional breeze. It was pleasant here in the morning with wisps of cloud just touching the mountain tops on the far eastern shore. From the roof of Mary's house on the western side at the lake's widest point, eight and a half miles shore to shore, Demetria stared out through a sparse grove of pine trees near the water's edge at the expanse of iridescent water beyond.

"Nice up here, is it not, girl?"

Demetria did not respond, but only closed her eyes, willing this moment in solitude not to end.

"Come. Sit."

The roof deck was stacked with diverse baskets filled with fruits and vegetables that had been dried in the hot sun. Utensils not being used were stored here, too, bowls, pitchers, an extra hand mill, everything for the kitchen. In the evening people sat on the roof after dinner to relax and enjoy the air as it cooled.

With a sigh of resignation Demetria turned toward Shoshanna. They sat down on covered reed baskets sturdy enough to hold their weight.

"I remember when Mary's father—Aaron his name was—added the outside stairway to this roof. He built the room below, our bedroom now, for his parents. His father was growing quite frail and his mother could no longer care for him alone, so Aaron and Rebecca brought them here to live.

"The children and their friends had great fun playing on the roof, running up and down the stairway. Endless games it was then."

Demetria thought Shoshanna's chatter an odd opening to the news that she would be banished from the household.

"Demetria, there is something you must know," Shoshanna said, examining the girl's face, watching for her reaction. "Our mistress is unwell."

"Our mistress," Demetria thought, still concentrating on herself. *She would not say that if I were to be sent away.*

"She is plagued with demons. Headaches, insomnia, terrifying visions. The worst is when she rants against herself."

Shoshanna had Demetria's full attention now as she tried to grasp what she was being told. Shoshanna paused to let it sink in.

"I do not understand. Demons, visions, ranting."

"She tries to hurt herself."

"Why does she want to hurt herself?"

Demetria's mind was flooded with images of Mary's lovely face, her divine demeanor, how she loved everyone and was loved in return. Then she was plunged back to the day she and her mother had been separated from her father and sent from Sicily to Rome. There she was stripped from the arms of her mother and shipped, alone in the world, from Rome to Tiberias. What would happen to her next if Mary hurt herself? And, like the child she was, Demetria started to cry.

The surly Shoshanna looked with tenderness on the suffering of this girl. She hugged Demetria to her ample breast and gave herself over to the compassion that had been building in her all morning. There they sat, woman and girl, Jew and Greek, while Shoshanna told the story.

"When the mistress was fifteen, she was betrothed. Somewhat older than many, it is true, but her parents were in no hurry to part with her, and she was determined to delay until she would find a husband who pleased her. Finally she fell in love with young Hanani ben Jahdo. Aaron and Rebecca rejoiced that their daughter had made a fine match. Hanani was—is—a blacksmith, skilled and hardworking, and, I might say, a feast for the eyes as well. He was completely love-struck, poor boy," Shoshanna chuckled. "Everything was being readied for the marriage celebration with families from both sides coming to Magdala for the week of festivities. What a mountain of work there was! Cleaning, cooking, trimming the garden, buying wine, hiring musicians, arranging accommodations. And making her beautiful dress."

Shoshanna paused to catch her breath, but Demetria couldn't wait.

"What happened?"

"Reuben died."

"The mistress' brother. She told me that."

"Did she?"

"Well, she did not say more, only that he died. She seemed very sad remembering it."

"Oh, yes. Sad she was. Inconsolable. It is hard to believe, but Mary was more devastated than their parents. For a couple to lose their only son—a tragedy beyond speaking. But Mary and Reuben were so close, inseparable all their lives. Twins, you know. Aaron and Rebecca grieved for Reuben as long as they lived. But Mary was changed; she never recovered."

"What do you mean?"

"From early childhood Reuben was a pensive little boy. As the years came on, his brooding deepened into sadness until finally he was despondent almost all of the time. Hearing his laugh ring through the courtyard became a rare event that we all cherished. Aaron sought the help of physicians from towns and from caravans. Rebecca prayed night and day. They made offerings. It was all in vain. Only Mary could coax her brother occasionally from his terrors, until at last he eluded even her." Salty water pooled in Shoshanna's eyes from tear ducts that Demetria had thought to be useless, dry as pine needles on a thirsty forest floor. "His closest friends deserted him."

"Why?"

"They did not want to risk contamination by association."

"But *why?*" Demetria moaned, suffering now with Shoshanna and with poor Reuben, whom she did not know.

"Why else? They thought him possessed. If a man loses control of himself, goes beyond the ken of physicians and priests, he is possessed by demons. God is punishing him for some great sin."

"What great sin was Reuben's?"

What, indeed? thought Shoshanna reverting into the depths of the puzzling enigma that beset her. She knew that the LORD punished sin. She knew that the greater the sin, the greater the punishment. She knew that sometimes even the sins of the parents were visited on the children. What she did not know was where the sin lay within this righteous family. She had been with Aaron and Rebecca for decades. She was a second mother to Mary and Reuben. She respected the grandparents on both sides. Who among them had sinned? It was beyond all knowing.

"I do not know his sin, child."

When a few moments had passed, Demetria said, "What of Mary?"

"After Reuben died, Mary withdrew. She spent most of her days sitting in lonely spots along the shore of the sea or seeking the solitude of the forest. She broke both her betrothal and the heart of Hanani ben Jahdo, who begged to see her, but was refused. She spoke little, only 'Yes, Abba'; 'thank you, Mother.' Her parents, having borne the loss of one child, now faced tragedy in the other's life. They did not know how severe the tragedy would become. One morning, Mary did not come to the kitchen to help prepare the breakfast, so I went to fetch her. Aiee!"

Shoshanna's face collapsed into her palms. Timidly, Demetria patted the old woman's shoulders.

"I found her limp in a chair in her room. There was blood everywhere, still flowing from gashes at her wrists, a shard of pottery fallen from her hand. I tore strips from my apron and tied them around her wounds. I moved her gently onto her bed before I called for Aaron and Rebecca. What an anguish!

"We knew that we must keep her condition hidden, because it would certainly be put about the village that Reuben's demons had taken up residence in Mary's body. Everyone would shun us, and the family would be ruined. That day, we committed our lives not only to doing whatever we could to help her, but to keep the secret. And so we have done."

Shoshanna put her face close to Demetria's. The tears were gone from her eyes and, in their place, ice. She gripped the bones of the girl's shoulders and dug her fingers in deep.

"Can you keep this secret, girl?"

"Yes," she whispered through the pain.

Shoshanna stared into Demetria's mind, taking her measure. "Swear it."

"I swear by all the gods," said Demetria and then gasped.

"Pah! The best you can do, I suppose," said Shoshanna releasing her.

"I'm sorry."

Gravely, Shoshanna instructed, "Demetria, the mistress must never go alone outside the house. And within the house we must know where she is at all times. Mary has agreed to this arrangement. Mummius and I are in charge of the watch, but one or the other of us may ask you to help at times. Do you understand?"

"Mummius does not like me."

"You must ignore that. Mummius is essential to Mary's health. Besides, you have adult responsibilities now."

Demetria was changed. She felt safer. What was more, she felt significant. She had been entrusted with an important confidence, and she would do everything in her power to be worthy of the trust that had been placed in her. Months would pass before that resolve would be called upon.

For a time there was peace. Demetria monitored Mary for signs of disturbance, watching for an opportunity to display her heightened sense of responsibility. But Mary seemed quite well.

Demetria settled into a comfortable routine. She was learning to weave, and Shoshanna was, as Rachel had predicted, an excellent teacher, especially now that she had relaxed her harsher attitude towards her. Demetria thought that her joy was surely complete until, one day, Mary called her to the courtyard. The warm eyes of the mistress danced as she patted the stone bench where she sat indicating that Demetria should join her there.

"Do you know what this is, child?" she asked displaying a large, well-used scroll.

"A scroll, Lady."

"Well, yes, a scroll, but no ordinary scroll. This is the Book of Moses given to him by God. Demetria," she said slowly, "would you like to learn to read?"

"I, Lady? Read?" Demetria's wondering eyes searched Mary's face for signs of a cruel tease.

"Why not you?" Mary said, laughing.

"Oh, Lady, could I, really?"

"Of course you could. I will teach you myself."

Just then Demetria saw Rachel passing through the courtyard. She jumped up and ran to her, grabbing Rachel's hands and spinning around.

"Rachel, the mistress says that I am to learn to read!"

Then the ecstatic Demetria watched Mary open her Greek translation of the Hebrew scriptures. Mary put her finger on the beginning line and closed her eyes. When she spoke the ineffably beautiful words, her voice turned melodious and lush. It seemed to come not just from Mary's mouth, but from deep inside her.

"In the beginning God created the heavens and the earth. Now the earth was formless and empty, darkness was over the surface of the deep, and the Spirit of God was hovering over the waters."

She paused, and it seemed that Mary was in a kind of trance, that, behind closed eyelids, she had gone somewhere beyond Demetria's reach.

Fearing that Mary's momentary silence was a signal of the imminent disaster she had been told to watch for, Demetria asked anxiously, "How can you read without looking, Lady?"

"I know this part by heart," she whispered.

Demetria could see that something both disquieting and irresistible took hold of Mary when she read the sacred scriptures. She did not know what it was, but she wondered if it would happen to her, too. She wondered if it was something that came with learning to read. From then on, she watched for it every day.

CHAPTER 4

As the months went by, Demetria made progress in her lessons, learning to read Greek, and to write a bit as well. When they were studying, no one bothered them, and Demetria imagined that Mary was exclusively hers during their time together. She was annoyed when, on one of their afternoons in the courtyard, they were unexpectedly interrupted by Mummius.

Smiling and offering no apology for the intrusion, he held out his hand. "A letter from Severus, Lady," he said.

"Excellent, Mummius!" Mary replied, taking the scroll. "Sit with us, please, while I read."

She flicked off the familiar seal with her thumb and unrolled the letter.

"Marcus Quintius Severus to Mary of Magdala, Greeting." Mary read aloud, then silently to herself for a moment. "Oh, listen to this!" she exclaimed, "I shall arrive in Tyre in two months' time from the date of this letter, and from there on to Magdala. It is with great anticipation that I imagine our reunion...." Mary blushed and read silently again.

Demetria glanced at Mummius and saw that everything about the Egyptian's demeanor, the softness of his face, and his forward-leaning posture, even sparkling eyes beneath the kohl, announced what effect the news of the impending arrival of Marcus Quintius had upon him.

Mary continued aloud, "Please tell Mummius to set aside time for review of the accounts of last year and estimates for the next. Soon I shall be able to turn these matters over to him entirely, as he has proved himself to be quite a worthy manager. To dear little Demetria, say that I am proud of her accomplishments at reading and weaving and look forward to seeing her again."

With that phrase, "seeing her again," Demetria placed another piece into the puzzle of her own life. She had heard that it was Marcus Quintius who had originally sent Mummius to Mary's household. He also must be her own connection between Tiberias and Magdala, though no one had ever told her so. Marcus Quintius could certainly have been one of the continual flow of important visitors to the domus in Tiberias. At most he would have seen her dancing, unless—had he been one of her unnamed lovers? Generally the master had kept her for himself, but occasionally she was offered to a special guest. Or, perhaps, he knew her in her brief passage from Sicily through Rome. Mary had told her that Marcus Quintius had business interests in Sicily. Maybe he knew her father.

What manner of man was he, this fantastic Roman? Did he sail around the Great Sea picking up piteous slaves and bringing them to a welcoming, Galilean mistress to be redeemed? Little did Demetria know that her question was oh-so-close to the mark.

Five years before, Marcus Quintius Severus had stepped gingerly off the boat that had carried him from Rome to Alexandria, a voyage of just over the customary two weeks. Standing on the dock, weaving slightly as he regained his land legs, he looked out at the Egyptian metropolis which had begun to rival Rome herself as queen of the Hellenistic world. He loved Alexandria—second to Rome, of course.

The magnificent city was founded three and a half centuries before by Alexander the Great, who used his Greek architect to lay it out with orderly, right-angled streets. At the crux of the two central avenues there developed a locus of culture and politics worthy of the name and reputation of the great young king. When Alexander died, Ptolemy, one of his Macedonian generals, became satrap. Nineteen years later he declared himself King of Egypt, establishing a royal line that would rule for almost 300 years. Under the Ptolemies, Alexandria continued to develop into a leading literary and scientific center. With the death of Queen Cleopatra, last of the Ptolemaic line, the Romans swept in and made it the hub of world commerce.

Marcus Quintius found every excuse to visit the great Egyptian city to further his growing business enterprise. If, at 41 years old, he was able to take pleasure in the plays at the theater and to soak up the treasures in the museum, all the better. As he walked the familiar streets of the massive emporium with its thousand shops and bazaars, the heart of the noble Roman surged as though this were his first visit.

He had been brought here by his father one spring when he was fifteen, just old enough to don the toga of manhood. He remembered struggling to master the art of keeping the heavy wool garment in place and properly draped. It had no sleeves, no seams, and no closures, so it was hard not to fuss as it kept slipping from his shoulder. He imagined his embarrassment should the toga unwind itself completely and fall to the ground, leaving him standing in his tunic, the toga piled up unceremoniously around his leather sandals.

"It just takes practice, Quintius," his father encouraged. "You must learn to relax. You must never appear to be ill at ease, especially wearing the toga. Shoulders back, head up, elbow bent at 90 degrees. That's it. Good. *Dignitas*, son, *dignitas*."

These many years later, as he turned with anticipation onto the Street of the Jewelers, Marcus Quintius' toga was as much a part of him as his thick brown hair and his stunning smile that showed straight teeth white as new ivory.

No one can create jewelry like an Egyptian, he thought, as he paced the shops and stalls. The day was hot, but he and the other shoppers and merchants were kept cool in the shade of vast awnings hung from miles of massive colonnades. He carried a dozen designs for which he sought artisans. At each stop he compared motifs and quality and made mental notes about which jewelers' craftsmanship most closely matched the individual pieces he wanted, necklaces with intricate inlays of multicolored glass set in fine gold, filigreed bracelets dripping with quartz ornaments, blue chalcedony and red carnelian, buckles and brooches set with feldspar and calcite crystals, rare pearl earrings and, as a surprise for his father, a thick ring with a large, flat turquoise.

By the time he had made his choices it was late afternoon. He turned to his steward and said, "Lucius Gavius, find me a scribe. I will take a cup of beer at that tavern across the street and wait for you there. Be quick."

Marcus Quintius liked to travel light. He kept his entourage to a minimum, two assistants, one in charge of logistics like lodging and transportation, one a personal valet to see to his clothing and toilet, and the venerable Lucius Gavius, who managed his business affairs. Like most noblemen of Rome, he did not like to get too close to the details. Lucius Gavius had learned his managerial skills under Quintius' father and knew more about commerce than Quintius ever would, by virtue of which he was the most valuable slave of the household. Marcus Quintius mused about the old man's future. He would certainly grant Lucius Gavius his freedom at retirement, but for now he was irreplaceable.

Marcus Quintius settled onto a short bench at a table in the front of the tavern where he could watch the street and catch the breeze. The deferential owner served him an excellent local brew, and then another. Customers came and went, Egyptian, Arab, and Nubian men, all of whom sat well away from the only Roman in the place.

He passed nearly an hour in the tavern, his eyes glistening, imagining his jewelry designs. At length, most other customers had departed and were, by now, probably making their way home for the evening meal. Tables were empty and a boy was sweeping the floor. Marcus Quintius paid no attention to the uneasy owner who was eager to close, but not eager to ask the Roman to leave.

At length, Lucius Gavius arrived at the tavern, scribe in tow. Wearing a sly smile, he stood next to his master's table and announced, "Marcus Quintius Severus, may I present Mummius, scribe of Alexandria."

"It took you long enough to find him. I hope he is worth the effort," grumbled Quintius, looking him over. Having served Rome in her legions, Marcus Quintius recognized fitness in a man when he saw it and wondered if the impressive Egyptian who stood before him had perhaps trained as an athlete.

"His fee is quite high, but the choices were few at this hour," said Lucius Gavius, still smiling.

"How much?"

"One hundred lines for thirty-five denarii, Lord," answered Mummius.

"What? Lucius Gavius, you have brought me a robber. Surely twenty denarii is the going rate," said Quintius in disbelief. "How do you dare, scribe?"

"I am the finest scribe in Alexandria," replied Mummius, without emotion.

"Is this a jest?" laughed Marcus Quintius.

"No, Lord, no jest," said Mummius.

Quintius thought of the skilled and famous scribes of Alexandria, who had once copied the entire corpus of the precious manuscripts of Greece, Aeschylus, Sophocles and Euripides. The vast records of the pharaohs. Curious works such as a history of Babylon written by a Chaldean priest, Buddhist writings from distant India, and the first translation of the Pentateuch from Hebrew into Greek, so essential to the large Jewish community in Alexandria. This young one thinks he is the finest of them all?

"Your arrogance knows no bounds, scribe. I will not associate with you. Find me someone else, Lucius Gavius."

Mummius turned to go. But Lucius Gavius held the scribe by the arm and took from his hand a small papyrus scroll. Without speaking, he unrolled the sheet and held it close to Marcus Quintius' face as if to say, "You have never seen anything like this before!"

Quintius' expression betrayed his surprise. Upon the scroll was written in five languages the following: *Gallia est omnis divisa in partes tres.* The opening line from Gaius Julius Caesar's history of his Gallic military campaigns: "All Gaul is divided into three parts." It was not impossible that this Egyptian would know such a thing, he supposed. Marcus Quintius read the line in Latin and Greek, and he recognized the third line as Egyptian, though he could not read it. The other lines were in languages with which he was unfamiliar.

"You speak all these?"

"I speak and write ten tongues and dialects, Lord."

"How is that possible?"

"They say I have a gift, Lord. I learn one, another follows."

Quintius examined the scroll again. It was only now that he saw the true significance of what was before him. Every line in every language was rendered with such precision and beauty that it seemed divinely made, more like an inspired work of art than a tedious piece of commerce. It must have required hours of uninterrupted effort to produce this scroll.

"Have you ink?" asked Quintius, thinking to fault the scribe with a test.

From his sleeve Mummius produced black tincture, a pen, and a scrap of papyrus. Lucius Gavius brought water to dilute the inky substance. Taking up the challenge, Mummius held his pen in readiness, and looked Marcus Quintius directly in the eye.

"Lord," he said, as though he had been waiting for the Roman to begin.

"Greetings, Father," he challenged back, dictating in Latin at a somewhat faster than normal speaking rate. "We are safely arrived in Alexandria just this morning. As we approached the harbor, the city shone at her best with the sky above as blue as the sea beneath, seeming all of a piece, and the buildings in the distance emerging directly out of the sparkling water." He paused.

Instantly Mummius stopped writing and turned the scroll around for inspection. Quintius could not believe his eyes. There was his letter in perfect Latin, masterfully inscribed and, what was more, a Greek translation written simultaneously below each line! It, too, was flawless.

"Jupiter's eyes, scribe, how do you do it?" he exclaimed, shooting an incredulous glance at Lucius Gavius who looked on with his smug smile.

"Your approval honors me, Lord."

"Approval is an understatement, Scribe," he replied, elevating Mummius' title by an admiring change of tone. After a moment's reflection, he said, "Have dinner with me."

"Dinner, Lord?" Mummius did not yet realize what manner of man Marcus Quintius Severus was: a man who went where he pleased, to do exactly what he pleased; the kind of man whose wealth bought autonomy unknown to others, the kind who could violate normal social restrictions, even of his own class, with impunity. If he wanted to have dinner with a common Egyptian, so be it.

"Yes. We will go to my quarters, where I will dictate my inventory to you—pay your exorbitant fee—and take the evening meal together."

Eager to agree to this surprising invitation, Mummius went off with Marcus Quintius anticipating a sumptuous dinner.

"Have you always lived in Alexandria, Scribe?"

"I was born in Bubastis, Lord…"

"I know that city."

"…into a family of some privilege. I studied at the Greek school there and proved to be quick at languages. My tutor insisted that I take also the curriculum at the Asclepian…"

"The temple of Asclepius, the Greek god of medicine?"

"Yes. There I studied dream *therapeia*, as well as Egyptian pharmacology and other healing methods of the physician-god Imhotep."

"You are physician, then, as well as scribe?"

"Yes, and I have incorporated music into my healing practices."

"Go on."

"I was attached as scribe to the household of a friend of my father. I loved his daughter. Maret. We were to be married." Then, quickly changing the subject, Mummius said, "I wish to repay your hospitality in some way."

"No need, Mummius. My pleasure, I assure you."

"At least let me show you around Alexandria."

"Thank you, but I have been coming here many years. I know the city well."

"Not as I know it, Lord."

Marcus Quintius thought. He was going to be here for several weeks while the jewelry was being made. He was always looking for fresh diversions. Mummius was a remarkable character. Why not spend some time with him?

"If you are amenable, yes, I would like that."

"More than amenable!" said Mummius. "Shall I call for you tomorrow?"

"Until tomorrow, then."

"May you sleep well, Lord."

In the weeks that followed, Mummius revealed his Alexandria. Marcus Quintius' prior experiences had been confined largely to the emporium at the center, with forays into the southeast quadrant with its grand museum, unrivaled in all the world, the tombs of the Ptolemies, Greek temples, the royal palace, and splendid parks where he loved to wander. He knew little of the Jewish northeast quarter and the north- and southwest sections, which held mixed populations dominated by Egyptians.

King Alexander had envisioned a great, egalitarian society blended from Greek, Asian and Egyptian cultures. That grand concept was soon abandoned by the Ptolemies, whose sole interest was the increase of their own power and wealth. With an efficient government and advanced technology, they had organized Egypt into a major economic machine, the proceeds of which they took for themselves through high prices, rents, taxes and tolls. Everyone from peasant to noble paid dearly into state coffers. Most of this wealth flowed through the city of Alexandria, producing its glories. The country became divided along socio-economic lines with Macedonians and Greeks at the top of the chain just below the pharaoh-god-king. They lived in a luxury that surprised even the Roman ambassadors who were sent there. Down the chain in decrementing status were Egyptians, Jews, Persians, Anatolians, Syrians, Arabs, and Nubians. It was into this multifaceted world that Mummius introduced his Roman guest.

In the Jewish quarter, Marcus Quintius observed a thriving community that elected its own leaders to a senate, or *gerousia*, and practiced its religion freely. Temples, which served as schools and meeting halls, as well as houses of prayer, were called *synagogai*, places of assembly. Marcus Quintius visited one of the *synagogai* and listened to a reading of the Law in Hebrew, followed by an interpretation in Greek, necessitated because many Greek-speaking Jews could no more understand Hebrew than he!

"How came such a large Jewish population to Alexandria, Mummius?" Marcus Quintius inquired after a day of touring the Jewish section.

"Numerous reasons, sir, over the centuries, but many thousands were forced to immigrate as captives from Palestine by the first King Ptolemy.

Even though his successor freed them, most stayed of their own accord. Their descendants have built the prosperous life you see around you now. They are much admired as artisans and businessmen."

"In Rome we much admire their fleets and the Egyptian grain they feed us with," laughed Marcus Quintius. "Why do they separate themselves within their own section of the city?"

"They are greatly attached to their ways. And they are jealous of their religion. They worship only one god, you know. He frowns on mixing their blood—and their money—with others'. Though they have been here for hundreds of years, they are still allied with their homeland of Palestine."

For all his familiarity with the entire city, it was in the Egyptian section of Alexandria that Mummius was most at home. He took Marcus Quintius out to the fringes, where many local people still maintained old religions and antique customs of dress. Mummius was known and favored everywhere they went.

"I envy you, Mummius," said Marcus Quintius during an evening of drinking and arguing politics in a series of taverns they visited. "Friends and freedom. If I did this in Rome, it would be bruited about the city within hours."

That night, their festivities continued until they found themselves part of a mob, shouting encouragement to combatants in a street brawl. Marcus Quintius would have taken a blow to the head save for Mummius, who pushed him aside and dragged him out of harm's way.

"Still envious?" asked Mummius, out of breath and doubled up with laughter. "Come on, let's get out of here. I have a friend for you to meet."

"It is very late to be calling on friends," responded Marcus Quintius.

"Never too late for this friend." They strolled to a particularly affluent part of the city and entered a palm-lined promenade bordered by a row of impressive houses. "Here we are."

Marcus Quintius was skeptical as they ascended a broad stone staircase leading up to one of the magnificent houses and approached the entrance. From nowhere a servant appeared.

"Mummius, welcome!"

"Haremsat, friend. It is good to see you. May I present Marcus Quintius Severus. Marcus Quintius, this is Haremsat, Chief Steward of this house."

"Welcome to the abode of Tais," said Haremsat, bowing formally.

He led them into a garden, lit by a dozen mounted torches which created an ethereal, jungle-like scene.

"Honor us by taking some refreshment," he offered, gesturing to a table laden with epicurean delights and legendary Egyptian beer. "The mistress will be out shortly."

Haremsat backed out of the room, and when he was gone, Mummius said, "Come, let's eat. No one in Alexandria offers a finer repast than the Lady Tais."

The night of revelry had left Marcus Quintius famished. He finished one plateful and was halfway through the second when Tais appeared. Marcus Quintius choked on his pastry and had to gulp down the last of his beer to clear his throat.

She was stunning, middle-aged to be sure, but self-confident enough to stand before him in a diaphanous linen gown that left her breasts bare and showed every luscious curve of her lower body beneath the finely pleated skirt. At her throat was a broad inlaid necklace with a winged Isis and, encircling her left wrist, a wide bracelet of hammered gold. Tais' already large eyes were rimmed with kohl making them larger still, and enchanting. Her nipples were rouged and taut.

"Close your mouth," whispered Mummius to Marcus Quintius as Tais approached them.

Tiny bells tinkled on her ankles as she stood on tiptoe and lifted her cheek to receive Mummius' kiss.

"Darling," she crooned, "whom have you brought?"

Not waiting to be introduced, the Roman stammered, "Marcus Quintius." And when she turned to gaze at him, he fell instantly into the magnetic burn of one of the most renowned courtesans of Alexandria.

"A man of Rome. Well, let us be entertained. Come." She led the way to a music room and indicated a couch where Marcus Quintius should lie down. She took another next to him. "Have you heard Mummius play?"

"I have not. Does he play well?"

"Like a god. What will he choose?" she pondered, as Mummius walked among the instruments. "The ugab, the oud, one of those lutes—kinnor or kithara—tambourine, rababa…? No, no, no—yes, the mizmar!"

Mummius picked up a bamboo woodwind instrument from a table and started a haunting tune, still slowly pacing the room. "Watch," said Tais to Marcus Quintius. She tossed a pair of brass cymbals, which Mummius caught in his left hand and began to strike, adding to the melody of the mizmar.

"That is not possible," said Marcus Quintius.

"Nor is this," responded Tais, seeing that Mummius had sat on a stool in front of a tabla with a goat skin top and a body inlaid with mother-of-pearl and ebony. He struck the drum with his right elbow, adding a pulsing rhythm underneath the melody.

Mummius was renowned for playing multiple instruments apparently simultaneously. In truth, he played them sequentially, but at such a rate and with such skill that, to his captivated audiences, he sounded like a trio of musicians performing in concert. Soon Tais moved to Marcus Quintius' couch and placed a goblet of beer in his hand. She stroked his face and whispered in his ear. When the song was ended, Tais rose.

"I'll be right back. Don't move, Roman!"

"Don't worry," he said.

When she was gone, Mummius also rose. "I'll leave you two alone." He slipped a small glass vial into Marcus Quintius' palm. "Drink this. You'll need it."

Many hours later Marcus Quintius exited Tais' house to return to his own rooms wanting fresh clothes and, truthfully, needing a break. The uninterrupted erotic escapades with Tais had left him drained. Indeed, every room in her house, every couch, every table, every carpet and wall had played host to their gripping passion. Marcus Quintius was in dire need of sleep. Mummius was waiting for him at the door.

"Going home so soon?"

"Oh, I'll be back," said Marcus Quintius. "Just want a short reprieve, that's all. By the way, Mummius, what was in that drink?"

"A simple pleasure potion," said Mummius, convinced that his remedy would have increased Marcus Quintius' sexual performance beyond his wildest dreams, and, thinking with a satisfied superiority, *If you only knew what I can do without the potion.* "I trust it did not disappoint."

"No, indeed it did not." He was suddenly aware of a ravenous hunger. "Let's eat. I'm famished."

Before long, Marcus Quintius was chewing poached fish, washing it down with wine and regaling Mummius with a detailed report on Tais' performance. Then, blithely, between bites, he asked, "What happened to prevent your marriage to, what did you say her name was? Maret?"

Mummius was caught off guard. How could he answer this question in such a moment? Could he say that the night before his wedding ceremony he went to sleep, a happy bridegroom eager for the morning? That he woke up in an evil dream that altered his life forever? Mummius' eyes grew dark; the muscles of his jaw pulsed with clenching and unclenching. He started to sweat as the tragic ordeal unfolded again in his mind.

On that night of nights, he had been awakened from sleep with a blow to his right temple. A man with a covered face shoved a cloth into his mouth, while another man bound his hands. As the assailants dragged him through the streets, he tried to think what was happening and who they were, but he was half senseless from the blow to his head and suffocating gag. By the time they pushed him through the door of a dungeon not far away, Mummius was in a frantic struggle for breath.

Someone spoke, a third man, from the shadows. "Put him there."

Torches on opposite walls of the dungeon cast a dim light upon a grisly table in the middle of the room. Heavy leather straps hung from its corners. His captors shoved him down onto the table, a relief, he hoped, but the hope was quickly extinguished. He could see the face of the third man now as he approached, holding a knife, which glinted in the torchlight, rotating the blade in front of his eyes, inspecting its edge. Mummius was about to die.

Up against the moment of death, he summoned every ounce of will and fought to escape, bending both legs and kicking hard. It felt like a massive lunge to Mummius, but the captors only laughed at his weak effort and forced him back down.

The man with the knife again. He said nothing, but nodded to the other two. They forced apart Mummius' legs and tied the leather straps in place. "No!" he screamed, but the gag constricted his wild plea into a muffled scream—the last sound he heard before a final blow to the head.

Mummius woke up on the floor of a small dark cell, stinking of urine. Mercifully, a clean blanket had been spread out for him to lie on. When he lifted his head, a terrible, throbbing pain forced it back down. When he turned over to tuck into a more comfortable position, a sharp pain in his groin caused him to wince. He put his hand between his legs, and there was the evidence of the awful, unthinkable truth.

Holding his aching head and wounded groin, he sat up and looked around. *Water,* he thought, seeing a small jug on the floor next to him. He drank gratefully and began to take stock of his injuries. Rubbing his scalp, his fingers came away marked with dried blood. Not much, so there would be no infection there. A big lump and a deep bruise, certainly. More bruises at both ankles where he had strained against the straps. But no lacerations. *Could not have been much of a struggle,* he thought.

Then, the worst. He spread his legs and looked. Strangely, Mummius' thoughts went to the tunic he had to pull up to stare at himself. He had been sleeping naked when the kidnappers came, but someone had put a tunic on him. A clean blanket, fresh water, clothing. Small kindnesses. From someone he would never know, someone like Maret. He pushed the thought of her aside and, resisting the anger that moved like a whirlpool deep beneath the surface, brought his attention back to what he was seeing.

He examined the cuts, short and precise. Not much to them really, skin mostly, made by a very sharp blade, quick and simple, eerily bloodless. Castration was nothing to the man with the knife, only a job to him.

"Lucky to have *you*, I guess," he said to his limp organ, which, when he spoke to it, surged a little, with its own, irrepressible life. And in that moment Mummius' rage was born.

It came up from between his legs, molten lava flowing into his gut and his lungs, searing everything in its path and spewing with a wild shriek from his mouth, like an erupting volcano. With a knife in his own hand, he saw himself holding each assassin by the hair, pulling back the head, slicing ear to ear and dropping the body on the floor of that dungeon. First one, then another, then the last, the butcher with the blade.

Standing over his personal battlefield, enemies lying all around, he watched their bodies emptying of blood, spreading out in deep pools. He walked among them, slicing off their loincloths and mutilating them, one by one, as they had done to him. Holding the bloody trophies in his hand, Mummius took a deep breath, surveying the holocaust around him. In the aftermath of the warfare within, his own soul slain in the carnage, the final battle was joined—the beginning of the war that would never end. Is this what he would become, a butcher himself, consumed with rage, devoting his life to vengeance? Then, uninvited, another image—of Maret. *I don't want her to see me like this!*

He felt the feathery Maret curled up in his lap, her small, soft arms around his neck and her warm breath in his ear. Mummius was plunged into the dark cave of his losses, and he wept. He wept for his manhood, for his beloved, for his future. He cried till his breath was only dry heaving sobs and every muscle had been used up in the effort. In that abysmal moment, there was only one decent thing he could imagine—he must give her up. For love of Maret, he would leave Egypt.

Now, these five years later, having accomplished much that made him so superior to other men, Mummius gazed at the admirable Roman who had befriended him.

Marcus Quintius' voice was softer now, asking once more, "Mummius, what happened?"

He answered simply, "I was abducted in the night and gelded."

"You are a eunuch?"

"None other."

Who could have known from appearances? Mummius seemed to be a man among men, muscular and fit, towering physically and intellectually above all others, not weak and soft as eunuchs were generally thought to be.

"Who did that to you?" he asked, unconsciously slipping a protective hand between his own legs.

"Someone who wanted to prevent our marriage, no doubt. Not her father; he would have chosen me for her himself. Maret had rebuffed another suitor, who was preferred by her mother. I think it was not beyond that woman to execute such a plan. I am sure they did it together."

"How came you to Alexandria?"

"I was nursed in a prison cell until my cuts healed. Then, with a chest of my belongings and a few coins, I was put upon a barge on the Nile and warned never to return to Bubastis. Alexandria seemed to offer the best prospects, considering my circumstances."

"Why did you not return to avenge yourself, and to recapture Maret?" said the Roman, whose lodestar was justice.

"Upon whom would I avenge myself, Lord? And if I did return, would I not risk further assault, or even death, from sources unknown? As for my beloved, I cannot give her children. I would rather free her to marry another than deprive her in that way."

"She must imagine that you abandoned her without a word," observed Marcus Quintius, immediately regretting his clumsiness. Intending to be kind, but only making things worse, he said, "Many eunuchs turn to lives of sexual service for men, do they not? At least you have managed to stay out of that."

"I would not be a whore, Lord," said Mummius, through gritted teeth.

Marcus Quintius Severus looked at the young Egyptian and saw an image of himself, a man of the world, a man destined for a life of letters, a husband established in a noble house with a loving, well-bred wife surrounded by lusty sons and beautiful daughters. Only Fate had tragically changed his course, a mere toss of the dice by some heartless deity, toying, as they do, with humans.

In a burst of enthusiasm, Marcus Quintius Severus exclaimed, "Come to Rome with me!"

"My lord?"

"Come to Rome. I could use a man of your talents."

"I know nothing of Rome, Lord."

In truth, Mummius had longed to go to Rome, to put as much distance as possible between himself and the country of his grief. When he turned his back on Bubastis, he had taken a Roman name as a pledge to make his way there. He was smart enough and cunning, but he needed a patron, and here was one delivered into his very lap. The Roman was already beholden to him, having experienced the sexual prowess imparted by his potion. There would always be that weight on the balance scales of their relationship. Mummius formed an idea that, just days ago, would have been absurd.

Mummius was not the only man ever to sell himself into slavery, but it was by no means the norm. Slaves came from everywhere. They had to, because slavery was a great engine, which fired the economy of Rome and sustained her social structure. As many as one-third of the people in Rome and Italy were slaves. Even Romans of very modest means owned a slave or two. The imperial household and the civil service used thousands of them. The City alone had 700 slaves just to maintain aqueducts and keep the water flowing. The rich sometimes owned many hundreds, often motivated more by ostentation than necessity. In fact, Marcus Quintius' teacher had been a distinguished scholar from Greece, a man who, in order to earn a living, had sold himself into slavery as a tutor for boys of the highest rank.

Because the average life expectancy of ordinary slaves in the Empire was probably less than twenty years, hundreds of thousands were required every year to replace those who died. The slave population was not sufficiently self-propagating to satisfy the need, so Rome stretched out her arms and raked in a vast human harvest. Often after a war, disposal auctions were held during which soldiers could buy prisoners of war as slaves. In hard times throughout the Empire, parents were known to sell their children into slavery, and men their wives. It was not uncommon for individuals to be sold for non-payment of a debt. Penal enslavement arose from a conviction in law for grave crimes. Because infant abandonment was widespread, foundlings provided a considerable number of replacement slaves. Even the Roman aristocracy sometimes exposed unwanted children to the elements, particularly baby girls. Slave traders were proficient in collecting these children, discarded so heartlessly. Such was slavery in the Roman world.

But for a man like Mummius there were benefits to being under the protection of a wealthy and influential Roman, benefits that no man without the citizenship could hope to gain. Mummius seized the moment—and the man. He did not require social freedom. His was the freedom of the mind. He would indenture himself to Marcus Quintius Severus as a slave.

Quintius eagerly accepted Mummius' offer, and they spent the next hour agreeing on a contract. There were specific conditions restricting his duties to business affairs and allowing him to work for others at his own discretion, which would enable him to become financially independent. He would have a prominent place in the household and a salary in addition. Any work outside the household would be paid directly to Mummius at fees negotiated by him with his clients, never, of course, to interfere with his primary duties to his owner. He could not be sold without consent. He could buy his freedom, if he chose, after seven years.

Their negotiations completed, Mummius committed the agreement to papyrus. Putting away his implements and looking at Marcus Quintius, Mummius declared, "So it is done, Lord!"

But Marcus Quintius astonished him.

"Friends don't call each other 'Lord' in Rome, Mummius."

What did this mean? All he expected was passage and a patron. Now he had a friend?

"How shall I address you then?"

"Call me Severus," he said.

Satisfaction draped over Mummius like a cape. His relationship with Marcus Quintius did not fit ordinary categories. Mummius was too intelligent for that and Marcus Quintius too generous. Over the years they would become ardent comrades. Marcus Quintius would offer manumission to Mummius time and time again, but Mummius would refuse to be freed. Every time Mummius spoke to Marcus Quintius, or wrote to him in a letter, he felt it rise again, the ineffable satisfaction of hearing him say it that first time, "Call me Severus."

CHAPTER 5

Six weeks had passed since the arrival of Marcus Quintius' letter spun Mary's household into a flurry of preparations. Meal and entertainment planning was underway. Shopping and washing were incessant. Housekeeping was so comprehensive that even storage areas were undergoing rearrangement. The weavers tittered as Mary inspected their inventories again and again and pressed them to complete their orders. She was frequently to be found in the guest room that she was making ready for his stay.

"Rachel, have Demetria help you with these baskets. They need to be relocated, those to the loom room," Mary said, pointing out several, "these to Mummius' work room, and those three to, oh, my room, I suppose. How did all this clutter collect in here?" She surveyed the room. "And, Rachel, make sure Shoshanna airs the bed linens."

"She has already done so, Lady."

Demetria had never seen her mistress so unrestrained and wondered what kind of man it was who could stimulate such high spirits in her soft nature. Late one afternoon, Mary announced abruptly that she wanted to go into Magdala to do some shopping.

"The shops will be near closing by the time you get there," protested Shoshanna.

"I'm sure there will be plenty of time," said Mary lightly.

"But Mummius will not return from his trip to Tiberias until tomorrow morning. There are things I must complete here by this evening. There is no one to go with you. Wait until tomorrow. Please."

"Don't be silly, Shoshanna. Little Demetria here will come with me. Will you not, my dear?" said Mary, cupping the girl's chin in her fragrant palm. "She is overdue for an excursion."

Demetria looked at Shoshanna with a face full of uncertainty. She had never been entrusted with the responsibility of accompanying the mistress away from home. She wanted to go, but she was apprehensive, too.

"Oh, all right," agreed Shoshanna hesitantly. "Get your cloak, Demetria. I will prepare a purse and water bag."

On the way out Shoshanna took Demetria aside. "Don't worry. It will be a short trip."

"Shoshanna, I'm not sure. What if her demons...?"

"Mary will be fine, has been fine for weeks now. Just keep her in view at all times. And, Demetria, I trust you. You're a good girl."

Demetria glowed in the unfamiliar light of Shoshanna's praise, but she was very uneasy.

On the energetic walk to Magdala, Demetria relaxed a little, enjoying the lady's chatter and the fresh, open air.

"The Greek name for Magdala is Taricheae," said Mary.

"The place of salted fish."

"Yes. It has been famous for its preserved fish industry for many generations. In fact, the Sea of Galilee is so abundant that, during festival times, fish are exported to Jerusalem to feed the masses who go there to celebrate."

By the time they went through the eastern gate Demetria and her mistress were laughing, making faces at the smells and shouts and good-natured fish-tossing by workers in the processing area.

"No wonder this is called the Fish Gate!" Mary joked as they passed through.

Shopping with Mary was different from shopping with Rachel. They did not go to the main market outside the city wall to the west. Instead, Mary frequented small, somewhat exclusive shops that dotted the old city center. When they entered Mary's favorite jeweler's shop on the Goldsmiths Street, Demetria couldn't help gaping at the gleaming rows of bracelets and rings. On a high shelf behind the shopkeeper there was even a pure golden goblet, something that might be found in the domus in Tiberias.

Trays of earrings were produced from behind the counter. Examining them in a polished brass mirror that she held in one hand, Mary tried them all on, until finally she found a pair that suited her.

"Do you think Marcus Quintius will like these, Demetria?" she asked, shaking her head this way and that, causing the earrings to jump and sparkle.

Seeing Mary admiring herself in the mirror, Demetria was swept back to an image of her Roman master as he adjusted his toga and summoned her. "Demetria," he had said, his voice husky with lust, "I want to look at you." Obediently she slipped off her tunic, and let it slide to the polished marble floor. She smiled up at him, as she had been taught to do. "Leave the earrings on," he said.

"Oh, yes, Lady, what man would not?" she replied, her knowledge of Roman men's desires going far beyond what it should have been in so young a girl.

Mary took coins from the purse that Demetria carried and counted them out for the shopkeeper. When they left the shop and walked through winding streets, Demetria watched her mistress touch the new earrings. Shake her head. Touch the earrings again. And again.

Shortly they crossed the town square, filled with people and busy shop stalls and booths that were all different and yet somehow looked alike. Demetria lost her bearings. Mary took a right turn through an alley and stopped before an imposing building.

"Here is the synagogue, Demetria. I want to go in and offer a prayer. You must stay here. Pretty little pagan girls are not so welcome inside," she said, an unfamiliar edge in her voice. "I'll be right back."

"But, Lady, it will soon be dinner time. Shoshanna made me promise…," Demetria protested, alarm bells sounding inside her head.

"Shoshanna is a busybody. Don't argue with me, Demetria. Just do what I tell you. Sit down now and wait for me to return," ordered Mary, putting her hand on Demetria's shoulder and pressing her down onto the steps.

Her mistress had never given Demetria orders before. She had never been impatient with her. She had certainly never spoken ill of Shoshanna, except in a loving tease.

Demetria's concern must have showed in her eyes, because Mary's tone softened. "Really, my dear, it is quite all right. I will only be a moment."

Demetria sat on the lower step of the synagogue and waited, munching on a honeyed sweet that Mary had purchased for her at the bakery and watching the hustle of the square. Licking her fingers and listening, she made a game of picking out languages from within the polyglot of Greek, Latin, and the local Aramaic Chaldee, mixed with other languages that made no sense to her.

All sorts of people passed by with purchases carried home from the large market on the other side of town. She had been there with Rachel watching bales of spices and silks from the East beyond Damascus being unloaded and stacked at shops up and down the street. She remembered seeing carpets with intricate designs being unrolled and examined. She saw a man carrying one on his shoulder now, still fuming at the shopkeeper who haggled over prices, swearing against highway robbery, but secretly glad to pay any sum for his Arabian treasure.

After a time, Demetria grew impatient. She noticed that the sun was falling low on the western horizon and, for the first time, she was aware of how long she had been waiting. People had already gone home to prepare their dinners around the family fires. The smells of baking bread and roasting meat were wafting through the air. *Time for the evening meal*, she thought.

Stalls were folding up around her, and a vague apprehension began to mount in the waiting girl. The comforting sounds of bleating lambs on tethers and cooing doves in cages were gone from the streets. The chatter of commerce and politics slowed and was replaced by the mushrooming din of nightlife. The mix of languages developed into cacophony, sharp and threatening. Prostitutes set off on their night's trolling and rough looking camel drivers started drinking. Several of them leered at Demetria as they stumbled from a nearby tavern. Instinctively she pulled her knees up tight to her chest and tucked her cloak in around her.

Demetria leaned harder into the tall column that helped to support the portico of the synagogue and hoped that her position at the house of prayer would afford whatever protection she might need. She watched the door of the synagogue as though her staring might cause it to open and reveal her mistress. What was taking so long? Finally Demetria could wait no longer. She crept up the stairs to the front door of the synagogue. She reached out one trembling hand and touched it. Would the Hebrew god be angry, she wondered, when he saw what she was doing? Bravely, she shook off a shiver of fear and pushed open the great door. Demetria did not need to venture inside. One peek told her that the building was empty. Surprised and confused, she closed the door quickly and slipped back down the stairs. Why would her mistress abandon her in front of the synagogue? Where had she gone?

When Mary deposited Demetria on the steps outside and went into the synagogue, she intended to return shortly. She moved quietly inside and whispered the affirmation for entering the portals of the synagogue, "Through thy great loving-kindness I have come to thy house, O God; with reverence I will worship thee in thy holy shrine."

Mary passed by a few others who paid her no attention, lost as they were in their own prayerful concerns. She slipped unnoticed into a secluded corner and bowed her head. From the time of her babyhood, under the watchful eyes of her doting parents and grandparents, Mary had lived as a faithful Jew. She had been praised for her good qualities, never allowing her beauty and intelligence to eclipse her obedience and industry. What had she done to deserve her punishment, the raging demons, the visions, the voices, that the LORD seemed bent on delivering to her? Why did God so often fill her heart with love, only to abandon her at times to the torture of evil spirits? She sighed as she began her never-ending supplications, the ancient prayers of the faithful of Israel.

"I confess, O LORD my God, to all the evil I have done and the evil path whereon I have set my feet." Mary sank into her entreaties, repeating them again and again until she was hypnotized by her own whispering voice. "Give me pardon, O God, for all my transgressions and grant atonement for all my sins."

"What sins are those, Mary?" purred a voice inside her head.

"Get away from me," she hissed in reply. "Hear my supplication, LORD our God, with pity and compassion. Accept my prayer with love, O God, who hearest the prayers of the faithful."

"God does not hear one who is guilty of a twin brother's murder, woman."

"That is not true! I loved Reuben. I would gladly have traded places with him."

"What, would you have flung yourself from the mountain?"

"Come to my aid, O God, source of my strength."

"Your strength comes not from God! It comes from your own power."

"I had no power to save Reuben."

"Of course you didn't," cooed the voice.

"O LORD, regard my supplication and leave me not to this evil one!"

Mary was swinging back and forth like a bell inside her own head, swaying between the seduction of the voice and the silence of God. A dark disquiet settled into the place between her eyes, and she frowned. The voice was right. God would not comfort her, not forgive her this day. She must leave the house of God. *I must go home now.*

Distraught, pursued by her one thought of escaping the voice and the emptiness, Mary dashed to the nearest way out. Leaving by a side door, with no recollection of the young slave girl watching in vain for her at the front of the synagogue, Mary became disoriented. She walked the familiar streets of Magdala, but it was as though she had never before set foot on them. She looked at shops where she had made many purchases and wondered who owned them. She passed by government buildings where she paid her taxes and did not know them. Mary, recognizing nothing, wandered aimlessly and, finally, was lost. Here in the town, which had been her home for forty years and from which she had rarely strayed, she was hopelessly confused.

As she roamed the city trying to find the way home, the awful panic was swelling. She struggled to fix her drifting mind on a single thought, find the Fish Gate. The sun set. It grew cold. And then, the shadows descended.

Not knowing what else to do, Demetria set off searching for Mary. She took a path away from the boisterous crowds. She remembered Rachel's warning about the streets and alleys of Magdala, with their drunken cut-throats and pinch-purses. No place for a Greek child of twelve, with the promise of womanhood just blushing onto her cheeks and soft breast buds coming into flower beneath her coarse cloak. But so great was her desire to find Mary and bring her home safely that the girl forgot her own security.

Demetria decided to try to make her way back to the Goldsmiths Street. She was not too familiar with this area of the city and had not paid attention to the route they had taken earlier, so she spent precious time drifting off course, south to the city wall when she should have gone directly north. Trying to retrace her steps, Demetria searched for her absent mistress, occasionally thinking she recognized a landmark, but never able to ascertain precisely where she was. She was painfully aware of the passing hours but helpless to slow them as she paced the streets, looking this way and that, trying to imagine where Mary might have wandered.

Shops and taverns closed. Activity drained from the town as people went home to sleep off their excesses, or engage in them, until finally the threatening crowds were displaced by utterly deserted nighttime streets bathed in an empty silence. Demetria was completely alone now, with no idea of where she was. She was furious with herself, first for disobeying Shoshanna's instructions and losing sight of Mary, but more urgently now, for being so lost. Magdala was only one square mile in size. Why could she not find the High Street? She decided to organize her search in a crisscross pattern. That plan soon failed. There were no orderly Roman right angles; everything meandered or came to a puzzling dead end.

She stumbled on and at length arrived again at some portion of the city wall. She decided to follow it, knowing that eventually it would lead her to the High Street, which divided the city in two and intersected twice with the wall. This time her plan was successful. Exhausted, but triumphant, she had made it all the way back to the High Street and the Fish Gate. Now she could walk directly west to the Goldsmiths Street. She stepped into the road, and was startled by a blast of chill wind that blew the hood of her sinuous woolen cloak from her head, whipping her hair into a halo lit golden by the rising moon. She struggled to regain control of the hood.

Within the lonely hush of night Demetria finally arrived at the corner of the Goldsmiths Street. She paused to catch her breath, but there was no time. The quiet was broken by the heart-stopping growl of a pack of wild dogs, one of dozens that scavenged through the city at night. Demetria had heard tales of people assaulted by dogs, dragged down and attacked, their throats ripped out and.... She wondered how close the dogs had come. Then she saw them, and stood stock still in terror. There were five, all grey in the moonlight, with vicious mouths and yellow eyes. They were loping toward her, and she looked hysterically for a way to escape, a stairway or ladder or even a wall to climb to get away. Then they stopped as quickly as they had bolted. They were falling upon a meal, some discarded meat or dead animal that drew their attention away from the hapless girl.

Demetria backed slowly to the nearest building and stepped sideways to the corner of the building and then around it. She stood frozen there on the cobblestones at the crossroads of the High Street and the Goldsmiths Street, a chill wind blowing off the Sea of Galilee in the middle of a winter night. She could not know that just steps away the mistress whom she sought was stumbling, trance-like, toward the same deserted crossroads. Demetria raised her head and looked, hoping the street would be empty and safe. What she saw caused her to gasp.

Mary! Not twenty paces distant, standing rigid upon the limestone pavement, barefoot, her blue cloak discarded in a heap on cobblestones filthy with mud and excrement, the inevitable result of a town whose daytime streets were shared with every manner of domestic animal and beast of burden. Mary's bare arms were raised straight and stiff, like arrows, to the lustrous sky, its brilliant stars and moon unimpeded by artificial light. Her arms glistened with a moisture quite unnatural in the cold, drying wind. What could it be? Flowing down the skin inside each silken forearm, blood! Demetria felt dizzy. She put out one hand to brace herself against the building. She stared, horrified, as Mary's leaden hands fell to her sides. The crossroads dogs sounded again.

"Let them come!" cried Mary into the void around her. "What are mangy street dogs to me? I am ravaged by fiery wolves!"

Demetria watched as Mary's last, thin thread of control snapped. She watched as Mary threw back her head and wailed the visceral, mad wail of the possessed.

The sound pierced the night around Demetria. She screamed, then clamped one hand over her mouth. She trembled uncontrollably, trapped between wild dogs and the mad devil that was her mistress. Vacillating between fear for her lady and fear for herself, Demetria wanted to run. But she held fast, then took the few, last, tentative steps toward the terrifying vision who stood motionless before her.

"I must not think about the dogs," she whispered to herself. "I will go very slowly. Not scare her. She will recognize me. Surely not hurt me."

These bits of self-encouragement offered little reassurance to Demetria, but they did give her enough to keep going, one step, then another and another, toward, what? She had never seen her mistress *in extremis*, but she had heard about it from Shoshanna who spoke of Mary's darkness, a grave gloom that descended slowly like a storm approaching from the desert eastern shore of the sea. Shoshanna spoke of her helplessness when she watched the ominous clouds thicken and gather around Mary. She spoke of the demons that entered, demons that only Mummius could command at times and even then only temporarily. Well then, where were Mummius and his lute now?

Demetria spoke Mary's name softly at first, repeating it slightly more loudly when there was no response. Finally she was standing close to Mary, looking up into her face, a face distorted beyond recognition, and for a fleeting moment she thought she must be mistaken, that this was not her mistress at all. Mary turned hard on Demetria, teeth bared, eyes blazing. *Those horrible dogs*, was Demetria's last thought as she put her hand protectively over her throat.

Mary looked at Demetria with a questioning stare and then sank down to the pavement, seeming to faint.

Praying to all the gods to protect her, Demetria knelt beside her mistress, reached out her hand, and touched Mary's shoulder. "Lady," she said. Demetria heard an angry howl gather inside a white vapor that whirled around her mistress and then rolled like a fog down the street and disappeared as mysteriously as it had arisen.

"Demetria?"

Demetria released her breath and gasped for more. She could only say, "Lady."

"Child, what are you doing here? It is late. You are not safe alone in town at night. Let's get you home now."

Demetria drew Mary's arm around her own small shoulder and, as she did, noticed blood congealed all over her lovely hand, blood clotting in the creases of the joints of her fingers and drying under her fingernails, nails that Demetria had manicured that very morning. She had filed and polished the delicate ovals, gently pushed back the cuticle with an olive wood stick, exposing pale pink moons, and massaged oil into the skin. Now, this horror. Mary must have used her nails to scratch and claw at her arms, for what purpose Demetria could not imagine.

The evil spirits mysteriously gone now, Mary leaned against Demetria for support. The girl staggered under the weight, but found her footing. When they arrived at the Fish Gate, it was closed and locked. Of course. What city gate would be open in the middle of the night? They would have to go single file up the narrow pedestrian steps to the top of the wall and down the other side, Demetria half-dragging Mary's limp body. *Demeter, Great Goddess, if you have ever looked on me with kindness, do it now and give me strength*, she prayed silently.

Demetria bore the near dead weight of her mistress on the painful walk home, first to the Roman road, and then another mile north to Mary's house. It had never before seemed long, but now she was in pain, her shoulders screaming and her legs quivering from the exertion.

Shoshanna met them at the door. She had waited for hours in ever-mounting fear, imagining all kinds of horrors, but even she was not prepared for the sight of them. "Come in. Quickly!"

Demetria could tell from the look on her face that Shoshanna was shocked, that she thought she had seen Mary at her worst over the years of her care. But the old Jewish woman had never seen her darling like this before.

Demetria very nearly collapsed as she turned the weight of Mary's body over to the stout woman. The three of them passed through the loom room. Demetria saw the manger where a baby had slept that morning. *I will never sleep that way again*, she thought miserably.

Demetria watched Shoshanna bear Mary's buckled body to the bedroom. She watched the old woman place the mistress in a chair and arrange her arms and legs in ways she thought were comfortable. Shoshanna poured water from a pitcher into a basin and placed it on a low table beside the chair. She took a clean linen cloth from a shelf. Demetria remembered seeing Shoshanna with the laundry that day, how she had washed and dried and carefully folded all the towels and table linens. She understood how loyal Shoshanna was to Mary, how committed to creating beauty and peace all around her. Demetria understood that all these ministrations were against the day—or night—when something like this would happen, when the demons would seize Mary away from home, out of reach of the protection it provided her, and beauty and peace would vanish like the illusion they were.

As Shoshanna washed Mary's arms and rinsed the cloth and washed again, dripping water made rosy with blood, Demetria stood by, wanting nothing so desperately as to crumple into bed.

Shoshanna glanced in her direction. "How did this happen?"

"I should not have let her out of my sight."

"What do you mean, out of your sight?"

"She wanted to pray in the synagogue, and I couldn't go in."

"So you let her go alone."

"She said she would return quickly," explained Demetria, choked with regret.

"How could you!" accused Shoshanna, instantly repenting of her tone for Mary's sake.

"She insisted, Shoshanna. I waited too long. It was stupid of me. I am so sorry," moaned Demetria.

For the second time since Demetria had arrived in Magdala, the girl's suffering and shame gripped Shoshanna's heart, and she said, "No. The fault is mine. Go to bed, Demetria, you are weary."

Demetria turned to go.

"And, child, thank you. What you did required strength and courage."

Demetria stumbled from Mary's room and out into the dark courtyard. She walked across the mosaic where the mistress and she had sat all the previous summer for her reading lessons. It needed cleaning now, its luster spoiled by the rains of winter, golden tiles of MAGDALENA smeared with mud and almost obliterated. Demetria did not feel courageous or strong. She knew that neither she nor anyone else would ever be able to fend off the evil spirits from her mistress. Demetria had joined the ranks of Mary's family, the helpless, the tormented.

CHAPTER 6

The next day Mary was still in bed, sleeping, when Mummius arrived from Tiberias at midday and heard the story.

"By Bast, woman, why did you let them go?" he hissed at Shoshanna, trying to strike a balance between bellowing and keeping his voice low so that Mary could not hear him rant. "Why did you not send someone to search for them?"

"Do not call upon your gods, Egyptian! Do you not think I sent after them? They could not be found."

He turned on Demetria. "How did you say the demon went out of her?"

Confused and mumbling, the girl tried to explain. "It was a cloud. No a fog. Or more like a mist. Oh, I don't know, I have never seen anything like it before. It swirled around her for a while and then soared away, with great haste."

"A sound emanated from it, you said?"

"Yes, a howl, like a creature frustrated, or angry, like a jackal robbed of a meal."

After a moment's contemplation, Mummius muttered to himself, "I have to think," and swept from the room.

Passing silently from the kitchen, across the courtyard, through the office and into his sleeping cubicle, Mummius was deeply concerned. When he came to Magdala, he had intended to treat Mary's condition, perhaps even to cure her. At first she responded well to his precisely mixed and balanced herbal remedies. He was always able to soothe her into deep relaxation, often sleep, with the music that she heard as song, but within which he concealed potent incantations. She improved to the point that frequently months would pass between her episodes, and when they did occur, they were less severe and shorter-lived than before. But if Demetria had reported the incident of the past night correctly—and there was no reason to think that she had not—these latest symptoms were more extreme than ever. Perhaps Mary's condition had progressed beyond his skill to aid her. He shuddered. He did not wish to lose his grip on the lady or on the household. To say nothing of Severus' high estimation of him.

Before he could deal with the story of the demon, Mummius must attend to Mary's physical wounds, the lacerations to her arms that Shoshanna had described. He perused his wall of vials and pouches, jars and small boxes, and considered the options. He reached for a pot of honey and poured some out into a wooden bowl.

It would be many centuries before the science of antibiotics was understood, but every physician like Mummius knew that wounds well cleansed and then treated with honey were less likely to fester. He used it as a base into which he stirred aloe vera, good for burns and diseases of the skin. Scanning the shelves for pain relievers, he took down three, belladonna, thyme, and poppy. He bobbed the containers gently in one hand. *Best to use the poppy.* He measured the opiate into the mixture and, taking the bowl into the palm of his hand, began to swirl the ingredients together with a short ivory spatula. Mummius had just stirred the topical remedy into a warm and fragrant compound when he heard a scratch at the doorway.

"Come."

"She's awake now."

Mummius looked up from his completed work to see Demetria holding back the curtain. He squinted suspiciously. What had happened to *her* during the course of last night's events? She seemed less timid, less—deferential. No surprise, he thought. Such an experience could have but one of two results, increased fear or increased strength. Perhaps there was more to this weepy girl than previously known.

Carrying his medicine bowl, Mummius followed Demetria to Mary's room. He tossed his head slightly, indicating to the girl to leave them. Alone there, with the light of the late afternoon sun casting long shadows around them, Mummius walked to Mary's bedside. He knelt on one knee, bending the other, and resting his forearm on his leg, he leaned forward toward her. He lifted her slack wrist and cupped it in the long, slender fingers of his right hand, touching his fingertips to her pulse. She looked at him feebly and started to speak.

"Shh. Shh." He turned Mary's arm over tenderly, pulled back the linen that Shoshanna had used as bandages, and saw the wounds.

Mummius' heart pounded inside his chest. His breathing grew rapid and shallow. Crimson circles flushed the rims of his eyes. And without warning, the bride he had left behind upon the banks of the Nile floated over the pavement of another courtyard, climbed eagerly into his lap, and whispered, "Darling."

Laboring to regain control of himself, Mummius coughed and cleared his throat. "Lady," he said, "I must examine you. I will try not to hurt you."

With utmost care, Mummius washed and patted dry the gashes in Mary's arms, alert for signs of swelling and color that would portend infection. Grudgingly, he admitted to himself that Shoshanna had done an admirable job. Satisfied, he applied the soothing honey mixture and clean linen wraps. Then Mummius summoned Shoshanna and furnished instructions for food: weak garlic broth at frequent intervals to strengthen her body against spirits and as much water as she would take.

"Keep sandalwood incense burning in here. The headaches will undoubtedly begin soon."

As Mummius turned to go, he glanced back at Mary in a sudden inspiration and said, "Send Demetria in to read to her." Mary's weak smile pierced his heart almost to breaking. He returned her smile and left quickly.

Mummius retreated to his own chamber assured that, with proper care, Mary's wounds would heal without difficulty. It was easy enough to treat the external wounds of the body. The internal suffering of the mind was quite another thing. Mary was the model of melancholic humor, cold, dry and pale, with heightened sensitivities and the resulting visions. Often Mummius had medicated her with tinctures and teas appropriate to melancholy, and they had worked—to a point. He thought how weak she was as she lay in her bed, how debilitated of spirit; he would need something far greater than saffron and asafoetida to help her now.

Mummius spent the rest of the afternoon and evening consulting all the relevant ancient texts, both Egyptian and Greek, even Indian. He read and reread annotations from his discussions with every itinerant physician who had passed through Magdala in the past year, as well as notes from a conference of physicians that he had attended recently in Tiberias. The search revealed nothing that he had overlooked. Alternatives were melting away. With Mary at her weakest, the risk was great that, next time, the demon would return to take up permanent residence within her. He began to face the inevitable; he would have to exorcise Mary's demon, and soon.

Mummius did not often resort to magic. Yes, he had attended the classes at the Asclepian in Alexandria. Yes, he had learned the basics from master magicians. But he had long since abandoned the path of magic, a path of "whatever works," that offended his scientific sensibilities. Mummius relied on uncompromising hygiene, wisely compounded herbal remedies, and his talent for music, color and dream interpretation. He was a brilliantly endowed son of the line of Imhotep, the venerated, divine healer of Egypt. Mummius was no magus, nor did he aspire to be. Besides, the last time he had used magic to bend another to his will it was disastrous, and even Severus' considerable influence in Rome could not protect him.

He should be there still, luxuriating in his status as a member of Severus' household. Instead, he had been forced to make an abrupt and unfortunate departure, fleeing the accusations of that lying whore, Livia Valeria. She had become over-greedy—magnificent, attentive lover that he was—until finally her jealousy forced Mummius to use any and all means to rein her in. She retaliated and brought charges against him, charges of theft and fraud that he was powerless to refute, Roman noblewoman that *she* was. Severus solved the problem by offering to send Mummius to Galilee, temporarily he promised, for his own protection, as much as for his desire to help Mary in every way he could. Mummius shook the unpleasant, distracting memory of Livia Valeria from his head.

He was resolved. He took a key from his belt and went to his trunk. Bending over, he opened the lock and dug through the ordinary contents of the trunk to find a hooded robe, secreted beneath. He pulled it out and laid the garment carefully on his bed. He walked to his inventory of scrolls. It took some time to find the magical papyrus among the baskets that held so many scrolls stored on end. Long unused, the cord which held it broke in his hand when he sought to untie it. A bad omen.

At his work bench, by the light of an oil lamp, Mummius unrolled the papyrus and read the recipe for exorcism: "oil of unripe olives mixed with sacred herbs-not-to-be-revealed, and fruit pulp, boiled in colorless marjoram." He located and took each ingredient from its place on his shelves, lit the burner and set them to boil. Reading on in the instructions, he took up a stylus and inscribed upon a piece of tin a list of divine names. He pierced a hole in the amulet and threaded a small leather thong through the hole, tying it securely. When the amulet was ready, Mummius turned to the bed where the garment of the magus was waiting.

The moment of last resort was upon him. Holding the robe high, with a deep inbreath he slipped it over his head. A current flashed and sparked through Mummius' body as the folds of the robe fell out in what seemed like a timeless motion down his great height to his ankles.

Returning to the boiling mixture, Mummius began a low, growling recitation of a list of names of many gods of many nations, including even the god of the Jews, an impenetrable jumble recognizable to him and him alone. Stirring and reciting, he swayed to the sound of his own voice, rising in pitch and intensity. When he was ready, and only then, Mummius cried out the invocation that would summon his divine aide, and also, inevitably, the demon that would be his battle enemy.

"Come, God of all gods. Enter me and do for me what my soul desires. We are one, Great God, you and I. Whatever I command must occur, for your name is an amulet in my heart.

"Come, Daemon! No being will prevail against me. No spirit will defeat me in battle."

Surrendering himself to the hand of god, Mummius took up the oily substance and the magic amulet and, thus armed, went out in search of the evil that he knew awaited him in the room of his mistress.

To the women who watched him pass by, Mummius seemed a disembodied shade from the netherworld. They huddled together across the courtyard, speechless and terrified, as his black cloak merged with the shadows. Later they would report that his eyes glowed red like bits of hot coal within the concealing hood. It was easy to see how he might have become a legendary conjurer in Egypt. There was power in his erect posture, aloof and hypnotic, that would have been irresistible to women, men, too, in their different ways. He was older than most when they castrated him, but not yet married, not yet a father. Young men like that turned to evil: they sold themselves to those who took their bodies, or cut the throats of others who tried; they plied their drugs among the rich, who begged for more, and then withheld the prize to watch them suffer. Rarely, rarely, did they forgive the pain, use their knowledge for some good purpose, or learn to love.

Silently the fearless Egyptian pulled back the heavy curtain of Mary's room. The darkness was relieved by the light of only one small lamp, which caused shadows to flicker and flare against the smooth, whitewashed walls. Mary stood across the room, warbling to herself, her eyes downcast at the floor. She was naked except for the bandages he had so tenderly applied and a short shift of diaphanous cotton, torn at the neck to reveal one breast which she cupped softly in her palm. He had never seen her thus disrobed, and it took his breath. The ebony river that was her hair flowed over alabaster shoulders that the sun had never touched; tiny bare feet with a circlet of bells at the ankle called out to be kissed. And in that moment, Mummius the magus almost lost the first battle to Mummius the man.

Preying on his desire, Mary looked at him with lust, still crooning, still cupping her breast. He took a step forward. Gripping the thong in one hand and holding out the magic potion in the other, as though to bribe and bridle a wild horse, he said to her, "Drink this, Lady."

Mary lifted her hand, seeming to take his offering, and instead back-handed the bowl, struck it with a force that sprayed its contents into Mummius' face and across the front of his robe. Caught off guard and momentarily blinded, he staggered back as the bowl clattered onto the stone floor leaving an oily trace. When she spoke, her voice was a deep, bass tremolo.

"You think we are your lady?" the spirit spat out from Mary's mouth, slowly with tightened, twisted lips.

Mummius wiped his face with the long sleeve of his robe. "Name yourself!"

"You cannot know us, Magus."

"I command you, release her!"

"She is ours," said the voice, hard and insistent.

Seizing the possessed body of his mistress with a fiery glare he began his incantation: "Daemon! *Parhon kniphou breskul bremanten...*"

At that, Mary's body was flung at Mummius with full strength.

"*...bresephri rezar Kraphi Bamesen!*"

Mary struck, scratched and pounded Mummius' eyes and head. He fought to contain the force, grabbing and twisting, catching a shoulder, an arm, reopening her wounds, spraying blood. In his violent reaction to stave off the attack, Mummius heard the unmistakable sound of a fragile bone snapping in two. The broken clavicle distracted the demon momentarily, and Mummius was able to slip his small leather thong over Mary's head. The demon flew against the wall letting out a cry of rage. Mummius chanted the divine names inscribed upon the tin loudly, again and again, as the demon struggled to remove the thong burning around its neck, Mary's lovely neck.

Mummius repeated his incantations. The demon pitched at him, clawing, tearing open a gash on the side of Mummius' neck, narrowly missing the jugular. Unfazed, he kept up his chant. The demon flew back and forth crashing into Mummius, withdrawing, crashing again, in a relentless attack until Mary's body seemed more like a bundle of rags than flesh and bone. Mummius sensed that if the battle raged much longer she would surely die.

The demon must have known it, too. Abruptly it abandoned its instrument, dropping her in a heap upon the bloodied floor. A sound like wild jackals rose all around him and, for a moment, Mummius feared that the thick fog that contained it would overtake him. It was instead sucked from the room through Mary's window leaving only the black velvet sky and brush of stars in its wake.

It was with a massive effort that Mummius straightened the body of his mistress, adjusting the broken shoulder on the hard, supporting floor, causing her to wail in pain. He dripped opium into her mouth. Finally, giving in to exhaustion, Mummius collapsed beside her.

It was Shoshanna who found them. When she heard the animal sound and then Mary's suffering cry, she could bear it no longer. Leaving Rachel and Demetria with orders not to move, she marched across the courtyard like an advancing army toward Mary's room praying frantically, "Arise, O LORD, and come to my aid."

Shoshanna entered Mary's room and nearly fainted. There was blood on the floor and walls, two spent creatures crumpled and unconscious, dead perhaps, on the cold limestone. She stepped over the litter of broken furniture cast like matchsticks around the room. Falling to her knees between the bodies of Mary and Mummius she searched her uncomprehending mind, as the stench of blood and oil and herbs soaked into her dress and her nostrils. She held her breath and closed her eyes against the overload.

A bony hand came up and seized her arm.

"Aieee!" she screamed.

Shoshanna opened her eyes to Mummius' looking up at her weakly. But for the forearm and hand that gripped her, he seemed unable to move.

His voice was a barely audible rasp. "Don't touch her."

Shoshanna leaned closer, her ear to his dry mouth, almost fainting again with the revolting, sulfurous odor that was his breath.

"Cover her. Must sleep. One hour, saffron."

Then he was gone, slipped into what Shoshanna hoped was his own oblivion, a respite from whatever foul event had taken place here.

Shoshanna was old and hard. She had not wept since the day Mary's mother died. She had learned to brace herself against suffering, for Mary's sake. Now, though, as she rose and gathered blankets, her grief flowed out in unabated tears. She covered Mary's nakedness, and knew there was nothing more to do for her.

As for Mummius, she looked on him with horror, with gratitude, with hatred, with uncertainty. She would do as he instructed. What choice did she have? Was it he who had almost killed her darling? Or was it he who had saved her?

Shoshanna covered Mummius with a blanket, tucking it in around his feet and shoulders. She noticed that the kohl with which he lined his eyes was smeared and running. Had he been crying? She imagined his awful struggle with Mary's demon. In her own ways, for many years, she, too, had been in combat with that vile spirit. As warning to the sleeping Mummius, she said, "It will be back."

CHAPTER 7

In the early morning hours, Mary woke. Listening, she heard no sound. She imagined that they were all tiptoeing around the house, whispering. Or no one was up yet.

Someone had changed her bed linens, and Mary felt the softness of the sheet on her arms and neck. Fine Egyptian cotton, a luxury she had come to love, along with the crisp, clean laundry smell that lingered there. But today she didn't care.

Her body felt heavy, like an anvil. Her arms were so immobile that she half expected to see leather restraints holding them down. Her head felt stuffed with batting, like a child's doll. Her vision was blurred, and when she glanced around the room, her stomach churned. She closed her eyes.

If I cannot care about anything, if I cannot move or think or see, what is the point of living? Mary agonized to herself, and, then, to God, in fragments of a half-remembered Psalm, *"Thou hast laid me in the lowest pit, in darkness. Thy wrath lieth hard upon me. I am afflicted and ready to die from my youth up. Thy fierce wrath goeth over me; thy terrors have cut me off."* Mary's tears formed straight, salt traces down her temples and into her hair and ears.

What had happened to her, last night, was it? Or the night before? She remembered being in the town with Demetria. The familiar bad feeling that had stalked her and sent her into the synagogue seeking God. Voices. Scratching her arms. Walking home late at night. Mummius giving her medicine.

Then what? The voices again, when she was in her room. She remembered getting out of bed and pressing up against the wall, begging to be left alone. Then, everything disappeared into a fog of shame.

Mary hated what she had become. The people she trusted—her parents, Shoshanna, now Mummius—excused her, saying it was not her fault.

They were wrong, wrong, wrong. They did not understand that it was her own vile nature that created this unending agony.

She wanted to end her worthlessness. But how could she face God if she killed herself? *I am so weary of this,* she thought. Then, giving in to the weight of mind-numbing fatigue, she fell back into the mercy of sleep.

A few hours later, she woke again, to Mummius' voice. "Lady, can you hear me?"

While Mummius checked her pulse and administered medication, Mary saw that he was ashen, that he had not shaved or applied his kohl. In response to her questions, he spoke briefly of the events of the prior night, editing the story for her benefit. Having an indistinct recollection, she was forced to accept her chief steward's abbreviated account. When he insisted that she not move from her bed, she agreed; in truth, she could not. Besides, even in her hopelessness, Mary still clung to one desire: she wanted to be vibrant and lovely when Marcus Quintius arrived—any day now—so she would rest until he came.

Mummius, himself exhausted, could do little more than care for Mary and then find refuge in his own healing slumber. It was left to Shoshanna to supervise the final preparations for their guest's arrival. This she did with dispatch, and, when the last shelf was dusted, the last towel washed and folded, the last bronze plate polished, they waited. And continued to wait.

At last a messenger arrived from Magdala announcing that the Roman had spent the night in the town and was even now en route to Mary's home. Mary responded by tossing her blankets aside and sitting up. Too quickly, she tried to stand, and wobbled. Mummius barely reached her side as she swayed into his arms, wincing with pain.

"Lady, you mustn't," he said, supporting her easily as he, at least, had recovered fully during the three days of their waiting.

"Mummius, help me. I cannot greet Marcus Quintius like this. Give me something to fortify me. Send Shoshanna to dress me. Please."

Mary's reluctant guardians did as she requested. When all was done, Mummius propped her up with pillows in a chair by the window. Shoshanna adjusted the flowing skirt of Mary's best silk gown. Its bodice of Tyrian purple hid her wounded shoulder and mirrored the new amethyst teardrops at her ears. A delicate scent of lavender had been applied in the folds of her elbows and knees. Mummius and Shoshanna marveled at Mary's fragile beauty, a beauty now polluted in their minds by the shared image of her ravaged body lying naked on the floor. Then and there, they locked away the shameful truth within an unspoken pact never to tell her they had seen her thus.

"Leave me for a moment," she said, and before they had entirely exited the room, Mary's eyelids drifted shut.

Marcus Quintius found her there, dozing. His footfall at the doorway woke her. Mary stood to welcome him, bracing herself against the chair and bestowing her smile on him—her friend, her savior. He tossed the long, leather cloak that protected his clothing from the weather onto a stone bench outside the door and shook his hair to rid it of the mist that had fallen on him on the way from Magdala.

At 46 years, Marcus Quintius still glowed with health and energy. His posture was erect, and he moved easily within the remaining layers of his heavy traveling garments. The carved muscles of his shoulders and back, developed during the military service of his youth, remained a source of envy in younger men. Women loved him—with his dark brown eyes and wavy hair, worn just long enough to fall over his forehead when he looked down at them. The thin lines that creased the outside corners of his eyes from a lifetime of laughter made him all the more appealing. The goddess Fortuna smiled on Marcus Quintius. He expected to live forever.

As he entered, the room brimmed with his presence, the four walls barely able to contain him. He moved toward Mary, like a welcome gust of wind, like the arrival of Rome herself. Here was the son of a nation inspired by a law both self-created and self-imposed—unique in a world governed by tyrants—and devoutly enshrined within each of her citizens. A man steeped in the best Roman ideals of piety, liberty, personal authority, and fidelity. A man trained to assign importance to important matters only and not to trifles and, once committed to some purpose, to keep constant to that purpose. A man who, in a promise to her late father, had committed himself to the welfare of Mary of Magdala, daughter of Israel.

"My dear," he said, reaching out for her with both arms. And, as he did, he saw not the matron, but the bright-eyed girl of sixteen who had ambushed his heart a quarter century before on the loading dock at Tyre.

Unwilling and unable to push aside his embrace, she gasped when he took her in his arms. Stepping back, Marcus Quintius observed with alarm Mary's tightened lips and her involuntary tears of pain.

"My shoulder. It is broken."

"Jupiter's eyes, Mary! Why did you not speak?"

She tried to rescue him. "It is not too bad. I just need to stay a bit quiet is all. And avoid being hugged by Roman bears!" Then she whispered, "It is so very good to see you, dear Marcus Quintius."

He helped her back into her chair and pulled up another for himself. Their knees touched as Marcus Quintius leaned forward and took Mary's hand in his. Her small fingers and palm disappeared within his grasp. His hair, thick and shining and boyish, fell into his face and caused Mary's heart to jump, as it always did. She noticed grey beginning at his temples and was charmed.

"Tell me what happened."

"I was doing so well." She looked down into her lap where he held her hand. "Thanks to the excellent Mummius. He is a wonder, Marcus. How can I ever thank you for bringing him to me?"

He shrugged off her gratitude. "You were doing so well, and…?"

"And a few days ago, just as we were preparing for your arrival—I was very excited, thinking of it." She blushed. "I went to the town to buy jewelry." She moved her head slightly, causing the earrings to swing weightlessly. "Demetria went with me. What a darling girl!"

"Stick to your story," he chided gently, his patience stretching.

"Marcus," she said, beginning to tremble, "a voice spoke to me in the synagogue. It warned me that God would not forgive me, that God blamed me for Reuben's death." She shuddered. "Mummius told me that I was possessed by my demon, and that I fought with him, or the demon did." Mary squeezed the hand of her friend till his massive signet ring bit its imprint into his finger.

Marcus did not flinch but expended his energy keeping a tight rein on his raging frustration. What in life had been beyond his power to control or change? His family fortunes and his own fine intellect, enriched by the favor of the gods, all these had furnished him with the means to have whatever he desired. Only Mary had escaped him.

Years ago he had begged Aaron for his daughter's hand in marriage, but was refused.

"You already have a wife, Marcus Quintius."

"She is barren. I need sons."

"What is to prevent you from putting away my daughter if she, too, displeases you in some way?"

"Draw up whatever marriage contract you desire. It does not matter. I will give Mary everything. I will love her until I die."

"Marcus Quintius," said Aaron with compassion for the man who loved his daughter, "Mary will not have you, even if it were permitted for her to marry outside our faith. She has already broken the only betrothal she would accept."

And Aaron told his friend the story of Reuben's suicide and its effect on Mary. The demon that possessed the brother before his death had moved to the sister. Having suffered with her brother for the fifteen years of their life together, Mary refused to inflict her torment upon a husband. She certainly did not want to carry her tragedy into the bodies of her children. She broke off her engagement to poor, confused Hanani ben Jahdo, vowing to live forever unwed and childless, the worst curse life had to offer a woman of Israel.

"Do not pursue her. It would only increase her anguish," said Aaron awash in misery for his children.

"I will find the best physicians."

"No."

"Is there nothing I can say to persuade you, Aaron?"

"I forbid you to speak of it," said Mary's father, and the door was closed.

Now, in this moment when Marcus Quintius' eyes locked onto Mary's face, all that had transpired—all that had brought them together, all that had kept them apart—flooded over him. Twenty-five years of desire, twenty-five years of iron discipline.

"Magdalena, listen to me. You had nothing to do with the death of your brother. Do you not remember the years of his suffering, when you and you alone saved him from his gloom? Do you not remember the hours of dedicated ministrations, singing, petting, praying that you devoted to him? Do you not remember how he loved you? Indeed, you were Reuben's anchor."

Mary offered no response. Marcus Quintius was wrong; they all were. They thought she had been an angel to Reuben. But she had not done enough. She was selfish, and God was punishing her.

"Do you not trust me, Magdalena?"

She nodded weakly. "I do," she said, wanting it to be true.

"Then believe what I tell you. You are innocent." Marcus Quintius desired above all things to take Mary's suffering upon himself, and could not. "You should rest now," he said.

He slipped strong arms underneath her, cocked his head and raised his eyebrows as if to inquire whether it hurt her shoulder. Lifting her as though she were made of fragile glass, he carried her to her bed.

"Give me a drop of that potion," she said, indicating a vial on the bedside table.

Marcus Quintius examined the liquid.

"Is this opium?"

"For a few days more only."

A slight furrow sketched itself briefly onto his forehead as he gave her the drug.

"Stay a while," she said, drifting off.

"I will."

Moments later, seeing that Mary slept, Marcus Quintius Severus stood and, as quietly as his thick sandals would allow, tiptoed from the room, sucking the drop of blood that Mary's clutch had drawn from his finger.

Everyone was waiting for him in the courtyard. They were bundled up against the winter chill, but no one wanted to miss the first opportunity to see him. He went immediately to Shoshanna and lifted her off her feet, spinning around with her.

"Shushu, you are beautiful as ever, I see! Did you miss me?"

Shoshanna sputtered and giggled.

Demetria's mouth flew open, and she covered it with her hand. Eyes big as moons, she looked up at Rachel, who only smiled.

Releasing the stout, old woman from his massive grasp, Marcus Quintius turned to Rachel.

"Shalom, Marcus Quintius," said the cook.

"And peace be to you, Rachel. Seeing you makes my mouth water! Have you made your delicious lentil soup for me?"

"As a matter of fact, I have. It is ready, whenever you are," Rachel replied, her cheeks coloring.

"Is this Demetria, then?" he asked next, as Rachel pulled Demetria from behind her skirts and pushed her slightly forward into the enthralling Roman presence. "Lady," he said with pleasure and bowed in a formal way, elevating her from child to woman with his ceremonial manner.

Demetria choked. She remembered the last time a rich and powerful Roman had spoken to her; she remembered how he stared at her, salivating with lust; she remembered the pain that he thrust between her legs that traveled up through her stomach and into her throat as though a fence stake had been driven there. In Mary's home she had thought herself safe from Rome, but here was Rome again, threatening her. She pressed into Rachel's protecting body. Her mouth was clamped shut, but her mind was screaming, *Don't let him touch me!*

Marcus Quintius took a step back.

Mummius intervened. "Ungrateful slave! Do you not know that, but for the grace of this gentleman, you would still be locked up in the domus at Tiberias?"

Marcus Quintius held up his hand. "Never mind." And then to Demetria, "No one will harm you here, little daughter."

Everyone was relieved when Marcus Quintius turned his attention to Mummius. "Old friend," he said, grasping forearms in the Roman manner, and clapping him on the shoulder. "Come, show me to my room."

Mummius led the way across the courtyard to the guest room so recently cleaned and reorganized for his comfort. Marcus Quintius handed the still damp leather cloak to Mummius and stripped off layers of clothing, first, the hooded *cucculus*, the big, outer garment he used for travel, and then the lighter weight *laena* that was secured by a golden *fibula*, pinned at his shoulder, richly decorated with a cat with sapphire eyes stalking two birds. Finally he tossed his belt on the bed and, standing in his tunic, stretched out his arms with a great sigh.

Mummius said, "I have put your two men up in comfortable quarters in the servant house."

"Thank you," he replied, and then took a cup that Mummius handed to him.

"Good Egyptian beer? Why, Mummius, you have outdone yourself!" He quaffed it in a single gulp and held out the cup for more. "Tell me now, what has happened to our Mary?"

The two men exchanged a look eloquent with familiarity. In Rome they had shared a life of camaraderie, a relationship that transcended all the boundaries that defined master and slave. During that time, Mummius had pitied his friend for the suffering affection he held for the unattainable Mary. Then he met her. Working for her, caring for her over the past two years, Mummius had come to understand Marcus Quintius' devotion. He felt it, too.

Mummius told the story of his fight with Mary's demon. Showing his battle scars, he said, "Severus, I am alarmed."

Again Marcus Quintius felt the unfamiliar helplessness. Never before had his confidence in Mummius wavered. He thought of their meeting in Alexandria on the shore of the Great Sea when he first saw the genius of the man: scribe, musician, business manager, physician. Could it be that even Mummius, master of all affairs, was powerless when it mattered most?

"Do you remember my telling you of Amenwahsu?"

Severus thought, then shook his head no.

"He was the greatest of the clan of magi who taught at the Asclepian. His power was so immense that it seemed there was nothing in the natural world that was beyond his ability to command. He had league with gods and spirits of every force and locus. Spent his entire life developing it."

"By Jupiter, Mummius, let us bring him here!"

"He is dead now, Severus. Besides, in the end he was seduced by evil. In truth, you would not want him near her."

For a moment Mummius' face clouded with darkness remembering the night when he had been forced to test his strength against the infamous Amenwahsu. In the subterranean vault of the great school in Alexandria, he had wrestled with unseen powers, and very nearly lost his life. When Amenwahsu finally released him, the teacher said only, "A worthy opponent," and vanished from sight, leaving Mummius alone in the suffocating dungeon.

With an unconscious movement of one hand to protect his throat, Mummius shook off the memory and continued, "What I learned from Amenwahsu leads me to conclude that Mary's situation is dire. Her melancholic and sensitive disposition makes her naturally vulnerable to spirit possession. That, combined with the loss of her twin brother, whom—as you well know—she loved deeply, further weakened her. And above all, she is consumed with devotion to this god of theirs, the one they call LORD. She believes that he holds her responsible for Reuben's death. This devastates her and thus opens wide the demonic threshold. I am afraid I used all my power to challenge her demons three nights ago."

"Demons? More than one?"

"Yes. There were three, perhaps four. A ravaging spirit like that comes and goes in repeated visitations. As the possessed body weakens, it becomes more accessible, and the demon brings with it cohorts until as many as an entire legion have taken up residence in the host body."

"What are you saying, Mummius? The demon goes out and recruits its fellows? Preposterous!"

Mummius, his face set like granite, insisted, "It is not a laughing matter, sir. I felt it myself. The demon's grip upon Mary was so severe that, in truth, it did seem to multiply. I was certainly dealing with powers that gathered force as we struggled. Legions of demons indeed are rare, but, mistake not, cases are well documented. They are very difficult to drive out. Understand, Severus, I have reached my limits. The cycle must be broken—and soon."

Marcus Quintius resisted what Mummius had already accepted. They continued to argue until finally Mummius did what he had never done before. He led Marcus Quintius to the inner sanctum of his rooms and laid out the evidence: records of demon possession from Egypt, Greece, and the East; remedies of all kinds, potions, incantations and spells; notes from his discussions with other exorcists; and finally, a journal he had kept of his own experiences with Mary's demons and his efforts to strengthen her against them.

"What more can be done, Mummius?" the Roman asked, finally beginning to grasp the full meaning of Mummius' report.

"I know of nothing, sir. Unless...."

"Unless?"

"Unless we can find one of their own."

"What do you mean?"

"The Jews have a long history of exorcising demons. Perhaps there is something peculiar to these lands, their history, even their religion, that might be effective."

"More effective than you and your Amenwahsu?"

"Your cynicism is unworthy, Severus." And after a pause, "There are many stories of their prophets' driving out evil spirits. Even their legendary Father Abraham is said to have had the gift. I must seek out someone of their line. Let us pray that I can find help before it is too late."

CHAPTER 8

That evening, when everyone gathered for the evening meal, the household looked normal. Mary came to the dining room for the first time since her episode. Playfully ceremonious, she ceded her place at the head of the board to Rome. She was unaccountably animated, even allowing for the presence of Marcus Quintius.

Mary was aware that she was fidgeting. She could not keep herself from twisting her hair and playing with her jewelry. Her voice was too loud, her laughter too shrill. She knew that her agitation worried the others. Still, the meal continued without incident until, finally, Mary managed to adopt her normal reserve, and they sat with their sweets and last sips of wine and spoke gratefully of ordinary things.

All was going well until Demetria, unused to wine, seized a momentary lull in the conversation to blurt out, "Sudi's face looked just dreadful today, did it not?"

A dead silence followed, and everyone looked to Mary. Everyone except Shoshanna, who burned holes in Demetria with her eyes.

"What on earth do you mean, child?" asked Mary.

Rachel reached out for Demetria's hand under the table, and squeezed. More silence.

"Explain this to me," Mary insisted, frowning at each member of her household in turn.

Rachel rescued Demetria from her blunder. "Mistress, Sudi's face is cut and swollen." Rachel paused, but it was clear that Mary was waiting for more. "Apparently, her betrothed struck her."

"Oh, the poor girl." Mary hung her head for a moment and closed her eyes, thinking of dear Sudi, with her baby-soft skin and delicate features. Mary had made her a gift of gossamer fabric for her bridal veil and imagined how beautiful she would be on her wedding day. Would her face be ruined? And what of the inner scars that would result from such treatment?

"Mummius," Mary said, inquiring of her chief steward, "did you see her wounds? Could you do anything to heal them?"

"She would not let me touch her, Lady. I appealed to her mother, but the elder Sahadia also declined my assistance. From looking at the cut I believe no bones were broken and that the bruising, though deep, will fade in time for her wedding. I gave her some colchicum to reduce the swelling."

"Why would Eber do such a thing?" Mary asked of Shoshanna, who was privy to all the secrets of the weavers.

Shoshanna hesitated before answering. "The truth is that Sudi has taken to following a teacher, seems quite smitten with him, and Eber is threatening to break off their engagement if Sudi does not renounce this rabbi. She is equally emphatic about not giving him up."

"And he would beat her into submission?"

"So it would seem."

"What about Sudi's mother?"

"A complication. Sahadia, also, listens to this teacher. And *her* husband is fuming, too. Though their son has taken up with the man as well. The whole family is in turmoil," Shoshanna explained.

"Why did you not tell me of this? I might have been able to do something to help."

"We had thought it best not to trouble you with this, Mary dear, until you were stronger."

"Do I know this rabbi?" she said, her irritation rising.

"I do not think so, Mary. He lives in Capernaum and only recently visited Magdala."

"There are many teachers. What is so special about this one?"

Another look at Mummius and Marcus Quintius; another choice for Shoshanna. "They say he is a miracle-worker."

"Sowing dissension within families, this is his miracle?"

"He cures illness. Lame, blind, lepers, they all come to him to be healed."

"You believe this, Shoshanna?"

"Sahadia does. Says she has witnessed it. Avireina, too."

"Avireina, too?" Mary frowned as she began to see how much had been kept from her, how cut off she was from others, how they had isolated her. Had she lost the ability to manage her own household? She had always feared that her malady would one day destroy her life. She was being treated like a child, and, in truth, she felt like one.

"Mary, the entire town goes to see him. Of course the weavers do not want to be left behind." Understanding that Mary was distressed at their dissembling, Shoshanna added, "We were only doing what we thought best, Mary."

At that, all the physical, emotional, and spiritual pressure of the past week bore down on Mary, and she gave way. In a swell of pain and anger and frustration, she found herself shouting, "Who are you to choose what to disclose to me? It is for me to decide what will be done and what will be refrained from being done! Am I no longer mistress in my own house?"

Shoshanna made an effort. "Mary, dear...,"

"I'm sorry," Mary said, looking around at people she seemed suddenly not to know. "I must meet this teacher for myself, to see what manner of man disrupts the peace of my household. I want to go to Magdala tomorrow morning."

"Out of the question, Mary!" said Marcus Quintius. "You cannot possibly walk to the town in your condition."

"Then I will ride."

Mummius added his objection. "Lady, no. The movement of the donkey will too severely stress your shoulder."

Aware that her physical condition would indeed prevent her going into Magdala, Mary tried to exert an authority she did not feel. "Then you must bring him here," she said, to the company at large and to Mummius in particular.

As well as she could, Mary rose to leave the room. "Come, Demetria," she said.

Demetria put her arm around Mary's waist and helped her from the room.

Marcus Quintius was the first to speak, "Jupiter's eyes! What was that?"

"Not a demon possession, if that is what you are thinking," said Mummius.

Marcus Quintius voiced the question that was in all their minds, "Well, what *did* get into her? Shoshanna?"

"Just imagine what your response would be if you caught the members of your household staff withholding the truth from you, Marcus Quintius," said Shoshanna, still smarting from the angry outburst that had been directed at her.

Seeing the blood rush to Marcus Quintius' face, Mummius redirected their attention. "We must find this teacher."

Not knowing what more to say, they went to their separate rooms, perplexed and worried.

On an impulse, Marcus Quintius walked to Mary's door and peeked in. Intending to charm her, he put on his softest face and impish smile, "May I?"

"You may," she said, "but, be warned, I am very angry."

"I can see that."

Demetria had been brushing Mary's long black hair, and it shone in the lamplight.

"Goodnight, Demetria," said Marcus Quintius.

"No. She stays."

"All right," he said slowly.

"Don't humor me, Marcus Quintius." The sobs she had been holding back began to shake loose. "I do not know what is going on. If they think that I cannot bear the truth about Sudi, what else is being kept from me? I can trust no one."

"Not so, dear lady."

"Well, you, yes. Perhaps."

"They were just trying to help you."

"Hiding the truth does not help me! I have agreed to be watched, to be accompanied wherever I go. But this… I feel like a fool."

"They are acquainted with the fact that you are no fool."

"Can you not understand? The weavers are my children. They are women with difficult lives who have made something of themselves through their long labors here. Throughout all my own difficulties, I have never lost sight of my desire to provide a safe haven for the downtrodden. God expects it, and I have been faithful. You of all people should appreciate this, Marcus, having sent Mummius and Demetria to me in their time of need. How can I fulfill my promise to God if secrets are kept from me?"

Mary wiped her face with a damp cloth handed to her by Demetria. "Thank you, my dear," she said. "They trust me to protect them. I will not betray that trust. And surely I will not have the peace of my home shattered by some roaming ninny of a man who wanders by."

"Pax Magdalena?" he asked.

"Well, yes, if you want to put it that way," she responded, succumbing to his irresistible mischief. "The countryside is filled with teachers, good ones and bad ones. They blow in, they blow out. Typically they do no harm.

There must be something different about this one—imagine Sudi jeopardizing her marriage! I will not have it. I need to know what this man is up to."

"Very well then. I will find this 'roaming ninny' for you," said Marcus Quintius.

"And bring him here tomorrow."

"And bring him here tomorrow," he promised.

They embraced and said goodnight, and Marcus Quintius left the room, embarrassed by the surge in his loins that came on him as he gazed at Mary and Demetria lying innocently next to each other, sleepy and, for the moment, content.

Early next morning the men breakfasted quietly. Fifteen centuries into the future, the entire eastern Mediterranean region would be strewn with coffee houses serving up the pleasures of fine, roasted Arabica. For now, coffee was uncommon, so Mummius dispelled their sleepiness with a brew of khat leaves infused with milk and sweetened with honey. He munched on a few figs, while the ever-hungry Severus ate liberally of cheese and dates and last night's bread. When they were finished, leaving their dirty dishes on the table, they stole from the house, glad to be out before the women had stirred.

The rising sun could not banish the dull grey of heavy skies as they stepped from the front door into the street. A chilly wind gusted off the sea, and the early March air was wet with drizzle. It would be another full month before spring was evident. They drew their woolen hoods over their heads, and, leaving the hills behind, started off on the soggy, flat road to Magdala. Within the first quarter mile of the well-worn path, their feet were coated with mud.

"What do you think of the reports, Mummius?"

"Hard to tell. Some of these teachers do possess healing powers. Or, it could be a kind of mass hysteria—women are gullible."

"You know what Mary called him? A 'roaming ninny'!"

"Ha! Ha, ha. Well, she does not take kindly to interference with her weavers."

"She would be furious to know the real reason we are going to seek him out."

"Indeed. She likes to think that I have things under control. She would not appreciate having her situation revealed to outsiders. But what choice do we have?"

Then, as men will do, they spoke of business matters to pass the time.

"You have done well with the accounts, Mummius. Mary will have an excellent profit this year."

"And yet it could be so much better."

"How is that?"

"In truth, Severus, she does ever squander money."

"What? I never knew a woman more frugal."

"It is not on herself that the lady spends. No. The first ten percent of both the crops and the sales income she gives to the priest, for the religious tithe. That surely goes directly into his pocket. Even worse, she insists upon taking in every stray who comes by. The weavers are good enough, that is true, but you should see how she burdens my field operation with the weak and lazy ne'er-do-wells who come around begging a day's work. She turns no one away, and then she insists on paying them higher wages than her own workers. Everyone for miles around is familiar with this ill-advised practice. By Bast, they know how to take advantage!"

"Can you not persuade her to stop?" Mummius rolled his eyes, causing Severus to laugh. "Of course not. What powers would a man like you have over such a woman?"

"And you, noble Roman, what help are you?"

"Whatever do you mean?" asked Severus, a counterfeit innocence playing over his face.

"Most particularly, I mean Demetria. Mary lavishes her with unnecessary extravagances—books, jewelry, soft, doeskin shoes completely unfit for walking—disgraceful."

"Tell you what, Mummius. I will deposit five talents in a private account from which you may cover Demetria's extra expenses, so as not to strain your budget," said Severus, pleased with himself.

"What! So much?"

"Just keep them happy, Mummius."

Mummius loathed Mary's pampering of Demetria. She had too many privileges, and she knew too much. The first time the mistress had sent Demetria to summon him, an ordinary moment really, it had put him on guard. Since then he had felt his supremacy in the household slipping by inches, his cozy relationship with Mary being undermined by Demetria. The mistress treated her like a daughter. Severus encouraged it, so Mummius was forced to hide his resentment.

"Your wish is my command, Great Lord," replied Mummius, drawing his head further within his hood.

Their long strides gobbled up the mile to the town, and shortly they arrived at the Fish Gate. The morning's catch was being unloaded as soaking-wet fishermen hauled their heavily laden creels from the lake to the processing plant outside the city wall. Women elbowed each other, examining the fish piled in the large, loosely woven wicker baskets, choosing what they wanted for their families' dinner tables, bargaining hard for the best price. As the trades concluded, tired fishermen flocked to the public eateries in the town.

"Where shall we look?" wondered Severus out loud.

Mummius nodded toward an inn a few paces beyond.

Joining the noisy crowd that pushed into the low stone building, they scanned the room for an empty table. Finding one in a back corner, they made their way there and sat down. They didn't have long to wait until Mummius recognized someone he was looking for.

"Aristoun! Over here."

In an aside to Severus, he whispered, "He is Greek. Knows everything. Drives a man crazy with his witless jesting."

"Welcome, my brother. Let me present Marcus Quintius Severus, just arrived from Rome. Join us, won't you?"

"You're a fisherman, Aristoun?" inquired Severus, forcing himself not to cover his nose against the fish stink that came off him.

"Yes, and a good day for it, too. Heavy catch."

The three men drank cups of strongly brewed khat and soon became garrulous. After the customary and interminable Galilean pleasantries, which sent the no-nonsense Severus to the edge of his endurance, Mummius finally broached the subject.

"I have heard of a new Jewish teacher passing through Magdala, Aristoun."

"The streets are full of rabbis, Mummius. Who can keep up with them?"

"This one is said to have, uh, special talents."

"Don't know what you're talking about."

"A wonder-worker?" coaxed Mummius, laying a coin on the table.

"Oh, you must mean the chap who heals lepers and blind men," Aristoun said, pocketing the money. "Never heard of him."

"Do not toy with me, rascal."

"Let me see now," mused Aristoun, dragging it out. "What *is* his name?"

"Think, man, think," said Mummius, playing along.

"Something about Moses. You are Egyptian; you know Moses."

"As you know Socrates, you Greek loon!" replied Mummius.

After a short pause, "Ah, yes, now I remember. The old prophet Moses had a follower named Joshua. Popular name after that, Joshua. Over time, what with one change and another, the name became Jesus. Nowadays, lots of baby boys named Jesus."

Severus forced a laugh, trying to join the amusement of the younger men, but it was too late. "Where can he be found, Aristoun?"

"Ah, the impatience of Rome! Eager to get down to business, are we?"

Severus held his tongue.

"Oh, all right. This Jesus stays at the house of Menahem the tanner when he passes through Magdala. He is there now, I am certain. But you will have to hurry to catch him. Even as we speak, his boat is on the shore waiting to take him home to Capernaum."

"Let's go," ordered Severus, pushing away from the table.

"Wait," said Mummius. "What sort of fee does this wonder-worker charge?"

"Does it matter?" asked Aristoun, eyeing a purse at Severus' waist.

Severus and Mummius stood.

"By the way," offered Aristoun, "you should know that an acquaintance of mine was at a wedding in Cana recently...."

Severus looked at him as though to say, *And so?*

"In the midst of the festivities, the bridegroom's family ran out of wine. It is said that Jesus replenished the supply by turning all their water stores into wine—six water-pots full! And not that vile, pepper-enhanced, juniper-laced swill made locally for export, but the good stuff of Amminean grapes."

Marcus Quintius Severus roared with laughter. "This just gets better and better! Farewell, Aristoun."

They made straight for the house of Menahem, Mummius in the lead and Severus fairly pushing him from behind.

"I had no idea you were bribing spies."

"Nothing is free in Galilee, sir."

"Nor in Rome."

"Business is business...." Then, turning down a winding alley, "The third door there is the entrance to Menahem's insula."

"Ah, the insula. Yet another excellent Roman idea transplanted!"

"This individual one is not so excellent, but it is serviceable. Six poor families live here in separate apartments and share the central courtyard."

At that moment, twenty paces ahead, a small crowd—eight men and two women—emerged from the apartment house. They seemed in high spirits, laughing and talking together as they walked. Noting their mended garments and crude appearance, Severus turned up his nose and looked questioningly at Mummius, who perused their faces.

"I recognize Menahem, his wife and daughter. The others—no, I have never seen them before," he whispered in Latin.

Mummius picked up his pace and, switching to Aramaic, hailed the tanner. "Peace be unto you and your family, Menahem."

"Mummius," he said with a deep reserve in his voice.

Mummius knew that, along with many other observant Jews in the town, Menahem disapproved of the way Mary ran her household: gentiles and pagans living there, in violation of the Law. Still, out of respect for Mary's dead parents, they made certain allowances. Furthermore, like so many in their community, Menahem had been a recipient of Mary's generosity when times were lean. He owed her what she had no intention of collecting.

"I—we—beg to make the acquaintance of your guest," said Mummius.

At that, six of the men made a circle, a kind of barrier around the seventh.

One said, "We are late. The master has no time to tarry."

Severus took up a position, legs spread, feet planted firmly, arms folded over his chest, the bag of gold hanging prominently from his belt. Mummius breathed deeply and prepared to deliver the oily diplomacy that he had come to rely upon with Jews.

Instead, the rabbi spoke. "Let them come, Philip."

"But, Master," objected the six in unison. "They are gentiles," one whispered, as though this fact were not easily discerned from Mummius' hair and eyes and Severus' Roman dress.

The teacher stepped out of the protective circle of his followers. "What is it you desire?"

Mummius scrutinized the rabbi as Severus spoke.

"Are you the one called Jesus? The wonder-worker?"

"My name is Jesus, yes," he responded to the first question, chuckling at the second.

The simplicity of his long tunic and traditional Galilean turban gave Jesus a modest appearance and relaxed demeanor that took Mummius by surprise. He thought of the men he had known from Alexandria to faraway India who possessed great mystical powers. He counted himself among them. Such men were defined by some common characteristics. They were defined also by the lack of certain characteristics: They were not humble. They were not relaxed. Specifically, they were not given to chuckling.

Severus continued. "I have urgent need of your assistance."

"My friends and I are even now returning home to Capernaum from a journey."

"Can you not delay one day?"

"For what purpose?"

"May we speak privately?"

With one hand over his heart and the other gesturing toward the insula, Menahem offered, "You are welcome to my abode, Master, lowly as it is."

"I thank you, brother," said the rabbi.

The entire company turned and entered Menahem's home, all trying to crowd into the main room, the place for cooking, eating, socializing and every manner of communal activity.

When Jesus requested that they be left alone, Menahem and his family made to withdraw, but the others fussed. Jesus addressed each one in turn. "John, Andrew, James, Nathaniel, go now. Peter and Philip, you, too. I will be but a moment." Buzzing petulantly, they retired to the courtyard.

Jesus sat down with Severus and Mummius on the threadbare carpet, which covered the hard-packed dirt floor of their meeting room. Again Mummius fixed his attention on what lay beneath the rabbi's outward appearance.

Severus began. "We have heard that you are a wonder-worker. Is this true?"

"I bring the power of God to the children of Israel."

Mummius recognized this statement as typical of the insular superiority that Jews felt for themselves and their god. They were the special, chosen ones, sole inheritors of God's personal attention. Yet they had been conquered, dispersed and ruled by Assyria, Babylonia, the great Alexander and, now, Rome. That should tell them something about the kind of attention they were getting from their God.

Severus continued, "But can you drive out devils?"

"Evil spirits are under the command of God, as are all things."

"Speak plainly, man!"

Concerned that Severus' tone would spoil their opportunity, Mummius knew he must intercede. When he cleared his throat to begin, it drew Jesus' attention, and immediately Mummius felt the rabbi's gaze bore into his eyes and down into his heart. No amount of painted-on kohl could protect him from that look. He said, "I sense a power in you, Jesus."

When Jesus said, "And I in you, Mummius," the Asclepian underground materialized in Mummius' mind, his struggle with great Amenwahsu, who had acknowledged his talent and wanted him as a disciple, and his decision to turn his back on black magic. Was Jesus another Amenwahsu to be rejected?

Mummius went on. "We greatly desire that you would consent to visit my lady, a woman who suffers tragically, being possessed by many demons."

"I told you, I am for the children of Israel. What have I to do with you?"

Mummius laid a restraining hand on the rigid arm of Severus, and he brought out the key that could unlock the rabbi's reluctance.

"My lady Mary is a devout daughter of Israel. She loves and fears the LORD as is prescribed in the Law."

"But not the whole Law it would seem," replied Jesus.

"Would you hold the flaw of her generosity against her, great teacher?"

"Why do you call me 'great,' Mummius? God alone is great."

Mummius had stumbled on his ego. He made the mistake of seeing Jesus as he saw himself. It was so foreign to him, this notion of not taking credit for one's own achievements.

"Will you see her, or not?" demanded Severus.

Jesus turned to him. "You are a good man, Marcus Quintius Severus. One thing is lacking: patience." Then to Mummius, "Tell your lady I will celebrate the Sabbath with her."

"Three days hence? So much for your rush to get back to Capernaum!" protested Severus. "I will pay any price if you come today."

Mummius, hoping he had chosen an acceptable mode of address, added, "Honored teacher, I implore you, her demons may return at any moment. Just last evening at supper she began to be agitated, a sure sign that the threshold is opening in her."

Jesus was unmoved. "Tell Mary I shall come on the Sabbath."

Mary's ambassadors rose to go, and Jesus with them, into the muddy street. As they parted, Jesus said quietly, "And, Mummius, fear not."

What does he mean by that? wondered Mummius, insulted. There was nothing in Jesus' tone to indicate that he meant to insult or patronize. He was just standing there in the street, as any colleague would do, as though this were an ordinary conversation, implying, *All is well. Until Friday, then.*

Mummius both admired and resented Jesus' confidence. The man seemed unconcerned about the growing strength of the demons that threatened Mary. Did Jesus think that Mummius had the power to face Mary's demons alone for three more days? Was his power so great that it rendered time irrelevant? Or, was Jesus nothing more than a charlatan?

"He did not seem like much of a wonder-worker to me," observed Severus.

Mummius knew better, for he had seen it in his eyes and felt the power of mutual recognition.

When Marcus Quintius and Mummius arrived home, they walked into a throng of eager women waiting for them in the loom room. Mary and the household servants were joined by all the weavers in assaulting them with the kind of inquisition that men dread.

"Where did you go?" "Did you see him?" "What was he like?" "Did he perform any miracles?" "Who else was there?"

"Ladies, ladies," begged Marcus Quintius, holding up his hands, palms toward them in a gesture meant to halt the phalanx that moved on him. "Sit down, and I will report to you all that has transpired. Just give me some room, please."

Marcus Quintius sat upon the raised platform at the back of the loom room, his thick legs and sandaled feet dangling down.

"I am going to make tea," declared Mummius.

"Have you no mercy?" asked Marcus Quintius.

"Fare well!" he replied and left the room.

Marcus Quintius looked around at the women, some sitting, some standing, all waiting, and knew they would be hanging on his every word. Mary sat beside him with her feet tucked up under her skirt, leaning slightly to keep her broken shoulder comfortable. The young Sudi—how many years was she, twelve, thirteen?—perched on her heels, eyes shining in spite of the angry bruise on her cheek. Rachel stood some distance away, protective arms draped over Demetria's shoulders. Shoshanna had taken up a position blocking the doorway, like a centurion, bent on keeping order.

What had brought them to such a moment? Marcus Quintius wondered. Honestly, he was confused. He was accustomed to knowing answers, to having people around him, particularly women, look up to him, rely on him. Now, all he could do was report the facts and let them fall as they might.

He told the story, step by step in every detail, just as the women desired, not skipping to the end, but stopping just short of it. There was silence as everyone deferred to Mary.

"Is he coming, then?" she said.

"Yes, he will come."

The room was filled with sighs of relief and pleasure, praises to the living God, even giggling.

"Let us make ready!" said Mary, starting the painful rise to her feet.

"Wait."

She sat back down.

"As we departed, he said, 'Tell your lady I will celebrate the Sabbath with her.'"

"What? You promised you would bring him today, Marcus Quintius," said Mary, pulling Sudi towards her protectively. "There is no time to waste. The safety of this child is at stake."

Marcus Quintius' heart shuddered. He knew nothing of this supposed wonder-worker. There was no guarantee at all that Jesus could help Mary. It didn't matter: all that Marcus Quintius cared about right now was that she not be disappointed. He had made a promise to Mary, and he had failed her.

Subdued, he went on, "He said he will come in three days, to celebrate the Sabbath here, with you. Wait for the Sabbath."

CHAPTER 9

Why in the name of all that was holy had Jesus chosen to come on the Sabbath? Mary wanted nothing more than to give this home-wrecking rabbi a piece of her mind. Now, she would have to find a way to curb her resentment and welcome him, even give him the place of honor at the Sabbath table.

Every week of her life, Mary looked forward to the celebration of the Sabbath. It represented the sacred covenant bond of love between Jews and God. Her memories of its beauty went deep into her childhood, glad times with her parents and grandparents, the sweetness of her brother, the sanctity of their family. The laws of the Sabbath required a loving heart, centered on God, and provided a welcome respite, one day in seven, from the slavery of earthly demands. This week it would be spoiled by some rabbi she already resented.

Mary really did not have much choice in the matter. It was common for traveling teachers to take meals at the homes of seekers and disciples. It was considered a great honor to be chosen. She was not a disciple of this teacher, and she did not feel honored. But she could not say no.

Among Jews the code of hospitality was one of the supreme laws of honor. According to this code, uninvited guests could rely on a host to welcome them into his tent, where their feet would be washed and they would be fed. Their camels would be cared for. They could stay the night, or longer. Even sworn enemies had certain rights under the laws of hospitality, handed down through millennia of desert living. Out of this background, Mary's responsibilities were clear.

Added to duty was the fact that everyone else, even Marcus Quintius—even Mummius—seemed eager when the subject of Jesus' visit came up. And she did not know their underlying motives for bringing Jesus here.

On Friday afternoon, before the Sabbath began at sundown, preparations were under way. The house was swept. Weekday things were put away. Everyone washed. Mind, body, and soul cleansed.

Because no work could be done on the Sabbath, including the kindling of fires and cooking of food, Rachel prepared a delicious stew of juicy lamb, beans, barley, potatoes and onions late in the afternoon. Not being Jewish, Demetria was banished from the kitchen that day, because Shoshanna insisted that the regulations for food preparation be strictly adhered to for the Sabbath. So Rachel worked alone. Tasting carefully, she added garlic and pepper, then just the right touch of paprika, until she was satisfied.

Just before sunset all stood around the table dressed in their best clothes. The table was spread with a beautiful white cloth and set with special occasion dishes and tableware. A choice goblet filled with good wine was placed next to two loaves of challah, the sweet, eggy, braided bread which everyone loved. The challah was covered with a fresh linen napkin reserved for this purpose alone. The second trumpet blast had sounded from the roof of the synagogue, warning merchants to close their shops. Erev Shabbat, Sabbath eve, would begin in exactly twenty minutes. Where was Jesus? Mary looked at Marcus Quintius and Mummius with *I told you so* in her eyes.

Then, like the woman of every other house in the entire Jewish world, Mary covered her head. She pulled a pale blue silk veil over her long, black hair and remembered her grandmother, whose scarf it had been. At times like this Mary seemed like a girl again. The evening light erased the tiny lines from around her eyes. Because she had never added the weight that followed other women's continuous pregnancies, she looked diminutive within her robe. She was erect, without the incipient dowager's hump that bent so many women as they aged. Her hair was still a black shining river and the burnt umber of her eyes deepened, making them all the more extraordinary. When the gossamer blue silk shimmered around her face, she looked like something from paradise. In another time and place she might have been a royal princess, at home in King David's palace, perhaps. It had never been said that Mary's imperfections could be seen from the outside.

Hearing the third trumpet telling all to kindle the Sabbath lights, Mary lifted a taper and lit two small oil lamps, the Sabbath lights: *zachor* and *shamor*, to remember and to observe. With the lamps flickering before her, Mary covered her eyes with her hands and as everyone around the table, Jew and gentile, male and female, old and young, slave and free, listened reverently, she pronounced the blessing:

"Blessed are You, our God, King of the Universe, Who Has Commanded us to kindle the Light of Shabbat."

Mary was silent for a moment, allowing a solemn quiet to settle in around them. Just as she was about to continue her prayers, the silence was interrupted by footsteps. *Well, finally!* thought Mary, as they all looked up to see Jesus standing at the entrance to the dining room.

Mary took stock of him: early thirties, neither tall nor short, dressed like everyone else in a long, grey woolen robe, thick sandals, and white turban. Her eyes went to his slim waist, cinched in by a belt. But not too thin. The weavers had told her that he ate and drank well, liked to have parties with his friends, laughed a lot.

Mary was indignant. *Who comes late to Erev Shabbat?* she grumbled to herself. Not late, but not early either. Exactly on time to light the menorah lights, to recite the *kiddush*, and pray over the challah. She had been irritated when she thought he was late; now she was irritated that he was not.

"Peace be unto you, Mary," Jesus said.

"And peace be to you," she replied, gesturing coolly to the place reserved for him, the place that, in other homes, was occupied by the husband of the household.

Mary continued with prayers for the welfare of her family. She named the names of those who stood at the table. She named the names of the absent weavers, emphasizing Sudi and Sahadia. As she did this, she opened one eye and looked at Jesus wanting to see, perhaps, some recognition, some glimmer of responsibility for the turmoil he had created among them. But the rabbi only stood, eyes closed, hands folded, head bowed.

After her prayers, she nodded to him, indicating that he should begin his duties. Jesus put a hand into the sleeve of his robe which served as a pocket and withdrew a carefully folded tallit, a wide, white prayer shawl. He shook it out and placed it over his head and shoulders, and prayed, "Blessed are You, our God, Creator of time and space, Who Enriches our lives with Holiness, Commanding us to wrap ourselves in the Tallit."

Even from where Mary stood at the opposite end of the table, she recognized that this was no ordinary shawl. It was made of the finest wool, soft, white and evenly woven, an exquisite thing. As Jesus recited the Sabbath prayers, Mary heard nothing, for she was transfixed by the tallit. She stared at the stripes which decorated the ends of the shawl, horizontal stripes of black and dark blue alternating with white and—yes—purple. Her purple! The dark, rich Tyrian purple that she loved. *I know that tallit,* she thought. Mary looked at the face that was framed within the folds of the prayer shawl, and wondered. Jesus—such a common name among Jewish males. There had been no reason for her to suspect his identity before this moment.

Mary's eyes moved to the long white fringe swaying beneath the stripes. She felt her fingers tying the knots which, by tradition, bound the one who tied them to all others who were part of the fabric of her life. Then, the irrefutable evidence, embroidered within a purple stripe just above the fringe, meticulously stitched in gold, "Magdalena." Mary could not believe that Jesus was wearing the matchless tallit she had made long ago to please her mother. *Is it possible that he is the one?*

Mary could feel the boundaries of time and place loosening within. She was watching faraway happenings, distant, childhood memories from deep burial grounds in her mind.

Ten-year-old Mary and her brother Reuben had been in the town center and seen it all. It was 748 A.U.C., *anno urbis conditae*, "in the year from the building of the city," as time was reckoned in Rome. Octavius, Imperator Caesar Augustus had issued a decree of colossal proportions. Imperial messengers were dispatched throughout Palestine. They stood on high places, blew trumpets, and proclaimed in loud voices: "Every man shall go to his own natal city and be enrolled there. It is the command of CAESAR!"

The twins raced home, and found their mother in the kitchen where she was working. They interrupted each another with their eager story.

"Mother, you should see! The messenger stood on the steps of the assembly hall..."

"and everyone in the town gathered around. He had a scarlet cape and a long brass trumpet...."

"It was so loud, and when he finished, he handed it to a page who handed him a scroll in return. He unrolled the scroll..."

"and read it out so all who were assembled could hear. It was really something." "A messenger from Caesar!"

By now the children had spun down and stood, still panting, staring at their mother with big eyes.

"What does it mean, Mother?"

Rebecca looked to her husband.

Eyes fixed on his wife, Aaron said, "It means that we will go to Beth-el to be counted."

"Beth-el!" whooped Reuben. "We can visit our cousins there, can we not, Father?"

"Yes, son, I suppose we can."

Reuben and Mary turned and ran to find their friends and share the news.

Later that night, when the children were finally asleep, Rebecca and Aaron talked in low tones.

"Must we all go, Aaron?"

"The imperial decree is quite clear that I am to appear in person, and you with me. With whom can we leave the children? Our parents will be gone, mine to Beth-el and yours to Shechem. Everyone we know will be traveling to his natal city, wherever that might be."

"But why?"

"I thought something like this might occur when King Herod died and Caesar divided up the kingdom among Herod's sons. Now, the Romans must recalculate the tax rolls to reflect the holdings of the three rulers. They have to take a census to prepare for taxation."

Taxation! The Land Tax already cost property owners ten percent of their corn each year and twenty percent of grapes and fruit. The Poll Tax was collected on everyone in the entire population. Those were just two of the onerous duties levied by Rome. In Magdala, as in the rest of Palestine, reaction to the census reflected the range of people's attitudes towards a half century of Roman occupation. Some wanted to keep the peace at any cost; others wanted to launch a full scale rebellion; most were somewhere in between.

If Rebecca and Aaron harbored resentment of Rome's domination of their homeland, they kept it to themselves. For one thing, they did not want to raise their children in an atmosphere poisoned by rebelliousness and dissension. For another, Aaron had important business connections with the Severus family in Rome. He and his wife would make the best of this latest imperial demand.

And so it was that Mary's family, parents and children alike, undertook the mandatory trip from Magdala to Beth-el, Aaron being of the ancient tribe of Benjamin to the south. Their first stop would be Nazareth, fifteen miles southwest of Magdala, where they planned to join grandparents and friends for the three-day trek that would take them through Samaria to Beth-el. If things went smoothly, they would visit Jerusalem for a day or two after their enrollment. It was, after all, just one more day's journey beyond Beth-el. Spending the Sabbath in the Temple at Jerusalem—that would make it all worthwhile!

The next few days saw a flurry of activity. As the children buzzed and scurried, Rebecca tried to keep a steady hand on the household. She considered what they would need for their journey. They were in the middle of the short, dry period of late December, which always interrupted the long, rainy winter. The weather would be cool, but not wet. Nonetheless, she would take plenty of extra clothing. She packed food: salted fish, dried figs, barley cakes, almonds. She filled goatskin bags with water, which would be replenished along the way.

In Beth-el they would stay at the home of relatives, where they would be welcome for as long as they desired to stay. Rebecca wanted to take excellent gifts for them. After careful deliberation, she chose three, the first a small alabaster box with pomegranate fruits carved around the edges. Next she packed a translucent glass vial containing a bit of fragrant oil of myrrh that she had managed to acquire from Arabian traders. For a third gift Rebecca desired something made in their own home, of their own labor. She decided on a white prayer shawl with a border of colored stripes of different widths that had been made by Mary. The tallit was her daughter's most ambitious weaving project to date. Rebecca was dumbfounded when she saw the intricacy of the pattern that Mary had designed.

The girl had an eye for restrained embellishment. She had insisted on using just the right quantity of Tyrian purple thread to enhance the shades of blue. At first Rebecca thought it a vanity that Mary requested permission to use rare gold thread to embroider a kind of signature in tiny letters, but when it was done, she had to admit that the "Magdalena" above the fringe was tasteful. With deep satisfaction Rebecca watched her daughter tying off the ends of the tallit, creating a knotted fringe that would bind her in love to everyone close to her throughout her life. Indeed, it would be a grand honor for the girl to have her handiwork included among the hospitality gifts representing the very best that their family had to offer.

When Aaron and Rebecca were satisfied that all was ready, they set out on the road to Nazareth, two adults and two children, along with two donkeys, Alazar and Mikmik by name. Aaron went on foot leading the massive and feisty Alazar who was heavily laden with provisions—food, blankets, extra clothing, water, and the hospitality gifts. Rebecca rode the older and diminutive Mikmik. Reuben and Mary took turns holding Mikmik's reins and keeping their mother company.

When the family reached Nazareth they found it full of excited travelers most of whom, like themselves, were determined to make the best of the hated census by enjoying the trip and each other's companionship. Mary's family group soon swelled to a dozen people, along with their animals and provisions. All together, the people of Galilee became a throng of hundreds traveling south to their various natal cities to be counted. It was almost 9:00 o'clock in the morning when they set out from Nazareth, but they could still make twenty miles before sundown, if they kept the pace.

The travelers settled into the comfortable routine of a journey, mostly catching up with news of who had gotten married, who had died, and an assortment of babies joyfully handed around to be cooed over. Reuben was soon off with a crowd of other boys. Mary preferred the company of her father's parents, whom she didn't often see. She walked between the donkeys ridden by her mother and grandmother, listening to their talk, absent-mindedly petting Mikmik's soft, furry ears, and dimly aware of being on the brink of womanhood. Her parents were disappointed, she knew, to have such a small family, two children only, so she strove to be everything they expected of her and more. Reuben tried, too, but his efforts were hindered.

Mary rejoiced to see her twin brother playing with others, enjoying himself now, but who could tell when he might start to brood? He became so gloomy sometimes. Only she had access to him then, invested with the special intimacy of life shared within the womb. Mary seemed to have been born with a secret knowledge of how to soothe Reuben, pacify him, and help him manage his distress till it passed. She held to the hope that someday he would grow out of it, be whole and healthy.

She would never have believed now that his moods would continue to darken, become more powerful until finally, in five short years, at only fifteen years old, he would fling himself from a craggy mountain outcropping to the Jordan River Valley below and die in the flower of his youth. Suicide—the worst kind of sin under their Law. And Mary certainly could not imagine that a darkness like Reuben's would later descend upon her own mind like an unexpected storm in the night, forcing her to break off her betrothal, and alter her course forever.

In this moment, on the road to Beth-el, life was very good. They were walking with light hearts, singing a psalm from ancient days:

"Sing joyfully to the LORD, you righteous;
    it is fitting for the upright to praise him.
Praise the LORD with the harp;
    make music on the ten-stringed lyre.
Sing to him a new song;
    Play well, and shout for joy!"

Tambourines and lutes, small lyres and flutes, emerged from bags and donkey packs. Soon everyone in the train was singing and dancing in time to the music.

Only the malcontent Azarias bar Jonah and his band of grumblers held back at the edge of the company. They were mostly younger men fired with the fervor of rebellion that was growing all over Palestine. They would not celebrate in the face of Rome's oppressive census!

Mary's family spoke of Azarias bar Jonah that night at supper. They had found lodgings at a comfortable *khan*, one of several inns along the way that catered to travelers like themselves. They sat in the common dining room, savoring their meal and relaxing after the long day's walk. A boisterous bellow from a portly man approaching their table interrupted them.

"Well, well, well, this must be Aaron! At last I make your acquaintance. Yep, look just like your father, you do."

He was well-dressed in a long robe covered by a woolen cloak woven with the customary wide, alternating stripes of brown and light grey and slits at the shoulders for his arms. He wore the national headdress, a white turban loosely wrapped around his head and draped over one shoulder.

Aaron's father made the introductions, "Aaron, Rebecca, this is Josiah of Nazareth, my business associate."

"And these youngsters—who might they be?" brayed Josiah, holding out his fleshy arms.

"Our twins, Reuben and Mary," replied Aaron.

For a moment Rebecca imagined that the man might embarrass her children by embracing them, as he seemed to be tipsy with wine. But he only wriggled onto their bench and made himself comfortable, not pausing for an invitation.

Sitting close to him, Rebecca could see that he had dripped mutton grease on the front of his robe, its stains spreading down his chest. He arched his back and, with a satisfied belch, loosened the girdle around his waist. When he removed his turban, Rebecca saw that his hair was oiled into ringlets, an affectation of the rich, which made her cringe. Her nose told her that he had perfumed his beard, with a substance she judged to be sandalwood fixed into pomade with galbanum. It effused a sweet odor that she found repulsive so soon after their meal. He seemed interested in flaunting a gold ring, which held a large beryl stone—a costly, deep green emerald. He was crude, this Josiah, so unlike her elegant father-in-law, who was now speaking.

"Josiah knows something of the young rebels, do you not, my friend?" said Aaron's father.

"You mean Azarias bar Jonah and his crowd?" asked Josiah. "Oh, yes, he is one of those rabble rousers whose fondest wish is to throw out the

Romans. Harebrained idiots. Imagine our waging a war against Rome! It's laughable. Hey, boy, more wine!" ordered Josiah, jiggling the cup in his right hand and flashing the emerald ring.

"It does seem out of the question," said Rebecca. Then, thinking the conversation was not for young ears, she said to Mary and Reuben, "Children, go to our room and make yourselves ready for bed. I will be in shortly for your prayers."

Knowing better than to whine, they obeyed, but reluctantly, eager as they were to be in on the talk of war.

Josiah continued, "These people are crazed with the idea of Jewish independence. They despise the Sadducees—who will get under the blanket with any whore of a conqueror—as long as they can keep control of the Temple. Naturally."

The Nazarene was beginning to slur his words, but Aaron wanted to learn as much as he could from Josiah. "What do they think of the Pharisees, then?"

"Even the Pharisees are not radical enough for that crowd. In truth, it is hard not to respect the Pharisees, minding the Law to the tiniest detail so that all God's promises will be fulfilled. Well, let them keep the rules and wait for the Kingdom of Israel to be restored."

"And what of the radicals?" asked Aaron, impatient for the kernel of news in Josiah's political dissertation.

"Well, those now. They will do anything to be rid of Rome. They are ready for another Maccabean revolt! Why? Because if they strike the first blow, God will come to their aid against any odds. Ha! They are indeed reckless fanatics, but, mark my words, they will grow in numbers. Eventually there will be a showdown. Rome will not tolerate them, and there will be a massacre. It is surely just a matter of time."

With this pronouncement, and a full cup of wine, Josiah ended his speech, bade his listeners good night and staggered off to his room.

Mary's family went, too. Disconcerting as Josiah's story was, everyone was tired and so went to bed without further discussion. They needed to be well rested for the next day's journey, the longest uninterrupted day of travel through the region of Samaria, not particularly friendly country.

Long ago, the Jews in old Samaria had a history of rebelliousness. In order to control them, a series of conquering nations had systematically denationalized them. Colonists had been imported from places like Babylonia and Arabia, bringing with them their cultures and, more important, their gods. Over the centuries, ancestral idolatries had blended with the worship of God in Samaria, which revolted most Jews. By the time Mary's family walked through Samaria on the way to Beth-el, the Samaritans were practicing a reformed religion that had no essential differences from the theology of the Jews, particularly the Sadducean sect. But, because of their historical dissension, they reviled each other as people, and Jews sought to have nothing to do with Samaritans.

To Mary, the Samarian countryside seemed hospitable enough. There were plains and rolling hills terraced for crops. Crisp, bracing, winter air and beautiful, clear blue skies made her impatient.

"Mother, may I walk ahead in the train for a while?"

"Yes, but don't go too far. Be back before the midday meal."

"Yes, Mother, I will."

Mary walked idly through the train, watching. So many animals, so many people. She noticed that some had fallen into groups. There were families, of course, but something else divided them. She realized that it was their clothing. Yes, that was it. Some of the well-to-do people had separated themselves from others, and everyone in their groups was dressed in fine clothing. Many wore elaborate jewelry. None of the prosperous women walked, but rather sat upon fine fringed blankets on the backs of young donkeys. The donkeys had decorations on their reins. Some of the babies were held not by their mothers, but by nurses.

Mary saw groups of people who were not so elegant. In fact they were poor. All but the most frail walked. Fewer animals, fewer provisions. She moved along the edge of the caravan trying to make sense of the situation around her until at length the train slowed, and people began to draw water from a nearby spring. They were settling down to rest and eat. Mary realized that she was late and started to return to her family when she noticed, off to the side, all alone, two people and a small donkey—a woman struggling to dismount and the man trying to assist her while holding the donkey still.

Mary drew closer. When the woman's feet touched the ground, Mary heard a deep sigh of relief and saw the woman lean briefly against the man to catch her breath. The woman was large with child and, also, very young. Not so much older than Mary. Why were they off by themselves? Mary was surprised when the mother-to-be spoke to her.

"Peace be unto you, sister."

"And peace be to you," Mary replied. She felt shy.

"Come, join us."

Mary looked to the man, who nodded in assent.

"What is your name?" asked the woman.

"I am called Mary."

"My name is Mary, too! This is my husband, Joseph," she said, smiling. "Where is your home, Mary?"

"I live in Magdala with my father and mother and Reuben, my brother."

"Ah. In Nazareth we enjoy the excellent fish that come from Magdala," she said. The man supported her weight while she lowered herself to the ground. "Hard for me to get comfortable these days. Oww!"

Mary backed away a little.

"It is all right, sister. My little boy is so active! He runs footraces in there. Would you like to touch?"

"Oh, I don't think...," Mary demurred, though she wanted very much to feel an unborn baby moving.

"Come on, sit here beside me."

Mary gave in to the invitation and sat down eagerly. The young mother took Mary's hand and brought it to rest on her swollen belly. Mary touched too softly, so the other Mary pressed her hand down hard over a tiny foot. Under her palm Mary felt the surge of life yearning for expression.

"It kicked hard!" she said, amazed.

"Yes. But 'it' is a boy," said the baby's mother.

"How do you know?"

"Oh, an angel told me."

Mary's eyes grew wide with wonder. She knew, of course, that God sent angelic messengers to those with great faith, like patriarchs and prophets. But she herself had never known anyone who had been visited by an angel.

"The angel also told me his name."

Mary's amazement multiplied when Joseph shrugged and said, "It is true."

"His name is Jesus," she said. "A common name for a very uncommon child."

"Why do you call him uncommon, Mary?"

The mother of Jesus closed her eyes. She seemed to be praying, and when she opened her eyes, light shone from them.

"Mary," she said, "an angel of the Lord came to me in a vision and told me that I could bear a son who came directly from God. The angel said that this child would be emmanuel—"

"God with us?"

"Yes, God with us! The angel asked if I would accept this wonderful thing willingly for my love of God and God's plan for all people. I tell you, Mary, I was so scared, but at the same time I felt so much love that all I could do was say yes.

"It was hard for me in Nazareth after that. My family and the whole town thought I was wicked to be pregnant and not married. My dear Joseph silenced them by marrying me anyway. Now we are alone together, waiting for God's special child, Emmanuel."

Mary knew as much as any other girl about having babies. She knew that the most important thing she could do in life was to protect her purity until marriage and then, with her husband, to have many children. She thought that the worst thing in the world would be to become pregnant by someone other than her husband, yet here was this other Mary, speaking of her sin that was not sin, saying that God had asked her to have a baby—not Joseph's baby—and she had said yes! Mary did not understand why any woman would agree to such a thing. Why would any man?

Mary was awed by Joseph's love for his wife. She was awed by the serenity in this other Mary's face, the peace that surrounded her and seemed to come from her heart. Mary desired what this couple had: devotion to each another, a special child on the way, and the deep peace that comes with certainty. In fact, Mary loved them.

Mary continued to talk with Joseph and Mary until suddenly she remembered the promise she had made to her mother. One last time, she laid her ear down on Mary's belly and listened. With Jesus' heartbeat resonating inside her head, she tore herself away.

By the time Mary found her family, Rebecca and her mother-in-law had already drawn water and spread out the noon meal. Aaron rebuked her.

"Where were you, daughter, while your mother and grandmother prepared our meal and your brother and I took care of the donkeys?"

Mary threw herself onto the ground beside her father and took his hand in the way that always melted his heart. She turned to the women.

"Forgive me, Mother, Grandmother. I lost track of time, but I met someone. A girl from Nazareth, traveling with her husband, just the two of them, all the way to Beth-lehem. That is even farther than Jerusalem, is it not, Abba?"

Aaron nodded.

"She is thirteen and pregnant already! Her husband is quite a bit older, but they seem very much in love. He is worried about her."

"Why is that?" Rebecca inquired.

"He worries that the baby might be born before they reach Beth-lehem. Will you come to meet them, Mother? Please. You will see how different they are from other people."

Rebecca lifted her brows with an indulgent air. "I'll think about it. Perhaps when our meal is finished."

"Oh, Mother, thank you!" said Mary, not quite understanding why this was so important to her, but feeling very relieved.

After they had packed up the remnant of the meal, Rebecca and her daughter set out to meet the new friends. "What are their names, dear?" asked Rebecca.

"Mary, like me. Mary and Joseph. And the baby's name is Jesus."

Rebecca smiled. "You mean, if it is a boy, his name will be Jesus."

Mary replied, "She knows it is a boy. His name is Jesus."

Rebecca had not imagined that there was anything extraordinary about this couple, but she was wrong. She saw the concern on the man's brow when he helped his wife up to greet them; she saw the calm in the pregnant girl's face; she saw the light in her daughter's eyes when she introduced them. Rebecca considered what it would be like to be in advanced pregnancy and young, traveling with a man she probably did not know well, married or no. Without women to help her. *A plague on these Romans!* Rebecca cursed under her breath. She knew what she must do.

That night Aaron and his father tried several *khans* before they were able to secure two small rooms for the six of them. The traveling company had continued to swell along the way and the pressure for accommodations with it. The men had to overspend in order to coax the innkeeper to part with an anteroom—not much more than a closet, really—for Mary's grandparents. Here, as everywhere, business was business, and the highest bidder had the advantage.

When the donkeys were relieved and tethered for the night, Aaron missed Rebecca. He found his wife in the courtyard of the *khan* whispering to his mother. When she noticed him, Rebecca walked resolutely in his direction.

"Husband, we must help the poor young mother."

"Which poor young mother is that?"

"You know, the girl Mary was talking about."

"She has a husband. I am sure he is taking care of her."

"You men! You know nothing of waiting for a child to come," she complained with uncharacteristic impatience. "They are sleeping outdoors with not so much as a tent, only wrapped in their cloaks."

"They have made it this far."

"She could give birth at any moment."

"There is nothing I can do. There are no more rooms available. Father and I had to grease the palm of that thief of an innkeeper with ten denarii above the price just to acquire what we have."

Rebecca moved to her husband and pressed her body lightly against his, took both his hands in hers and held them tightly at her sides. Embarrassed, Aaron looked around to see who might be watching their indiscretion, particularly his own mother standing across the courtyard.

"Aaron," said Rebecca softly, "do you remember the night our twins were born?"

Aaron tried halfheartedly to pull away, but she held him fast, and pressed her case.

"Remember the warmth and safety of our little house that you yourself had built? The midwife there to help me, and all the women of our family. Remember you pacing around outside? Other men with the experience of many children trying to calm the uncalmable?" Rebecca smiled her radiant and devoted smile.

"Release me," Aaron said.

"I will. When you agree to help."

"How?"

"By giving the couple your parents' room."

"What! Would you have Father and Mother be the ones to sleep outside on the ground wrapped in cloaks, woman?"

"No, husband. They will share our room. The children can sleep outside. I have discussed it with your mother. She agrees completely."

Aaron was exasperated. "If they are so poor, how can they pay us for the room?"

"They cannot," she said.

That was it. There was just no end to Rebecca's determination to help someone in need. And not only people, animals, too, weak lambs abandoned by their mothers. Aaron remembered that once she had tried to splint the broken leg of a rooster. She had been known to nurse even sick plants back to health that should have been dug up and thrown on the fire. Now she had recruited his own mother in the service of some unknown Nazarenes. Looking at Rebecca's face, Aaron knew it was over. The truth was, he adored her, far beyond what was seemly for a man in his position, any man for that matter. He could not deny her. Well, nothing for it, then, but to move everyone around.

"Outside? We get to sleep outside?" said Reuben and Mary in unison.

"Yes," said Aaron, irritated that this agreement was bringing so much pleasure to others. "Your grandfather has arranged for you to sleep in the camp with people of his acquaintance. They have a tent full of children with room for the two of you."

Reuben whooped his whoop and ran for the camp. Mary went to her mother.

"Thank you for doing this good thing, Mother," she said.

"The honor is yours, daughter."

Soon everyone was ready to retire, exhausted from their long trek. Rebecca took pains to attend to her own family, wanting to mollify Aaron and draw no further attention to the couple they had helped. With brief "shaloms," all went to their assigned accommodations.

Next morning, well breakfasted, the family packed for the final day of their journey. Again, Mary was missing. As her parents' frustration was building, she appeared with that determined look on her face.

Mary pulled her mother aside and whispered, "I want to give her a present."

"Who?" asked Rebecca, at once wondering and knowing.

"Mary."

"Daughter, what has gotten into you?"

"Mother, you talked to her. You could tell there is something unusual about her, could you not? Joseph, too. I want to give them a present for their baby. A way to remember us."

It was true, Rebecca had sensed something quite extraordinary about the girl from Nazareth. She was no more than a child, really, but she had an uncommon serenity. Well, life on the road with a newborn would change that soon enough.

"Mother, let us give her the prayer shawl."

"Mary, that tallit is a gift for our host family. We must not part with it."

"Mother, with respect, was it not I who made the tallit? Is it not mine to do with as I will?"

Another mother would have slapped her in the face for insolence. But Rebecca recognized something in her daughter, something of herself, something no one around her had ever completely understood: the deep cry of her heart to reach out to others in need, to help them if she could. People had ridiculed Rebecca all her life for her unnecessary sacrifices, asking nothing in return.

Rebecca of Magdala looked into the mirror that was her daughter Mary and said, "Go ahead then."

Clutching the exquisite shawl to her chest, Mary skipped over to where Mary and Joseph were packing meager belongings onto their donkey.

"Thank you for assisting us last night. Mary slept well for a change," Joseph said, his voice heavy with regret that he could not do better for his own wife.

"It was my mother, really," said Mary, modestly. Then, on an impulse, "Joseph, bring Mary to Beth-el with my family. You can stay there until your baby is born. I am sure our relatives would be happy to help." With the innocence of a ten-year-old she added, "My aunt in Beth-el has many children. She will know what to do!"

Mary of Nazareth wrapped the girl from Magdala in her arms, pressing her as close as she could with a squirming baby inside and said, "May you be blessed by God for the purity of your heart, Mary. But we must continue on. Jesus is to be born in Beth-lehem."

Joseph helped his wife to her seat upon the donkey. The loving good-bye Mary had practiced in her mind was stuck in her throat. With both arms she had been holding the shawl against her chest. She remembered selecting the blue and purple thread, matching the colors of each skein to contrast with the undertones of the fine white wool she had chosen, the hours she had labored at her loom and the prayer she had prayed into each fringe knot. When she asked permission to embroider her name in gold and her mother had said yes, she rejoiced that her mother had recognized the wonderful thing she had accomplished. Mary knew that she had created the magnificent shawl for this moment, this mother, this baby. Still unable to speak, she lay her thin arms against the bristly fur of the donkey's neck. In her palms, she felt the softness of the wool as she stretched up to offer the tallit. She felt the shawl streaming from her arms as the mother of Jesus leaned over and, kissing her hands, received her gift.

When they parted, Mary heard her say, "Farewell, Mary of Magdala. And, dear one, don't be afraid for us."

Mary's fear would not be held at bay. When her family left the train at Beth-el, northwest of Jerusalem, the hour was late. It would be dark when her new friends arrived in Beth-lehem, twelve miles farther south.

Mary fretted to her mother, "I wanted them to come with us to Beth-el and continue their journey after the baby is born, but they would not. They said that their baby must be born in Beth-lehem. Why would they say that, Amma? The *khans* are completely full. What if they cannot find a place to stay in Beth-lehem?"

"Shh. Hush now. You have done what you could. Besides, they probably have relatives there. Leave them to God. He will provide," said Rebecca, forcing some assurance into her voice.

"I think they really liked the tallit," Mary said, her voice trailing off.

At Beth-el there was anticipation in the air. The closer they got to Jerusalem, the more the crowd grew edgy. That great capital city, the center of Jewish political and religious life with its magnificent Temple, was like a magnet pulling them with increasing force. Everyone in Mary's family, man and beast, was in some stage of exhilaration and weariness when they arrived at the home of their relatives. Mikmik showed signs of exhaustion.

"Poor Mikmik," said Mary as she helped to remove the little donkey's blanket and bridle. She wiped sweat from his neck. She laid her head against his and stroked one ear.

"You have the largest and furriest ears in all the world of donkeys, Mikmik," she whispered to him. Then to Aaron, "Abba, do you think Mikmik is sick?"

"No, Mary, not sick. Just tired. The trip has drained the old boy. He will be all right with a few days' rest."

That evening after dinner the men went to the bazaar to meet others and get the latest political news over cups of khat, strong enough to intoxicate them as the night wore on. The women stayed home washing dishes and preparing beds. Mary worked diligently helping her hostess clean up after what had been a great feast in celebration of a long overdue family reunion. Her ears burned, listening to the compliments paid to her mother: a dutiful daughter, she was, and lovely, too. She will grow into a beauty, no doubt. A good catch for a worthy man someday. The young girl dreamed that these predictions would indeed come true for her.

When the work was finished, Mary put on a cloak and climbed the outside stairs to the roof of the house. She stood alone at the low wall surrounding the roof and gazed out at the landscape. Much of Judea was desert wilderness, but Beth-el was tucked into the western slope of a hillside, green even now in winter with forests of pine. The undulating hills provided olive crops and summer pasturage for sheep and goats. It was pleasant, thought Mary, but nothing so beautiful as her home in Galilee. She sat down with her back against the wall and, hugging her knees to her chest, closed her eyes. She thought that Mary and Joseph would surely have arrived in Beth-lehem by now. "Please, God, protect them," she prayed, drifting into a light sleep.

The hour was late when Mary opened her eyes. All around her the night was hushed. Above her the sky was an indigo blanket thick-sequined with stars. And still there was more light than stars could reasonably give. Then the unexpected, in the sky to the south, a celestial fire of such great brilliance that Mary had to shield her eyes. With each succeeding glance, she took in more until finally she was able to stare without interruption at the sight of it: an immense star with a shining tail that reduced the entire host of heaven to insignificance beside it. What could it be? Mary wanted her mother and father to see the star, but she was transfixed by the heavenly light. Her whole body alert and tingling, she was held within the moment by unseen forces, wrapped in a bliss she did not understand.

These thirty years later, seeing Jesus wrapped in the tallit she had given to his mother on the night of the wondrous star, Mary felt that bliss again.

Wearing the prayer shawl, Jesus left his place at the head of the Sabbath table. He walked toward Mary, passing behind the women standing motionless on one side of the board, the men on the other. Mary examined him as he approached. She saw features she thought she recognized: tendrils of his mother Mary's wavy, dark brown hair peeking out from within the shawl, the full, even shape of his mother's mouth. His stride and the way he carried his shoulders were exactly like those of his father Joseph. The remarkable self-assurance and the mysterious light that radiated from him were his exclusively.

Jesus stopped next to Mary, their faces close enough for her to feel his clean, sweet breath on her cheek. Mary reached down to Jesus' thigh and closed her fingers on the edge of the shawl. She lifted the fringe to her lips. Her head bent back slightly, and her eyelids floated shut on the long ago image of another tallit, another Mary, another Jesus. Another extraordinary night. As she held the prayer shawl to her lips, Jesus covered Mary's hand with his own hand and, when he did, a cry of rapture escaped from her.

CHAPTER 10

The strain of the days of waiting for Jesus, the initial irritation, the shock of seeing the tallit, and now recognition, all this bewildered Mary. Her excitement changed to agitation. Pressure built inside her skull. Then the familiar force that pulsed relentlessly down, down into her body. Mary's face grew sharp, her eyes wide and flashing. Her beautiful lips twisted into a grimace. Her limbs tensed, her fingers went rigid, and, impossible though it was, she seemed to gain stature.

Observing Mary's appalling alteration, everyone stood stock still, as though nailed in place, fearing to act, even if they had known what act could help her. Mummius became frantic. Why had he not seen this coming? He had done nothing to prepare himself, and now it was too late. He knew that the next voice that issued from Mary would not be her own. But even Mummius had never experienced a sound such as that which shook the Sabbath night. It was like the shriek of a thousand tormented souls thrashing in the grip of evil. Mummius clutched vainly at an amulet around his neck.

Marcus Quintius, too, was terrified by the sound. It was the roar of a legion in battle, six thousand foot soldiers with cavalry, thrown against an enemy bent on his destruction and the destruction of his men. Even that could not compare to the thunder that rolled over him now. Marcus Quintius' hand went instinctively to a nonexistent weapon at his waist. Stupid. What use was a blade against such a force?

Across the table from the men, the sound erupted in Shoshanna's ears like a raging storm she had once experienced on the Galilean Sea. That tempest had echoed ruthlessly back and forth between the hills, over the turbulent waters, breaking men and vessels into splinters and casting them in heaps upon the land. Shoshanna wished she had died on that shore rather than endure the unholy din that engulfed her now.

As though the demon had multiplied ten fold, the roar surged to a painful level, and surged again. Poor Rachel and little Demetria could only cover their ears with their fists, adding their own screams to the furor.

An insufferable heat rose from the place where Mary and Jesus stood. Mary was changing before them: her lip was pulled back in a teeth-baring sneer, her eyes flamed red, and she growled like a rabid jackal. Finally, the transformation was complete, and the vile being standing at the table was no longer Mary, but a demon wrapped absurdly in her veil. When the revolting, acrid smell of burning sulfur detonated in the room, threatening to blister their eyes and lungs, they couldn't help it—they fled the table. Choking and coughing, they pressed their backs against the walls and watched, terrified.

Jesus, too, wanted to escape. A wave of adrenalin surged through him. Beads of sweat erupted on his forehead. He started to panic, wondering if tonight might be the night when vicious Evil would overwhelm him. His body stiffened with resistance. How much easier it would be to turn his back on this, to flee to Capernaum, to take refuge in his friends!

But when Jesus saw Mary's grotesque transformation and felt the weight of her suffering, it tore at his heart. He pulled himself together. Standing his ground, he took hold of Mary's shoulders to control her body, which had begun to writhe and flail. He kept his face close to hers, and, with increasing power from within, spoke directly to the demon.

"What is your name, Evil Spirit?"

The voice cried out in a roar of angry jackals, "My name is Legion. What do you want with us?"

"You must come out of this woman!"

At that, the demon lashed out, and, using Mary's body as a weapon, kicked and pounded at Jesus. Caught off guard, Jesus took a sharp blow to his temple, which splattered blood into his eyes. He staggered. With difficulty, he regained his footing and blinked away the blood that blurred his vision. The demon wailed again, thrashing, struggling to break free. Jesus tightened his hold.

The Legion tried a desperate bargain. "We know who you are, Jesus, Son of the Most High God. Swear that you will not torture us!"

From within her submerged consciousness Mary could hear the alien voice issuing from her mouth. Her mind was already dissolving when she felt Jesus calling her to return. His plea was filled with love, but also with pity, and not just for her, but also for the demon he was about to expel. His empathy struck her as odd.

Mary did not know if she had the strength to answer him—or the will. In the instant before succumbing to the force that had finally bested her, she saw her life as nothing more than a petty drama. Her elaborate efforts to hang on seemed self-indulgent now, and empty. And the fragile Pax Magdalena? Well, that too was foolishness, as if her tiny cup of water could stave off a long summer drought. Her brother's leap from the pinnacle, Shoshanna's attempts to save her: the effort to die, the effort to live, both completely futile. She was ready to let go.

Jesus locked his eyes onto the eyes of the evil that inhabited Mary. With his left arm, he pinned her body against his own, immobilizing it. He spread out his fingers and pressed his right hand onto her pallid face. He breathed a deep breath, filling his lungs with air and proclaimed in a loud voice, "Legion, be gone!"

From her tiny, hidden place under the crushing force that had squeezed her down to the brink of extinction, Mary felt Jesus calling her again. She wanted to help him. When she heard Jesus' command to the Legion, she pushed as hard as she could and regretted it instantly. She felt her skull crack open. She heard her own agonizing screams as her insides were ripped out through the top of her head. Then—darkness. Mary's body crumpled in Jesus' arms. She was dead. Or so it seemed to those who witnessed it. It seemed that way to Mary, too. She was suspended in a black, lifeless void. The pain was gone, but so was everything else.

Jesus held up her limp body, its head twisted alarmingly to one side. He pushed back the tangled hair, damp with sweat, put his lips to her ear, and whispered, "Mary, come here."

Somewhere within Mary's slumped form, life stirred. Her body filled slowly at first. Then, like a huge bellows, it swelled, rapidly, almost to bursting, almost too much. She shuddered violently and gasped and choked until again it seemed to those who watched that she might die. Jesus continued to support her in his arms. Gradually her breath returned to normal. Eventually she was able stand on her own.

From within the circle of his arms, Mary gazed up at Jesus as if to question what had happened.

"It is over," he said.

"Over?" she said, hesitant, unsure of what he meant.

"Forever," he said.

Jesus had pulled her back from the edge of extinction. But into what life? Was there to be no more suffering, ever? For the first time in recollection, Mary's mind was quiet. The scattered energy that had required a quarter century of unremitting effort to rein in was under her control. At his command, had she truly been set free, restored?

Bathing in the calm of Jesus' embrace, Mary closed her eyes and was transported back in time. She was a small child of six or seven years, before modesty, before responsibility. It was a warm spring day, and she was skipping through the garden with bare feet, wearing only a short, loose tunic, which left her free to run and play at will. Her thick, black curls tumbled over her neck and shoulders as she bounced down onto a patch of soft moss in the garden. Mimicking the profusion of lilies and narcissus that bloomed all around her, she tilted her face to receive the splendid, beckoning warmth of the sun. So thick was the air with henna that she could feel its scent tingling against her bare skin. Breathing deeply, she felt sunlight and flowers flow into her, filling every fold and crevice till she could no longer distinguish inside from outside. Thus she sat when the beloved voice of her father called to her.

"Mary," he said, approaching her on the path.

"Abba!"

She rushed to greet him. He caught her in his arms as she jumped, knocking him off balance. She wrapped her strong, brown legs around her father's waist and covered his face with kisses. She put her hands on his cheeks and her nose close to his, enchanting him.

"Is it not a glorious morning, Abba?"

Mary opened her eyes and looked around wonderingly. She saw the table in her own dining room, the dishes that had been prepared for the Sabbath meal, and the empty benches. She saw her friends pressed up against the walls and the terrified looks on their faces, so incongruous with her own deep peace.

She sat down at the table. One by one they released their grip on the wall. Hearts pounding, breath shallow, they took mechanical steps, their eyes darting from Mary to Jesus and back again to Mary. They slid cautiously onto the benches around the table and eased themselves down. Jesus sank onto the seat at Mary's right hand and labored to take a few breaths. His shoulders sagged. He seemed about to collapse.

Rachel poured him a cup of wine. "Master, you are not well?" she asked. Her hand shook, almost spilling the wine.

Jesus took a sip from the cup. "Thank you, kind woman." When he weakly smiled his gratitude, Rachel thought she might faint for love of him.

From his position directly across the table, Mummius tracked Jesus' every move. Jealousy was at the top of the heap of churning emotions that threatened to erupt like a volcano within him. Mummius knew that he could not have been the victor a second time against Mary's demons. The vicious assault of last week had left him depleted. It was inevitable that when the demon returned to Mary, reinforced as a Legion, it would have defeated him.

Jesus, on the other hand, had sought out this confrontation and had planned his arrival to coincide with the demonic visitation. Mummius was certain of it. The passage of three days' time was meant to ensure that Mary would be weak and receptive so the Legion could come in easily. Jesus would be guaranteed an opportunity to demonstrate his spectacular skill.

It was more than skill. Mummius replayed the scene in his mind, scrutinizing the details. Jesus had used no rituals, no potions, and no prayers. He simply restrained the flailing body, took in a breath, and ordered the force gone. He did not go into a trance, but seemed rather to locate the power he needed from within. The battle had tired Jesus, surely, but that was nothing compared to Mummius' earlier experience: he had lain on the floor unconscious for hours and then required three days and three nights of rest and fortifying potions to restore himself. Jesus was already recovering, dabbing at a trickle of blood on his head.

Mummius guessed that there must have been some kind of connecting link between Jesus and Mary that channeled his power directly into her. Or had Jesus actually taken Mary's suffering into himself and transformed it? A bond between magus and seeker? Never! What magician would allow that kind of unprotected access to himself? There was no question that the demon had begged for mercy just before Jesus ordered it gone. What was the basis of his authority? What manner of man could command such a force with just a word? The demon had called him by name, and title. "Jesus, Son of the Most High God." Mummius' jealousy turned to anger. He was frantic to leave the room, but did not want to draw attention to himself, and so he waited.

After a few moments, Mary spoke. "I am at peace," she said to them. "I do not understand it, but I feel more truly and completely free, than I ever imagined possible. What it must have cost you, my dearest friends, to contend with this over these years of agony! Be comforted now. I rejoice that you, too, can be released from all your suffering on my behalf."

Tears glistened on Mary's radiant face as she went on. "There is something else you must know." She reached over and touched the tallit draped around Jesus' shoulders. "I myself made this prayer shawl when I was ten years old."

Shoshanna gasped. She remembered guiding the young Mary's hands and heart in the creation of this magnificent tallit decades ago. She had been shocked when the family returned from Beth-el to learn that the extraordinary gift had been squandered on strangers. The old woman who loved Mary was dizzy with confusion.

Mary continued. "I know you must be wondering what all this is about. I, too, am bewildered. All I know is that I need to be alone with Jesus for a while." Mary stood up and bade everyone Shabbat shalom.

Jesus followed her out. Passing by Demetria, he laid his hand momentarily on her head. "God bless you, little daughter," he said. "Sleep well."

The rest remained for a while in silence, staring at the table or at their own folded hands. Eventually everyone moved away and retired. But on this night of nights, none would sleep.

Alone in his quarters, Mummius paced. He scanned the shelves of remedies lining the walls. He fingered mystical scrolls standing in baskets. He sat on the trunk that contained his secrets. Herbs, amulets, incantations. What good was any of this? The Egyptian rested his elbows on his knees and cradled his face in his hands. His mind seized on the moment of recognition, when the demon had called Jesus "Son of the Most High God."

Not a particularly unusual characterization, "son of god." Everywhere in the world the offspring of gods had walked upon the earth. On any whim a god might inhabit a mortal body and modify it with divinity. Or a god might copulate with a mortal and beget a hero-god. Mummius himself was connected to the god through his healing profession, which traced its origin to the god-born Asclepius, son of Apollo. Mummius stood, and resumed his pacing. Jews, too, designated certain holy men as sons of god. Some of their ancient prophets, and others who were able to see into another world, carried the title. Mummius had heard that even now a few such men were active in Galilee. There were accounts of heavenly voices proclaiming them to be son of God. They served as a kind of human emissary to the Spirit world, often interceding as healers. Demons recognized and feared them. They were said to be intimate with the LORD.

Oh, the passionate desire of men to become like gods! They could not help themselves. Egyptian, Greek, Roman, and Jew, all the same. They wanted to live forever, and so, the "sons of god" were everywhere in their stories—and in their desiring hearts. And here was Jesus, a Spirit-filled mediator, who bridged worlds and had extraordinary gifts. *They will make him a god,* Mummius thought bitterly.

While Mummius paced in his room, Marcus Quintius sat naked on the bed in his, sipping Egyptian beer. Being Roman, he saw everything through political eyes. Already people were flocking to be near Jesus, to hear his message and be healed. It would not take long for his adherents to become a multitude. There would be a groundswell of support and—devotion.

Marcus Quintius had known that kind of love once. As a young military leader, he had been successful and popular. His men followed him as though he were possessed of some divine power that would protect them in battle. Under the intense light of their adulation he had come to think of himself, sometimes, on the eve of battle, as godlike. Only loyalty to Rome prevented men like Marcus Quintius from succumbing to the temptations of hubris.

Jesus had no such loyalty. It would be risky to allow a man like that to move around unchecked in a Roman province. Particularly this province. Palestine was a thorn in the side of the Empire, strategically and economically important, but hard to control because of the rebelliousness of some of its people. They could be so radical, these Jews! They were ripe for a charismatic leader.

What if Jesus were on the throne here? A real Jew, not like that pompous Herod with his half-breed bloodlines, and now his incompetent sons. A self-possessed man who could hold the people in thrall, curbing their seditious tendencies and enabling Rome to keep her easternmost territories at peace and wealth flowing into her coffers. The Jews wanted a king of their own blood. Could Jesus be persuaded to accept a Roman crown? *And if not, what then?* wondered Marcus Quintius tossing back his beer.

In the women's bedroom, the mood was nothing like the men's. Demetria and Shoshanna listened quietly as Rachel talked, her face warm and bright.

"Did you see how he looked at me?"

Indeed, Jesus had watched Rachel intently. When he addressed her, it was to thank her for her attention. In all her life, no man had ever spoken to Rachel in such a manner.

When she was barely grown, her hateful father had given her in marriage to a man she did not know. She served her husband as little more than a slave, submitting to his nightly brutality, until, in less than a year, he abandoned her. Her father blamed Rachel for her husband's cruelty and refused to give his daughter refuge. She was left to the streets, facing a life of prostitution, her only alternative. Mary had found her on the Bench of the Prostitutes outside the city wall and brought her home.

Here Rachel had found solace in the company of women, and she did not care if she never spoke to another man as long as she lived. Rachel tolerated Mummius because she had to, and the feeling, she knew, was mutual. As for Marcus Quintius, he was good to her, yes, but in a benevolently condescending way, as though she were a household pet whose absence would scarcely be noticed if one day she turned up missing.

This man, this Jesus, had softened her callused heart. In him Rachel saw a man worthy of love, a man who might love her back. Her pulse raced with the thought of his presence up the short flight of stairs to the upper room. She was ready to do anything he asked.

Enveloped in her joy, Rachel at first did not notice that Demetria's face was wet with tears.

"Little Bit, what is wrong?" she asked at last.

"I miss my papa."

Rachel knew the facts of Demetria's story, but she had been blind to the anguish of it. Now she began to recognize the painful truth more fully as the girl buried her head in the bed covers and sobbed.

Rachel remembered that Demetria had come from a loving slave family in an idyllic setting on Sicily. In her mind she saw a doting father who had watched as his wife and daughter were ripped away from him by a heartless Roman master. She imagined a brief sea voyage to the mainland and on to Rome where Demetria's hysterical mother was sold to another. Then a scene in which the terrified child was shipped off to Tiberias, there to be violated and ruined. Here in Galilee, Demetria had transferred her affection to the mistress who rescued her, but she never stopped longing for what she had left behind in the wheat fields of Sicily.

"Papa always knew what I needed. He watched to see if I was happy or sad. He gave me sweets. Sometimes he brought ribbons for my hair. When I was sleepy, he used to put his hand on my head and send me to bed. Like Jesus did tonight." Demetria cried like a four-year-old.

Shoshanna's eyes narrowed, mulling over what had occurred this night. Unlike Rachel and Demetria, she was thinking not of herself, but of Mary. She remembered everyone's baffled reactions when Jesus addressed the Legion. Even Mummius seemed not to understand it. The look on the Egyptian's face had told her that his scheming mind was racing over the implications. Shoshanna recalled the horror when the demons spoke to

Jesus, naming him Son of God. But what happened next had been even more terrifying. Jesus ordered the demons gone, and they obeyed him instantly. Was this the divine deliverance she had longed for, the day when Mary would be released from God's cruel punishment? Or was it the worst kind of sacrilege?

In the midst of the furor, there was one thing that Shoshanna, and only she, comprehended. When the demons called Jesus "Son of the Most High God," blasphemy had been uttered in their presence. She did what the Law required in the face of blasphemy; she tore her veil. Shoshanna fingered the rips she had made. It was all she could do to restrain her impulse to rush upstairs and pull Mary from whatever sacrilege Jesus might be carrying out even now. Clearly Mary believed that Jesus had healed her. There was some perplexing connection with the past and with the tallit. Over the years, Shoshanna had seen it all. She had hoped in physicians and cures of every kind. She had prayed continually to God to lift his incomprehensible curse. Mummius had provided Mary's only relief, and because of it, Shoshanna risked even more divine displeasure by sharing control of the household with an unclean gentile. There was nothing she would not do to help Mary. Knowing *what* to do was Shoshanna's dilemma. *Who is this Jesus?* An instrument of the Evil One or an instrument of God? *Confusion upon confusion!*

Shoshanna gazed at Rachel and Demetria, holding each other and rocking softly back and forth. Soon they were sleeping. *Silly girls. Life is hard. Life is painful. They should accept that.* Shoshanna knew what was hard and painful about life, and it wasn't one's own suffering. It was to endure helplessly the suffering of a beloved. Many hours of restlessness passed until Shoshanna gave up trying to sleep. She left the room, abandoning Rachel and Demetria to their mutual comfort.

Passing through to the dining room, Shoshanna hardly noticed the uneaten Sabbath meal. She was thinking only of Jesus. His ways seemed gentle enough. But addressing demons? Being addressed by them? Perhaps she should report the blasphemy to the priest. She did not dare. That would mean revealing the carefully protected details of Mary's affliction. To expose Jesus was to expose Mary.

It was in this state of confusion that Shoshanna heard quiet voices from the next room. She tiptoed to the doorway leading into the loom room and peered in. What she saw froze her in the shadows. Jesus and Mary stood at the entrance to the house, their silhouettes backlit by the pink glow of the sun just rising on the Sabbath morn.

Jesus had his arms around Mary and he whispered, "Peace be unto you, dear lady."

Mary answered, "Farewell, Rabbouni."

Rabbouni? She calls him Rabbouni?

Before Shoshanna could recover from her shock, Jesus was gone, and Mary was standing beside her saying, "Dear, dear Shoshanna, is he not wonderful?" Then, picking up her skirts, Mary floated off to her room leaving Shoshanna in a pool of despair.

The old woman sank onto a bench in the dining room. She was dimly aware of a background of muffled noises—people arising and moving about, dressing for Sabbath services. Mary's whispered "rabbouni" reverberated in Shoshanna's ears, dominating all other sounds.

Jewish teachers were sometimes called "rab," a general term of respect meaning "master." "Rabbi" meant "*my* master" and implied acceptance of a teacher as one's own spiritual guide. But "rabbouni." It was a title reserved for the most intimate and sacred of bonds between teacher and devoted disciple. It meant "my lord and my master."

Can it have gone this far? Shoshanna wondered, not realizing that it could go so much farther.

CHAPTER 11

After leaving the Sabbath table, Mary had led Jesus to her private upper room, a small place divided from the rooftop storage area by the courtyard below, and accessible only from her bedroom. Here they could be undisturbed, and no one could overhear them.

It was not the custom for Jewish women to be alone with men. Through her business activities Mary had somewhat more experience with men, but still she was not often in intimate company with them, except for two. Mummius, steward and physician, had private access to her home, her affairs, even her body. Though she cared deeply for him and was grateful for his ministrations, Mary had never thought of Mummius as anything like a lover.

Marcus Quintius was an altogether different matter. Mary adored him, and would have desired him, but by the time they met she was already determined not to marry, so terrified was she of burdening children with her affliction. The potential for desire had never entirely left her, but the last twenty-five years had transformed her love for Marcus Quintius safely into the kind of affection reserved for a devoted uncle.

Alone now with Jesus, Mary took a seat on a cushion, embarrassed by the feelings that stirred within when Jesus folded his lean frame down beside her. She watched him settle onto a pillow close to her, tucking his feet under him and arranging his robes gracefully. His skin still glistened with the effort he had expended on her behalf. Was there something else? She became aware that Jesus was staring at her. He seemed a little breathless, and Mary wondered why. Self-conscious and wanting to move to familiar ground, she stroked the tallit lying across her lap.

"It has grown soft," she said.

Jesus continued to stare at her a bit restlessly, but followed her lead. He would not press her to go where she was not ready.

"Years of wear," he responded.

As he spoke, Jesus put his hands to his shoulders, just at the place where they joined the base of his neck, and squeezed. He rotated his head gently from side to side, trying to alleviate the tension there.

"Would you like some wine?" Mary offered.

"No, but thank you. It will take a while for this to pass," he said.

Mary waited, and finally he offered a thin smile that invited her to speak.

"How is your mother, Jesus?"

"She is well. She lives happily in Nazareth surrounded by her children and grandchildren," Jesus said, rubbing his eyes.

"And Joseph?"

"Dead. Fifteen years."

"Ah."

Mary coiled strands of fringe around her fingers, noticing that the knots remained secure after all these years. "I wonder if she remembers me."

"Mother? Of course she does."

Jesus recounted the story that his mother had told him from childhood about a caring, young girl in a caravan who had given her a prayer shawl on the way to Beth-lehem where he would be born. She had received other gifts that day, rare objects from curious strangers, but none so cherished as the little girl's offering. She had swaddled her newborn son in the shawl as she held him to her breast. She had draped him in it for his bar mitzvah in the Temple at Jerusalem. When he left home to begin his teaching, she gave it to him in remembrance of the night of his birth and the devotion of a child from Magdala.

"I have been wrapped in your prayers my whole life, Mary. Your gift to Mother and to me."

A secret grin tugged at the edge of Mary's mouth.

"Why do you smile?" he asked.

"Mother was at first appalled when I suggested we give away this tallit. She had brought it as a hospitality gift for our hostess in Beth-el. I told her that, since I had made it, I should be able to decide to whom to give it. Finally she agreed."

"You have always done as you please, then?"

"Are you teasing me?"

"Yes, a little," he said, and for a moment Mary was reminded of her brother Reuben and their childhood banter.

"My parents taught me obedience. It was not difficult to abide by their expectations, so deep was my love for them. They also taught me to think for myself and to follow the instincts of my own heart."

"And this has been a problem for you."

"Why do you say that?" asked Mary, a bit defensive.

"You have gentiles living under your roof as family members; you accept an Egyptian as physician. Surely your parents did not teach you that."

She studied his face with its neatly trimmed beard and deep olive skin darkened even more by years in the strong Galilean sunshine. His wavy brown hair framed black eyes that looked into her as though nothing in the world were as important as her response. His unusual interest in her opinions made him seem remarkably attractive. No rabbi listened to the thoughts of women on matters of the Law.

"Do you not think that God loves all his human children, then, Jesus?"

"You dare to question the rabbi, woman?"

Unsure whether or not he was serious, and thus unable to keep the defiance from her voice, she challenged him. "If the rabbi thinks I should put people out because they were born with different blood, then, yes, I do question him."

Jesus laughed. "You are a rare woman in Israel, Mary."

Mary looked him in the eye. "Rabbouni?"

Jesus hesitated. This was the moment when people hearing him for the first time either received what he had to say, or did not. He wanted Mary to understand his message about the Reign of God. He pursued her gently.

"Most people think the Law is quite clear; in Israel we must live pure lives, keeping strictly to ourselves, shunning others and the unclean ways of the world."

"I do not think of my household as unclean, Jesus. Mummius and Marcus Quintius are my dear friends. They have loved and accepted me far beyond the boundaries of our faith. And dear little Chloe and the vibrant Jamileh—not daughters of Israel, but surely daughters of God who made them. To say nothing of Demetria, my own daughter now."

Jesus shook his head slightly.

"Is this so wrong?"

"Wrong? No, dear lady," he said, taking her hands in his. "I was just thinking how different life would be if Pharisees and scribes were blessed with Wisdom such as yours."

Although his compliment surprised and pleased her, Mary perceived that this was a great deal more than flattery. She tried to take it in, allowing his high regard for her to penetrate as fully as she could.

Mary had always been compassionate. She was in many ways a captive of her own heart, taking in the outcasts of society and making them her own. Jesus did this, too, seeking out and lifting up the pariahs who hovered around the edges of the social order. Mary and Jesus were alike in this particular way: they looked at the whole world with the eye of love, the kind of love that characterized the Reign of God, which God intended to disclose through them. Eventually, they would come to share a tolerant and sacrificial love that no one around them had the capacity to understand fully. But for now they felt only the quiver of an unknown, promised future.

Mary withdrew her hands. She reached into her pocket for an embroidered kerchief to wipe perspiration from her face and palms. Again she needed to ease the passion that was pulsing between them. Seeking safety, she returned to the telling of their mutual story.

"You know, when Joseph and Mary left for Beth-lehem I was deeply troubled. But that night, as I sat pensively on the roof of the house, I saw a great star in the sky. For a moment it took my breath away, and the light that shone from it streamed through me like a wave of peace. I understood nothing, but somehow I felt assured that your parents—and you—were safe."

"Believe me, I have heard about that star!"

"Yes, I suppose you have."

After a pause Mary found herself in the grip of an urge to tell Jesus everything that was in her heart.

"The star was not the only extraordinary event of that journey."

"Tell me," he said, again catching her off guard with his concentrated attention.

"Well, after registering for the census in Beth-el, my family went up to Jerusalem. What a trip it was! Father went there every year, of course, for Passover. He had taken my brother Reuben once or twice—the privilege of boys, you know—but it was the first time for me."

"Yes," he said, encouraging her.

"We arrived from the north and walked around the city by the eastern wall. As we approached, the Temple Mount rose before us, and when I looked up and saw the roof of the Temple with its adornments all around the parapet shining in the sun, I cried, though I could not explain why. We climbed the great wall and entered by the Shusan Gate into the Court of the Gentiles. Hundreds not of our faith were milling around there. I was surprised to see the signs in many languages warning them not to proceed. As we stepped through the Beautiful Gate into the Court of Women, I pitied the gentiles who were not allowed in.

"Father and Reuben and the other men in our party proceeded to the inner court. We women passed the time in the outer court watching people come and go."

"Did you not pity yourself that you were forbidden to enter the Court of Israel?"

"I suppose I never thought of it like that." She paused for a moment, reflecting, and then continued, "When the men returned from the inner court, Reuben was bursting with self-importance. I had tried every way imaginable to catch a glimpse inside the wall that divided us, but it was impossible. Though I could see the rising smoke and smell the offerings as they burned. I begged Reuben to report every detail of what he had seen. He described the large altar, the laver, the slaughterhouse and the many tables where the sacrifices were prepared. I developed a vivid picture in my mind, but even now I long to be admitted there to experience it for myself."

"It is indeed awe-inspiring."

"Following our visit to the Temple, we went to the home of relatives in Bethany, and, after two days, we packed our belongings for the return trip to Magdala. Reuben and I pleaded with Father to let us see the sights of Jerusalem one more time, so he agreed that we would walk through the city on our way home. I marveled at everything King Herod had built. His palace was bigger than the entire Temple enclosure. The theater was gigantic. I still do not understand why he built a Greek stadium so near the Temple Mount, knowing it would be offensive."

"Well, Herod loved his pomp. He imagined that by embellishing Jerusalem he could appease everyone, Jews and Hellenizers alike. So arrogant. Still, his building program did provide employment for many of our people for many years. In the end, it gave us the magnificent Temple Mount and you a treasured memory."

"Our trip to Jerusalem was not all a treasure."

Sensitive to Mary's fading spirits, Jesus waited.

"At the end of our sightseeing, we were on the main road out of the city to the north. Mother and I walked together. Father led our strong donkey Alazar, who was laden with provisions, and Reuben held Mikmik, the small one. Mikmik had been born on the very day of my mother's birth—that would make him, what? thirty years or so, old for a donkey—and she had loved him throughout her life. He was funny to look at, with legs too short—he never grew taller than four feet high—and ears too big by half, and so furry. I used to pet them all the time.

"Anyway, the streets were busy and noisy, you know, the way they are in Jerusalem. We were just taking it all in, trying not to get separated in the crowd, when we heard a ruckus ahead. People started pushing and jumping to the sides of the road. We looked up to see someone we recognized—Azarias bar Jonah, a rebel who had traveled in our company from Galilee—running past. Apparently, he and his followers had made a disturbance, brandishing weapons and causing the Roman guard to chase after him.

"Against our father's strict orders, Reuben had spent some time with those foolish young men and became fascinated with them. When he saw what the Romans were doing, Reuben shoved Mikmik's bridle at me saying, 'Hold this!' He ran off screaming in support of Azarias.

"I was terrified for Reuben when I lost sight of him in the fray as foot soldiers rushed past, followed by a chariot hurtling through the street. Stalls were knocked over and goods scattered and trampled in the melee. The chariot careened around the corner directly in front of us. Mikmik pulled frantically against his rein and I released my grip. To save myself, I let go. The rein floated away from me, above Mikmik's head and then down to the ground. Mikmik lunged and the chariot driver lashed him with a whip and drove into his legs.

"The next thing I knew, Mikmik was lying in the street and I was kneeling by his side. He was making little braying noises, trying to take breath. I petted his ears and beseeched him to get up. I was pulling on him, and he was struggling to rise, but…

"Soon my father was there, red in the face and clutching my brother by the neck. Father had dashed off after Reuben and seized him just in time to prevent his being swept up in the wide net of arrests the Romans cast over anyone suspected of association with Azarias bar Jonah.

"Father handed Reuben over to my mother and knelt down in the road beside me. He shook his head. I wailed as Abba stood up and reached into Alazar's saddlebag and found his scabbard. I shall never forget the few steps he took toward us as he pulled the knife and me screaming, 'No! No!' With the blade glinting in his hand, he knelt down and said, 'We must end his suffering.' I refused to release my hold on Mikmik's head as Abba drew the knife swiftly across his neck. I buried my face in Mikmik's fur as his lifeblood poured out onto the road."

Jesus leaned close to Mary, and she laid her head on his chest, weeping. "I can still smell it."

Eyes brimming, Jesus stroked her hair. "You were a loyal friend for one so young."

"If only I had not let go..."

Jesus held Mary until she was able to control her sobs and go on with her story.

"The rest was like walking through a swamp of reeds, slow and deliberate. I heard Father say, 'Rebecca, take the children and go out of the city by the Damascus Gate to the north. It is less than three hundred paces on this road. Outside the wall there is a vast timber market on the left. You can't miss it. Across the road from the market is a small palm grove. Wait for me there. I will arrange for a cart to remove the animal and join you as soon as I can.'

"Father held Alazar's rein out to me. 'Can you handle him?' he asked. I told him, 'Yes, Abba, I can,' though I did not believe I could do it. We started to walk, and I turned back for one more look at Mikmik. I could see only his big ears and the wide black stripes that outlined them. Poor, dead thing. What a way to end his life!"

Then Mary told Jesus what she had never confessed to another soul. "When Father handed Alazar's reins over to me, I felt responsible for everything, our family's provisions, my weeping mother, and my frantic brother. The warm stench of Mikmik's blood rose from my skirt. I was only ten years old.

"And, Jesus, it wasn't just Mikmik who lay dead in the streets of Jerusalem. A part of my brother lay there, too. The brutal arrest of Azarias bar Jonah changed Reuben. After that, the evil that had threatened him his whole life seemed to swell and engulf him. Over the next five years, it was free to come and go at will through the big hole that had been opened in him. It drove him to the cliff where he jumped off and died.

"In Jerusalem I lost my hold on Reuben. I couldn't save Mikmik from the legions of Rome nor Reuben from the legion of demons. When he died and the demons entered *me*, I thought it was my fault. I thought God blamed me."

After a long pause, Jesus asked, "And now?"

Under Jesus' watchful eye, Mary began to discern the truth. "Perhaps it was the Evil One who told me lies using the voice of God. I must have mistaken them, one for the other."

Mary examined the prayer shawl lying in her lap. "When I was young, I used to think God was in my weaving. I felt the soft wool in my fingers and saw fascinating designs in my mind, and I remembered God. I sang psalms as my small arms pushed the shuttle rhythmically back and forth through the fabric. I was so certain, then, of God and of myself."

"What changed?"

"I'm not sure. I know that after Reuben died, I began to suffer terribly. I took it for granted that God was punishing me. Sometimes when I prayed to God, instead of being comforted, I was pressed into a dark, terrifying place where God found me guilty."

"Mary," Jesus said, flooded with compassion, "your suffering was never from God."

"But the Law..."

More to himself than to Mary, Jesus said in a furious lament, "Are there no wise ones in Israel?"

Mary's look told him that she did not comprehend what he was saying.

"Do you think that when we suffer it means that we have offended God, and so God punishes us? Often people have no idea what their supposed transgressions have been. The scribes and the Pharisees judge and imprison us with their misguided interpretations.

"The Law is meant to serve the people, Mary, not the other way around. It is intended to show the way to God, not to be a substitute for God. Israel has fallen far from the truth in this matter. But you, dear lady, have diligently pursued the truth of God's love against every pressure to do otherwise. It is you who have been fulfilling the Law of Love.

"The Evil One is a great conveyer of God's words. He uses the Law against us. When we open ourselves to the Spirit of God, as you have, we open ourselves to evil spirits as well. It can be difficult to distinguish between them and even more difficult to embrace the One and refuse entrance to the other. It is a lifelong challenge."

Mary could see that Jesus was telling her this with the authority of one acutely aware of the challenge. She heard the reassuring words he spoke, but still she was troubled. Mary remembered the moment when Jesus had freed her from the near fatal clutch of the demons and called her back into life. Because she did not understand what he had done or how he had done it, she still doubted. Would she ever again be able to hear the voice of God and trust that it really was God?

"But if I open myself to God, how can I know that the Evil One will not come into me?"

"Dear lady, do you believe in me?"

"Yes, Rabbouni, I do."

"Then hear me when I tell you that through your faith you have received the freedom to choose."

"You are so confident in me?"

He nodded and said, "I am." Mary wanted it to be true.

It seemed natural, now, for Jesus to lay his head on Mary's shoulder, depleted as he was and longing for sleep. She put her arms around him, and he sank into her lap and closed his eyes and slept. He lay there, almost like a child, tired and safe. As she held him thus, a melody from Mary's childhood arose, a sweet, soothing song she had often sung to Reuben. Mary started to hum, and the fullness of her miraculous restoration swelled in her heart.

As her song went on, repetition after repetition, Mary's folded legs grew cramped and one foot went to sleep, making her uncomfortable, but she would not move for fear of waking him. She was relieved when, after a while, he stirred and she could stretch.

Jesus seemed disoriented when he realized how freely and fully he had relaxed into Mary's embrace. He straightened and cleared his throat and pushed himself away from her. Then he bent over and, holding out his hand to her, drew Mary up and put his arm around her waist. Mary allowed herself to be led to the window of her upper room where they looked out over the garden to the Sea of Galilee in the distance. As they stood close together, Mary felt flashes of fire where her body came in contact with his, at her hip and shoulder, around her waist and in her hand.

The energy that surged between them caught Jesus off guard. He turned to Mary and buried his face in her hair, breathing in the lingering scent of lavender. When she slipped her arms around his back and laid her head on his chest, a muted moan escaped from him.

Jesus had known such a force once before. On a mountain in the Judean desert in a vision he had surveyed Jerusalem and all it stood for. He became aware for the first time that he could seize whatever authority he wanted on this earth. He had the power to take the path that God intended for him or another path of his own choosing. Oh, how he had been tempted to yield on that mountain!

Hands trembling, Jesus picked up the tallit from the floor where Mary had dropped it. He covered his head and, wrapping the shawl around Mary's shoulders as he embraced her, lifted his eyes to heaven and prayed, "Abba, I give you thanks for the gift of this, your beloved daughter, and the great trust that you have placed in me. I return her to you, restored.

Now I ask you to give her all that she requires to fulfill her place in the Reign of God."

At the sound of Jesus' "Amen," Mary permitted herself to soften in his arms, uncertainty dwindling in the face of gratitude for his gift of healing.

Mary and Jesus stood together under the protective blanket of his prayer, lost in private thoughts. There was much for her to take in; she needed time to reflect, and so she was thankful when he said simply, "The sun is coming up."

Jesus breathed in the freshening air. "No rain today. And tomorrow, after the Sabbath, a pleasant boat ride to Capernaum."

"Must you go?"

"My friends are already beside themselves. They are a little jealous, I think, wondering why we lingered these three days. They had made arrangements to return home on urgent business—so many people waiting, they said. My brothers do not always understand my priorities."

"When will I see you again?" asked Mary.

"I am sure it will be soon," he promised.

CHAPTER 12

At the third hour after sunrise of that Sabbath morn, the trumpet sounded, summoning the faithful to prayer. Small groups arrived at the much-loved synagogue, its distinctive columns stretching up from a foundation of well-hewn basalt blocks to unpretentious capitals above. The remarkable columns of the synagogue in Magdala were a source of pride to the community. The architect who designed them, in some instinct for beauty exceeding mere function, had indented each one with a large notch, creating two graceful curves, mirror images of one another, that seemed to flow from the center and circle around to meet at a point on the other side, forming an imprint of what would in later times and places come to be known as heart-shaped.

The congregation, generally relaxed after the quiet Erev Shabbat, greeted friends and family as they entered the basilica by the western door. They spread out through the aisles, many choosing to separate casually into groups of men and women as they settled onto benches in the nave or on risers to the sides. The weavers found each other and sat together toward the front.

At a signal from the worship leader, two hundred people stood as one, and, along with hundreds of thousands of other Jews all over their world, covered their heads and turned to face Jerusalem. They responded "amen" after the recitation of each of eighteen opening prayers. They listened to the reading of the first lesson, "The Law," then the chants, and finally the second lesson, the *haphtarah* of the day. All these parts of the service were conducted in Hebrew, the language of Torah, barely understood by most people and spoken by even fewer, as generations of Diaspora had distanced them from the ancient tongue. The sermon that followed, an exposition of the lessons, was conducted in the vernacular; Greek, for example, in the synagogues of Alexandria, Aramaic in Magdala.

The congregation was ready for a sermon from Isaac, the priest, or Niqai, the scribe. But when Isaac rose to address them, it was to make an introduction. He said that this morning they were honored by the presence of a guest rabbi, a teacher from Capernaum. This announcement led to enthusiastic murmuring among the congregation: someone new—today it might not be so hard to stay attentive through the long hours of the sermon. Eagerly, the people watched the visiting teacher rise from a bench in the front and stand up to take his place at the center of a raised platform facing them.

Sudi grasped Avireina's hand. "It's him!" she cried in a rapture that caused them all to sit up and pay attention.

Jesus looked out at two hundred expectant faces and took a deep breath, wondering how his message would be received this day. He had only just begun his ministry in earnest, but already he knew that his gifts—the teaching, the healing—were more accessible if his followers believed in him. Here in Magdala many people had proved receptive. He was grateful for that.

Not like in Nazareth. He had tried to perform miracles in Nazareth, where he grew up. People said, "We've known this fellow all his life. He is the son of Mary who lives just up the street, and Joseph, the carpenter, peace be upon him. He used to play ball with our boys. And now he is healing lepers? Ridiculous." And so he couldn't do it there.

Jesus needed believers. When people came to him with faith, when they brought their broken bodies and minds, believing that life could be different, believing that he could do it, then he really could do it. He opened a conduit between the believer and his heavenly father, the One he called "Abba." He transmitted power one to the other, through himself. When it worked, it was dazzling.

It was not that when he was performing miracles he was telling people who he was. Rather, he was telling them as fully as he could, who God is. Jesus' miracles were evidence of what God intends for his children, the Beloved, evidence of who they were meant to be. This intention he called the "Reign of God."

Jesus' eyes fell upon a girl who sat near the front, not far from him. He smiled at her and felt the warmth of her adoring look wash over him, encouraging him. Then his eyes were drawn, as if by a tether, to the other side and farther back, to a young man who was staring at the girl from behind. Jesus recognized a vindictive resentment in that stare, and when the young man turned his eyes on Jesus, he gave the miserable youth a brief, compassionate nod.

Jesus opened his mouth to speak. "The Reign of God is like this...," he began.

It went hard with Sudi that Sabbath day. From across the aisle of the synagogue, Eber spied on his betrothed, whispering to her friends. Bad enough that he should be forced to witness the ardent attention she lavished on other girls. He never felt that eager energy directed toward him. So when Eber saw the worshipful glow on Sudi's face as Jesus stood to speak, it made him seethe. How could he wed such a woman? Throughout the sermon Eber's anger ripened until he could barely control his urge to drag her from the synagogue in plain view. He restrained himself until the final blessing ended the service.

The congregation was milling around, saying their goodbyes and passing the Sabbath peace, when Eber approached Sudi at the foot of the steps outside the synagogue. He seized her arm and wrenched it up painfully behind her back. The two of them disappeared down a side street before anyone could come to her aid, or would.

The next morning Sudi sat on a rug in the loom room surrounded by the other weavers. "Is he not extraordinary?" she said, effervescent with admiration.

Sudi's face, which had begun to heal to a dull yellow from the previous assault, was freshly bruised to red and purple. One eye was swollen shut. Though the arm that Eber had bent behind her back hung limply at her side, the young Sudi had never seemed happier. When Mary arrived to greet the weavers and saw what had happened, she was horrified.

"Oh, Sudi," she exclaimed, kneeling beside the wounded girl, "what has he done to you now?"

Knowing that no answer was required, Sudi instead asked, "Mary, why is Eber so jealous of Jesus?"

As Mary sifted through her mind for a response to the girl's question, her comprehension expanded. She was starting to notice that each time she thought of Jesus, some new idea, some new way of seeing things, drifted into her mind, spurred by her own healing. Had he not turned everything she thought she knew upside down when he told her that her suffering was not inflicted by God, as they had all been taught?

"Eber, I think, is jealous of everyone, Sudi. Jesus is especially irritating. He has radical ideas. If it were not for his power to heal, I fear many more would reject him."

"Jesus is peaceful and generous. What is so radical about that?" Sudi asked, wincing while Mary inspected her swollen eye.

"Jesus is like a prophet, very close to God. So close that he addresses God as 'Abba' when he prays."

The weavers were puzzled. Jesus called The Almighty, The Lord God of Israel, his "papa"? Certainly that was peculiar, but not exactly what could be called radical.

"He is also very learned. He knows Torah and loves it. He is not reluctant to point out to priests and scribes their misinterpretations of the Law. Can you see why this would be unsettling to people?"

The weavers buzzed and nodded. This they could understand.

"It is the healing that really causes problems. A rabbi with radical ideas might be dismissed as foolish or eccentric, but Jesus backs up his message with miracles. He says his power comes from God. If they don't believe it comes from God, they have to believe it comes from the Evil One."

Jamileh and Chloe, being pagan, made signs against the Evil Eye. Their Jewish sisters smiled, though they did not laugh.

Avireina asked the question that was in all their minds. "Mary, how did you come to know Jesus?"

Mary closed her eyes and allowed her thoughts to go back to two days ago, a brief passage of time that now seemed an eternity. One by one the weavers moved to surround her, creating a circle, and waited for her to speak.

"Jesus was here just last Erev Shabbat."

The weavers were impressed by this revelation and answered with "ooohs" and "aaahs."

"At my insistence, Mummius and Marcus Quintius had sought him out and persuaded him to visit me. Really, the reason I wanted to meet him was because of you, Sudi, and you, Sahadia. I had heard that you were attracted to his message and that your men were angry on account of it. I did not like anyone disrupting your lives. I insisted that Jesus come here so I could see what he was up to. The meeting was not what I expected.

"When Jesus covered his head for the prayers of Erev Shabbat, I recognized the tallit he wore. It was a prayer shawl I myself had made when I was but a girl of ten years. Imagine this: I had met Jesus' mother when she was with child. In her presence I was moved by an unseen force, a deep connection of the heart, to give the tallit to her in remembrance of me.

"Seeing the tallit sent me spinning, and I barely knew what was happening. It was then that the demons came into me, or so I was told. All I know is that I became so small that my body was not my body. My spirit was ready to flee. I thought I was gone forever."

Mary paused, remembering how she had shrunk to insignificance that night, how she had been ready to release life, had wanted to release it.

"But I heard Jesus' voice calling, telling me to come to him. Wrapped in the shawl that I had made, Jesus drove away the affliction that had plagued me for so long. He healed my wounded spirit and restored me. Then I knew, miraculously, that we were intended by God, after all these years, to be joined one to the other.

"How can I describe what I feel now? I am like a young girl with a dancing heart in the thrill of a budding springtime. No more suffering. Deep peace."

The sweep of a feather could have been heard in the hush that followed. Avireina buried her face in Mary's lap and Sahadia stroked her long, black hair. Chloe rose from her cushion on the floor and moved to stand before Mary. The silent Greek girl quivered as she thrust her hands spontaneously over her mouth and patted her lips.

"What is she doing?" asked Sudi.

Chloe pounded feverishly at her mouth.

Mary frowned in deep concentration for a moment. Then, in a flash of confidence, Mary spoke for Jesus and said, "Dear Chloe, yes, I am certain that Jesus will restore your speech."

Mary was thunderstruck when, in the next instant, Chloe fell to the floor, took hold of Mary's feet, and kissed them.

This is what it is like for Jesus! she thought as she pulled the elated girl up from her supplicant's position. Mary wrapped Chloe in her arms, and the other women closed their circle tightly around the two of them. After a few moments, Mary released her embrace and hopped down from the platform. She took Chloe by the hand and pulled her toward the courtyard. Mummius was blocking the door. He had seen the whole thing.

"Oh, good, Mummius. Here you are. I am taking this girl to the lake shore. Please go and give my apologies to Marcus Quintius and say that I shall return shortly."

Mummius did not move.

"Excuse me, Mummius. We must hurry now."

"Lady, you have not taken your medications," he said, as he might to a disobedient child.

Mary looked at Mummius as though he had become suddenly dim-witted.

"I no longer have need of medications, Mummius."

Mary saw what she thought might have been dejection on Mummius' face, but there was no time to waste. "Don't worry. I'll be right back," she said, pushing past him.

Mary pulled Chloe by the hand, the weavers following. Through the courtyard they ran, out the back door, over the garden pathway and into the olive grove, six women, veils loose, skirts flying, dashing through the trees to the seashore not far from Mary's house. When they arrived, Jesus' boat was nowhere to be found.

"Look out there," instructed Mary. "Does anyone see him?"

They scanned the waters frantically. Disappointment rose with each passing moment and each boat that was not his. Chloe was crestfallen.

"Keep looking," Mary insisted.

Then, just as they were giving up hope, Sudi cried out, "I see him!"

The women started jumping, waving their hands, and calling out, "Jesus, come back!"

Mummius was shaken. He did not have to follow the women to the lakeshore in order to visualize the scene there. Jesus would heal Chloe—probably Sudi, too—and they would all be following him around like sheep. He cared nothing for the weavers. But Mary—what now, if she no longer needed him? Mummius was losing his grip: on the household, on the mistress, on himself.

Shoshanna walked in on him leaning against the doorway and staring across the courtyard where the weavers had departed in Mary's wake.

"Where is everyone?"

"What do you think? They have gone off after the wonderworker." Mummius made no attempt to keep the rancor from his voice. "I imagine that Chloe will return with praises to the Living God upon her lips."

Shoshanna stared at him. Mummius could see satisfaction in her eyes when she probed, "What do you mean?"

"You know very well what I mean," Mummius replied as he swept away to deliver Mary's message to Severus.

Hearing no response to his knock, Mummius looked in and found the room empty and tidied. *Gone to the baths*, Mummius thought. *He has been here six days. He will have begun to offend himself with his own odor.*

Indeed, Marcus Quintius had left for Magdala hours ago and was at this very moment soaking and sweating contentedly in the caldarium, the hot room. When he began making regular visits to Magdala twenty years ago, Marcus Quintius had been revolted by the absence of public baths. It wasn't long before he had engaged the support of Roman residents there to construct a bath house, which he could use whenever he traveled to Magdala. Quintius himself had sketched out the design of the facility and given it to an architect who had executed the plan admirably. *Not bad, not bad at all*, he thought. As he soaked, he looked around at the walls and ceiling of the caldarium and imagined the elaborate hypocaust concealed within, a vast central heating system.

The principal component of the system was a huge furnace that warmed great volumes of air, which flowed, via convection, under the floors throughout the building and into flues that carried hot air upward, warming the walls. The furnace also heated water in a large boiler, which was then distributed to room-sized soaking tubs in the tepidarium, or warm room, and the caldarium where he was now. Of course, the hypocaust required an aqueduct, which brought water from the river to the north. Aqueducts and arches to hold them up—once Roman engineers had mastered those two concepts, there was no reason for any place on earth to be without an ample water supply.

As usual, Marcus Quintius had started his routine with a luxurious soak in the tepidarium, allowing his body to warm up slowly in preparation for the high temperatures of the caldarium. Easing down into the hot water, he nodded in passing to the few others who had come to the baths early, not particularly wanting to engage any of them in conversation. The heat of the water, and the steam that rose from it, lured Marcus Quintius into a languid daydream. It was in such reveries that Mary unfailingly appeared to him in visions. He willingly gave himself to these imaginings, because they offered him the only way he could possess her.

From the moment he had met her on the shores of the Mediterranean Sea at Tyre twenty-five years ago, until this very day, Marcus Quintius had loved Mary. It started as primordial lust, a potent urge that was kept in check only by his respect for her father, Aaron, and the risk of losing her altogether. Over the years, as he denied his hunger, it metamorphosed into an intoxicating desire that included elements of deep affection. Finally he begged Aaron for her hand in marriage.

Aaron refused, citing an illness that Marcus Quintius had not then begun to understand. Years later, on his deathbed, Aaron would extract a promise from Marcus Quintius—he must never confess his desire to Mary. He had also pledged that he would always protect her. He would see that she never wanted for anything. All this he had done without fail, in full measure.

In fact, Marcus Quintius had made Mary rich—or what would have been rich, if she would just quit spreading her wealth over every needy person who came her way. What was more, it appeared that now, at long last, she was healed of her dreadful affliction. *I did this for her,* thought Marcus Quintius with satisfaction, remembering that it was he who had gone to Magdala to insist that Jesus come to help her. Then, from within the mist of his longing, a barely recognizable hope floated across his consciousness, the hope that if Mary were someday miraculously to be healed, he would be released from his promise to Aaron.

Marcus Quintius thought of Mary's long black hair and the fragrance of lavender arising from it. He felt again her head resting on his neck, as he carried her to her sickbed the night he had arrived, and the soft silk of her dress in contrast to the rough skin of his arms.

He went on to imagine that which had not happened. He saw himself lying beside her and speaking to her of his love. He undressed her slowly, stroking each rising curve of her body as she was about to give herself to him at last. His body tensed with anticipation when a surge of steam from the hypocaust brought Marcus Quintius abruptly out of his daydream.

He shook his head vigorously. *Time for icy water.* He stood up and walked out of the bath on steps intricately tiled with images of sea creatures frolicking in waves. Not bothering to wrap himself in a towel, he walked down the dark hall to the frigidarium, the cold room. Marcus Quintius paused for a moment at the edge of this next bath, his hot skin releasing clouds of steam. There would be no easing into the chilly water for him. He took a breath and plunged in, feet first, submerging his whole body. Seconds later, when his head and shoulders reemerged, he let out an exhilarated howl.

"Why do you do that?" said a voice behind him.

Marcus Quintius turned to see Mummius leaning against the wall.

"Why not?" he said and howled again.

Mummius sat down on a stone bench close to the edge of the pool. "I thought I would find you here. Couldn't bear it another moment, eh?"

"You know, Mummius, I do not understand these provincials. With such excellent baths, you'd think they would learn to wash, as we do."

"There is much you do not understand, Severus. Their God takes offense at luxury."

"The pleasures of the bath, a luxury? More like necessity, I say," and holding his breath, Marcus Quintius submerged his head.

When he popped up again, Mummius said, "Meet me in the atrium when you are finished, Severus. I have something to tell you."

After a few minutes more, Marcus Quintius emerged from the water, his skin tingling pleasurably. He picked up a towel from the bench where he had tossed it and walked to the dressing room. When a slave had completed a brisk drying of his skin, he slipped on his tunic and went to find Mummius.

"You worry too much, my friend," he insisted, hearing Mummius' report of the morning's events.

"Severus, do you not see?" Mummius lowered his voice discreetly so other bathers who came and went could not overhear. "Jesus has the lady under his control now."

"Jupiter's eyes, Mummius! Two days ago you feared the demon would take her. Now that the demon is defeated, you fear the one who saved her? She says she is at peace. I, for one, am grateful for that."

"What kind of peace? We have no idea how Jesus will use his power over her. Even you may have lost your influence with her."

"Never," said the Roman, but there was no mistaking the note of apprehension in his voice.

"You have an old comrade-in-arms in Capernaum, do you not?"

"How do you remember such things?"

Taking the question for the expression of admiration that it was, Mummius ignored it and said, "I think it is time for you to pay him a visit. Let us go together. I, too, have, um, an acquaintance there."

Marcus Quintius finished dressing, and the two men set a brisk pace on the five-mile walk to Capernaum. As they approached the city, Marcus Quintius headed for an affluent residential area. Mummius had a very different destination in mind—an antiquated amulet shop in the old town. Different destinations, but one objective: to find out more about Jesus, each hoping in his own way that it was not too late to shape Mary's response to him. What they did not know was that Mary was already moving beyond their reach.

CHAPTER 13

Capernaum was the ideal location for an amulet shop, for that city, to judge from the part of it which surrounded the shop and jostled it, and stuck its limestone fingers into it, and smothered it, deserved the magic inside.

You couldn't walk about the neighborhood of the amulet shop as you could any other neighborhood. Groping your way through lanes and dark passages, you never once emerged onto anything that you would recognize as a street. In those days, nobody ever found the amulet shop based on verbal instructions. It was said that many people who intended a rendezvous there had set out on a wandering journey amongst the twisted pathways and, finally tiring, gave up and went home again, mystified. This gave rise to the persistent myth that the amulet shop was concealed within a labyrinth.

Surrounding the amulet shop, and threatening to engulf it, were other dilapidated shops, their courtyards covered in vines as thick as hedges. Groggy merchants sat on the ground outside their establishments, chewing khat leaves or drunk on wine, indifferent as to whether customers came in or walked on by. Blind men, and others ruined by fate, held out pathetic arms, begging for alms. Week after week, year after year, each one sat until at last he disappeared and another assumed his place, taking up his piteous wail in the same ragged clothes with the same nauseating stench. Their condition could hardly be said to have undergone any material change when they, in turn, were replaced by others.

When Mummius first went in search of the amulet shop, years ago, a kind of resignation came over him as he trod those circuitous mazes. He was about to give himself up for lost, when, unexpectedly, he noticed a pattern to his meandering. Amongst the narrow thoroughfares, he found an occasional lone paving stone, upon which were carved inscriptions of old, now barely discernible, worn down by the endless treading of sandaled feet.

Within the cryptic messages on each stone was inscribed a number, and if you could follow the numerical sequence, you would be led, inevitably, to the amulet shop.

Above each stone was mounted a wrought iron bar secured into the sides of nearby buildings, a series of inanimate limbs, metal arms with brackets that once held ewers of oil which, burning, would light the night and the stones below. Mysterious torch arms, offering rigid salutes to the seeker passing by and obscuring the probability that anyone anymore knew what they were there for. There were more torch arms in the small area near the amulet shop than you would think all of Capernaum would ever need.

Mummius no longer glanced down at the stones for guidance. Since that first perplexing visit, he had learned the way well, and had come here many times to acquire arcane additions to his pharmacopoeia and to get a dose of the old Egypt for himself. He made unerringly for the amulet shop, and entered.

"Siamun, you leprous son of a whore, come forth!" Mummius shouted in his best Egyptian voice and language. Waiting for the owner of the shop to emerge from its nether regions, he looked around, taking quick stock of the inventory.

If you came into the amulet shop to buy, you had to know what you were doing. To an untrained eye, the shelves, floor-to-ceiling and wall-to-wall, would have been as confounding as the very route that brought you here. They were crowded with every sort of vial, bag and box, most dusty, all unidentified. If you were not careful, you would end up with substances meant for one ailment, given for another, in unspecified doses, poisonous in some cases, efficacious in others. Or you might take home a talisman thought to bring good luck and end up murdering your wife. The owner certainly did not imagine that it was his responsibility to educate you.

Mummius, of course, knew what he was doing, so Siamun never tried to trick him, or, if he did, the trick was decisively turned back upon him. Once, in response to a sleight-of-hand with a substance, Mummius had left Siamun on the floor of the shop whimpering like a puppy for an hour while he went for a walk. He did not often resort to such trickery, but he knew it was what Siamun would understand. When he returned and released the spell, Siamun roared with laughter. Their friendship was forged.

Materializing from the back room, Siamun exclaimed, "Mentuhotep, welcome!"

Mummius winced. He was always startled to hear his Egyptian name, but Siamun refused to address him by any other. Mentuhotep—he hated the sound of it, but he loved it, too. It reminded him of the tragic events of his early life in Bubastis, and so he hated it. It reminded him that he was fully, truly and eternally Egyptian, and so he loved it.

Siamun and Mummius, different in many ways, were brothers in every way that counted: Egyptian first and last, proficient in medicine and magic, far from home, aliens in an inhospitable land. From a distance you would have a difficult time distinguishing them one from the other—tall, slender forms draped shoulder to ankle in tightly woven cotton robes of pure white, cinched at the waist, wigs of black hair combed into a severe style, which looked for all the world like caps, rather than hair, with bangs on the forehead and the outline of flares just below the ears. Only as they came nearer could you perceive their dissimilarities.

Mummius moved like music, graceful in restraint, drawing you into his floating cadence, whereas Siamun limped, just slightly, but enough to cause you to think "cripple" when you looked, and then looked away. Mummius' face was beautiful in its unlined symmetry and the care he lavished on his skin. The face of Siamun was marred by a ghastly crescent-moon scar, etched from forehead to ear, and on that side a bulging knob of skin where his eye should be. Mummius was fastidious, washed, polished, and fragrant. Siamun, though richly ornamented, was unkempt, his irregular teeth stained with khat, the tarnish of his inlaid brass collar rubbing off on the skin of his neck. He smelled of spilled grease and stale sweat, the odor of someone too long abed.

"What brings you to Capernaum?"

"That depends. What do you have of interest today, my brother?"

Siamun's good eye squinted at Mummius. "You want to know about Jesus," he said slowly.

"Ah, mind reader are you now, Siamun?"

"Who needs to read minds? No one speaks of anything else. All my customers want to know how he does it. I knew you would come eventually. And here you are! Sit."

Siamun motioned to large, tooled and fringed camel skin cushions circling a low brass table in the center of the shop. From somewhere a slave appeared with steaming cups of tea and a plate of dates and bread. He served them, and retreated.

Mummius lowered his eyes and stared into his tea. He breathed in the aromatic steam and sipped slowly.

"What do you mean, 'how he does it'? How he does what?"

"Come now, Mentuhotep. You surely know that he heals every category of affliction. That he does it publicly, without preparation of any sort, using neither amulets nor incantations. Pity. If he were an ordinary magus, he'd have been in here by now buying supplies." Siamun looked warily at Mummius, who was still staring into his tea. "What is it, Mentuhotep? What secrets lurk behind those hooded eyes, eh?"

Mummius decided to bring Siamun into his confidence, sooner rather than later. He laid a hand on Siamun's forearm and dug his fingernails in. "You must tell no one."

Unscrewing his arm from Mummius' grip and rubbing the sting off, Siamun promised, "Your knowledge is safe with me, brother. I swear it."

Just to be sure, Mummius made the secret sign, which placed a blood seal upon the lips, and waited. When Siamun responded in kind, Mummius whispered, "I saw him drive out a legion."

"No," Siamun said, his response barely a murmur, so astonished was he by this revelation.

"I witnessed it myself."

Well aware that Mummius was no exaggerator, Siamun just sat and let amazement sink in. Finally he asked, "Who?"

Putting his faith in the curse of their blood seal, Mummius admitted, "My lady, Mary of Magdala."

Siamun's eye squinted again as his mind sifted through the grit of the past. Mummius had kept the truth of his regular visits to Siamun's shop and the pattern of his purchases unclear. Today, he was grateful at last that Siamun understood not only the struggles he had endured over the years, but also the demands on him for secrecy.

Siamun's already high opinion of Mummius surged, and he dared to ask, "You tried to do it?"

"Yes. Well, not precisely. The legion was not at full strength when I drove it out. I tell you, Siamun, it almost took me. I knew that when it returned I would not be able to match it." For a moment, Mummius' inscrutable face softened, and there might have been moisture arising in the corners of his kohl-rimmed eyes.

"But Jesus was able to do it?"

"Yes. And it was as you said—no amulets, no potions, not a breath of incantation. He just laid his hand on her and ordered it gone."

Siamun shook his head and gave a low whistle.

Mummius sat quietly, drinking his tea, and waited for the full impact of his report to be absorbed. He himself was still in the process of acknowledging all that he stood to lose. He thought of Mary and how he had come to love her in spite of himself. She had entrusted to him her home, her fortune, even her life. Though he had not dared to hope for love from her, she gave him a deep and generous affection that warmed him body and mind whenever he was in her presence.

Now, spurred by the reopened wounds of his past, Mummius believed that life was about to deal him another near-fatal blow. He thought of Jesus with a combination of jealousy and reverence. And fear. Ironically, by healing Mary, Jesus threatened to rob Mummius of everything he had built. It was then that he set upon a course to break the bond between Mary and Jesus. In order to do that, he would have to know everything there was to know about the wonder-worker, and he would have to do it without exposing himself.

"I need your help," he said.

Siamun replied, "Anything."

While Mummius was passing the time with Siamun in the amulet shop, Marcus Quintius was visiting an old friend of his own. As the Egyptians were, so the two Romans were at once alike and very unlike.

In the world of foreign missions, whether diplomatic, military, or economic, there had always been, and would always be, those few renegades, cultural converts as it were, who come to prefer their adopted homes to the lands of their birth. Some such individuals "go native," as it is said, immersing themselves in the alien culture, seeking to become what they were never born to be. Others, having experienced the rewards that accrue to subjugators, make a more rational decision to stay on, enjoying the advantages of the host nation, but not completely severing ties to their homelands—privileges in both locations, responsibilities in neither. Such was Gaius Valerius, centurion of Rome. He was stationed in Capernaum at his own request and would retire here, of course never relinquishing his Roman citizenship, the most valuable benefit in the known world.

In Capernaum, Valerius was able to maintain and take pleasure in an impressive villa, a country home with extensive adjacent land, which would have been far beyond his means in Rome. Here it was that Marcus Quintius sat with his comrade from their earlier military days, drinking wine. He tried not to grimace as he took in the garish details surrounding him. Marcus Quintius was accustomed to luxury, and his own homes—two villas in the country and the domus in Rome—were certainly splendid. Everything about them was elegant, understated and manly. Like himself.

Gaius Valerius' taste ran to the extravagant, and that was putting a charitable eye on it. Ostentatious would be the better description, even vulgar. Like himself. His villa had the shape of a small temple with fine stucco walls and a patterned floor laid out in polychrome marble tiles. Its principal atrium had fourteen imposing columns and a massive fountain in the center. All quite tasteful, really, except for the embellishments. Everywhere, in statuary and mosaic, were scenes of men and women cavorting and copulating, not only with each other but with fauna of every conceivable type. Marcus Quintius' residences, on the other hand, were decorated with representations of the military feats, for example, of King Alexander. His flora and fauna were in natural settings doing what was *natural* for them to do.

Valerius and Quintius were different in personal appearance, as well. It was not uncommon for Roman men who were standing for political office to appear in public stripped to undergarments to display their battle scars, so that voters would be reminded of their heroism and desire them as leaders. Marcus Quintius did not need to disrobe to show his valor. Even now, covered in civilian clothes, his scars pulsed unseen, making themselves known by the very way he carried himself and the imagination of the observer. On the other hand, Gaius Valerius' uniform itself seemed affected, with gaudy metal trappings added here and there and polished to a high sheen. When he sat, his tunic had an odd way of falling off his left thigh to reveal the evidence of a deep wound, decades old.

Marcus Quintius wanted to tell him to cover up his leg. Instead, he kept to his business and asked, "How reliable is your source, Gaius Valerius?"

"Very reliable, I assure you. When Jesus started to draw crowds, I assigned one of my best men to follow him. He has gathered some interesting information."

"Such as?"

"For one thing, Jesus is not from Capernaum, but Nazareth."

"That backwater?"

"Yes. I believe they ran him out of town over there. So he settled here in Capernaum, probably thinking it more fruitful ground for the spread of his ideas—more diverse, less, well, less Jewish."

"Why should Rome concern herself with all this, Gaius Valerius?" interrupted Quintius, impatience, as usual, getting the better of him.

"Let me back up. Jesus has a kinsman, one John, who himself draws crowds in Judea."

"Judea!" exclaimed Marcus Quintius. "That could spell trouble."

"Yes. You know how all the area around Jerusalem breeds discontent. John is a perfect example of it. That idiot Pontius Pilate only inflames resentment against Rome. He has nothing but contempt for the Jews. Seems to seek out ways to offend them at every turn. By any measure he is inflexible and cruel. Not at all the best procurator for Judea. Why Tiberius appointed him, I cannot fathom." Then in a whispered aside, "Who can tell why Caesar does anything, right, my friend?"

Marcus Quintius smiled a wry smile, but said nothing. Criticism of Caesar would never pass his lips where the walls had ears.

"Many of the Jews call John a prophet. In my opinion he is completely mad, roaming the wilderness, scavenging, living on locusts...," said Gaius Valerius, pulling a face. "He is reported to dress in a coarse and stinking camel hair burnoose that hangs from his shoulders like a bag. Disgusting."

Marcus Quintius nodded. *What is it about these Jews?* he wondered. *They will take up with anybody who promises what they cannot have.* Imagining an unpleasant portrait of John, he thought how unlike Jesus he must be. Jesus, with his ordinary clothing, his shining face and his quiet manner...

Gaius Valerius was in mid-sentence. "...which makes even more remarkable the number of people who follow him. He baptizes them in the Jordan River down there. They swarm in from everywhere. It started around Jerusalem; then, as his fame spread, they came from all Judea, west to Our Sea, and finally from as far away as here in Galilee. Can't you just see ragtag groups of them traipsing all the way to the lower ford of the Jordan and wading into the water to be dunked by a wild prophet?"

Gaius Valerius chuckled and then paused to take a deep draft of wine before continuing. "That is how I first heard of Jesus. As you know, we have soldiers stationed routinely at all the river fords. Well, the guards there began sending in reports of John's activities. He was proclaiming that the Jewish Messiah was coming, that the people should repent and prepare, and that he, John, had been appointed by God to announce the arrival of said Messiah. Are you familiar with their Messiah tradition, Marcus Quintius?"

"I know that they have long anticipated a king who will restore their nation to power, and that their current hope is that this king will kick Rome off their land," replied Marcus Quintius, snorting.

"Precisely. And when Jesus went down to be baptized, it began to be rumored that *he* might be the long-awaited Messiah. That bit of news spread like flame through the ranks, I can tell you. Imagine my surprise when the same Jesus turned up here in Capernaum."

"Yes, imagine it." Marcus Quintius again became lost in his own musings. There was nothing unusual about baptism. Quite the opposite. Every religion he knew of involved some sort of ritual purification by water. Water was available at Greek and Roman temple entrances. The very word "baptism" meant "dipping" in Greek. Most important, he guessed, was the tradition that baptism by immersion was an integral part of most ancient mysteries. He was only slightly familiar with the Jewish *tebilah*, an ancient rite of baptism intended for gentile converts. He did not know that the polluted waters of the Jordan would not have qualified as clean water for this or any other Jewish purification.

"My man says that after he was baptized by John, Jesus disappeared for a time. When he reappeared, he began gathering disciples of his own. That was about three months ago. Recently, he and his followers returned here, to Galilee."

Marcus Quintius frowned in concentration, recalling his first meeting with Jesus at the insula of a man in Magdala, what was his name? Menahem. A tanner. Jesus had been accompanied there by six men who buzzed around him, fawning. Disciples. He could see that now. That was troubling, a man's ability to beguile people into devoting their lives to him. Marcus Quintius remembered that some of Mary's weavers were enamored of Jesus and their men were furious about it. Would Mary be tempted to follow Jesus in that way? She might be, after what he had done for her. He would certainly have to put a stop to anything like that.

"You have been most helpful, old friend," said Marcus Quintius, rising to go.

"My pleasure. Will you come again before you return to Rome?"

"Oh, I am quite certain of it."

"My villa is your villa, Quintius."

I would not have it, thought Marcus Quintius as he took leave of his former colleague and set out walking back to Capernaum. Eventually he found himself upon a little hill from where he could gaze out over the Sea of Tiberias, which the local residents persisted in calling the Sea of Galilee. The wharf was busy with ships, and he looked with pride on the Roman war vessels that dominated the scene. Like any man of Rome, Marcus Quintius considered himself owner of the fleet. Captains of their world, these Romans were, and wherever they went they reveled in the evidence of their ascendancy.

Riding on the water was a pair of sleek galleys, a vessel design that would span thirty-five hundred years from Phoenician and Greek antecedents into a future of as yet unimagined nations. The long boats were propelled by staggered banks of oarsmen and a large rectangular sail and steered with a pair of longer oars mounted near the stern. Below the waterline, under its bow, each Roman ship carried a heavy bronze ram capable of punching holes in enemy warships, if indeed there had been enemy warships in evidence. Upon the Sea of Galilee the imposing triremes were mostly for show. And they did show the capability of Rome to knit her far-flung, conquered provinces together, to govern her empire, and to place an army wherever rebellion might threaten the peace. Compared to those warships, the rough fishing boats from the shore towns all around were like bobbing rubbish. Even the gilded pinnaces, tenders from the palace of Herod Antipas at Tiberias, were as children's toys upon the water.

Capernaum was not called "Queen of the Lake" for nothing. It sat below a curtain of yellow limestone, the hillsides made glorious by a profusion of fruit, nut and fig trees and an intoxicating burden of fragrance coming off red oleanders when they bloomed. The many boats that called there gave proof of the importance of the town. It was a chief station on the direct route from Damascus to lower Palestine, the Mediterranean, and on to Egypt. All the great caravans passed through it, creating a market where fish were so abundant they seemed to swim in the streets as they were carted in hundreds of baskets and so much good olive oil a person might take a bath in it if he wanted. Mixed populations from places like Bethsaida just to the east and north to Caesarea Philippi at the Tyrian border crowded Capernaum, buying wheat, silk and ivory.

Marcus Quintius regarded the blend of people around him, the variety of costume and language that identified individuals as members of a discrete region or tribe. His head echoed with the words of Gaius Valerius concerning Jesus: Capernaum is diverse, "fruitful ground for the spread of his ideas." *Yes*, thought Marcus Quintius, *there is constant debating here, talk of the follies of government, what they call Roman oppression, and scandals in Jerusalem. A very good platform indeed.*

The sketchy outline of Jesus' activities provided by Valerius had left him with more questions than answers. There was still a great deal that Marcus Quintius did not know about Jesus. As Mummius had said, there was much he did not understand.

Remembering Mummius, Marcus Quintius consulted the sun and saw that it was nearing time to meet him at their rendezvous point. Mummius had given him directions to an amulet shop in the old town. "Go down to the east end of the wharf. There you will find a large paving stone against the wall of a tavern. It is inscribed with a number 'one.' Go five paces west. There, another stone, number 'two.' Turn north and find 'three.' Then east for 'four,' south for 'five' and so on. Look for torch arms and follow the stones; the stones will lead you to the amulet shop. You can't miss it."

CHAPTER 14

The Sea of Galilee was all about men. Water and shore, it was crowded with fishermen, their boats and their routines. Women were seen there, sometimes, passing by on errands, making purchases from the catch, or tending to some other temporary business. To have Mary and her weavers create a commotion on the shore by calling after Jesus was quite out of the ordinary. The men stopped and stared. Who were these crazed women? What were they doing here?

The boat carrying Jesus and his friends was sailing farther away. Finally someone among them must have noticed the women's hailing them because they reversed course, causing the weavers to cheer.

"They're coming back!" shouted Avireina.

"Thanks be to God," said Mary.

Against an adverse wind, the boat was slow to arrive. By the time it neared the shore where they stood, the women could wait no longer. Fighting their billowing skirts, which floated up around them, they waded out to meet it. They took hold of the edge of the vessel and looked in.

Six men sat in the boat that could hold a dozen, their lungs heaving with the exertion of sail and oar. Jesus held onto the mast, bracing himself in a wide stance.

"What are you doing?" he exclaimed, looking down at Mary and her women and barely able to keep from laughing.

"I want you to restore this girl's speech," she said simply, pointing to Chloe.

Jesus' friends gaped and grumbled. "For a gentile dog, we break our backs?" complained one.

Jesus ignored their protests. He, too, wondered at the urgency, the boldness, of Mary's request. But touched by her trusting naiveté, and not wanting to fail her, he steadied himself against the movement of the waves and knelt down in the boat.

Leaning over to Chloe, he asked her, "Do you want me to do this for you?"

Poor Chloe, bobbing in the choppy water, nodded her head.

The women moved aside to make room as Jesus swung one leg over the side of the boat into the water, and then the other. Holding onto the stout wale of the boat, he rested his weight briefly on his diaphragm and palms, and then slipped into the shallow water. He pushed up one sleeve and submerged his fingers into the lake. For a few moments, Jesus closed his eyes in prayer, and when he opened them again, it was to look unblinkingly at Chloe. He brought his hand up dripping with water and pressed his fingertips onto her quivering lips.

"Rejoice, and give thanks to God," he said, and released her.

The women looked expectantly at Chloe. But when she opened her mouth and moved her lips, no sound came out; she was as mute as ever.

Chloe took a deep breath and tried again. This time there emerged from her throat a soft croak that sounded something like "Praise to God." A great smile spread over Chloe's face. "Praise to God," she said again, her voice clearer. "Praise to God!" shouted Chloe, loud and strong, and the others joined in, till a chorus of women's praises rose up on the morning air and floated out over the Sea of Galilee.

"Master, let us go now," came a nervous voice from the boat.

Jesus turned to climb back in, but, buoyed by the success of her request, Mary held him. "One more thing, Rabbouni."

She nodded to Sahadia who pried Sudi loose from the edge of the boat. The girl and her skirt floated in the water as Sahadia handed her daughter over like a doll to Mary, who in turn handed her over to Jesus. Unable to protect her injured arm from their transferring her, Sudi cried out involuntarily when Jesus pulled her close.

Jesus studied Sudi's small, ravaged face and recognized her as the worshipful girl in the synagogue yesterday. Remembering Eber's cruel stare, he realized that Sudi had suffered on account of him and was touched by her devotion.

Then he did something unexpected. Still holding Sudi in one arm, he held out his other hand to Mary and drew her to him. Inspired by a collective impulse, the women let go of the boat and formed a circle with Sudi, Mary, and Jesus at the center, the cool waters of the sea lapping at their legs. One by one the women laid their hands on Sudi, her head, her waist, her shoulders, her back. Sudi could feel the warmth of healing begin to arise within her as she opened her heart to the love of the women encircling her.

Mary saw the confident smile on Jesus' face and wondered what he was doing as he guided her hand into the water. Together they lifted a palmful up to Sudi's face. Together they laid their dripping hands on her livid bruises. Then the command, "Be healed, little daughter." Jesus' lips were moving silently, mouthing the words. But the sound came from Mary. It was Mary who said, "Be healed, little daughter."

Jesus looked intently into Mary's eyes. Now she understood. Sudi's face was restored, yes. But there was more. Deep inside, where self-loathing had lived, there, too, Sudi was healed. The Reign of God meant that she would never again have to believe that she deserved the beatings that had brought her here. Small as she was, her life was nevertheless of great consequence. She was important, deeply loved, by God and by the women encircling her with that love.

Gently, Jesus unlocked Sudi's fingers from around his neck where she held him fast, her arm made well. "Your sins are forgiven. Return to your mother now," he said.

Unnoticed by the women who were focused on Sudi and hugging her, Mary stared at her hand, the hand that had washed healing power over the young girl's face. It seemed to belong not to her, but to someone—something—else. She touched her lips that had spoken the command to heal and looked to Jesus for an explanation, but he was already climbing into the boat.

Mary resisted a compulsion to climb into the boat with him. She wanted desperately to secure the peace that had swelled in her since Jesus laid his hands on her and made her whole. Even after these miraculous events in the lake, she was reluctant to put complete trust in what he had done. Was it just another temporary respite, as so many others had been? And that incomprehensible and unsettling business of using her hand to heal Sudi's face. Why had he done that? *How* had he done it?

Back home from the lake, the excited weavers removed their wet sandals outside the door and wrung water from the hems of their skirts. Mary made a half-hearted attempt to settle them into their work in the loom room. That was useless. They were all gathered around Chloe, who babbled incessantly, mispronouncing words and being corrected by the others who kept offering suggestions as to what to say next. They giggled with her efforts, especially the jubilant Chloe, who found the sound of her own laughter irresistible.

When Demetria and Rachel arrived to hear the news and join in the celebration, Mary gave up; no weaving would be accomplished in the loom room today. *Let them be happy,* she thought, as she stole from the room and went looking for Shoshanna.

When she heard that Marcus Quintius and Mummius had gone to the baths in Magdala, she was relieved. With everyone accounted for, she made some excuse to Shoshanna and slipped out of the house, satisfied that she would not be interrupted.

Wary nonetheless, she kept a close watch behind her through the garden and out into the olive groves. Soon she turned off the main path that led to the Sea of Galilee and took a wandering route through the trees until she came to the edge of the northernmost section of olives. Here she stopped and looked across an open, uncultivated area at a small, isolated, stone building where no one ever went. She hesitated, knowing that she should not be here.

Jesus had done everything she asked of him and more in the Sea of Galilee that day. Risking the displeasure of his friends, he had obliged them to turn the boat around and return to her. He had healed Chloe and Sudi, and everyone who saw it would by now have spread the story in towns all around the lake. They had made such a spectacle, jumping and screaming. Many would have interpreted Jesus' actions as yielding to the demands of self-indulgent women and thought less of him. But Jesus had made his choice and would live with it. Mary, too, had a choice to make.

She remembered the night in the upper room when Jesus held her hands in his, and energy surged between them. He had praised her. He had allowed her to hold him and sing to him till he slept like a worn-out boy. When he woke and led her to the window and embraced her, she thought he might desire her, as a man naturally desires a woman. But he had pushed her away. After that he prayed for her and then took her into his arms again.

Mary was awash in confusion that night, and she still was. She was troubled by her feelings for Jesus, to say nothing of his inconsistent behavior towards her. Worst of all, she was skeptical about her healing. She could see no alternative; the miracle of her healing would have to be put to the test.

Drawing her veil tightly around her head and shoulders, Mary took a step forward. She walked carefully, as if on broken glass, across the still-muddy area to the entrance of the building, and, with an effort, pushed open the door. Covering her nose against the stagnant air, Mary peered into the soundless room, waiting for her eyes to adjust to the darkness. On the wall opposite her, rough-hewn shelves came slowly into focus. Then ossuaries—small, stone boxes of old, assembled mute and cold upon the planks—took shape, containers for the bones of her grandparents and parents.

Leaving the door ajar to take advantage of the light outside, trembling with dread, Mary entered and walked to the shelves. Searching out the particular box in six that held the bones of her father, she fixed her eyes on it to give herself courage. When she was ready, slowly, slowly, she forced herself to turn slightly and look over to the right, where a seventh box stood alone. At the sight of it, Mary whimpered.

Stretching out a trembling hand, she traced its sad Aramaic inscription with her finger: "Reuben son of Aaron." With an effort, Mary pulled this box to her, scraping a trail in the dust of the shelf. Cross-legged, she sat down upon the damp dirt floor and cradled her brother's bones in her lap, grateful that her parents were not here to witness this offensive deed.

Mary had sat here like this once before, in violation of the Law. One year after Reuben's death; one year for him to decompose in the tomb and be reduced to bones that could be gathered into a small box and moved to their final resting place. Her parents had just performed the rite of purification to rid themselves of the extreme impurity transmitted by contact with tombs and things of the dead. Then they left their son's remains here within the family burial place. Mary had returned to the burial house and crept in, hoping to find a way back to her dead brother. Now, as then, Mary clutched Reuben's ossuary to her heart, and instantly the buried vault of grief in her broke open.

She rocked back and forth, staccato, sorting through scenes of their life together. She felt herself running through a labyrinth, chasing delusions, renouncing his death, imagining that if she could revisit a certain time and place, find a key to alter the past, he would return to her. She stumbled this way and that, and, as each figment of her imagination led to a black dead end, she moaned and frantically cast about for another possibility. Is he there?—no. Over here?—no. What about that way?—no, no, no.

"Reuben!" she wailed, and her cry crashed against the walls. She ducked involuntarily as his name echoed back and beat upon her head. Mary felt herself sinking down, down into the old despair. She braced herself for the voices that would send her raving. But there was only deafening silence.

She did not know what to do. She wanted to escape, but where could she go? She could not return home. Everyone would see that she was still their pathetic, wounded Mary, and they were still her pathetic, captive slaves. Twenty-five years of torment, then the cruel hoax of a counterfeit healing. So—this was the insufferable answer to her troubled questioning about Jesus. Reuben could not be found. Nothing had changed.

Mary was suffocating. God was choking the life out of her, mercilessly extracting the blood price for the sin of her brother's death. She might just as well have pushed him off the cliff herself. God had every reason to torture her.

Mary cried till tears soaked the bodice of her dress and little pools formed on the top of Reuben's ossuary, making muddy traces in the accumulated dust of a quarter century. She saw herself reduced to bones, crammed into the box with Reuben, where she belonged, where she could do no harm. Reuben's bones were suddenly a very heavy weight, holding her down.

The waters of self-condemnation rising steadily around her, Mary felt the building where she sat stirring with a deep, almost imperceptible, growl. The very earth beneath her seemed to shift and groan. She heard a whisper.

"Mary"

The final call to extinction. As though separated from her body and observing it from a distance, Mary thought how odd it was that her destruction had come, finally, in such a small, quiet voice. Not at all like the hideous, enflamed raging that had tortured her for so many years. Odd, too, how a whisper could radiate with power sufficient to shake the earth itself. Mary closed her eyes and prepared for the ground to open and swallow her misery.

The earth went still. She waited. At length she sensed that the cold stone clutched in her lap was turning warm. Opening her eyes, Mary was astonished by what she saw. The box was aglow with a light that became ever brighter. She thought it might be pulsing, as with a heartbeat. She wanted to thrust it from her, but the ossuary pinned her in place, and she could not move. Was it some demon, come to claim her? Was there to be no escape for her, even through death? A shadow of dread descended and thickened around her.

Again her name, "Mary," and again the earth shuddered.

This time, a flicker of recognition. "Reuben?" she said in a voice so low she did not know whether it was sound or only thought.

And from the now-fiery stone, "Rise, Beloved. Go to your brother, and live!"

Mary's breath came fast and shallow, and she felt her heart flinging itself against the wall of her chest. She was about to pass out. She stared at the stone box, fearing that it would burst into flame, burning her alive. *"Go to your brother,"* rang in her head. Was this, now, the true and terrible voice of God telling her to go to Reuben? To die like Reuben?

Then, as suddenly as it had happened, it was over. The ossuary that had burned in her hands was again stone cold, leaving her disoriented, unable to gather her thoughts. Was it Reuben's voice that had spoken from the box? She tried to remember exactly what the voice had said.

"Rise, Beloved."

Beloved. I? she wondered, struggling to make some sense of it.

"Go to your brother and live."

What? Am I to live and not to die?

Then, like the morning sun that first promises itself in a quickening aurora and afterwards springs bright over the far horizon to flood the earth, light dawned in Mary's heart. It was God who had spoken to her through the only means she could grasp, Reuben's love. Reuben would not want to punish her or hurt her in any way. Would the love of God be less than the love of a brother? Surely a compassionate God would not be vengeful to his own children. Jesus had tried to tell her this.

Mary was standing, as she had stood so often, on the edge of the terrifying abyss of Reuben's death and found herself unafraid. At last she was able to look into that pit and reclaim him, her brother, her twin, bound together from conception, body to body, soul to soul. He was no longer lost, but found, restored to her. She was free of the undeserved guilt she had felt for Reuben's death. It was his own act that had resulted in anguish to their parents, and to her.

Still cradling his bones, she heard herself speaking to Reuben. "I have sought you vainly these long years, my dearest brother, and have wished for death because I believed I had failed you. I wish I could have prevented what you did, but it was never within my power."

Mary stood from her seat on the musty earth and carefully replaced Reuben's ossuary in its resting place. And she wondered, was it possible that Jesus was her brother, too? Could she go to Jesus, and live, as the voice had said? Unsteadily, she left the dark building into the shaft of light at the entrance. She paused and looked back at the stone box holding the bones of her brother and said, "I forgive you, Reuben."

Neglecting to close the door behind her, Mary raced for home.

CHAPTER 15

By the time Jesus' boat arrived in Capernaum, at the northern end of the Sea of Galilee, the story of the miracles just performed had sailed up the lake as fast as fishermen could tell it from boat to boat. An eager crowd materialized, having dropped what they were doing to hear the news, to speak of it together, hoping to experience some miracle for themselves. Jesus could scarcely disembark for the throng that awaited him. Touching the many hands held out to him as he passed, he made his way to a dry place just beyond where the waves lapped. People sat about him on the ground and gathered in boats just offshore to hear what he had to say—and to watch him receive the broken and wounded, healing them and sending them home, amazed and jubilant.

The crowd would have held him indefinitely, but after some hours Jesus was drained. He sent them away with promises to return and went, with relief, to the house where he was staying as a guest. He ate his midday meal and then lay down to rest in the unexpected warmth of the late winter afternoon. Solitude. So he could think. Of Mary.

He could not quiet his mind about this woman. He should feel grateful that he had been able to liberate her from her long suffering, but, instead, he was angry. *Why did she have to endure so much for so long?* In a way, she was like him, suspended these many years, waiting to enter into The Reign of God.

Jesus went to the window. The freshness of the air reminded him of the breeze that had caressed them as they stood together in Mary's upper room. He breathed in the memory of her scented hair and felt its silken flow against his neck. Was Mary thinking of him, like this? Suddenly his face flushed. *What have I done?* he thought, trying to summon the details. He had fallen asleep in her lap while she sang to him some little song—a lullaby?

The truth was that Jesus was lonely. He tried not to be weighed down by it, but he was acutely aware that even his disciples, devotees who had turned over their lives to him could not assuage his yearning at the end of an exhausting day when all he wanted was to be held. He had felt desire for women before. What man did not? With the duty to marry pressing in on him at every turn, mothers were constantly thrusting their virgin daughters in his direction. He had resisted, cherishing the claim of God on his life more deeply than cultural claims.

That claim set him on a mission. While he did not know exactly where his path would lead, he had learned from the scriptures that power structures had always sought to suppress prophetic voices and always would. Even now, just as he was getting started on his mission, he knew it was inevitable that the powers of earth—Rome, the Temple cult—would seek to silence him in order to preserve the status quo that favored them so mightily. As he caught a glimpse of what he knew must come, Jesus shook his head to clear the thought. He had delayed too long. It was time to fulfill his promises to his Father-in-Heaven and act on his commitment to The Reign of God. The path he had chosen was no place for a wife and children.

Then why this plague of yearning? Why the image of Mary of Magdala pushing into his heart? Why take her hand in the Sea of Galilee and show her how to use her power to heal? *What must she think of me?* he wondered, surprised at how much he wanted her to have a good opinion of him.

Jesus' next thought was of his mother. *Just wait until she hears,* he thought, imagining the moment when he would tell her that he had found Mary, that she had recognized the tallit and that he had relieved her of a grievous affliction. Had his mother foreseen all this? Did she know something that he did not know about Mary's destiny, *their* destiny? Could it be that he was meant, after all, to lead the conventional life of a rabbi, with a strong family life? *Have I been so wrong about it?*

Seeing his mother's face, lined now with age but still radiant, caused Jesus to peer into the years of his childhood. He missed his father, Joseph. Jesus had spent his boyhood learning carpentry from Joseph and, in school, studying the Hebrew scriptures. Over the years, as he went on to gain an extensive knowledge of both his trade and the Law, he seemed fated for the life of a rabbi in Nazareth. Respected rabbis always combined the study of the Law with a practical trade: head in the heavens, feet firmly on the earth. In this regard, Jesus' ethnic credentials were impeccable.

Rabbis were expected, also, to marry and to be fruitful and multiply. But when Joseph died, what else could he do? He accepted the burden as firstborn son to support his mother. He turned himself into an able builder on construction crews all around northern Galilee. Responsibilities to his mother would leave neither time nor energy for the ordinary life of a householder. Nor would the demands of his divine call. What was his call, exactly? Jesus had not known at first. What he did know was a fierce urge to serve God, whom he thought of as Father-in-Heaven. The desire came on him early and strong. It had grown inside him from childhood, when he tried to keep it concealed.

It was widely agreed among people in Nazareth that Jesus was different. As a youngster, although he enjoyed playing games with other boys, amusement had never been his focus. When he was not working alongside Joseph in the construction business, he was staying after school arguing points of the Law with his teachers. He was known to help his mother with domestic chores. What ordinary boy would stoop to that? The thing that truly set him apart was the time he spent alone. Every day he would go off to some isolated place on a hillside and sit quietly, not moving, sometimes for three or four hours at a time.

"What are you doing out there?" his friends would ask.

"I'm listening to God."

"You're praying?" they said, rolling with laughter. "All afternoon?"

"Not praying! Listening."

By his fifteenth birthday, his father dead, Jesus was left to shoulder the financial burden of the family. For the next fifteen years, he felt unsettled, guilty about living such a small life, when he knew he was destined for greater things. Once his siblings were grown and well-established, able to take care of their own families as well as their widowed mother, it was time for him to answer once and for all the call he heard from God. He decided to begin by being baptized publicly by his cousin John.

So it was that Jesus left Nazareth, walking four days by the Samarian route to the lower ford of the Jordan River, where Joshua himself, successor to Moses and leader of the original conquest of Canaan by the Israelites, had camped with his army many generations before. At that very place, Jesus, Joshua's namesake, stood on the bank of the Jordan, stripped off his clothing and, laying it down on a dry rock, allowed himself to be laid down into the river by John. Jesus emerged from that river with its water running off his head and face, disguising tears of relief. He was at long last where he had yearned to be. Many who witnessed the scene remembered the words of the ancient scriptures, which told of the coming Messiah: "Here I am. I have come to do your will, O my God. It is my desire; your law is within my heart." It began to be spread about that Jesus was that long-awaited Messiah. Jesus, too, began to wonder if it were true.

Then, as it ever happened for prophets, he was led by the Spirit of God into isolation to be tested. That was the time of disappearance reported by military spies to Gaius Valerius, who told it in turn to Marcus Quintius, when Jesus had spent a period of forty days in the Judean wilderness, fasting. "Forty" was a number indicating the passage of a substantial, but indefinite, period of time. Everyone knew of Noah and his forty-day flood, Moses' forty-year wandering in the wilderness, and the mighty King David's ascending the throne at forty years old. The use of such a number was recognizable to all.

Seclusion after baptism was common to holy men, especially those of the nearby sect of the Essenes. Following that example, Jesus turned his back on the waters of the Jordan and walked five miles west into the Wilderness of Judea, from time immemorial a place of retreat for those wishing to withdraw from the world. Did he have the resolve, the commitment, the will to follow God above all else, to choose God's desires instead of earthly desires? Could he resist the lure of personal power? This was what he went into the wilderness to find out.

With each step the landscape grew more inhospitable. Flora gave way to rock and dust until finally there was no green left, only a vast sea of rolling, golden brown hills silhouetted clearly against the brilliant blue of the sky. From a distance they looked soft, but as he approached, he saw how rocky these hills were, etched with dry, ankle-breaking fissures. He put his hand to the goatskin bag that hung from his waist. It would have to last a long time. He turned to look back toward the waters of the Jordan and imagined them winding down from the Galilean Lake, through the semi-tropical rift-valley where lush tamarisks hung down into the glistening waters rippling around rock outcroppings. Then it became muddy and flat at Beth-abara near the Dead Sea where he had left John. He pushed on. Climbing one of the higher hills, he located a large, flat shelf of rock that suited him. As night fell, he wrapped his cloak around him and lay down to sleep under the stars.

The first days were easy enough, exhilarating in fact, as his body and mind began to cleanse themselves. He welcomed the deepening feelings of solitude and sanctity. On the morning of the third day, he woke up very hungry. Already lean of body, he had not much to fall back on. His stomach rumbled. He pressed it with his fist to quiet it.

The days wore on, and the desire for food was intensified by a relentless thirst. He huddled in his cranny in the rocks, apportioning his water and trying to conserve moisture, but the Judean sun blazed, turning the air into a greedy sponge. His lips cracked, bled and scabbed over. In the brutal midday, each breath was like fire from an oven, scorching his lungs from the inside out. At night the sun retreated, leaving a chill that stung icy cold by contrast. He shivered so violently that he thought some bone might break against the rock upon which he lay, his thin cloak inadequate to cushion him. He no longer slept. Night and day he sat half-conscious, staring at the sky above, the sand below. Predators soared in circles above, causing furry prey to scamper and dive into the protective earth.

On one such day he noticed a small scrub bush tucked under a rock, fighting for life. *Like me,* he thought, swaying on the frontier between life and death. It was then that he heard a voice, a welcome, familiar voice.

"Jesus, look."

He strained to see who was speaking and saw no one.

"Right here."

"Mother?"

She sat on the ledge next to him, cradling large round loaves in her lap. The aroma of fresh-baked bread rose up around her, as it always had at her hearth.

"See what I have made for you."

He squinted. Where had she come from? What was she doing here?

"I hate to see you suffering like this, son. Please, eat something." She held up one of the loaves toward him, and he saw that it was not bread but a large, round stone.

Inside Jesus, the power to change rocks into bread spun and whirled. He pushed it down. "I must not."

"Just a little, to keep you going."

His mother had always put his needs before her own. She would do nothing to cause him to stray. A few bites could not hurt, if she said so. His mouth watered in anticipation as he reached out his hand. When he saw what he was doing, he woke to the betrayal of his body and released an anguished howl into the desert air. He shut his eyes against the sight of bread, crying out, "No!" His renunciation reverberated against the hillsides beyond and back again, and at once his mother vanished.

He was again alone on the sizzling ledge, weak with hunger. He tried to remember why he had come here. Searching for God. Searching for himself, the true self that *is* God, not the false self that lusts and demeans and alienates. The true self that loves as God loves. *Merciful God, where are you? Do not leave me like this!* Jesus wept.

Days and nights passed. He continued to fight off a parade of desires. On the fortieth day, down to the last fiber of his will, he was seized by the ultimate temptation. He felt himself lifted from his perch on the hillside. He was floating in the air just off the cliff, even as he saw his body still sitting there. Someone's arm was around his shoulders, guiding him toward an image in the distance, soaring together through the air. His mysterious companion placed him on a pinnacle from where he could survey the land for miles around.

Another voice, silky and seductive. "You can have all this, you know," it said. At once he saw a vision of himself larger than life and all Jerusalem at his feet. "The people are expecting a king, Jesus, one who will restore the nation to greatness. Are you not a direct descendant of King David, as the Messiah is prophesied to be? If you were king, see how wisely and how well you would govern. You could bring peace and prosperity to the land, all lands for that matter. Just think of it."

He did think of it. God was allowing the people to suffer terribly under the burden of Rome. To say nothing of the harsh and misguided application of the Law of Moses. He could certainly do better than that. In his heart he knew he could be king. Why should he not?

"Do it!" the voice commanded.

At that, the ravishing image of his own royalty possessed him. He felt a crown encircling his head and robes of state falling from his shoulders. He saw himself presiding over a vast court where men shoved forward to be first to do his bidding and where women fawned over him, worshipping. He was king of all the earth.

No man could be blamed for covering himself in glory. Any man would take what he was capable of taking. Soon the hallucinations brought on by exposure and deprivation submitted another world in which he was not a king at all. Here, God was the king and Jesus only a servant. Goaded by hunger and thirst, and fighting to hold onto his crown, he thundered, "I am the Chosen One!"

And his heart replied, *If you become a king, you will be like any other, lording over those who love you and those who fear you alike. Seduced by power.*

He knew it was true. His life had been an unquenchable fire burning toward this moment and no other, and, when it came, he was faced with two unwanted choices—unworthy king or lowly servant.

"O God," he called out, "am I to be a slave?" In the silence that followed, Jesus knew that he, and only he, must answer that question. What kind of instrument could he be with no worldly power?

Jesus looked down at the rocky ground, empty except for one wild, desert flower, which, having bloomed against all odds in the hot, hostile air, had matured to a soft fluff of seeds. Jesus bent to pluck the lonely plant. Thinking to blow on it, he brought it close to his parched lips, but no puff of air came out. *Not enough power to help even this poor weed?* he thought, ready to toss the plant aside and let it die.

From somewhere within came a passionate longing for the flower to live. Already the stem was wilting in his hand when Jesus lifted the seed head to his face. With a great effort he took in a deep breath that burned his lungs and held it for a moment. He pursed his cracked lips and blew. The seed head bent before his little current of air, the fluff holding, holding, holding on until suddenly, it was free, each separate seed floating toward its own fate.

The stifling air freshened and a swirling wind arose. The seeds were swept downward to the city of Jerusalem below, then lifted on an updraft, and Jesus watched as they multiplied into a vast cloud, streaming westward to the Great Sea toward Rome and beyond. The wind stopped suddenly, and the cloud of seeds floated down, settling into the earth below.

How many will find nurturing ground? Jesus wondered, an intense desire for their success welling up in him. Jesus saw himself like a miniscule seed, blowing in dry winds, desperately seeking soil. *A seed that must dissolve in order to mature and flower and bear fruit.* Here it was, clear at last, God's call, stored within a seed. On a pinnacle in the Judean wilderness, Jesus made his choice. As warring visions blazed up before him, he said "no" to the selfishness of the world and "yes" to Mercy. He would live to bear the fruit of Mercy, the kind of Mercy that is not just forgiveness, but the gift of God's redeeming Love. He would give his life as an exemplar of what it is to be free from the desire for mastery over others.

Jesus reached up his hand for the crown that still rested on his head and tossed it down the hillside. Immediately, he was flung back upon his rocky ledge. The great test was over. Like a bundle of bones wrapped in thin sheets of sensitive flesh, but nonetheless ripe with certainty, Jesus emerged from the wilderness, back into the world, bearing the lamp of Mercy.

Now, months later in a comfortable house in Capernaum, subjected to the memory of his terrible ordeal in the desert, Jesus was soaked with sweat. Again he was tempted by images. He wanted to be with Mary with the same ferocity he had wanted to be king. He sought to justify his desire with the same premise: it would be so much easier to fit the expectations of others. He could marry and take up the contented life of a great teacher in Israel.

Will these struggles never cease! Jesus walked to the window. Shoulders sagging under the burden of desire, hands balled into tight fists, he mechanically scanned the scene below. Soon his eyes fell upon a small garden not far from the house. Relieved at the sight of it, he unlocked his hands and pushed back tendrils of hair that were stuck to his brow with sweat, then turned to make his way down to the garden to find some answers in prayer.

CHAPTER 16

A bewildered Marcus Quintius stumbled into Mummius near the street of the amulet shop. Mummius had stationed himself in a likely spot, aware that, by now, the Roman would be dizzy with confusion—and hopelessly lost.

"By all the gods, Mummius, what mischief is this?"

Mummius could never resist teasing Marcus Quintius, who accepted it graciously, as he had from the beginning in Alexandria.

"Had troubling finding it, did you, Severus?"

"I did not find it at all, villain. You found me, and you know it."

"Would it console you to learn that I got lost the first time, too?"

Marcus Quintius scowled.

"Come, let us go somewhere to talk," suggested Mummius, leading the way.

"Well, let it be far from this foul place."

They found a quiet inn with a garden and a trickling fountain where they could drink a cup of wine and Severus could regain command of himself. Much as they favored each another, today the men were made cautious by unrevealed reasons for visiting Capernaum. Marcus Quintius wanted to work out whether Jesus could pose some real threat to Rome; Mummius wanted to get close to the source of power of the strongest magus he had ever encountered. Both hoped to find a way to turn Jesus' power to their own purposes. Each one needed to know, above all, whether Jesus had really stolen Mary away from him.

"What did you learn?" Mummius inquired.

"Interesting particulars. My colleague had already posted a spy on Jesus. That was somewhat surprising. It means that he perceives a threat."

"Ah, turbulence in the waters of Pax Romana."

"Gaius Valerius has an enviable situation here, Mummius. Of course he would be wary of any man who attracts crowds and does miracles. What about *your* friend? Anything new?"

"Yes, well. He tells me that everyone in Capernaum, including all in our brotherhood, is talking of Jesus' powers. His miracles are everyday occurrences."

"Are you saying that what we saw in Magdala is common, Mummius?"

"I am saying that there is *nothing* common about what we saw in Magdala. No one I know could keep up an unending performance of that sort of thing. When I piece together all that I have seen and heard over the last few days, I must conclude that he is even more extraordinary than I had guessed."

"How do you mean?"

"Can you not see? Jesus is only just starting out, yet crowds follow him everywhere. He has the ability to thrill people—what the Greeks call *charisma*—a special gift of magnetic personal leadership."

"Great military leaders have *charisma*, Mummius. It is not so very unusual for ordinary men to be endowed with extraordinary powers at times. I myself have felt *charisma* on the battlefield," said Marcus Quintius, losing himself momentarily in the memory of the blood lust of his youth.

"Perhaps. But listen. Among Jews there is a tradition that such men are endowed with supernatural powers and have direct access to God, independent of the Law that governs ordinary humans."

"No Jew is independent of the religious Law, Mummius. Everyone knows that."

"Severus, what do you think Jesus is doing when he talks about the Reign of God?"

"I have no idea."

"Well, I think that he is trying to convince people that God is acting through him."

Severus scoffed. "What? He thinks he will be a king? Rome chooses who rules in Palestine. Jesus had better start making the right friends."

"Jesus doesn't want to be an ordinary king, with a throne and territory."

"You are talking in circles, Egyptian. Speak plainly!"

Mummius tried to explain. "In ancient times the Jews were a great nation. That greatness is long past. In their decline, they developed the idea that their god, the God who calls himself One, has been punishing them for their infidelity. But they hold to the hope of collective salvation in the form of a national restoration that will come with the arrival of a messiah."

"Yes?"

"Such a man would possess miraculous powers, would he not?"

"Certainly."

"His miracles would be accepted as manifested episodes of that future, but in the present time, would they not?"

"I don't know what you are talking about."

Mummius slowed down and chose his words carefully. "Jesus may actually believe that this so-called Reign of God is dawning in him, that his deeds are part of the end of the old world and the beginning of the new. He may think that the time of salvation is here, in the present, in him."

Marcus Quintius grew serious. "Do you believe that is possible?"

"I wish I knew. Still, the more immediate question remains, what does this mean for Mary?" Mummius said. *And for me?* he wondered.

He was soon to learn how unsuspected events in Magdala had already changed his life.

The tide of extraordinary happenings of the past few days had left Shoshanna baffled. Now she was worried, because, accustomed to monitoring Mary's every move, Shoshanna realized she had lost track of her whereabouts. Mary had disappeared rather suddenly, hours before, and could not be found. Shoshanna tried to remember where she said she was going—something about fig trees in the southern section. Reflecting on it, she realized that it had made no sense.

Pulling Demetria from the loom room, she asked, "Have you seen Mary?"

"Not since we returned from the sea, no. Why?"

"It is just that, well, I am a little concerned..."

Demetria put a hand on the shoulder of the old woman she had come to love.

"Would you like me to go in search of her?"

"Yes, Demetria, would you, please?"

"Of course I will."

"Try the path to the sea, dear."

Demetria had not gone far from the garden when she was nearly toppled by her mistress, rushing onto the path. Demetria was shocked by Mary's appearance. Her clothes were disheveled. She had lost her veil somewhere, and the lap of her skirt seemed scorched by fire. Her face was lit with a shimmering glow, burnished copper in the sun. Her eyes were fiery, like wolves' in the dark, and Demetria thought of the night of horror when she had encountered her mistress in the grip of demons, the horror she had ever feared might come again.

"Lady, what has happened?"

Mary took hold of Demetria's shoulders and fixed her with luminous eyes. When she spoke, her voice was sweet and strong, an odd mixture, nothing like the possessed ravings of old. She sounded both awed and confident, as though charged with some kind of mission. "The LORD spoke to me." Mary held out the folds of her skirt and said, "Look, Demetria, God has burned my robe."

Demetria tried to stammer out a question, but Mary, uncharacteristically brusque, hushed her.

"Don't worry, child. I will explain everything, but right now I must hurry."

At the courtyard gate, Mary rushed to her room. The astonished Demetria went to find Shoshanna and told what she could. Shoshanna went directly to Mary.

"What are you doing, dear?" she asked, her voice heavy with caution.

"Packing a bag. Here, help me, quickly." Mary was selecting traveling clothes from a basket, sorting them on her bed.

"Where are you going?" asked Shoshanna, picking up a skirt and folding it.

"To Capernaum," Mary said, not looking up.

"For how long?"

"Oh, I don't know. I haven't really considered that," she said, her answer accented with light-hearted laughter.

Pressure rising in her heart and in her voice, Shoshanna laid aside the garment she was folding. "For what purpose?"

"To be with Jesus, of course."

It was as though the very stones of the tower of Magdala had tumbled down upon Shoshanna, crushing her. She felt every bit the heavily burdened old woman she was, and looked the part. Her stout body, which had served so many people for so many years, sagged within her long tunic, accentuating the pain in her stiff knees. The grey in her hair, which had at last overtaken the brown, was dull. Her wrinkled face resembled nothing so much as the bank of a stream where rivulets of spring water had dried in the summer sun leaving deep traces.

"Mary, dear, I do not think that is a good idea," she managed to choke out. Then, her concern for Mary strengthening her heart, she warned, "No good can come from this. I beg you, do not follow this man."

Indifferent to Shoshanna's concern, Mary tossed a response, "Can you still doubt?"

Poor Shoshanna. Of course she doubted. Mary herself had doubted, and it had required nothing less than a personal visitation by God through bones in a burial house to vanquish her disbelief. What could be expected of this old and simple woman?

In the moments that followed, the silence was so profound, issuing from a kind of bereavement really, that the distracted Mary finally became aware of it and of her own unfeeling disregard of the cherished Shoshanna. "Come, dear heart, sit down. Let me tell you the wonderful thing that has happened."

They sat, and Shoshanna noticed with alarm the singed front of Mary's skirt, which had been hidden from her when they stood side by side folding clothes.

"I have heard the LORD," Mary whispered. Shoshanna gasped and was about to rend her veil against blasphemy when Mary took her hands and held them fast. "Do not be afraid, Shoshanna. Listen to me. I went to the burial house..."

Offense heaped upon offense!

"Reuben's bones spoke to me, or, no, Reuben spoke to me from his box of bones, or..."

Shoshanna's body twisted on the bed where they sat as she tried to extricate herself from Mary's grip, to no avail.

"I held Reuben's ossuary in my lap, and, as I did, the stone grew strangely warm. It pulsed as though it lived. Then it spoke. Or rather, God spoke from within it; yes, that's how it was."

Mary was struggling to put into words the earth-shaking, mind-cracking, body-spiraling experience of the burial house. She knew that God had spoken to her using Reuben's voice. She knew that God had burned her clothes with a fire that did not consume. She was trying to convey this knowledge to Shoshanna, to reassure her. She could not do it.

Shoshanna was pale with fear. The appearance of demons she understood. The appearance of God was completely outside her ability to understand. Her mind retreated from Mary's incomprehensible story.

"Shoshanna, through all my time of suffering, you held my head above the waters that threatened to engulf me. You were steadfast while

I crumbled, believing that I was responsible for Reuben's death and that God was punishing me for it. You assured me that I was innocent." Mary placed her fingertips under the old woman's slumping chin and lifted it gently. "You were right. God has told me so."

At this, water filled the dry crevices beneath Shoshanna's eyes and overflowed to roll unchecked down her cheeks, off her chin, and onto Mary's hand. In all their years together, from Mary's infancy, when Shoshanna had been her nursemaid, down to the latter days of agony when she held and soothed her, wounded and suffering like a child, Shoshanna had never before permitted Mary to see this. Shoshanna the rock, who, like a commander of forces, struck fear into the hearts of any who posed a threat to her treasure-child and held all Mary's enemies at bay, this very Shoshanna wept. Here, at long last, was acknowledgment of her life of self-sacrificing love, acknowledgment not just by the darling who had become her daughter, but by the very God of Israel.

Shoshanna could not have said whether it was fear, or loss, or anger, whether it was joy or relief, or something of all of them that caused her to yield to tears. But of one thing Shoshanna was sure; Mary was going to Capernaum, and nothing would ever be the same.

CHAPTER 17

On the road back to Magdala, the men walked as if on a forced march, staring into the space directly ahead. Mummius had that hooded look of his that carried the implicit command, "Say nothing." So Marcus Quintius held his tongue while his friend's thoughts raged.

Mummius' life had been a series of unforeseen crossroads, pivotal moments and irreversible changes launching him in undesired directions. He envied Marcus Quintius, whose pampered life always averted the unexpected. Stabilized by money and privilege, he seemed master of his destiny. Not so Mummius.

If only he could stand again with Maret at that first crossroads. He saw her now and felt her slim, brown arms slipping around his neck. He smelled her musk as she climbed into his lap and purred, "Yes," promising to marry him. Their future rolled out before him like a carpet of soft, delicious moss. But on a cold table in a dark dungeon, pitiless, knife-wielding men altered his course. Perhaps that fleeting moment with Maret had been a dream. In any case, it was a vanished dream. What would life hold for him, thus gelded?

He went to Alexandria thinking to discover some kind of future, and so he did. It was there that he realized his genius for medicine and music, there assumed a Roman name, and, as circumstance would have it, there met Severus, who offered him Rome, the center of the world. In Rome he grew strong in a new life until a love affair gone terribly wrong forced another turn. He saw that he must leave, for a time, until the storm blew over and the offended lady cooled off. He could see Livia Valeria blowing into Marcus Quintius' villa with her lies, her charges of theft and fraud. Imperious whore. Greedy for attention, jealous beyond all reason. Even the persuasive Marcus Quintius could not convince her to drop her charges.

She was determined to bring Mummius down—after what they had been to each another!

Again Marcus Quintius had provided him a way out, an escape to the Roman district of Galilee. Mummius hated the idea of such a place, living among unwashed and uneducated boors, a cultural backwater rife with political upheaval. But Mary had surprised him. In Magdala he found a lady who loved him, if not like Maret, at least for the man she thought he was. Indeed, he pretended to be that man until, through his acting, he had almost become the one she believed in, dedicated and honest. She had accepted him as physician as well as steward of her worldly goods, and he had eagerly received her swift and genuine gratitude. He was able to drop, sometimes, the posturing that kept him at arm's length from others. One day she had said to him, "Mummius, my friend, I could not live without you."

Now here was Jesus, standing at yet another unpredicted crossroads, threatening to knock him off his path and launch him into the unknown. Mummius was losing track of who he had become. Each moment of transformation, piling one upon the other over the years, had resulted in an abnormal being not of his own creation, but of the forces acting on his life and circumstances. All those other pivotal moments had led to this one. How could he release Mary to this Jew? To lose her would be to lose himself.

Flying on the angry wings of his reverie, Mummius was back at the entrance to Mary's garden before he knew it. "I'll be in my quarters," he said, knowing that Marcus Quintius would make straight for Mary's room.

Later, when he heard footsteps approaching, it was not the expected Severus who came to him. It was Mary.

"Mummius?" she said, asking permission to enter.

"Lady," he responded, bowing from the waist, surprised to see her fairly bouncing with excitement.

She sat down in a chair beside his desk and pulled another near, inviting him to sit next to her. He blushed and did as she asked. He felt like a young man just then, in her presence, basking in her light. She had that effect on him, forever causing him to let down his guard. She was remarkably radiant, and he wondered at the extraordinary glow that came off her. Her black tresses were pulled back from her face, revealing that the burnt umber of her eyes smoldered more than usual. *What has happened?* he wondered.

He noticed her simple house dress, not much more than a tunic, which lay in light folds over the curves of her body. He could not help himself; since the night he had saved her from the demons and she lay unclothed and disheveled on the floor, every time he looked at her he imagined her naked. *By Bast! I do love her. Why is she here?*

"Mummius, dear friend," she began. Instantly he knew what was coming. Beneath his elegant robe, his body became taut, alert for danger.

Sensing his subtle change, Mary hesitated, for she knew he would be wounded by what she was about to say. Subdued, she went on.

"I am going to live in Capernaum for a while."

Defenses up and locked into place, Mummius was silent.

"Will you take care of things here while I am away?"

Mummius had come to Galilee to help Mary at a time when she needed it badly. He had devoted himself to her, made sacrifices. He had done everything possible to keep her well and happy. Now he looked on her exhilaration, which had absolutely nothing to do with him, and loathed it.

Mary could see the sting on his face, even as he tried to suppress it. She wanted to offer him a sure pledge of her friendship. "You know I cannot do this without your help."

Here then, the pivotal moment. Like an actor in a Greek play, Mummius holds up the mask of tragedy to his face and waits plaintively for his cue. Mary has only to say an affectionate word, anything to reassure him, and Mummius will forgive her. With his face hidden behind the mask, she has no idea how she has betrayed him. He waits. She says nothing more. Finally, as a servant who has received unwelcome orders, he responds flatly, "Whatever you desire, Lady." For the first time in his life, Mummius knows how it feels to be a slave.

She rises from the chair and he does, too. She takes his hands.

"Thank you, Mummius," she says, wanting to believe that she has made him happy. "God's peace be upon you." And the glimmer of hope in Mummius' heart goes out.

CHAPTER 18

By mid-morning the next day, Mary had told everyone of her intentions and had hastily pulled together arrangements for her departure. Alone and pensive, she sat for a last time upon the stone bench in her courtyard. Someone had swept the pavement, picking up the multilayered debris of winter and washing away the mud. Spring was everywhere in evidence in tiny buds of carefully pruned plants, their pots temporarily restraining the inexorable awakening of life force within. Would her garden miss her as she would miss her garden? Without her devoted attention, would the plants, which were like children to her, withhold their abundance this spring, or would they bloom on defiantly?

Mary studied the mosaic at her feet, an altogether Roman device for, since Moses received the ancient command to create no graven images, Jewish use of certain decorative arts had been all but abolished. Mary's mosaic had been designed for her by Marcus Quintius years ago when her father died, as a pledge of his unwavering support, and she had accepted gratefully both the pledge and the art.

Every facet had been chosen with care, the fish-filled Galilean Sea with the Jordan River flowing in and out of it; blue-flowering flax and a loom; a fruit-laden fig tree; and the crowning grace, in a semi-circle of golden tiles, his name for her, MAGDALENA. Over time, the mosaic had come to represent Marcus Quintius himself and, thus, had been a lifeline for Mary. Many times she had come here bereft of hope and never failed to find encouragement; many times his confidence in her had pulled her back from the verge of giving up and going under. Now she looked to Marcus for affirmation of this, the most difficult choice of her life, and found him constant. In her lap, she rubbed the pad of her thumb over the flat side of the personal seal that he had given her, a miniature replica of the mosaic, painstakingly made in its tiny details, and thought of how she had matured from inexperienced girl to successful businesswoman. She owed him much.

Mary thought, with regret, of Jesus. *How could I have doubted him?* Yet she knew that she had to prove her healing and that the test would be as much a proof of her as it was of him. The voice of God that issued from Reuben's bones rose in her mind, and her body shook much as it had in the burial house. Mary was sure that for the rest of her life, whenever she remembered that moment, it would set her trembling. It had also pulled her, then and now, toward Jesus. What could she do but go to Capernaum in search of him?

The time for departure was near when Demetria appeared. Eyes red and swollen, the girl took a few steps forward, twisting a rumpled kerchief.

"I cannot bear for you to go," she said.

Mary's chest constricted with an awful heartache, and she held out her arms. Demetria came to her and was drawn down onto the bench where they had often sat, where Mary had taught her to read and write, where Demetria had been transformed from confused child to confident young woman, and where she had become, in the process, a daughter to Mary.

"You are not alone, Demetria. This is your home."

"You are my home."

A blonde curl had escaped from its pin and was dancing around the side of her face. Mary tucked it back in.

"Take me with you," she begged.

"Demetria, I cannot. I do not know what lies ahead."

Mary watched Demetria's jaw bulge out as she clenched her teeth and swallowed hard. Her trembling little smile and the wringing of the handkerchief told it all.

"Demetria, I need you here. Shoshanna needs you. You must help her manage the household. Think of Rachel—and the weavers. They are frightened. You can encourage them."

Mary was unsure when this had happened, that she had come to rely on Demetria. She was suddenly aware of the girl's maturity—and its price. It was time for her to assume the responsibilities of adulthood. Demetria looked down at the pavement, as though wishing away this moment, but at the same time consenting to it.

"Can you do this for me?"

"I can, Mistress," Demetria mumbled to the mosaic at her feet, then raising her head to meet Mary's eyes, "but when will I see you again?"

"I'll be back, surely, to visit." Smile creases showed at the outside corners of her twinkling eyes when she added, "You must write to me!"

"In Greek, Mistress, or in Latin?"

"Both," she said, and they laughed.

When Demetria came to Magdala she could neither read nor write a word in any language. It was thought a folly to educate any girl, especially such a girl as this, but Mary had insisted. Less than a year later, here they were celebrating her impressive achievements. Their laughter was subsiding into quick breaths and sighs when Mummius materialized.

"He is ready, Lady."

"Thank you, Mummius," Mary answered, then said to Demetria, "Go ahead, dear."

As Demetria moved away, Mary rose and drew her steward aside. She reached for his hand and pressed an object into his palm. She looked up at him, towering over her, and said, "Here is my seal, Mummius."

Like the roll of a hundred drums, excitement surged inside Mummius as he folded his long, slender fingers tightly over the precious implement. With this act, Mary was transferring all her authority to him. Bankers and suppliers, employees and buyers, every business associate from Galilee to Rome would know that he was in charge, that his decisions were enforceable, as though they were those of Mary herself. He pictured the soft clay oozing out from under the seal as he pressed it onto documents and felt its slight resistance when he pulled it away from the hardening circle of ochre left behind. As far as the world of commerce was concerned, he *was* Mary.

To say Mary's action was imprudent in the extreme would have been a gross understatement. Her own father, and later Marcus Quintius, had been adamant that she never place her complete authority into the hands of another. But Mummius had been good to her. There was nothing of greater consequence that she could do to show how much she loved him. In Mary, the desire to love had always been greater than the need to protect, and never more so than now.

Mary and Mummius held there for a moment, she looking up at him with perfect trust, he with a tight grip upon the mask that concealed his face from her. The "never, ever" command of her father gave way to the "always love courageously" example of her mother.

They walked to the front door through the loom room, where the weavers were squeezing each other's hands till their fingers hurt. Rachel and Shoshanna and Demetria, already having said goodbye, stood behind, stoic observers. Every eye was moist, every heart trembling with its own particular loss. Embracing each one of them, she was met with clinging and wailing, to which she responded with generous smiles and reassuring words. Mary was very nearly overcome with regret at the intensity of the pain reflected in their wet faces, pain that she was causing. She did not even try to hold back her own sad tears.

Mary was both shamed and torn by their dependence on her. Ever since Reuben's death she had longed to feel the freedom she felt now, and she wanted to be on her way to Jesus, the one who had released her. She had to believe that her loved ones would find the strength to adapt to the changes in their lives, just as she was doing. She had made provisions for them to carry on without her. They would grow into their responsibilities. They would be better for it.

When she was able to tear herself from their hugging, she turned to Marcus Quintius who held out his hand to help her onto the back of a young donkey.

"I prefer to walk, thank you, Marcus."

"Very well," and he nodded to his slave, who held the reins of a second pack animal loaded with Mary's possessions, "we are off, then."

It was an unimaginable sight: Mary leaving her home, turning her back on her family and her weavers, saying farewell to all that had given her life meaning. Nevertheless, there it was, and no one, not even Mary, could have foretold how sweeping this already momentous change in her life would become.

Mary and her Roman walked in silence for a while along the Empire's paved road to the north. When she was sure she would see no more of her house and garden if she looked back, she relaxed a little and was able to take deep breaths without fear of another outbreak of weeping. She indulged a quiet chuckle, and Marcus Quintius inclined his head quizzically.

"It is astonishing that you are doing this," she said in answer to his unspoken query.

"Doing what?"

"Escorting me to Capernaum. Your man there could just as easily have accompanied me."

They both knew he would not have agreed to that. Besides, he had never needed much excuse for any trip, and this was beyond a dream—traveling alone with Mary, suspended together in time and space in the way that only a shared journey can do. They might even be mistaken for man and wife by a casual observer.

Marcus Quintius took on a protective air. "I could not very well send you off on your own to find lodgings in such a place."

"You think I am incapable of negotiating a domestic contract, sir?"

Amused by her own feigned condescension, she laughed, permitting her sense of freedom to rinse away the residue of her sorrow. Always her illness had overhung their relationship, choking its air supply like a force of nature she could not override. Now she breathed liberally of Marcus Quintius' loving attention, which he, encouraged, wrapped around her like a cloak.

After a moment, she became earnest. "Marcus, I know that you think it is absurd for me to go to Capernaum. You have warned me against this. Yet in spite of your reservations, you support me. Truly I do thank you, not only for coming with me, but for staying to tidy up affairs in Magdala."

"Mummius will take care of everything," he assured her.

"Whatever would I do without Mummius?"

"Do not forget, my dear lady, who it was that bestowed him upon you."

"Never, Great Benefactor!" she replied with a nod of obeisance. "Here, give me those," she demanded, reaching for the donkey's reins.

He handed them over. A slight gasp escaped from the slave walking behind, so startled was he at the sight of his master's gallantry relinquished. Careful not to let Mary see him do it, Marcus Quintius reprimanded the man with a look.

As they walked, Mary found herself petting the donkey's long, furry ears as she used to do to Mikmik, and a cloud passed over her face.

"What is it, my dear?"

"I was just reminded of the road from Jerusalem when I was a child," she answered, unconsciously placing a hand over her stomach to keep away the nausea that gripped her whenever she thought of that trip—Mikmik's death when he was run over by a Roman chariot. Reuben's subsequent descent into the terror that ended in his suicide.

"A difficult time, Magdalena."

"But, now, I am alive again," she declared, shining her face on him.

It was mid-afternoon when they arrived in Capernaum from Magdala, a distance of about eight miles, made easier by the good Roman road. Mary was exhilarated as she led her donkey up a small hill to the north where they could survey the town and the seascape below. It was just yesterday that Marcus Quintius had been here, secretly, with Mummius, and thus was eager to get on with their business. Not so with Mary. It had been years since she traveled to Capernaum with her father, and she wanted to drink it in sip by sip.

She climbed a grassy knoll where the breeze picked up the edges of her veil, cooling her pinkened cheeks and whisking away the perspiration that had beaded on her forehead. The entrance to the city below was marked by a high portico, supported by enormous columns. The main street ran north/south a half mile long, cutting the city into two relatively equal parts, and there was a lovely white sand beach along the waterfront, busy with sundry boats and ships. Muted by the change in elevation and distance, the noise of crowded streets floated up to her ears. The slanting rays of the still-bright sun glanced off the gilded statues atop Roman buildings and set the city sparkling.

"Look, there is the synagogue," she said, pointing out the distinctive limestone building within a nest of black basalt houses, built close together and mostly whitewashed. Mary leaned her head lightly on his shoulder and said, "Oh, Marcus Quintius, everything is just as I saw it in my childhood."

From her perch above the town, if she had known where to look, Mary could have picked out the small garden where, at that very moment, Jesus was praying. She would have been surprised indeed to learn that she was the motive for his prayer.

All Jews prayed. Praying was so much a part of their lives and their sacred obligation that prayers of one kind or another were constantly on their lips. Like all boys, Jesus had learned to pray in school and at home. Early in his life, prayer had become far more than duty. To pray was to touch his Father-in-Heaven, the way another man might seek out his earthly father for help or instruction; the way two friends might pass an afternoon in a bath house taking stock of their lives and forging bonds; the way a young Greek slave might sit for hours with her mistress, learning to read. Above all else, Jesus desired to be in his Father's presence, uninterrupted, alone and listening.

So he prayed every day, some days more than once, in gardens or on hillsides, for hours at a time, sometimes all night long. Much later when his disciples, lifelong Jews who had prayed daily in the synagogue and in their homes, said to him, "Master, teach us to pray," what they meant was this: "Teach us to desire God as you do."

Today Jesus knelt in a garden in Capernaum, with Mary on his unquiet mind. *Who is she?* he asked God. Why did he react to her as he did? He had never known anyone remotely like her, neither wife nor mother, but a woman who lived in her own way, not dwelling on the children she had denied herself. It was partly those unconceived children that had preserved her body and her beauty. *She must be forty years or so,* Jesus thought, surprised that her age had not occurred to him before. Past childbearing now. *I don't care about that,* he insisted. Was it not possible for him to be both messiah and married? Throughout history the prophets of Israel had married, just as they were expected to. Should he be so different?

Jesus knew the Law; women were like property, and he didn't like it. In Israel the situation was not quite as bad as in Rome. There, men were *paterfamilias*, father of the family, wielding the power of life and death over their wives and children, even their widowed mothers, though the man who actually killed one of his own was generally frowned upon.

The Law of Moses institutionalized the subordination of women in its own ways. They could inherit money only if they had no brothers. According to the word that the LORD spoke to Moses, "If a man die, and have no son, then you shall cause his inheritance to pass unto his daughter." *So*, Jesus thought, *it was through her brother's death that Mary became heir to her father's estate. How that must have added to her burden of guilt!*

The women in Jesus' life, his mother and sisters, were fortunate in that their men were mostly generous of spirit. He thought of his adorable little sister Elizabeth, the baby of the family, whom everyone had spoiled into pouting self-indulgence. By the time she was fourteen and approaching marriageable age, their father Joseph had died, so it fell to the reluctant Jesus to be her father-figure. She didn't make it easy for him. She had pitched a screaming fit when their mother first offered an excellent candidate as a husband. Elizabeth threw herself upon Jesus bodily, begging him not to force her. Of course he would not. Soon after that episode, she announced that she had identified a man whom she would be happy to receive as a suitor, and Jesus offered a relieved prayer of gratitude to God that the one she had chosen was acceptable to their mother.

Like his father before him, Jesus set a permissive standard of freedom within the extensive legal rights that the men in his family held over their women. In return, the women submitted willingly to the code: an unmarried woman was subordinate to her father or, in his absence, her elder brother. Any personal promises or vows made by a woman could be annulled by her father or husband. A father could sell his daughter as a maidservant, hoping her master might take her as a wife, or pass her on to one of his sons as wife. Sometimes marriage required her consent, but a husband could always divorce his wife freely. The list was long, communicating without debate that women were far less than men.

The most telling article of all was embedded in the four circumstances for which the Law of Moses required personal purification. Tucked in among uncleanness contracted by contact with a corpse, uncleanness due to a gonorrheal discharge, and uncleanness of a leper, there it was: uncleanness of a mother after childbirth. Her period of ritual impurity was fourteen days for a girl, but only seven for a boy. For an additional thirty-three days for a boy and sixty-six days for a girl, she was prohibited from touching holy things or entering the Temple sanctuary. There was no doubt—women were unclean, even in their primary function of childbearing, even from the day they were born.

People did not regard these laws as anything unjust. Jesus knew that, at its root, the Law was intended to provide some protection for women in a world that held them less valuable than a good ox. Now as he prayed, his eyes, clear at last, saw this: a woman who was not subordinate, but equal, a woman who was filled, just as he was, with compassion so profound that it transcended all else. It was as though he could remember from some other time and place a community of love that they created, a community defending no boundaries, no separation; women and men equally honored within the Reign of God. He could feel Mary's kindness pouring out upon everyone who came in contact with her. He sensed the force of her will when she would take her place among his disciples. He loved her, but in what way? He did not know the answer to that question, but he was sure now that he must choose her.

But would she say yes? And yes to what? Wife? Disciple? And if disciple, how would the men react? Could they learn to accept a woman within their circle? Could he weaken the resistance that had been so deeply conditioned in them? *Remember Deborah!* he thought, rehearsing his argument. She had been Judge in the days before the kings, and the people revered her still, called her "mother in Israel." *And what about Miriam?* sister of Moses, prophet in her own right, whose very name was reflected in Mary's. One quarter of all the women in Palestine bore the name Mary in Miriam's honor; thus was her heroism esteemed to this very day.

Images of life with Mary flickered in Jesus' mind, ordinary moments alone with her, sharing a meal or talking late into the night, and extraordinary moments when he would take her hand and show her again how to channel life-restoring freedom into the heart of a wounded sufferer. He saw also pain, a jealous Marcus Quintius watching their every move, his own disciples rejecting Mary. Could he desire a life like that, a life that would not be easy, for him or for her? Restlessly, he prayed for some resolution, but could find none. He tried to turn his mind to other matters, but frustration drowned his efforts. He could see only imponderables heaped one upon the other.

Jesus was about to rise and leave the garden, but before he could say his last amen, an expression swept through his mind like the sound of a crystal chime in a gentle wind. He heard his own voice whispering, "Mary, the Wise One." He tried to follow the thought, but it had come to him uninvited and now, just as swiftly, vanished.

With a sigh, Jesus stood and turned to see his host, the man who owned the house where he was staying, excusing the interruption and gesturing toward the door.

"A woman here to see you, Master."

"What woman?"

"She says her name is Mary, of Magdala."

Jesus' neck and face turned crimson. His heart pounded in his chest, and he stumbled over an uneven spot in the pavement. No use trying to hide his reaction. It was too late, the man could already see.

"Shall I show her out here to the garden?"

Jesus cleared his throat. "Do you mind if we go to the upper room, brother?"

"Of course not, Master," said the man, motioning to the stairway.

Trying to regain his composure, Jesus strode over to it, too purposefully. "Thank you," he said, too formally.

He thought she would never arrive. It was only steps from the house to the outside stairway leading to the upper room where he waited. What was taking so long? He paced around like a grinding stone in an effort to smooth down the edges of his impatience.

"Rabbouni?"

A look at the light radiating from his face whisked Mary away to the roof of the house in Beth-el, on the night of the wondrous star, the night that Jesus was born. She had wanted her mother and father to see the star, too, yet was glad they were not there. She did not want them to see her like that, alert and tingling, wrapped in bliss a girl of ten years could not explain. She was held within the moment by unseen forces, transfixed by heavenly light. When Jesus opened his arms to her and exclaimed, "Dear lady!" she was covered again in that bliss of thirty years ago.

"What? How?"

"Are you surprised to see me?" she responded, walking to him, aware that the exertion of the trek from Magdala still glowed on her skin. She could see that she had pleased him.

He could not stop smiling.

"Are you going to ask me to sit down, then?"

He stammered an apology and reached to help her with her cloak. "How did you find me?"

"Everyone knows where you are, Jesus. I had only to inquire in the street."

"But how did you get to Capernaum?"

"I walked," she said, slipping off her cloak with an enchanting shrug of her shoulder. "Not alone, of course. Marcus Quintius accompanied me."

Wanting anything but to reveal his disappointment, Jesus tried not to glance toward the door, but he could not restrain himself and looked anyway.

"Oh, he is not here. He is off securing my accommodations."

"Your accommodations?"

Jesus could feel Mary searching him, watching for his reaction when she said, "I want to stay."

He closed his eyes. After a moment, she asked, "Do you not wish it?" and Jesus heard that her voice had fallen very quiet with the pain of disillusionment. How could she know that he had been imagining her all day? How could she know that he was shutting out the sight of her to deny his mounting desire?

Even Jesus was surprised by the fervor of his answer. "I do. I do." Cautiously, unsure what answer to want, he asked, "What caused you to come here like this, Mary?"

"Do you believe that God speaks to ordinary people, Rabbouni?"

He said nothing, only waited for her to continue.

"God spoke to *me*. I went to my family's burial house. I held my brother's bones in my lap."

"A grave violation of the Law, Mary."

"I should not have done it, but I had to be sure."

"Sure of what?"

"I am ashamed to say it, but I needed to test my myself. Test you." She looked down as if to avoid any reproach she might see in his eyes. "Facing my guilt about Reuben's death seemed the only way. If it were not erased completely, then I was not truly free." When Mary forced herself to look, Jesus' face was full, not of rebuke, but understanding, an invitation to continue.

"In the tomb I felt the power of the LORD aimed directly at me. I absorbed all I could bear, but I was so inadequate. I thought it was going to consume me, but it retreated, just in time, leaving me, I don't know, pregnant—with God's love. It left me with the strength to face Reuben's death without guilt and certain that my healing was complete. God told me to go to my brother. You, Jesus. The one who healed me. I wanted only to be with you."

What did he think of her now that she had confessed that he was more important to her than everyone else put together? His lips were parted slightly; he leaned in close. He seemed to be hanging on every word, not pulling back, not resisting.

"Yesterday in the sea when you said to Sudi, 'Your sins are forgiven,' I was astonished. How could poor, little Sudi be called sinner? And who are you, or any man, to forgive sins? Surely that authority belongs to God alone. I saw the incident again and again in my mind. Sudi's face was restored, yes. But after what happened to me in the burial house, I think I understand that something much larger was transpiring. Were you not saying, Rabbouni, that deep inside, where shame had lived, there, too, is Sudi healed? Did you mean that, small as Sudi is, her life is nevertheless of great consequence? That she is worthy, deeply loved by God?"

Jesus said something in response, but she did not understand him.

"I could not hear you, Rabbouni."

"The Reign of God," he said again. "In the Reign of God Sudi will never have to believe that she deserved the beatings inflicted on her."

"And I. I will never again believe that I deserved my years of suffering. In that way, Sudi's healing is just like mine. I, too, am cherished by God."

Mary saw that Jesus' eyes were bright with love, searching her.

"Mary, I want you to come with me."

"Rabbouni, where shall we go?"

Without hesitation, he declared, "Be my disciple, my witness."

Mary had not expected a proposal of marriage when she left Magdala to be with Jesus, but disciple, witness? Those were words from the Prophets. She was not in those categories. Mary was aware that her face was a mask of confusion and could not change it because she did not know what was going on in Jesus' heart.

She did not know that he, too, had been confused, but that now the answer to his prayer was crystal clear. His heart had been opened in love, and he knew why he had taken her hand in the sea to reveal her healing power. The deepest union Mary could conceive of was marriage between a woman and a man, but Jesus wanted a union of the spirit, unbound by ordinary roles and expectations, a union that would grow to surpass all they knew of human life and relationships. It was in their power to transform their desire for each other into desire for the Reign of God.

Mary had nothing against which to measure such a bond. She did recognize that he was inviting her into the extraordinary life he had chosen, inviting her to choose it, too. She did not know what Jesus saw in her that would make him want her in this way. But when he said, "Will you do this with me, Mary?" his appeal was irresistible, just as it had been when he called her back from the brink of extinction, saying, "Mary, come here." She had wanted desperately to help him defeat her demons, and she wanted to help him now. Drawn in by Jesus' irresistible confidence, she answered, "I will."

CHAPTER 19

Grieving at the door, those left behind watched Mary, Marcus Quintius, and the laden donkeys move down the road toward Capernaum. When the last glimpse of their heads dwindled in the distance, no one could find a word to say. The weavers melted into the loom room and took up their work. Mummius vanished into his quarters. Shoshanna slumped upon the bed in Mary's room, burying her face in the pillow. In the kitchen Rachel grumbled that someone still had to prepare dinner. Demetria sought solace on the bench near the mosaic. Thus the day of a thousand hours passed until at last the weavers folded their fabrics and left their looms for home.

In early evening the household wandered into the dining room and took their accustomed seats. All eyes were averted to avoid the emptiness of Mary's place at the head of the table. Throughout the meal, Demetria picked at her food and surveilled the others for signs of change.

Demetria watched Rachel's struggle to stay composed twist her pretty face into unpretty contortions, the muscles around her swollen eyes squinting and blinking, chin quivering, lips sucked in and bitten. She was repeatedly up and down, removing plates or standing in the corner with her back turned, feigning kitchen work. She fingered the fringe of a new sash, which cinched in her slim waist. Demetria guessed it to be a farewell gift from Mary. A striking belt it was, striped, multi-colored and embellished with gold thread. *I wonder why she didn't give me a gift*, Demetria thought.

Turning her attention to Shoshanna, Demetria imagined that the old woman's short, stocky body had turned to stone within her clothing, unmoving but for the one arm that, like a hinge, transferred food slowly from plate to mouth. Her head was swathed in a brown veil, practically covering her eyes. It was her common veil, of rough wool that scratched—to match her suffering. It was wrapped close to her cheeks and draped tightly over one shoulder so it could not move. Shoshanna was shrinking, as though she wanted to die. She probably felt no reason to live on, with Mary gone. *Leaving no one to shield me from Mummius!*

Mummius. His face more inscrutable than ever, if that were possible, the Egyptian seemed taller, even as he sat at table. The wariness that had always cloaked him was gone. He was smiling, not at any one of them, but to himself, a secret smile, which drew the corners of his mouth just slightly, not up, but back, toward his ears. Demetria was caught up in his jewelry, the foremost of which was a wide collar, resplendent with lapis and rare silver, recently polished. She counted three rows of feathers making up widely spread wings—the Egyptian vulture goddess, what was her name? The bird's talons were spread on Mummius' chest where they gripped certain symbols that she did not recognize. Where had this item been these past years?

A leopard skin belt was at Mummius' waist, held in place by an openwork brass buckle. Demetria examined it, risking his observation, trying to make out the design. She thought it was the image of some kind of priest dressed in a leopard skin mantle.

When Mummius reached to take a piece of bread from the basket, a bracelet fell from his forearm down to his wrist. It had a flexible band created by many rows of small, colored glass beads strung into links, which then held its primary object, the Egyptian udjat eye—the amulet that was said to have the power to restore the dead to life. No doubt Mummius would have performed some fantastic ritual as he slipped it onto his arm, supposing himself to be in complete control of the household now, holding the power of life and death over all of them. *Don't be silly*, she said to herself. *He's just a man.*

Hardly a word was spoken during that meal, but Demetria, watching all of them in their eloquent silence, had learned much. *What a relief!* she thought when it was over. They wandered away from the table, mumbling "shalom" to each other out of habit or because Mary would have expected it. Demetria stayed behind to help Rachel with the dishes, but the woman yanked a towel from her hands, saying, "Never mind. I can do it."

She was hurt by this bewildering dismissal from Rachel, who loved her. Was this to be her home now, a prison made friendless by Mary's departure? She wanted to flee, but to whom could she go? She decided to walk down to the sea.

Along Demetria's path, the air was still and cool, magnifying the distant sounds nocturnal hunters make. Coming to the shore, she made her way to a large, flat rock and sat down. From miles away, at the southern tip of the large inland lake, warmer air brought up a wind over the water, causing it to ebb and flow, simulating a weak tide. The waves lapped close, so Demetria tucked her feet in tight to keep them dry. She sat until the sun was gone and the moon rose to watch over the night.

The water's roll was hypnotic, each apex glistening silver, then sinking into a wet, black pool only to emerge and crest again to receive the kiss of the moon. Demetria was dizzy with the up-and-down action of the waves, as though she were sitting within a rocking boat. She put out her hands on either side to steady herself. But it was not the rock that was moving; it was she.

She was being tossed about by circumstances she could not control. Her entire young life had been dictated by other people. With Mary gone, once again she was stripped of the power to make her own choices. *I do not want to stay and help Shoshanna with the house,* she protested. Nor did she want to be an example to the weavers or a comfort to Rachel. Most of all, she did not want to be kept in check by Mummius, who, even at dinner, seemed to grow grander in the space created by Mary's absence.

All the people who had ruled Demetria's life seemed to dance upon the foamy platform of the waves, floating up one by one in light, then sinking below the surface—Father and Mother, the Romans who bought and sold her, and Mary. Up and down, up and down they moved with the waters of the sea.

Then, as the likeness of Mary sank from its silvery crest into the inky water, Demetria thought she heard the sound of her mistress reciting the ancient prayers she knew by heart. Mary's voice calling down the divine blessing of Erev Shabbat gave Demetria an idea. She got to her feet and stood upon the rock that jutted into the sea like a raft. Stretching her arms to the sky, Demetria spoke, as she had never before dared to speak, to the God of Israel, Mary's God.

"O LORD of Heaven and Earth, I call upon you," she cried out in the language of the scriptures. "I am in distress beyond all knowing." Demetria took a deep breath and spoke with all her power. "Save me from my desolation and I will worship you forever!"

Arms extended, expectant face to the stars, Demetria waited. She heard the sound of the waves, lap-lapping around her, and night creatures howling in the distance, but there was nothing from God, no sound, no sign. Was this what it was like for Mary when she prayed, utter silence? Or did the Lord God of Israel not listen to Greeks, slaves, girls? Was God revolted by the pathetic creature that she was—an unclean mixture of all three?

Demetria had given up praying to the gods of Greece. She had tried that for years after her wrenching abduction from her mother's arms. And Roman gods—never! Rome was the source of all her suffering; she would die before she would turn that way. Searching the skies, she tried again. "O God, I am nothing but a Greek slave girl, and insignificant before you. In your mercy, hear my prayer, I beg you!"

Still only silence. Demetria's arms were heavy. She could hold them up no longer. It didn't matter. God did not care about her—if there was a God. She was alone and trapped. Weighed down with hopelessness, she let her weary arms fall to her sides. There was nothing left to do but go home. The shadows on Demetria's path seemed menacing, the air too cold, the sound of predators too close. Nearly there, she was practically running to the house to escape the terrors of the night.

But for the wide beam of moon at the window, the bedroom was unlit. Shoshanna was mumbling in a fitful sleep. Rachel was sitting on her cot, closest to the door, her back to Demetria. Late as it was, Rachel was still dressed in her daytime clothes, veil closed around her head, and rocking back and forth in the dark.

"Put your things there," Mummius had instructed on the first day that Demetria entered this room. At the time it was a clear message. She was relegated to the center cot, scrutinized from both sides by women she did not know, without even an illusion of privacy. As time passed and their love grew, she had come to appreciate the presence of Shoshanna and Rachel on either side, their gentle sleep-sounds enfolding her each night. "Rachel?" she whispered. Receiving no answer, Demetria walked to her own bed, sat down opposite Rachel, and folded back one edge of her swathing veil. *She has not ceased weeping since dinner, poor thing.*

She moved to Rachel's side and put her arms around her. "Don't be afraid," she said.

On her first morning here Demetria had been allowed to sleep late. Rachel had waited for her in the kitchen, then fed her breakfast and was kind to her. She took her to Magdala to shop for food and talked to her like a sister. Rachel had been the first in Magdala to befriend her. Now it was for her, the girl-turned-elder-sister to the woman, to show compassion.

She helped Rachel off with her clothes and into bed and lay beside her, humming until Rachel's crying subsided. She lay still as a board, as one would with a fussy child, waiting for her to go completely asleep and hoping that she would not reawaken and start to cry again. *How could you do this to us, Mistress?*

When she felt sure it was safe to move, she carefully released Rachel's hand and slipped one leg backwards off the cot, and then another. When she pushed away, Rachel stirred and Demetria froze, half on the bed, half off. Rachel did not wake, only turned, so Demetria rose slowly and moved away.

Not risking a lamp, she tiptoed around the room in the dark, preparing for bed. Blindly she slid her hand along the edge of her shelf, feeling for a sleep shift. Patting the stacked clothing, she felt something hard among her folded clothes. She reached in and pulled out a box she had never seen before. *Strange*, she thought, lifting it from the shelf and carrying it to the window.

Holding the box in one hand, with the other Demetria slipped up the clasp that secured its top and pushed it open. Moonlight fell upon the magical contents, a cake of ink, two pens, a wax wand and, tucked into one corner, a small brass seal. Lifting the seal and twirling it in the light, she saw engraved upon it the lustrous image of the mother-goddess, Demeter. Mary's presence filled the room, as though she were standing right beside her.

"Mistress," she whispered, "thank you."

CHAPTER 20

Mary was as happy as the women she had left behind were miserable. She could not get enough of Jesus that day, nor he of her, drinking in the details of their lives.

"I want to know everything about you," he said.

"There is nothing special to say, Rabbouni."

"Everything about you is special. Tell me about your childhood."

"All right. Well, my childhood was very happy." Mary adjusted her skirt and wriggled to make her seat on the cushion more comfortable. Seeing how he took note of her every move, she wondered if she had done anything provocative. "I grew up in the house in Magdala. It was small at first, one room only, but Father's business prospered, so his parents came to live with us, then Mother's. The house grew rapidly to keep pace with the need. Reuben and I had a room to ourselves."

"Pampered children."

"Why are you staring at me so?" she asked, blushing.

"I am *listening*. Go on. Please."

"You are right. We were pampered. There were only two of us, after all, and we were doted on by both parents and grandparents. I realize now how unusual it is to have so harmonious a group of people in the midst of so much togetherness. At the time, it just seemed natural to be content."

"Surrounded by love. Natural, indeed, but rare," he said by way of affirmation, still not taking his eyes from her face.

"My only sorrow was Reuben's melancholy. When we were quite young, I was usually able to coax him out of it. Eventually, his malaise grew black and hard. It sharpened into the cruel blade that cut him down in his flower. Then, Reuben's demons took up residence in me, and...

"My parents tried everything to help me, but no remedy could be found. In due course, caring for me took down everyone in the house, until only poor, faithful Shoshanna remained."

"It brings me great sadness to think of your long suffering," he said, taking both her hands in his. "Was there no respite?"

"I did have one great joy during that time, my dear father, whom I looked on as my hero. He had always indulged me, but with Reuben gone, Abba turned to me as his special companion. He taught me everything concerning the farm and exporting. He began to regard me as a colleague as much as a daughter. I have sometimes wondered whether, within the awful depths of his heartache, there was a small portion of relief." Mary lowered her head, made shy by the praise her father had heaped on her. "In the end, Abba's greatest gift was the strong hand of Marcus Quintius."

Jesus cocked his head, puzzled.

"They had been business associates for many years; friends as well. When Father's health failed, he extracted a promise from Marcus Quintius to help me shoulder the responsibilities of the business when he was gone."

"I don't imagine that your father had much difficulty with that," interrupted Jesus, feeling suddenly grateful for the Roman who fretted over Mary. Even in the brief time Jesus had seen them together, Marcus Quintius' devotion to her had shone from him like the blast of a lighthouse fire, mirrored for the entire world to see.

"He has been better than his word," Mary continued. "He encouraged me to cultivate my weaving and showed me how to make it the core of my business. That way, I could do what I loved most—as well as employ my women and help needy people in the town. He calls it 'Pax Magdalena.' He developed a market for my cloth in Rome. Imagine that—a small-town Galilean girl receiving orders for fine fabrics to dress Roman ladies in!"

"It is no wonder you are so fond of him."

"I met him on a trip to Tyre, you know."

"What?"

"Yes. I was fifteen, but still so naive. Father and I stayed with Marcus at his townhouse..."

"Are you saying that your father took you, a girl, on business trips and you stayed in the home of Romans?"

"Well, yes. How else could I learn?"

"I wish I had known your abba, Mary!" he said, engrossed in his continuing discovery of the forces that had shaped this remarkable woman.

"You would have liked him, Jesus. I still miss him every day." Mary found herself uncomfortable with so much attention paid to her, so she said, "But, Rabbouni, tell me now of *your* life. I will stare at you for a change."

Having the tables turned on him, Jesus laughed, unable to keep down the color that seeped up his neck and onto his ears.

"What shall I say? My childhood was ordinary in some ways. I had friends that I played with, but they teased me because I was different from them, always wandering off, walking the fields around Nazareth by myself. Sometimes they ganged up on me. Typical boys. But, I was discovering things."

"What things, Rabbouni?"

"I learned that I could touch nature in uncommon ways. I remember the first time I felt it, lying under a tree in late spring, warm breezes moving wispy clouds overhead, a turtledove in the branches singing to its mate in a distant tree. 'Tor, tor,' they called to each other, loudly, then softly, back and forth. When they fell silent, I stared at the bird above me and felt a desire to be close to it. I willed it to come near. I thought it and thought it until the bird lifted off from its branch to soar in a large circle. Instead of flying away, the dove swooped back, descended and landed on a rock near my shoulder. I held my breath and slowly moved my arm along the ground toward the rock where it stood looking back at me. Mary, that dove hopped onto my open palm! It stayed there until I tired and my arm ached so that I had to move. When it flew away, I felt something being pulled from me and lifting into the air within the bird.

"My mother seemed troubled by my story and told me not to speak of the bird to anyone. And so I did not. But you can imagine that after that I spent most of my free time with animals of all kinds, and plants as well, everything in the natural world."

"Is it like merging with them in some way?"

"No, not merging. I suppose the best way to describe it is a feeling of connection, like a pipe or a channel, with the force of life flowing through it. When I realized that I had that power, which other boys did not have, I was separated from the group even more. I confess I played pranks sometimes."

"I cannot believe that you were ever mischievous."

"You can believe it, surely enough. My only excuse is that I was very young, six, maybe seven. I did things like cause them to stumble or change the direction of a ball they had thrown."

"Oh, how I would like to be able to make certain people stumble around! Or run them into trees. Are you not still tempted?"

"What do you think?"

Mary smiled.

"More often, I made things glow with light or jump from one place to another—to make children laugh, you know, because I wanted them to like me. My mother put a stop to that nonsense in a hurry! What might I have become without her influence? I hate to think of it. She taught me that great power brings great responsibility. She disciplined me concerning the forces of nature that came to my hand so readily. Respect and restraint—those were her gifts.

"Anyway, in my teenage years my father taught me his trade—he was a builder—and I worked with him on construction crews. Of course I attended religious school. I'm sorry to say that I became a little self-righteous in those days, showing off to teachers, that kind of thing. It was a way to deal with how different I was from other young men, I guess. I often wished I could be more like them, with no special power, no special call. But the fact was I couldn't wait to be alone. Well, not alone…"

"What do you mean, Rabbouni?"

It seemed a simple question, and yet, it was anything but simple. Jesus paused, considering how he should respond. The crowds that flocked to him now, they did not understand him, any more than his boyhood friends had understood him. They could see that he was a holy man and powerful before God, and they talked about him that way, but that did not mean they could comprehend his special relationship to God, however much he wanted them to. Jesus had begun to doubt that he would ever find a companion who could stand together with him in the light of God and not be blinded. Could it be that Mary was the one?

"You said that God spoke to you, Mary."

"In the burial house."

"God speaks to me all the time."

"What does God say, Rabbouni?"

"Mostly ideas about what my life on this earth is meant to be. You can understand that now, I think."

"Excuse me, Rabbouni, but I do *not* understand. When God spoke to me, I thought I was going to die. I do not wish for that again."

"God knows how much to give, and when," Jesus said, intending to encourage her. But Mary's furrowed brow and tight lips showed that she was worried, frightened even, so he said more lightly, expecting her to laugh, "Don't fear. You will grow used to it."

"I will never grow used to it; not I."

"I'm sorry."

"Just go on with your story. Please."

And so Jesus continued. "When my father died, I took up my own financial responsibilities—just as you did, Mary. I supported my mother and siblings for many years, but the pressure to begin my real work swelled in me. Recently, I realized that the time had come for me to leave Nazareth. It pained my family so much, but it was a choice I had to make. I didn't want to hurt them, but they have their own lives. They will find their way."

That is just as it was for me this morning, Mary thought, picturing her heartbreaking goodbye to the clinging weavers. She, too, had been compelled to leave, to come to Capernaum and embark on this new phase of life, whatever it might be. Listening to Jesus tell of being called by God to depart from Nazareth, Mary wondered if it were possible that God had a special intention for her life as well. Was that why Jesus was confiding in her? An unfamiliar awareness of being revered arose in her heart.

"So you came to Capernaum?"

"It is a home base, yes, but we are constantly traveling."

Blood rushed to Mary's face. "We?"

She had not considered the possibility that there were people in Jesus' life who were close enough to live and travel with him, people who were a "we." How could she have been so thick-headed? It should have been obvious. Rabbis often collected students who attached themselves to their teacher, those who were chosen to follow and learn so they could one day carry on his ideals and principles. Was she to be part of a "we"?

"Along my way I have gathered a few special friends who have left everything to follow me. You saw them, yesterday, in the boat. They are my family now. I can hardly think of life without them, though it has been only three months since I left Nazareth."

"So short a time?" she mumbled, still trying to grasp what he was saying about this "we."

"A lot has happened in that short time. The first thing I did was go alone to Beth-abara to be baptized by a man named John, a distant cousin of mine. Perhaps you know of this holy man. Everyone is talking about him."

She shook her head no.

"He lives in the desert and wears animal skins and eats honey, which he gathers in the wild, and locusts."

"He sounds disgusting," she replied, grimacing at the imagined stench of untanned skins and the crunch and squish of insects in her mouth.

"It is just that he has no interest in worldly things and disdains any pleasure. He has attracted the attention of Rome because many of his followers believe he is the Messiah."

"Could he be the Messiah?"

"John is an extraordinary man, a prophet devoted to God, but Messiah? No. He would not make that claim. What he does claim is that he has come to announce the arrival of the Messiah. He baptizes people by the hundreds in preparation for the Reign of God."

"He baptized you."

"Yes. I went down there to join the crowd. Everyone had removed their outer garments, men in loincloths, women in tunics, so I stripped to the waist, too. When it was my turn, I walked right up to John and stood before him. He folded my arms over my chest and told me to close my eyes and hold my breath. He laid me down in the river. I felt the water climbing over my ears, my temples, then my eyes, nose, mouth until I was completely submerged. I remember my hair floating freely around my head and how cool it was on my scalp. Water was dripping everywhere from me when John raised me up and I heard him dedicating me to the Reign of God." Jesus paused, feeling again his hair rinsing smoothly over his tipped-back head and down his neck when he was lifted out of the river. "Everyone in the crowd was crying and praising God. It was a crossroads, Mary—the point of no return."

"What does that mean, Rabbouni?"

Jesus laid a hand on her shoulder and the other over his own heart and said, "They were praising God for *me*, Mary. They had been longing for me, just as I was longing for them. I can never go back; I am living for the people, now... Does this make any sense, Mary?"

For years Mary had desired to feel God's love in the place of what she thought was God's punishment, years of waiting for the deliverance that Jesus had given her. "It is the only thing that does make sense to me, Rabbouni."

Jesus inhaled deeply, as though taking her answer into his lungs, and then let out a big breath. "After my baptism God called me into the Judean wilderness to fast and pray."

Jesus told Mary the story of his wilderness, stumbling over words and hesitating, as if striving to find language adequate for the event. As he spoke, he appeared to be lit with an internal fire that showed itself in a brilliance surrounding his head and streaming downward to wrap his body in a radiant blanket where he sat. Mary was reminded of her own blistering experience in the burial house and how she must have looked afterwards, frightening people with her singed skirt.

"I came out of that desert very much changed. Do you know what I found when I returned to Beth-abara? Four men from Galilee, the brothers, John and James, and Andrew and Simon, also brothers. I was overcome with love for them when I heard they had witnessed my baptism and had been waiting for me all the time I was gone. They said they had waited because they wanted to be by my side always."

"I know that feeling," whispered Mary, thinking of the irresistible urge that had pulled her away from home just to be near him.

"The five of us proceeded home to Galilee by the eastern route."

Jesus described that trip, saying that he spoke to small crowds wherever they stopped along the way. He told her that, back in Galilee, two other disciples joined him, in Beth-saida a man named Philip and then, in Cana, one Nathaniel. Those six men were the "we" that Jesus had referred to.

"I was on my way home from Cana through Magdala when Mummius and Marcus Quintius came to see me," he said, bringing his story to the present.

"Yes, I sent them to fetch you," she said with a quick, flirting smile, thinking to charm him with her secret.

"Excuse me, lady?"

"Well, my weavers had heard you teaching in Magdala. Some were becoming quite attached to you, and it angered their men. You were causing a disturbance in Pax Magdalena—I couldn't allow that! I wanted to meet you myself, see what you were up to, protect my women, you know."

Jesus was taken aback, for he knew that the men had come to him on their own initiative, asking him to drive out Mary's demons. Confusion showed on his face as his eyebrows drew together.

"What is it, Rabbouni?"

"They said nothing of your invitation. I believe they came of their own accord. I thought you knew."

It was as though Mummius and Marcus Quintius had burst rudely into the room, intruding on her snug, private time with Jesus. She wanted a fresh start with him alone, uncontaminated by anyone from her past, and their unseemly presence aggravated her.

"I did not know. But I want to know now."

Jesus reported that Mummius and Marcus Quintius had sought him out at the home of Menahem in Magdala.

"I know Menahem. Not a bad man, but rigid. He has accepted aid from me at times, but cannot bring himself to endorse the help I give to gentiles. He speaks ill of me for it. Why do you befriend such a man?"

Thinking it was not the best time for a sermon on how he had come to save not the righteous but sinners, Jesus kept to the topic. "They were desperate, Mary. Mummius had used all his powers, which are considerable, to wrest you from the demons. He could not have done more, believe me. His next attempt would have been his last, and it would have failed. And poor Marcus Quintius. He had a purse of money that he thought would settle everything. Very impatient, that Roman."

Mary had never heard "poor" and "Marcus Quintius" spoken in the same breath, and it was that which calmed her down a bit. It would be exactly like him to try to pay off the spirit world on her behalf.

Why am I so angry? she wondered.

Through the years she had put herself under the watch of others so as not to betray herself publicly or to cause herself irreparable harm. She did this voluntarily, if not enthusiastically, because she knew she must. What then did she expect of her caretakers? Of course they did things behind her back; of course they sometimes hid the truth. It was for her own good. She would have done the same, if the roles had been reversed.

Jesus spoke again, and Mary realized that he was asking for more than simple generosity when he said, "Can you forgive them?"

Dipping deeply into her well of compassion, Mary at last said, "I do, Rabbouni. I forgive them."

Her response offered Jesus what he needed next. He wanted her to understand what it would mean to be joined with him in the work he was meant to do. He began to tell her about his mission.

"There is much that separates people from one another and from God, Mary. And so little forgiveness. People are trying hard to obey the Law, but they do not understand it. God despises a slavish following of regulations. What God desires is an inclination of the *heart*, not something imposed from the outside. This is the real meaning of the Law. This is what I have come to say. God wants us to love in a way that breaks down selfishness, and leads to acceptance of others, and forgiveness. Just as you, dear one, have loved without reservation throughout your life."

Jesus had tears in his eyes when he said, "I heal their afflictions to give evidence that they themselves are forgiven."

It was then that Mary knew what had happened in the waters of the Sea of Galilee yesterday. When Jesus guided her hand into the water and together they lifted a palmful up to Sudi's face and lay their dripping hands on her livid bruises; when Mary said, "Be healed, little daughter," and Jesus' lips mouthed the words silently, he had brought her directly into his ministry of love.

Today he had declared that he wanted her to be his disciple and asked for her commitment: "Will you do this with me, Mary?" he had said. Now, she understood what her desiring heart had promised when she answered, "I will." Coming face-to-face with the life-giving joy of reconciliation, Mary of Magdala stepped over the threshold into her future and placed her feet permanently upon the way of Life, Jesus' way, and they began to speak, for the first time, of their life together. They would spread the teaching of forgiveness and love throughout Galilee, south to Jerusalem, even into Samaria!

At one point reality niggled its way into Mary's mind and she said, "Rabbouni, how is it that I, a mere woman, can be at your side, teaching and healing? Will this not turn many people away?"

He said, "Mary, how is it that the Reign of God can come to earth without women? Who will show the way, if not you and I?"

That was the key that opened the door and allowed Mary, at last, to wrap herself in his confidence and to set her heart upon his world-shattering vision. Before they knew it, they were making plans about their travels. The more they talked, the more animated their conversation became. Their excitement soared, so that by the time their host interrupted them, they were breathless with possibility.

CHAPTER 21

"What, back so soon?" Gaius Valerius exclaimed.

Marcus Quintius had showed up with the startling news that he had returned to Capernaum in the company of Mary of Magdala, a companion of the very Jesus upon whom he, Valerius, had been spying. Craving the particular pleasures of Roman bath and table, Quintius was glad to accept Valerius' hospitality, for the time being.

"Come in and welcome, comrade."

The situation was complicated for Marcus Quintius. He wanted only to ensure that everything went smoothly for Mary in Capernaum; at least that is what he alleged to her. The truth was that he was edgy about the circumstances unfolding around Jesus and how they might affect his own plans for a future with Mary. He needed to keep a sharp eye on that Jew. In addition, there was the matter of Gaius Valerius, who would no doubt press him for information that he was not prepared to give. He did not wish to lose Valerius' trust. Even less did he want to put Mary under any kind of Roman military suspicion. Marcus Quintius found himself balanced precariously on a tightrope, one end held by Jesus, the other by Gaius Valerius. Being a generally straightforward man, he disliked evasion, and it was hard for him to keep track of the details that were inevitably produced by partial truths. Nevertheless, he would do what was required, and the first requirement was to locate a residence for Mary.

With Gaius Valerius' help, that very day he found something that would suit her perfectly. Though built in the style of a Roman domus, it was modest, situated on a quiet street near the market. It just felt right when he stepped into the atrium, a typically large room that served as a reception hall and gathering place. Passing through the atrium, he entered the peristyle, a central garden courtyard surrounded by a colonnade, and lush with plants. He could see Mary bending lovingly over each one, pinching off spent foliage and watering. How often had he imagined her bending over him and cooing as she did to her flowers.

He explored the peristyle with a critical eye as to the condition of pavement and paint, walking around it again and again, pacing off its length and width. He came to rest near the fountain in the middle, the thumb of his left hand tucked into his belt, right hand at his face, considering the columns and arches of the portico. The peristyle had a certain understated grace, and the unusual feature of a few tall trees stretching up above the roof to attract birds, but he wondered if it might smell a bit too much of Rome for Mary.

Attentive to every detail, he continued scrutinizing the house for features to recommend it. Opposite the entrance to the courtyard lay a row of four tidy *cubiculi*, small sleeping rooms, and a commodious lavatory with running water. To the left and immediately adjacent to the well-appointed kitchen was a rather large dining room. *Oh, yes,* he thought, *she will have this place filled with dinner guests in no time.* But he was confused about the furniture.

He turned to the land agent who was conducting his tour of the property. "No couches in the triclinium?"

"Barbaric, is it not?"

Quintius dismissed the distasteful comment with an impatient shake of his head, causing the man to carry on quickly.

"The house was built by a Jew and his wife from Alexandria. His family had lived in that city for generations. Apparently they acquired a taste for Roman architecture, but not our habit of reclining at table."

"Yes, I see. That explains the lack of murals and mosaics throughout."

"Indeed. A pity, really."

"Hmm," responded Quintius, lips pursed under his hand.

"We have many skilled artisans here in Capernaum, sir," the man added, grasping at the potential sale he felt slipping away. "You could easily have it decorated to your own impeccable tastes."

Marcus Quintius was already sold. He rubbed his hands together and said, "No, no, my good man, this is quite suitable! I'll take it." Without quibbling, he paid the asking price in full and handed the astonished agent a draft immediately redeemable at the local bank. He received in return the deed to the property.

The business transaction thus concluded, Marcus Quintius stood for a moment rehearsing his return with Mary: dramatic pause at the front door and an instruction to cover her eyes, then leading her into the spacious atrium for her first speechless glimpse into the garden courtyard beyond. Vibrant with anticipation, he gave a list of hurried directions to the agent and was off, the deed safely secured within his belt.

Setting out to find the house where he had been told that Jesus was staying, he made his way along the streets of Capernaum, a ten minute walk, which he reduced to seven with long, lighthearted paces. Locals stared as he passed by—a happy, whistling Roman? Remarkable! When he came to a pedestrian stairway leading down to his destination, he took the steps two at a time, big feet turned outward, the better to negotiate the narrow steps, thick-soled sandals tapping a confident, rhythmic beat as they landed in time to the music in his head. He felt lithe as a Greek dancing boy.

Identifying the house he sought, he went directly to the doorway and called out, "Hail, within!"

The owner met him at the door and said in a questioning voice, "Peace be unto you."

Insensitive to lesser men, Marcus Quintius could not see the revulsion on this Jew as he confronted a Roman who seemed determined to enter his home. Nor did he recognize the relief brought on by his inquiry about Mary, which meant that at least his contaminating presence would be confined to one room only.

"This way," said the man, ushering the unwelcome visitor around the house to the outside stairway. He had barely announced, "A Roman here for you, lady," when, driven by those Roman privileges, Marcus Quintius pushed past him and stood under the arch, covered in self-satisfaction, his wide shoulders filling up the narrow door.

Then it was that Marcus Quintius Severus laid eyes on a sight that blew him apart. She was sitting on the floor, his sweet, unspoiled Magdalena, glistening with perspiration and in high color, if not in the embrace of a man, certainly just released. She was leaning close to Jesus, not touching, not needing to touch, as energy pulsed in the space between them. They were gazing at each other in total absorption, unable to suppress their smiles.

"Magdalena!"

Mary rose to greet him. He stepped toward her and with one hand pulled her to him, roughly. The other hand went to a leather scabbard at his waist. The long-buried blood lust of the battlefield surged in him. His gorge rose. At the slightest provocation he would have driven the blade of his dagger to its hilt into the sternum of the man who had defiled Mary and thought nothing of it.

The object of his rage did not move, only spoke, softly, and kept speaking until some of the fury in Marcus Quintius seeped away.

"Marcus Quintius Severus," said Jesus from his seat on the floor, "peace be unto you. It is good to see you again."

Still pinning Mary to his side, he choked out a stiff acknowledgement, "Jesus."

"Mary has just been talking about you."

"Has she?"

"Yes. She tells me that she is deeply indebted to you. That you have guided her in her endeavors over these many years since her father died and, without you, she would have been at a loss."

Marcus Quintius relaxed his grip on the scabbard, but only slightly. "Aaron trained her. I was not much needed," he replied, dissembling. He became aware of his cruel hold on Mary's arm. "Magdalena, forgive me," he said and released her, realizing that he had surely left the mark of his fingers on the delicate skin beneath her sleeve.

Mary was rubbing the place where his hand had been, and he saw that she was gaping at him as if he were someone she did not know. Unable to stem the tide of emotions within, the undone Roman stood mute, every muscle clenched, until he heard Mary's voice saying, "Come, Marcus, let us go now," and felt her tug on his forearm. He allowed her to guide him out of the room, down the stairway and into the street, leaving Jesus behind.

The walk *through* Capernaum could not have been more different from the walk *to* Capernaum. Marcus Quintius set out at his seven-minute pace. "Please slow down," Mary pleaded, but, so trapped was he in his internal storm, that he only looked at her furiously and kept moving.

Images of all the women with whom Marcus Quintius had ever lain flashed through his mind. Their familiar look of ecstasy was the look he had seen on Mary's face when she was with Jesus. How long he had girded himself in patience, delaying his own pleasure, waiting to hold her in his arms, lie with her, be the man who would pleasure her first and last. What right did the Jew have to all this?

Mary abruptly came to a stop. "Marcus," she said, turning him around by the shoulders to look up into his rage-blind eyes, "what is wrong with you?"

Veins in his temples stood out, pumping blood. He glared at her with an unfamiliar face, twisted with contempt.

And she knew.

"Marcus Quintius Severus! You cannot think that Jesus and I have lain together."

"But, I...I... You...." He had become a stammering youth.

"Marcus, this is beyond belief."

Did he imagine that she would betray her virginity after a lifetime of purity, however much she might have been tempted? She pulled him into a side street, deserted now as shops had closed for the day.

"Listen," she began. Ready to wound him with accusations of her own, the sight of him brought her up short. Marcus had fairly collapsed against a wall, pushing the weight of his upper body against it, knees bent, and slumping, so that he was eye to eye with her. He showed her another face that she had never seen before, a wronged, grief-stricken face with moisture in the corners of its eyes, threatening to spill. Her anger supplanted by compassion at the sight of this face, she placed her warm, open palms on his cheeks, fingertips resting lightly on the surging veins beneath. "Shh, shh," she soothed.

It was many, many moments before Marcus Quintius recovered and then only because of Mary's insistent, repeated assurances that they had done nothing of the kind, that they were only speaking of their lives and their God of mystery. She continued fussing over him until her persistence caused him to yield.

Like a boy seeking reassurance, he said, "You did not...?"

"Must I take an oath? No, Marcus, we did not. You know better, surely."

"I am worried about you. I don't understand what you are doing with a man like Jesus. He healed you, yes. You are grateful to him for that, as I am. But to follow him, to be alone with him..." Then, seeing that he had become ridiculous in her eyes, he said, "I have offended you. Can you forgive me?"

And she, wanting above all to restore him, said readily, "You great Roman goose, of course I forgive you."

He pressed both her hands to his lips. "Darling Magdalena."

Mary had not thought it possible that the man she regarded as her savior could come unraveled. She had the sense to allow him an unobstructed exit from the dilemma in which he seemed cornered.

"Can we go now?" she asked. "I feel a chill. And I am starving."

Marcus Quintius pushed his damp hair back and wiped his face. He seized the opportunity to regain command of himself. "Yes, of course," he replied. "Shall I call for a cart?"

"Don't be silly," she responded and started walking. After a little while of silence and calmer breathing, and still looking for signs that he had recovered his stability, she asked, "Marcus, did you find me a house?"

In the wake of his outrage, he had forgotten his primary task. At great pains to move beyond the history of the last few moments and wanting to obliterate the memory of his lapse, he spoke blithely, as if it had never happened.

"Just wait until you see it!"

They finished the walk to Mary's new house at a more comfortable ten-minute pace. When they arrived at the door of the domus, "Here it is," he declared with a grand gesture.

In the evening dim, the dressed limestone construction of the house did not fill Mary with awe, but, seeing him so pleased and not wanting to agitate him, she replied, "It's very nice."

According to his plan, "Cover your eyes," he said, and, with one arm around her waist, guided her into the atrium. "You can look now."

Marcus Quintius heard the rush of pleasure in the intake of her breath as she took in the sight. Lamps had been lit behind each of the columns of the peristyle beyond, casting graceful reflections onto the tiled floor and around the fountain, whose soft, trickling sound floated to where she stood. She closed her eyes again to let the fragrance of flowers fill her up.

"Come. Let me show you," he said, completely in love with the moment he had created for her.

They strolled around the house, Marcus Quintius pointing out its various amenities. They came to the triclinium, which was exuding delicious smells of a supper laid out for them. *Good man,* remarked Marcus Quintius to himself, remembering the instructions he had left with the agent.

"Would you like to eat?"

"No, not yet," she said quietly.

Their circuit of the house finished near the southern wall, where he paused and said, "See how these windows open to the winds off the sea. You will be cool in summer."

"Marcus Quintius, my best ally," Mary said. "It is most agreeable, only…"

"Only what?" he asked, troubled that he might have disappointed her.

"Only, it must have cost dearly."

Marcus Quintius made light of her concern with a story about the owner's need to sell the property hastily, drastically reducing the price to a figure that she could easily afford and to which she could not possibly object. He kept to himself the true cost, having paid the difference from his own pocket.

"Then I confess; I love it," she said, poking her head through a window to let moonlight and the evening air bathe her face and hair. Marcus Quintius turned her around gently and placed the deed to her new house into her hand. As the scroll passed from his hand to hers, for a moment they held it together, and Mary felt the flare of a wick, lighting up a long-empty lamp in her heart. "If ever I were going to spend my life with... Now that I am free of my demons..." She looked as though she might start to cry.

Marcus rescued her. "Ready for supper now?" he asked softly.

"Beyond ready," she said, grateful to move on.

They went to the dining room where the meal was laid out, food that had been prepared according to the Jewish Law.

"How did you manage this?"

He told her about the Alexandrian Jew who had built the house, and the Jewish servants he had left behind, a man and his daughter, who were even now praising God that their employment was to be continued under the new owner.

Mary and Marcus sat close by one another and ate, the air around them pervaded by an unspoken agreement to say nothing of the ugly scenes with Jesus and in the street. The exertions of the day, the walk from Magdala, and the rope whip of emotions faded. Fatigue and food made them sleepy.

Mary's gratitude for Marcus Quintius was rock-solid. He had never failed her, and he had not failed her this day. She had met him on the beach at Tyre, where her father had taken her in hopes of lifting her spirits after her brother's death, after the demons came into her, and after her broken betrothal to Hanani ben Jahdo. On the trip with her father, she had been free of demons. She was ready to be happy, as a fifteen-year-old girl should be happy. From the moment she saw how the handsome, worldly, self-assured Roman looked at her, she loved him.

She had determined never to marry, but, even if she had not, Mary knew that, as a gentile, he would be forbidden. Still, she dreamed of him as a suitor, a safe fantasy, well out of reach. Over the years her youthful dreams had been woven into the tapestry of what she believed to be a mature, mutual, and respectful devotion.

"How God has blessed me!" Mary said in a silky contentment. "This is the life I have longed for, a quiet home, love..." She stopped, conflicted, remembrances of the man who had freed her overlaid on the visage of this man who cherished her. Then, no longer able to keep open her heavy eyelids, "It is time for me to sleep," she said.

Marcus Quintius walked Mary to her sleeping cubicle, his hand resting lightly on the nape of her neck under her hair.

"Are you going to Valerius' house," she asked, "or staying here?"

"Staying here. Only this one night," he insisted, "to ensure all is well and safe with the house."

"Very well then." She kissed him on the cheek and bade him shalom.

Marcus Quintius had long ago grown accustomed to exercising restraint where Mary was concerned, but when she turned and was already loosening her sash to undress for bed, he almost followed. Who would know? In a massive show of self-discipline, he retired to his own cubicle. He dismissed his slave, who had waited to undress him and put away his things. He took a deep draft from a full cup of unwatered wine left for him by the slave, swirled it in his mouth, and swallowed. Alone now, he lay naked on the bed, arms folded behind his head, legs crossed at the ankles, staring at the ceiling.

Upon the smooth, white, unadorned plaster above him marched a file of images from this improbable day, purged pictures that told a redacted story, all repugnant details conveniently expunged. Every time a thought of Mary with Jesus threatened to come into focus, he banished it, leaning heavily on her assurances. He drank again from the wine cup and concentrated on their supper just past.

Throughout the meal Marcus had believed that Mary's glow and her ebullient laughter were on his account, the house and everything he had provided for her. Blinded by his own wants, he could not even consider that her euphoria had anything at all to do with Jesus. Through the blurry haze of strong wine, he pictured himself gazing at her, the frame of her hair flowing loosely around her lamplit face like a waterfall of liquid ebony. The heavenly, burnt umber eyes with their long, thick, black-lash fringe, casting their spell on him. He had stroked the back of her hand, rubbing his thumb softly over the translucent skin. When he raised her hand to his lips, she had leaned forward to receive his attention without flinching. In his wine-fueled desire, he took this to mean that she wanted him, as surely as he wanted her, but was kept from saying so by the modesty that made her all the more alluring. Her demons banished, she was free now; she had said it herself. Was he not free, too, from the sacred promise he had made to her father never to speak to her of love? "Marry me," he could almost hear himself saying, but the moment had not been exactly the right moment, so he checked the impulse. *Not yet, not yet.*

The more Marcus Quintius pushed away the thought of being wedded to Mary, the more the tide of that rebellious thought surged back. He could see them sharing the intimacy of home and bed, while a pageant of love paraded across the ceiling over his head. He became a muralist, drawing in details and embellishing his pictures with vibrant colors. As he did so, his heart pounded and his breath became shallow and rapid. He began to lose track of the boundary between his body and his mind until, finally, Marcus Quintius rose from his bed.

His bare, callused feet made no sound upon the tile, but he tiptoed anyway, past the two doors that separated his cubicle from hers. At her entrance, he paused momentarily with his back against the wall, and then slowly lifted the drapery and peered into her room. A single torch had been left burning in the peristyle. It was enough. What he could not see, he could imagine. The gentle rising and falling of the form on the bed told him that she was asleep, lying on her side, cheek resting on the pillow, hip pushing up the blanket into an enticing mound. Holding his breath, he moved to her side and looked down. One arm was wrapped around her pillow and, uncovered, shone as though someone had poured out a stream of milk from a pitcher. A shadow marred the sheen: the purple mark made by his own hand.

Seeing the bruise he had inflicted triggered something unpredictable. He remembered how it felt to grab her and pull her to him. He could feel his fingers pressing deeply into her unresisting flesh. Even in his rage he had been aware of her trembling, how vulnerable she was and that some part of him had wanted to hurt her. His guilt was twisting into arousal, and he felt himself wanting to hurt her now. He rested his weight on a bent knee upon the mattress and pulled her covers down. Shockingly, she, too, was naked, an unheard-of, immodest thing for her to sleep unclothed, which could only mean that she had been waiting for this.

Mary woke, and he hesitated, not reluctant but savoring, witnessing with physical eyes her uncovered beauty, the pearly skin, the hills and valleys of her body, the crest of soft lamb's wool at the entrance to paradise. In his head he had seen it a thousand times, and done it a thousand times more.

Kneeling beside her on the bed, he pushed gently on her shoulder to lay her on her back and set out tasting her; the remnant of honeyed figs on her mouth; lavender at the indentation of her throat where her pulse was beating; the clean, salty dampness between her breasts. Then he lowered his head between her legs and tasted her there. When he heard her cry of ecstasy, he could wait no longer. He moved his body on top of hers and pushed into her, hard.

Again and again they loved each other through the night until, at last surfeited, he could do nothing more but allow her to kiss his battle scars wherever she found them. When she was finished, he flung one arm over her body and, covered in sweat and drained, he slept—and slept on.

"Marcus Quintius?"

The sound of his name arrived from the courtyard on the wings of birdsong. Barely able to come into consciousness, he reached out to pull her close to him. Face half buried in the bedclothes, "Yes, my darling?" he answered, a vague wondering in his mind about why her voice seemed to have come from afar, along with the sound of the birds.

"Come see the beautiful morning!"

Still lying on his stomach, he felt around gently, then more urgently, for her body next to his. She was not there. His eyes popped open to stare at the wall opposite. He was in his own room! His clothes were folded on a chair. One wine cup stood on the table near him. There was no sign that she had ever been here, or that he had ever left.

"Are you decent? May I come in?"

Marcus Quintius sat bolt upright and covered himself.

"No, wait! Please."

All that separated them was the curtain that hung at the doorway. He stared at it, willing her to stay on the other side until he could make sense of his startling situation. His head pounded and his stomach churned from last night's drinking. He looked around again, trying to remember when he had left her, when he had returned to his own bed. Had he ever really been with her?

"Have no fear. I won't look in; you never know what you might see peeking into the bedroom of a Roman," she teased.

His heart sank beneath the stinging truth. *It was all a dream!* "Jupiter's eyes," he said in a gravelly whisper.

"What did you say?"

"Nothing, dear. I'll be out soon."

He dressed as quickly as he could and stepped reluctantly out into the courtyard. His first sight of her was from behind, bending over a potted plant, asking it lovingly what sort of flower it was.

"Good morning," he said, clearing his throat.

"Good morning, at last. Not like you to be so long abed. Bad dreams?"

"Something like that."

"You're already dressed," she said, moving to a table that had been set up for them and handing him a cup of tea.

Normally, on a private morning like this, Marcus Quintius would have come to breakfast in just a tunic and belt, but today he was completely covered in a *laena*, a cloak secured at the shoulder with a metal brooch, and his big, hooded *cucculus*, an outer garment used for travel, draped over his forearm. No amount of clothing would have been sufficient to cover the humiliation he thought must surely been plain to see. He might have shown up within the sanctuary of a toga if only he had not left it in his baggage at Valerius' house.

He took the offered cup in a hand he couldn't keep from trembling. "Mustn't give the servants reason to gossip," he said, sitting down and laying the heavy *cucculus* over his lap. Registering Mary's look of incredulity, he said lamely, "I have business with Gaius Valerius this morning."

Marcus Quintius gulped some tea and rose to leave.

"Will you be back for dinner?"

"Yes, yes, of course, my dear," he muttered, and was gone.

CHAPTER 22

Mary perched upon a stone bench at the edge of the peristyle, still, like a cat. Around and above her, early morning birds flitted and dove, coming as close as they wanted. Only her eyes moved to follow them while they fed and sang. *Why are you so fearless?*

Every day of her first week in Capernaum, Mary had come here for her early prayers while it was still dark and then would sit, taking in the wet break of morning, and wait patiently for the rest of her world to rise and stretch. In the dawning of the day, birds, habitants of the garden, woke and appeared one by one among the plants and trees and sang until their chorus reached such a pitch that her contemplation was broken and she could only add her laughter to their song.

In Magdala, Mary's garden was a floral showcase that bloomed in splendor throughout the growing season, marking the calendar like a moveable feast around the grounds. She herself had chosen each plant and its location and overseen its cultivation so that each was, in a way, like a child to her. Here in Capernaum the select, interior garden of this new house was producing unknown flora that had been planted by others before her. Every day now another would wake from its slumber and burst open with surprising, dewy gifts.

When Zimzi arrived to serve morning tea—an indulgent, mild brew of khat—"Thank you, my dear," she would say, and Zimzi, painfully shy, waited to be dismissed. Today, the serving girl, eyes downcast, thrust out a small scroll. Mary nodded kindly and Zimzi turned and fled, scattering the birds and nearly toppling the tea tray.

The small wax impression of Demetria's seal upon the scroll was immediately recognizable. Eagerly, Mary lifted it with her thumbnail and unrolled the papyrus. Seeing it covered with the young author's native Greek, she began to read.

"Demetria of Magdala to the lady Mary in Capernaum, Greeting. How is that for a start, Mistress? Quite proper is it not? I do want the first letter I have ever written to make you proud."

The corner of Mary's mouth lifted in a half-smile as she thought of the countless occasions when Demetria, overhearing her dictation to Mummius, had apparently been learning proper correspondence forms. *Smart girl, excellent girl.*

"I cannot find words to express my thanks for your gift. I never imagined such a treasure, and it came at a time when I surely needed to feel your presence. The very next morning I went early to Mummius and asked for a small sheet of papyrus. He looked at me oddly and said he would bring it to me later. I did not want to wait, so, I hope you don't mind, I went into your bedroom and took some from your desk. I didn't sit at your desk. I just took the sheet to my room and sat on the floor to write.

"When I told the weavers that I was writing a letter, Avireina said her husband was going to Capernaum in a few days, so I gave it to her to give to her husband. She said he promised he would deliver it, but of course I cannot be sure. I hope that you will soon write back to me. I like to think of you opening my letter and reading. I never realized before that letters could bring people close together when they are far apart.

"We miss you very much here, Mistress, but we are doing our best to carry on without you. I try to help Rachel all the time, but she seems a little angry. Maybe you could find her a husband in Capernaum. Shoshanna's knees are hurting her, especially the right one. Mummius gave her a balm to rub on, but she won't use it. You know how she is about his salves and potions.

"Speaking of Mummius, you should see his new jewelry, Mistress! I don't know where it has come from. Most of it is decorated with Egyptian gods. They are scary looking, so I try not to think about them, but I can't help staring.

"The weavers send you their love and say to tell you that they are completing all the orders on time. I am still working on my shawl, but it is going slowly. I am making more mistakes than ever, so that I am afraid it will be fit only to wear around the house. Mostly I sit on your oak bench in the courtyard and read. I wash the mosaic every day to keep it sparkling.

"I will close for now, Mistress. Can you not come home soon? Your devoted girl, Demetria."

The edges of the scroll curled up around Mary's hands as she held it in her lap, trying to read between the lines of the tidy, childlike script.

The tone of the letter was somewhat immature, not consistent with the grown-up young lady Demetria had become. Well, it was her first letter and she had not yet learned how to transfer her thoughts and feelings elegantly into the written word. It would take practice for her to become as skilled at writing as she was at speaking. Still...

What was Demetria trying to say? Mary read and reread, searching for a word of cheer in a morass of allusion. Finding none, she was forced to admit what joy and precipitous action had blinded her to. It was not so easy for people left behind to "find their own way" as she had blithely expected of them. Although she could not find it in her heart to regret her decision, she did regret the hurt she had inflicted on them by following *her* own way. The image of Demetria on her hands and knees washing the treasured mosaic brought her to the edge of tears, and action.

"Zimzi!"

"Yes, mmmistress."

"Send Joachim out to me, please."

"Yes, mmmistress."

Within the hour Mary was sitting at a table in the atrium piled with writing materials, which had been secured by the resourceful Joachim. She smoothed out a long strip of papyrus and sat for a moment collecting her thoughts, absentmindedly clicking the end of her pen on her front teeth.

"My dearest Demetria," she began. "I have just received your letter, and what a delight to hear from you! I had hoped that you would enjoy the surprise of the writing set I left for you. Now, dear, you must use it often. Take as much papyrus as you need. As a matter of fact, tell Mummius and Shoshanna that I have given you permission to use my desk. I enjoy the thought of your sitting there practicing your writing skills. From now on, you may give your letters to Mummius for the courier, if you like.

"Let me tell you about Capernaum. On the very day of our arrival Marcus Quintius found the most charming house for me. It is smaller than the house in Magdala, but certainly large enough. I love every aspect of my new home, but as you would expect, I am most pleased by the garden. It is located within a central courtyard surrounded by the kind of portico that the Romans call a peristyle. It is filled with rare, flowering plants, unknown even to me. And, Demetria, the tiny birds that frequent the courtyard—truly remarkable! Marcus Quintius is staying with his colleague Gaius Valerius, but he usually comes by in the morning for a while to tend to business matters associated with the house, or we have our midday meal together."

Then, Mary thought, but did not write, *though he seems a bit distant at times. If I did not know better I would think he is avoiding me.* Instead, Mary described the house, the servants Zimzi and Joachim, the weather, the city, the waterfront and details of her daily life before getting to the news she was most eager to convey.

"I have spent these first days becoming acquainted with Jesus' friends. There are six men who are close to him, students is the best word for them, and I pass most of my time in their company.

"I like his friends well enough, though they seem sometimes like impressionable youths, following him around as witless sheep might a shepherd. Now, Demetria, you must tell no one that I am saying these things. They are secrets between us girls!

"At first I liked Andrew particularly. He is the youngest of the six, slight of stature, with very dark skin and big, soft, languid eyes that remind me of a goat I once had as a childhood pet. He is shy, especially around his older brother Simon, a big burly man whom Jesus has taken to calling Peter. No one knows whether Jesus is teasing him by labeling him "Rock," least of all Simon himself.

"Simon Peter is larger than any other man I know. He reminds me of a great bushy-haired, Syrian bear. He loves to eat and has a tendency toward corpulence—do you know this word 'corpulence'? It means stoutness, in Peter's case around the midsection. Fortunately, his corpulence is kept in check by how very hard he works. Peter and Andrew come from Bethsaida. Along with two other brothers, John and James, they are partners in a fishing business on the Sea of Galilee. Demetria dear, you should keep track of these locations. Go and get the papyrus map from the chest in the loom room and find Capernaum at the northern end of the sea and Bethsaida three miles distant.

"I think you would find Peter amusing, once you got used to his bluster. He clearly supposes himself leader of the group, is usually first to speak, and vociferously, like the bear he resembles, causing others to move back and wait their turn. Jesus spends a lot of time talking to Peter and asking him questions, but *I* think that it is John, in his adoring silence, for whom Jesus has particular affection. Yes, he's the favored one, I am sure.

"Philip and Nathanael are newest to the group and tend to keep their distance from the other men. I imagine that they are trying to find a way into the inner circle of four. As for me, a woman in their midst, *all* are cautious."

Mary did not tell Demetria that she wondered what the men, observing Jesus' favor, really thought of her. He had made it clear to them that she was an important part of the trusted "we" that he was gathering to his side. It must be apparent that she was no servant, but what, then? She did not flaunt her special status; neither did she hide it under a bushel. It was Jesus who included her, asking her opinion on significant matters equally with the men.

The first time he had moved over to make room for her next to him in their circle the unspoken expressions of disapproval were obvious—raised eyebrows, straightened spines, clenched lips, downcast looks. Reluctantly she sat and busied herself tidying her skirt. When she was settled, he said, "Mary, tell us what your understanding is of The Reign of God," and then ignored the ice that froze their circle in disbelief.

Each day she and the men would go to the hillsides outside Capernaum where Jesus spoke to groups of mostly ordinary people who clustered around. They watched, amazed, at the way the people listened, as though they had an insatiable hunger for his very words. It was such a simple message in simple, everyday language about God's love for every one of them. So different from the scribes and Pharisees, who could speak only of complicated rules and regulations and the burdensome impossibility of following every minute detail of the Law. Inevitably, when he finished speaking, by throngs they would present their sick so he could lay his hands on them.

Toward the end of one such day, Andrew, observing Jesus' fatigue, said to Peter, "Can we not stop him? There is no end to the line today. Let them come back tomorrow!"

Mary's heart fell when she heard that. She, among them all, was the one who had received healing from Jesus. She would not try to stop him.

"Brother," she said softly to Andrew, "for many years have they suffered. Some have traveled great distances to see the Master. He will surely not want them to wait any longer for release from their afflictions."

Andrew said coolly to the space straight ahead of him, "How is it you speak for the Master today, woman?"

Before she could find her voice to answer such a question, she saw John lay a restraining hand on Andrew's arm and heard him speak.

"He wouldn't listen, brother. You know how he is. Let it alone."

In their first conversations, when Mary was still struggling to see her future as a fully fledged disciple, she knew it would be like this. She had warned Jesus that it would be hard for men to accept her. He told her that he had been over it in his mind many times. He reminded her of the legendary women of Israel. He assured her that, through her leadership, she would show the way for others. She wanted to refuse. "I would do better in a role of service to others," she had said. To which he had replied, "This *is* your role of service. To lead. To prove the equality within the Reign of God." Again she argued and again he insisted, "Your heart is big and your mind is free."

She had agreed to do what Jesus asked, but she doubted that all would turn out well in the face of this kind of resistance. She would take it one step at a time. She had always been good at making room for people to be who they were. She would have to do that now, with these disciples. Mary wetted the nib of her reed with ink and continued writing.

"I am using my womanly wiles to win them over. (Another secret between us, Demetria.) Men can't resist a good meal, so I started right away feeding them. You know I haven't cooked in years, but I am cooking now. Actually, I enjoy planning meals and shopping the market on my own each day. My mother was an excellent cook, and I learned from her. I am happily surprised by how much I remember. Apparently it is good enough—they seem quite content to take all their evening meals at my house now."

Again Mary paused to reflect. Her new-found domesticity was pure joy: to be unencumbered, with no one following her around and monitoring her activities, no medicine, no headaches, no fabric deadlines, and no problems. After supper when everyone moved into the atrium and talked into the night, she never got tired, never had to worry about demons, or anything else.

Into the night they would sit on the floor or recline on cushions while Jesus disclosed more about the Reign of God and their essential part in it. His expectations were high. If they were to be his disciples, they would have to become better than they were, he told them. They would have to become "perfect in love." Not only for each other—that was the easy part. To be perfect in love meant including everyone, just as their Father-in-Heaven was perfect in love for all his earthly children. Sometimes when he said this, Mary caught some of the men casting glimpses in her direction, and she thought, *It means you must learn to love women as he does. You might as well start with me.* Then she thought, *I must love you, too, as he does.*

Like the crowds gathered on the hillsides, the companions never wanted to leave Jesus, but, here, in her home, they came to accept the fact that Mary was his guardian. Finally, she would shush their entreaties and push them out the door.

"He needs to rest. You must leave now. Go on. The sooner you sleep, the sooner morning will come," she would say.

In return, they offered counterfeit grumbling, but in the end took her mothering gracefully and went, hearts and bellies satisfied, to tents they had pitched around the city, it being still too wet in early spring to sleep outdoors. More often than not, a weary Jesus just fell asleep at Mary's.

In such moments she would cover him carefully, permitting herself to gaze secretly at his handsome face and slender limbs, folded up, too long for the cot. Her body yearned for a man, this man. She was trying to channel her desire for him into desire for the Reign of God, because that was what he expected of her. But in the dark, quiet, lamplit nighttime, she still wanted to lie down beside him. She did not write that to Demetria.

"If I expected to spend a leisurely spring and summer settling into my delightful new house and harvesting flowers and cooking, I was soon to learn otherwise," Mary wrote. "Jesus is already planning a trip to Jerusalem for Passover, just a few weeks from now. Consult your map, dear. Jerusalem is easy to find right at the center. I had not even enough time to set up housekeeping completely before he and his friends were chattering about the journey.

"After being so long confined to Magdala, it seems I have become quite the vagabond, first dashing to Capernaum to stay little more than a month, and then leaving again on a trip to Jerusalem. How happy I am! It is many, many years since I have traveled to Jerusalem. I told you the heart-breaking story of Mikmik's death there. This trip will help to cleanse me of that memory; I am certain of it.

"Thank you for all you are doing at home, Demetria. Tell the weavers I miss them terribly and give to each an embrace. Say to Mummius, Shoshanna, and Rachel that I will write to them soon. To you, I send my deepest love. I remain, as ever, your mother-in-spirit, Mary."

She rolled and sealed her letter and gave it to Joachim for the courier with instructions for a rapid delivery. Eager to prove his mettle, the zealous Joachim made sure that the scroll did, indeed, arrive in Magdala that very afternoon.

"Put them there," Mummius said curtly, indicating the floor near his chair.

He had been at his desk working on the books of account when a servant approached, announcing his presence with a quiet, "Chief Steward?" The servant who, as usual, had collected all the day's mail into a basket and was now delivering it, did as he was told and backed out of the room.

Having no reason to expect anything extraordinary, Mummius finished the ledger he was working on, then stood and stretched slowly to release the tension in his tightening lower back. *Maybe a visit to the baths later,* he thought. Bending his tall frame over the basket of incoming mail, he fingered the scrolls, glancing at their seals to make a quick assessment and sort by importance. Four from agents in Rome who were undoubtedly confirming orders—they could wait. Two from Tyre, probably concerning some problem with dyes—they would need immediate attention. The odd one remained—a lovely thing of good papyrus with finely finished edges, tightly rolled and tied with a silk ribbon. Of all the ridiculous... Wait a moment.

As Mummius lifted the scroll, the unmistakable fragrance of lavender rose from it. And suddenly he was sitting on a platform in her bedroom, finishing the letter she had just dictated to Marcus Quintius. "Put a drop of lavender oil there in the corner, Mummius," she had said, pointing. "I like for him to know it is I before he sees the seal."

Mummius closed his eyes and turned the letter slowly. There it was—an impression that clearly belonged to Mary, not like the universal seal she had bestowed on him, but hers nonetheless.

Had he expected to hear from her? No. Every day this week he had looked eagerly through the scroll basket, to no avail. He had tried to give up wanting. Now, here was the letter, at last. In his enthusiasm, he flicked off the seal carelessly and unrolled the papyrus. His eyes fell upon the salutation.

"My dearest Demetria...."

From within his belly a hollow wail rolled up and escaped through Mummius' clenched teeth. *No! No, no, no, a thousand times no!* He was on the verge of twisting the sheet, tearing it to pieces, destroying it as he would like to destroy Demetria's hold on Mary. He had gained everything he wanted here. Why did he care about that any longer?

Mummius did care. He cared because he still did not have the one thing he truly desired, a place in Mary's heart. Severus had a place, fool that he was, not realizing he had been diminished by Jesus. Jesus had a place, with good reason; she owed him her life. But for a stupid girl to receive the kind of lavish affection that Mary bestowed on Demetria, while he had none—he could not come to grips with it.

Mummius had given himself to a woman only twice. The first was Maret, his betrothed, lost to him forever in Bubastis. Mary was the second, and she would be the last. He had known from the beginning that he would not pursue her as Severus did. What kind of suitor would he be as slave, gentile, eunuchus? For a while he had given her what no other man could, relief from her suffering. In return he wanted her to look at him with eyes of love, as she looked at Severus and, more recently, at Jesus. He had her respect. He had her trust. What were those, when what he wanted was love?

Mummius thought back to Demetria's request for papyrus, days ago, which he had ignored and then forgotten. Her Greek darling had written to Mary, and this was the lady's reply. How had the girl managed to send a letter to Capernaum without his knowledge? Mummius' face hardened as he stretched the scroll out to its full length and read on.

When he was finished, he took the scroll to his room, the inner sanctum, and placed it upon his work bench. From a small storage pot he pinched off a bit of soft clay and held it next to Mary's seal, comparing its color. Taking a vial of umber dye he added it drop by drop and kneaded it in his palm until he had a ball that matched exactly. He rolled the scroll to its original size, tied it with the ribbon, and deftly covered the stain of the first seal with a pinch of new clay. Then he pressed it closed and modeled the soft circle with a stylus so that it resembled well enough the original impression. Satisfied with his artistry, Mummius secreted the scroll in a private basket until he could determine the moment when it would be advantageous for him to deliver it to Demetria.

CHAPTER 23

Two days after writing her letter to Demetria, Mary, in great haste, wrote another, to Mummius. She was careful to stay on safe ground. He had been so guarded when she left home. She did not want to make things more difficult for him by telling him of her new-found joys.

"To Mummius, Chief Steward, from Mary in Capernaum, Greeting. Forgive me, my dear Mummius, for what must seem like a long delay in writing to you. As you can imagine, Marcus Quintius and I have been extremely busy setting up the new household. How I wish you were here to work your administrative magic upon all these details! But then I would not have your steady hand on the oar in Magdala and all would be lost there. Among your vast talents, could you not arrange to be in two places at once?

"My chief reason for writing to you today is to inform you that I will soon be traveling. Jesus is taking his companions up to Jerusalem for Passover, less than a month from now. We will go by the western route around the sea—which means Magdala! It will be good to see everyone. As well, it will provide an opportunity for us to discuss any business matters that need attention before Marcus Quintius and I go on to Jerusalem. I see the surprise on your face as you read this. It is true: our dear Roman will indeed be traveling to Jerusalem for Passover. Wonder of wonders.

"Let me see, I will need you to prepare the guest quarters for Jesus and his companions, seven men in all. Marcus is undecided where he will stay. He is the soul of courtesy, maintaining a respectful distance between himself and my now-very-Jewish household. He comes to visit me most mornings and we sometimes take our midday meal together, though not as often as I would like. He is conscientious about not imposing his presence on my guests in the evening. The truth is, he prefers the company of Romans and is more comfortable at the home of Gaius Valerius. He does occasionally join the crowd that gathers to listen to Jesus talk, but he is less interested in the message than the miracle-working—like everyone else.

"Anyway, I am trying to persuade him to use his room at home when we return to Magdala, but if he decides to stay in town, we will give Jesus the room in the house and then there would be only six in the guest quarters. My goodness, this sounds like such a muddle. It is just that I am thrilled about the trip to Jerusalem and can hardly keep my mind on business. I know you will straighten out all these matters in due course.

"Once again, faithful Mummius, thank you for your stewardship of my worldly treasure. I am completely in your capable hands. Your devoted mistress, Mary."

So, thought Mummius, leaning over the papyrus spread out upon his desk, *they are going to Jerusalem. Good riddance.* The farther Mary was from Magdala, the better. He was adjusting to her absence and knew that being in her presence, reminded of the intimacy they had shared as physician and patient, would be painful and disorienting.

She writes as though nothing has changed, he thought, *with her little flatteries, which border on lies. She is perfectly content without me in Capernaum, presiding over her new home, ordering Severus about and charming Jesus with sweet talk and adoration.*

He did not want to see her. He did not want to watch Severus making a fool of himself over her. He did not want the "companions," those fawning disciples with their conceited religiosity, anywhere near him. Most of all, he did not want to *be seen,* particularly by Jesus.

Mummius had slipped easily into his new position. Though he did not sit at the head of the table—that would have been too obvious, as well as unnecessary—he was, without argument, head of the household. He had no desire to relinquish his role even for the brief duration of the impending visit, but it was essential that he adopt an obsequious attitude. It would not be difficult to deceive Mary and Severus; he knew them better than they knew themselves. But there would be no deceiving Jesus.

Mummius was mired in ambivalence. He respected Jesus, was awed by his skill, particularly as it was combined with that inexplicably modest temperament. Not even in the Asclepian in Alexandria had he encountered anyone who could do what Jesus could do. Certainly no one there would have been unpretentious about it. A man who could control the demon world as he did would no doubt have the very forces of nature at his command. What would it be like to have Jesus' powers? Under other circumstances, he surely would have sought him out as teacher and colleague, but not now.

When Mummius lost his manhood in Bubastis, he had been faced with the specter of a lifetime of degrading servitude. Instead, he chose to reconstruct his life along lines that were compatible with his extraordinary intellectual gifts. He did not regret his decision, but he had been so gravely wounded by his losses, that he chose also, then and there, to conceal the deepest aspects of his life. This was his power. Mummius would allow no one to pierce the shield that protected his inner world; not even Severus had earned that privilege. He had the feeling that Jesus could see right through him, into his very heart. As much as was possible, he resolved to stay away from the rabbi and hope that the visit would be short.

Within a few days, more letters arrived from Mary, meant for Shoshanna and Rachel, which Mummius opened with great care and resealed with his own clay when he had finished reading. *I am becoming quite good at this,* he thought, putting the finishing touches on his final forgery.

One evening, after what had become the habitually glum scene of their supper, he cleared his throat and said, "I have good news, women." Gloating over the attention his peculiar pronouncement evoked from them, he brought out scrolls from under the table and waved them overhead. "Letters from Mary!" He stood up, reveling in their bright-eyed eagerness. "Hmm, let me see if I remember the courier's instructions—this one for Shoshanna." He hesitated, deliberately tormenting them. "This, I think, for you, Rachel; no, wait, it is the other way around—that's right; and Demetria, the one tied with silk is for you, no mistaking that," he said, finally handing over the scrolls to the intended recipients who were bouncing gleefully and holding out their hands as though they were being presented the keys to some royal treasury.

"I, too, have received a letter. The lady informs me that she will be visiting us soon. We must make ready for a number of guests. I imagine that she tells about it in your letters, also."

At that, the women jumped from their seats, and Mummius watched them rush to their room to read, abandoning the supper dishes to take care of themselves.

Silly prattlers.

They clustered together on Demetria's cot and opened their scrolls, one at a time, like common property. Bonded in grief over Mary's absence, now they clung to each other in joy at the prospect of her return, reading the letters aloud, drinking them in, as women thirsting in the desert might gulp from a pool.

Mary had written to Rachel and Shoshanna in Aramaic, which both could read, although somewhat haltingly. She used simple wording for their benefit, but occasionally they found it necessary to turn to Demetria for clarification. Demetria's letter was written, naturally, in Greek and, when it was her turn, she translated into Aramaic, which slowed her down. When she came to the part about Jesus' friends, saying they were following him around like witless sheep, her eyes skipped ahead and found Mary's instruction, "Now, Demetria, you must tell no one I am saying these things." Fortunately, she caught it in time to give the others an edited translation, smiling inside at Mary's shared secrets. Coming to the end of her long letter, she read, "Tell the weavers I miss them terribly and give to each an embrace. Say to Mummius, Shoshanna, and Rachel that I will write to them soon."

"Is this not odd?" Demetria asked. "It appears that my letter was written some time before yours. When Mary wrote to me, she did not know she would be traveling through Magdala on the way to Jerusalem. Yet in your letters, she gives detailed instructions for housekeeping and meals for guests."

"Probably she waited a few days to mail yours along with ours," offered Rachel.

"Or the first courier was late," said Shoshanna.

"Perhaps," responded Demetria, unconvinced. Something was wrong, but she could not put her finger on it. Well, she was too excited to worry about that just now.

The weeks passed quickly. Spring weather brought farming activities into full buzz, which would have kept everyone busy enough, and now there was the additional work of preparing the house for guests, floors to sweep, linens to air, foodstuff supplies to replenish. The knowledge that Mary was only passing through did not prevent the women from behaving as though she were returning home to stay, their collective energy giving the house a heartbeat, a hidden hope that she would return to it for good. Mary had been gone a short time; it was easy enough to believe that she had not really moved away. Her letters had renewed that faith.

Every afternoon, her chores finished, Demetria climbed the steps to the roof to act as lookout. In the first days of her watch, she had known that it was far too soon for Mary to arrive. As the time of Passover grew nearer, she would run to her post, sit on a sturdy, overturned basket made of reed and lean over the short wall of the roof to survey the surrounding area, believing that at any moment her mistress would appear in the distance. Finally, it happened.

"They're here!" Demetria flew down the stairs, around the house, and into the loom room. "Come and see!" she called, running past the weavers to the kitchen searching for Shoshanna and Rachel. Within moments all the women were making an excited ascent to the roof, Shoshanna bringing up the rear in a slow but determined effort to catch a glimpse of Mary.

Demetria was the first to call to her, "Mistress! Up here!" and soon all were shrieking and waving, but the arriving party were mere dots in the distance and could not hear. The women relaxed their noisy vigil and watched as the figures came closer and took on distinguishable shapes.

Sudi, whose heart had been filled with longing for Jesus since that day in the sea, cried out, "Look, he sees us!"

They turned their attention to the figure of a man who was looking up and pointing their way.

"Let's go out to meet them!" Demetria said.

In a swarm the women ran out to the road, Shoshanna again lagging behind, but nonetheless following as best she could. Laughing and crying, they hugged Mary. The elfin Sudi threw herself at Jesus, causing him to catch her in his arms before he placed her on the ground beside him and held her hand. Chloe, who had become once again mute, this time from joy, walked close to him on the other side. The six male companions fell to the rear and put some distance between themselves and the unseemly hubbub of women.

Shoshanna, limping valiantly, caught up. "Shushu, what is wrong with your leg?" Marcus Quintius asked, offering his arm. "Lean on me," he insisted. "I'll get you home."

It wasn't until they were settling down in the courtyard and Rachel was serving refreshments that Mary thought to ask, "Why, where is Mummius?"

None of the women answered; they neither knew nor cared.

"I'll find him," said Marcus Quintius. Going to Mummius' quarters, he stuck his head into the empty office. "Egyptian!"

Mummius pulled back the curtain to his sleeping room, where he had been waiting for the uproar to subside. He wanted no part of it. "Well, well," he said, looking Severus up and down. "Come in. Would you like a drink?"

"Gratefully, yes," he said and sank into a chair.

"You look awful," said Mummius, handing him a cup of the good Egyptian beer Severus liked best.

When Severus closed his eyes and let out a deep sigh, Mummius knew he was at the end of his wits, that he had had enough of watching. Enough of not being able to control the situation. Enough of Jesus.

"You need a respite from all this."

Severus did not respond.

"I have informed the custodian to expect you."

Severus shook his head slowly from side to side. "I am going to stay here, in the house."

"No, Severus. Truly, go to your rooms in Magdala for a few days. Nothing will change here. It will all be waiting when you return."

"Perhaps you are right."

"I am right," replied Mummius in a moment of genuine concern for his friend. "I'll walk with you. Go on, tell her."

Marcus Quintius finished his beer and went back out into the courtyard to whisper something in Mary's ear.

"Oh, Marcus, do not. Truly, it is not necessary."

He put two fingers to his closed lips and shook his head slightly. Then, looking to the gathered company, "Farewell, all," he said. "I am off to the town. Enjoy your dinner. Shalom."

Mummius and Marcus Quintius, saying little, made quick work of the walk into Magdala, and were greeted by the custodian at Marcus' rooms.

"Welcome, sir."

"Thank you, Rufus Gaius," he replied, entering the house more relieved than he had expected to be.

Mummius lounged in the small atrium while Severus washed his face and changed his clothes.

"That's better," he said, flopping down onto a couch next to Mummius and picking up a goblet of watered wine.

"Had enough of Jews, eh?"

"By all the gods, Mummius, they are pompous!"

"Pompous? Nay! Their situation is so very humble," Mummius replied, baiting him.

"Oh, please. How *can* they regard themselves as superior to the rest of the entire world? It is so offensive."

"It is God that tells them so."

"What has their god done for them lately?" Severus snorted.

Relieved to be in each other's company again, the friends spent their time bantering and drinking, but a careful observer would have noticed that the Egyptian sipped while the Roman drank and grew loquacious.

"I am astonished by the crowds he draws."

"Who is that?"

Severus gave Mummius an exasperated look. "Truly, you should see them, by the hundreds, gathering every afternoon on that grassy hillock just west of the town. All he talks about is how much God loves them. He says they will be honored citizens of something he calls The Reign of God. They are poor; they have nothing. What are they doing, listening to that nonsense?"

"You are listening aren't you? What are *you* doing?"

"A plague on you, Mummius!"

After a while Mummius looked at Severus, who had fallen quiet, and demanded, "Out with it."

"What are you talking about?"

"I am talking about whatever is boiling in your pot."

"Stop penetrating my mind, Egyptian."

"I am penetrating nothing. It is lying over you like a cloak."

It was useless to resist Mummius' probing. Anyway, he needed to confess, so Severus admitted, "I do not know how much longer I can control my desire for her."

"What are you saying?"

"I am saying that I think of nothing else. I dream so vividly that when I wake it is as though I have lain with her."

"*Have* you lain with her?"

"What do you think?"

Mummius shook his head.

"Of course not. But she senses that something has changed. I have begun avoiding her for fear of discovery, or worse." Severus drained his cup and called for unwatered wine. "I want her desperately, Mummius. I do."

"Nothing new in that," Mummius replied with a dismissive grunt.

"Have you no sympathy?"

Mummius despised what he thought of as Severus' degrading pursuit of the unattainable, but he could not help feeling compassion for the agony he was in.

"Sympathy is not what you need, old friend. A deep draft of truth is the medicine you must swallow."

"What draft of truth?"

"The truth that it is Jesus she loves."

"No. She does not. Not like that."

"How do you know?"

"I know."

"Severus, whatever it is you think you know, you must accept the fact that she is beyond your reach. Why can you not see that she belongs to Jesus now? When he healed her, he bound her to him in ways you cannot fathom."

Severus shook his head. "Look, I am going with her to Jerusalem. As soon as the novelty of him wears off, as soon as this trip is finished, she will come back to herself and be ready to settle down. With me."

"Don't be a fool, Severus. Leave her alone or you will do something you will regret. Hear what I say. Everything Jesus comes near will be torn apart. It is the nature of his effect on people."

"Enough!" said Severus, storming from the room. "I'm going to the baths."

Mummius followed, but, before he left the house, he pulled Rufus Gaius aside to give him instructions. A pair of beautiful Nubian women would be waiting for Severus when he returned from his soak. Along with a plentiful supply of Mummius' performance potions.

CHAPTER 24

It is good to be home. Mary was once again in her expansive garden in Magdala, collecting a basketful of fresh greenery and dewy blossoms to decorate the house. She had been out here since sunrise, the alone and quiet time that had been so long denied her, before her healing, while respectfully surreptitious people watched over her. Lost in the cherished solitude, she was doubly surprised by the sound of an unfamiliar voice behind her.

"Mary?"

Hearing her name, she turned and, seeing the woman at the gate, dropped the small knife she was using to cut with.

"Dear lady? Can it be?"

Jesus' mother opened her arms, and Mary rushed into her embrace, neither of them having a care for the dirt-streaked front of her outdoor work tunic. Mary held her out at arms' length, examining her happily.

The older woman's hair had been pulled back into a bun and was greying, but was still thick and luxurious. Her shoulders were wrapped in a soft, well-worn, woolen shawl the color of pale hyacinths, which contrasted with her olive skin and set it glowing. Her eyes were dark as charcoal, and there were lines around them, which deepened when she smiled, as she did now. It was the serenity of the face which had not changed. Mary's hand flew to her own face, and she wondered how she looked to one who had not seen her for more than thirty years.

And suddenly she was a ten-year-old girl again, back on the road to Beth-el, where a chance encounter had brought them together. Jesus, yet-to-be-born and curled tightly within his mother's warm body, was restless, and she had asked if Mary wanted to feel the baby inside. "Oh, I don't think so," had been her hesitant reply, but the young mother took Mary's hand anyway and placed it on her swollen belly. When a tiny foot moved under her hand, she had felt astonished and happy to be included in the about-to-happen miracle of birth.

"You look wonderful!" Mary exclaimed now.

"Don't be ridiculous, dear," said Jesus' mother, patting her voluptuous, round hips. "All these children and grandchildren of mine have changed me. You, though, are as beautiful as you promised to be when you were a child!"

Mary's face colored at the compliment, and she quickly changed the subject. "Jesus did not tell me you were coming."

"He wanted to surprise you."

"And so he did, Amma, and so he did."

Mary was just three or four years the younger, but it felt natural to call her by the intimate "mama," as was common among extended or honorary family members. They had met only that one time on the road to Beth-el, but even then Mary knew that, already married and heavy with her special child, here was a woman wise beyond her circumstances and righteous beyond her years.

Suddenly Mary woke to the truth. This was the mother of the man with whom she was sharing her house! Until now, Mary had steadfastly refused to give heed to the problem others saw in her relationship with Jesus—unmarried and unchaperoned—and their domestic arrangement. She had become weary of the warnings, first from Shoshanna, then Marcus Quintius, and would not listen. Even the better judgment of her own mind had been quashed by her response to Jesus. It was not that her passion for him was no longer physical, but now her focus was on his message and his ministry. Together they were forging a unique, convention-breaking relationship that would transcend the accepted rules of daily life.

Mary knew how people talked, what they would say about her, but so long had she lived by her own compass that she did not care, frankly, what they thought. She had overcome challenges about which other people knew nothing; she had battled demons; she had sheltered outcasts. No one was going to tell her how to live. The God of Israel alone was her judge, and God knew the purity of her life—heart and body.

But she had not faced his mother. Suddenly Mary saw herself in a new and unforgiving light that showed her flaws, an unwelcome mirror. She felt her too-bright earrings and wished she could cover herself. She bent to retrieve her knife and spent longer than necessary tidying the trimmings left by the flowers she had cut and trying to catch her breath. *How much does she know? She will surely judge me. What should I say?*

The two of them walked arm in arm into the kitchen. Mary turned her back and, putting the flowers into a bit of water, paused a little too long. She held the vase tightly with both hands to keep them from shaking and placed it on the table.

"Your flowers look splendid, dear."

"I cannot take credit for them really; they seem to grow themselves," she said stiffly, motioning for her visitor to sit. "When did you arrive from Nazareth?"

Mary took a seat opposite, her eyes glancing around the kitchen, the shelf of towels, some dust collected in a corner of the floor, anywhere but the woman's eyes.

"Just yesterday. We spent last night in Magdala," she answered. "Is something wrong, dear?"

"Excuse me. No, nothing is wrong at all," Mary responded, forcing herself to look at the shining face across from her. "What brings you here, Amma?" The intimacy of the word seemed presumptuous now. She wished she could draw back the breath on which it had left her mouth.

Reaching across the table, Jesus' mother took Mary's hands in hers and, with a wide smile, announced, "I am going to Jerusalem with you."

"Why, this is wonderful news," Mary replied, swallowing hard.

"And some of my other sons, too. When Joseph was alive, he took our family to Jerusalem for Passover every year. As eldest son, Jesus has continued the tradition. Since his father's death."

Mary saw a cloud of sorrow pass over her face. "You miss him," she said quietly.

"Joseph was my defender, my champion," she said sadly. "But no tears today! Imagine it, Mary, Jesus leading us on a Passover journey together, after all this time."

Imagine it, indeed. Though her hands were no longer trembling, Mary was shaking inside. How could she explain her relationship with Jesus to his mother? She thought of the moment Jesus had reached into her soul and pulled her back from the brink of annihilation; she thought of the time he showed her how to heal little Sudi in the Sea of Galilee; she thought of her irrational flight to Capernaum and her nights with him there. The desire to be near him had started as a compulsion. When he said he wanted her as a cherished disciple, she agreed to follow, not knowing then, or even now, all of what that would mean. What would his mother think? To her, their uncommon intimacy would surely seem impure. Could she possibly understand? Mary was in a terrible bind, but she would not, could not, give him up.

"This year it will be different," Mary said cautiously. "We are on his path now."

Jesus' mother said, "We have been on his path since before he was born."

Hearing that simple, eloquent response, Mary felt tears of relief blossom in her eyes.

"There is something you must know, Mary. Jesus is not the son of Joseph's body. While we were betrothed, I was visited by an angel of the LORD who said that I was to bear a son. Joseph and I had not lain together, so I did not know how this could be. The angel told me that this son of mine would be very great, that he would be called Son of the Most High, and that he would inherit the ancient throne of David. He said the Spirit of God would come upon me and accomplish these things, but only if I was willing.

"I was so young, thirteen, you know? I had never heard of such a thing, but I was overcome with an ecstasy I cannot to this day explain. I replied to the angel, 'I am the servant of the LORD. I will do what you have asked me to do.' At that moment, I gave myself completely to the Reign of God through Jesus."

Mary could only stare in amazement at what she was hearing.

"Now he needs what I do not have to give, a companion in the work God has for him and that he, in return, has chosen. You are that companion, Mary. It seems that you, too, have chosen, just as I did. There is no other who can take your place. There is no way to know the implications of God's plan until it comes to pass."

Mary, still hoping for approval, said, "I was fearful that you would think me impure. I worried that you would judge me."

"Judge you? Why yes, of course I judge you—with the judgment of honor. And gratitude for helping him. Do you not think I know how people talk? Remember to whom you are speaking. I was a pregnant, unwed girl when Joseph rescued me! I know all about people's cruelty. Do not fear, Mary. I will be faithful to you; we will be faithful to him."

The two Marys looked at each other—they who loved Jesus as no other could love him—while solidarity put down roots into the ground they had cultivated. They knew they were on the verge of a sea change in their lives, beginning with the pilgrimage to Jerusalem, a journey that would, indeed, be different from all others. Jesus had emerged as a public figure; there would be an entourage, a gathering crowd as they walked the hundred miles south to the great city. Four days, possibly five, would they walk.

They did not know what would come to pass; but now, surprisingly, they had found each other. Throughout the coming days, their friendship deepened as they prepared together for the journey to Jerusalem. They could not have predicted what Jesus was planning.

One evening after dinner, as the day of departure was fast approaching, Mary went looking for him. She recognized his voice coming from the upper room over her sleeping quarters and walked slowly and respectfully to the doorway. As she drew near, she overheard him say, "The matter goes deeper than this, Mother."

"Excuse me," Mary said, walking in on two people obviously in the midst of a tense confrontation that had been going on for some time. They were face to face in aggressive stances, chins stuck out, and backs ramrod straight. Both had abandoned their outer garments and their faces were flushed and a bit damp with perspiration. "I will come back later," Mary offered.

"No, come in, please. Your help would be appreciated." As if to start over, Jesus took a deep breath and let it out with a sigh. "Mother and I have been talking about Jerusalem, and..."

"...*and* I am angry because he is planning to call the religious leaders to account," she interrupted, her face turned suddenly bleak. "It is too soon for this, Jesus. The time is not ripe."

"Mother, with respect, the time is overripe." Jesus' stance softened, and he held out his hands toward his mother, palms up, a look on his face that communicated a desire for her to agree with him. "What sense does it make to deliver a message of love and peace to the people and leave the other side of the coin unexamined?"

Mary still had not grown accustomed to the way Jesus sought out and valued the opinions of women. It was obvious that his mother had been one of his primary confidantes for a long time. Mary wondered if the men knew about his consultations with his mother in moments like this. Silence hung in the air so long that Mary's bewilderment got the best of her. "Would one of you please tell me what you are talking about?"

Jesus let out an exasperated sigh. "It is time for me to correct their erroneous interpretation of the Law."

"The way I hear it, you have been arguing points of the Law with your elders your whole life," Mary teased.

His mother groaned. "Making an endless nuisance of himself in the process."

"I just cannot tolerate the burdens that are placed on the poor by men who have been designated by God to help them. It infuriates me!" Then, more gently, he said, "Don't you see? By the time we arrive in Jerusalem, hundreds—thousands, probably—will be following. They will have heard me speak about the Reign of God, backed up with healings, and they will be leaning on my promises. News of my arrival will precede me into the city. The priests and scribes will be waiting to see what all the fuss is about. When it dawns on them that I am not just another wild-eyed fanatic and not so easy to dismiss, they will have to listen. What better time to point out their errors?"

Jesus grinned; it worked a small miracle upon his thin, serious face, which suddenly looked very young and mischievous. When Mary saw that look, an alarm bell went off in her. Was this some kind of petulant reaction that would endanger him? His mother seemed to think so when she said, "Do not think you can charm me, Jesus. If you get into a cauldron of boiling water, it is because you jumped in willingly, with your eyes open wide." Mary thought she heard a hint of resignation in her voice.

The tussle of wills was prolonged a few moments more, but there was never any doubt as to who would win when Jesus was doing the pushing.

"I know perfectly well how to conduct my life," he said.

Mary looked from the man to the mother and back again, beginning to appreciate their conflict. Mary knew what Jesus could do to a crowd when he spoke; she had been watching it in Capernaum for weeks. She had felt what it was like to be released by him from a lifetime of suffering. All that she had known of him to this time seemed so wonderful, so greatly desired. Now, she felt a moment of panic. Her heart beat wildly for a few seconds as she imagined the graver consequences of Jesus' actions. His message, by necessity, had to include a condemnation of those who had distorted God's plan for God's people. If the poor and the suffering were to be uplifted in the Reign of God, apparently that meant that the grand and mighty were to be brought down to make room for them. All the tables would be turned.

Mary was in the midst of a scene that would be painted on a vast canvas and could possibly involve every aspect of Jewish life. Jesus was larger than he had seemed before, even to her. She had just begun to feel comfortable in the role of devoted disciple. Was she now to be part of some kind of revolution? This was not what she had agreed to. How could she be the right person for this? Well, she *had* violated many social and religious customs in her own life, that much was true. But Pax Magdalena was only a small, domestic rebellion. She had certainly never taken a revolution to the street!

While her mind raced considering these things, she heard Jesus speaking to her, as though from a distance. "Mary, dear one?" She had been staring at him, and beyond him, and the sound of her name seemed to rouse her.

Her thoughts still swirling, she awakened enough to pay partial attention to him. "Yes, Rabbouni?"

"Do you understand me?"

"I think I do, Rabbouni."

Mary looked at his mother and, for the first time, fully comprehended what she had meant when she spoke of giving her life to the Reign of God. It meant being repeatedly surprised and challenged. It meant breaking not just small rules at home, but big ones in the very seat of power. It meant forever being scared.

Jesus put his hands firmly on her arms and, holding her eyes with his own, he said, "You do not have to do this."

Mary had been holding her breath and her heart was pounding hard. She took in an involuntary gasp and her respiration began to return to normal.

"If you are not ready, I can go to Jerusalem without you."

She looked him in the eye. "Never," she said.

When the time came to depart for Jerusalem, everyone was keen to get moving. Warm spring weather lay over the land, so they would travel lightly, sleeping under the stars, eating unleavened bread and water, easy to carry and replenish.

"Chloe, come quick!" Demetria called into the loom room as she sprinted by.

Chloe left her weaving and hurried to catch up. "What is it?"

"Have you seen all the people out there?"

A procession of hundreds of people was camped within sight of Mary's house. They had come down from the north and east, beyond Beth-saida. They had crossed the Jordan on a sandbar at the upper end of the sea where the river flowed into it, their numbers increasing as they came down the Roman road to Chorazin and to Capernaum. They had walked along the edge of the sea southwest to Gennesaret and came to rest at Magdala.

"It's frightening. I wish they would go away."

"It doesn't frighten *me*. For days I have been begging to join the crowd."

"What? No. Demetria, no!"

"Yes, yes. I have just come from the mistress' room. Jesus was there, and Mary said to him, 'Demetria wants to go with us. Do you think it would be all right?' I thought I saw her wink at him, but I could not tell from the sound of her voice whether she favored the idea or not and so I stood still waiting for his answer." Demetria drew herself up to full height, stuck out her chest, and with her little fists on her hips, imitated Jesus' rich baritone, "'So, the Greek maid wants to go to Jerusalem today, eh?' he said. 'Well, why not?' I breathed in hard and laughed at the same time. Imagine it, Chloe, I am going to Jerusalem!"

Chloe looked incredulously at the small bundle of belongings that her friend was retrieving from under the bed. "You were already packed."

"I was hoping they would say yes. Oh, Chloe, I do so want to be part of this."

So it was that Demetria joined the throng en route to the Passover celebration that day. It was both exhilarating and, despite what she had said to Chloe, a little frightening.

They departed Magdala by the lakeshore road, Jesus leading them southward in the direction of Tiberias, three miles distant. This was Herod's capital city, an unclean place shunned by Jews because of its location on the site of a long disappeared "city of the dead." Building upon cemeteries meant nothing to Romans, so here on the western shore of the Sea of Galilee, called by Romans Lake Tiberias, Herod Antipas, son of Herod the Great, raised up his city and, currying favor, named it for Tiberius Caesar. He lined the streets with immense, colonnaded buildings supported by granite columns in the Grecian style. He built an amphitheater and imported entertainments of all kinds. He erected a magnificent palace and adorned it with carved images of animals, birds, gods and heroes—all abominations in the eyes of Jews.

Just north of the city, Demetria felt her stomach swirl unexpectedly. As they got closer, the swirling turned to clenching. Even though they gave it a wide berth, by the time they were skirting Tiberias, bitter, stinging bile was collecting in the back of her throat; she swallowed again and again in a vain attempt to wash it away and keep it down. Within those city walls lay regal residences filled with every imaginable luxury, and one of those magnificent houses was the site of her shame. She had never wanted to come near this place again.

In Tiberias, she had been forced to dance almost naked in front of dinner guests, who reclined on damask-covered couches, stuffing themselves with food and getting drunk on wine. That was just the beginning. People tried to convince her that she was particularly fortunate to have a wealthy Roman fancy her and take her to his bed. She should be grateful, they said.

The first time it happened, the other girls had tried to help by giving her ointments to numb and lubricate herself, but still the pain was terrible. The master did not care about that as long as her screams were disguised as the cries of pleasure, and so she learned to do that, too. She bled when he forced himself on her and insisted that she smile while he did it. Sometimes he gave her to his friends while he watched. To Jews, Tiberias was just an impure idea, a religious construct. To Demetria it was a physical reality of pain and humiliation. She knew what being unclean really meant. It had nothing to do with God and everything to do with men.

Demetria wrapped her shawl tightly around her head and face, leaving only her eyes uncovered to stare down at her sandals. One foot in front of the other, one step at a time she walked, concentrating on her feet. When she thought the vile city must finally be behind her, she turned and looked. She could barely see the tops of the towers of the wall, so she opened her bag of water and took a few sips. It stayed down, cooling her raging throat. Gradually, her stomach returned to normal until, eventually, the fresh air and the high spirits of the crowd lifted her out of her painful reverie. When they reached the southern tip of the lake, six miles beyond Tiberias, in the resilience of her youth, it was forgotten. Here, where the Jordan River flowed out of the Sea of Galilee, they found a bridge teeming with life.

Crossing the bridge in both directions were travelers and merchants, donkeys and camels, horses and war chariots. Pleasure yachts and fishing boats animated the glistening lake. Demetria stared with big eyes at all the activity until an excited shout rose above the noise and attracted her attention. "There he is!" and suddenly the cry was taken up by a crowd from a white sand beach just beyond their path. Demetria felt Mary's protective arm slip around her waist as another two hundred people converged on them. She watched Jesus walk over to a small rock outcropping and stand for a moment, casting his eyes over all the people gathered. A thousand souls fell silent, waiting for him to speak.

Everywhere they went it was the same, the crowd swelling by the hour as they walked, the crowd drawing close to Jesus in the evening when he talked. Eventually, Demetria found herself ignoring the swarm of people that in the beginning had so captivated her and turned her attention instead to the spellbinding marvels of nature.

In the bright, spring month of April, everything was fresh and fair through the valleys. Along the path, wild flowers grew. Hyssop poked through cracks in walls and poisonous, majestic oleander bloomed near every stream with large, dark, leathery leaves and flower clusters of white and red nodding their showy heads when the breeze blew by, filling the air with thick perfume. The nearby hills were covered with living green mantles of oak and cedar, cypress and palm; the valleys burst with roses, marigolds and tulips of every color.

Demetria most loved the farms. Vineyards promising to be heavy with grapes; thick groves of olives, figs, almonds and pomegranates; fields flowing with grain, white for the spring harvest, stretching out as far as she could see. It was—Sicily!

A Roman hand came to rest unexpectedly on Demetria's shoulder.

"Aieee!" she screamed and twisted away.

The startled Marcus Quintius lifted his hand quickly and held both arms up slightly and took a step back. "I did not mean to frighten you."

Seeing it was he, Demetria blinked back a surge of tears and tried to swallow, but her throat was dust.

"I'm sorry," she said. Then, indicating the wheat fields with a nod of her head, she mumbled, "Sicily."

"Oh, I see."

Walking with Marcus Quintius through wheat fields that reminded her of home, gentiles in a sea of Jews, she felt safer now. He pulled a small bag of dates from his belt and held it out to her.

"I didn't think people were allowed to bring extra food."

He laughed at her naiveté and winked. She took some of the sweet, chewy fruit and munched contentedly. When Demetria slipped her small hand into his, his heart grew strangely warm. To delight her further, he said, "Jerusalem is a great city. You will be amazed." Marcus Quintius did not know how much more than celebrated architecture awaited them in Jerusalem.

With each hour that brought them nearer their destination, the crowds pressing toward Jerusalem thickened. At the city walls they had become a human sea. Pilgrims from every land pushed through the Damascus Gate, funneling into the city, where they were immediately beset by sellers of sacrificial animals, crates stuffed with living doves, immense flocks of sheep, and herds of cattle and oxen maddened with thirst, lashed by their drovers to keep them moving through the overcrowded streets.

"Stay close," Marcus Quintius instructed Demetria, but there was no need to say so; Demetria was stuck to him like whitewash on a stone wall as the company from Magdala, collected in a tight circle around Jesus, was propelled forward by the mass of humanity progressing toward the Temple.

Only in Rome had Demetria seen such grand sights, and yet no such sights as these, for Roman streets were straight and square, with manicured gardens and fountains everywhere. Nothing would be allowed to befoul the boulevards of Rome like the thousands of animals being led to slaughter in Jerusalem. When Demetria felt her foot slip, almost taking off her sandal, she did not look. She wanted to think it was mud that had caused her to slide, but in the warm, dry weather, what could it be but excrement?

Demetria was pained to see many doves doomed to die, packed into cages, scrambling for a place, their feet or wings or beaks sticking in and out, in and out, seeking relief. She wanted to free them, set them soaring into the hot, blue sky. From the street below the great Temple, she saw the smoke, rising, swirling, then dispersing till it vanished, all that was left of the spirits of poor, cooing things that once had lived and now were dead, an offering to the Living God. Then, for the first time, Demetria saw the Temple itself.

Anyone looking at the Temple of Herod the Great would be astonished, which is what that king intended when he built it, mistakenly thinking it would result in respect from the Jews he ruled. Though nominally a Jew by religion, Herod was only half Jewish by ancestry. He was a friend of Rome. Worst of all, he had obtained his throne by overthrowing and executing a Hasmonean king, a monarch from the pious Maccabean family, which had reigned in Judea for 130 years and under whom the festival of Hanukkah had been instituted. As king, Herod was a tyrant. His outrages, both domestic and political, were legion. Intrigues and assassinations wrought havoc all around him.

There was another side to the reign of Herod. He made an enduring contribution to the architecture of his day, and that was what earned his label "the Great." He founded whole cities at Samaria and Caesarea, and rebuilt many others. He constructed temples and amphitheaters throughout his territory and erected new fortress strongholds and refortified and embellished others, such as Masada. His most magnificent achievement, without doubt, was the reconstruction of the Temple in Jerusalem.

The design for the Temple was copied from King Solomon's original, which had stood for four centuries until it was destroyed by the Babylonian army almost six hundred years earlier. Herod began his reconstruction with ten thousand skilled laborers. Because only priests were authorized to enter the sanctuary, one thousand of them were assigned to build the central edifice. It took them a year and a half to accomplish that task. Others took up the labor of building structures of ever-decreasing holiness out from the center and then surrounding the whole by a wall, which formed the Temple enclosure and separated it from the rest of Jerusalem. The Temple proper stood upon the highest ground in the enclosure. Its walls were built of blocks of white stone that shone in the sun like a snow-covered mountain. People came from all over the world just to look at it and marvel.

The Holy Place was secreted deep within the central building. Inside that, the most sacred chamber of all, the Holy of Holies, was closed off by a veil and could be entered only once a year, on the Day of Atonement, and then only by the chief priest. The Holy Place was an awe-inspiring 135 feet high and contained a golden altar for incense, a table for sacred bread and golden candlesticks. Its access was through a pair of golden doors, also 135 feet high and 24 feet broad. It was hung with fine linen and a drapery of blue, purple and scarlet. Its outer wall was embellished by a golden vine from which were suspended clusters of golden grapes. Twelve steps descended from the vestibule of The Holy Place down to the Court of the Priests, which surrounded the sacred building.

In the Court of the Priests stood the altar for burnt offerings; around the Court of Priests lay the Court of Israel; around the Court of Israel, down fifteen steps, lay the Court of the Women; and around the Court of the Women was a very thick barrier, like the wall of a fortress. Here no gentile could enter, on pain of death. Around the restricted area lay the Court of the Gentiles, where all could enter. And this they did, Jesus and his mixed party of Jews and gentiles.

It wasn't as though they did not know what to expect, for most had seen it many times. It did not surprise them that the twenty acres of The Court of the Gentiles had been turned into a scene of irreverent chaos. What surprised them was Jesus. He walked a few steps and then came to a standstill, causing the rest of them to stop as one. For a few moments he looked over the raucous scene, disgust showing in his clenched teeth and rigid shoulders. Mary saw it, too, as though for the first time.

Thousands of sheep and oxen had been brought in from the streets and were penned within the consecrated court, and birds without number. The bleating, bellowing and cooing of animals combined in a noisy stew with the shouts of pilgrim and seller making their deals in Hebrew, Greek, Aramaic, Coptic Egyptian, and Latin. Worst of all was the stench, which assaulted the senses, and rose in waves from the stone pavement as the heat of the day was building.

In their various locations around the court, potters hawked clay vessels and portable ovens for cooking the Passover lamb. Traders shouted the value of their wares, wine, oil, herbs, salt, vinegar, and everything else needed for sacrifice. And there were money-changers.

Originally, the money-changers had been established at locations from Jerusalem's eastern gate, called Shusan, up to the outside wall at Solomon's Portico, the only portion of the original Temple still standing. Over time they had pushed upon the Temple itself and into the sacred Court of the Gentiles. Between the quadruple lines of Corinthian columns, cages of doves were stacked and along the aisles created by the cages sat the money-changers at their banks, which were flimsy benches long enough for a man to sit on and pile his coins beside him. If a man failed in his obligations or was caught in acts of dishonesty, his bench was demolished—his bank was broken—and he was denied the right to do business.

What business did money-changers have here? A very lucrative one in fact, for everyone entering the Temple was required to pay a half-shekel tax, and it was the bankers who provided the only coinage that was authorized by the priests for payment of the tax. They exchanged foreign currency from all over the Empire.

Here within the consecrated courts of the Most High, in the very Temple precincts of the Living God, Jesus, and Mary along with him, watched the unholy scene and grew more offended with each passing moment. Because he stood so long unmoving, eventually everyone in his company was looking to him. The glare on his face told them not to speak. They watched, disbelieving, as he picked up some leather cords from the floor and began twisting them together, slowly, deliberately. When it was finished, he held the makeshift whip at his side where the end of it lay coiled on the floor at his feet, like a snake. His silence was frigid, but his eyes were fiery within his crimson face.

Mary glanced around for the disciples and found that they had moved some distance away from Jesus and the inexplicable rage that had descended on him. She laid a hand on the whip that Jesus had made and asked quietly but firmly, "Rabbouni, what are you doing?"

"I have to stop this," he said.

Mary thought of how he had argued with his mother about teaching the religious leaders a lesson. It would be futile to interfere with him now. Turning to Marcus Quintius, she handed Demetria to him saying, "Take her away." To Jesus' mother she said, "Stand over there beside Peter," and pushed her in his direction. When they had been moved to safety, Mary released the whip and, nodding her approval, stepped out of the way.

Even if Jesus had been all alone there, he was ready to act. But Mary was with him in what he was about to do. She had not backed down. Taking courage from her presence, he turned to the scene in the Court. Slowly, as if in a dream, he raised his whip over his head. He cracked it hard and brought it down onto the floor with a sharp snap.

The sheep nearest him started to trot in confused circles. This caused some oxen to look around with wild eyes, close to panicking. They roared and began to run, a few at first, then more and more until there was a herd threatening a stampede. Alarmed shepherds and drovers yelled and beat the animals with canes, directing the frightened beasts as best they could toward the exits. The frenzy of the animals seemed to fuel Jesus' wrath. Sweat broke out on his forehead as he pointed his whip in a circle around the Court and commanded, "Remove these cages!" The hapless dove-sellers tripped over each other in an attempt to obey.

As the animals and their keepers fled the court, Jesus turned his attention to the money-changers. Some were frantically scraping stacked coins into bags, their faces masks of surprise. Some were frozen in place by fear, not knowing whether to run or to resist. Those who still dared to sit on their benches he lifted off and tossed aside. He went down the aisles, ferociously breaking the banks as he went. Some of the bewildered money-changers, and many greedy on-lookers, scrambled around on the stone floor for the coins that were scattered, bouncing and rolling on the tiles.

From atop Solomon's Portico a few particular men, who happened to be standing there, looked down on the Court of Gentiles at the man gone wild, who was turning everything upside down and yelling, "What do you think this is, an auction market?" and "Get out of my Father's house!" Only Mary seemed to notice them and realized from their dress that they must be members of the Council, that bickering collection of Pharisees, Sadducees, and priests who ruled the Jewish people as the supreme political, religious, and judicial body in Judea. She could imagine their questions. "Who is that man? By what authority does he enter and call the Temple the house of his father?"

This is it, she thought, her eyes fixed on the men of the Council above. *This is why we have come. To clean up the mess they have made.* The blood drained from her face. It was apparent now that Jesus was determined to cast out demons from the very Temple itself. When she caught the eye of his mother, standing off a way with Peter's arm around her, Mary recognized the anguish that had caused her to argue with Jesus. Her son, her first-born, had begun a revolt from which there would be no return.

Wondering what this violence had to do with her, Mary was filled with fear. Fear for herself. Fear for Jesus.

An eerie silence began to spread. All who remained within the massive court, those watching from the galleries above, those inside the Temple who had heard the ruckus and had come out to see what was happening, all fell silent as Jesus stood alone, motionless except for the heaving of his chest.

Mary went to his side. "Rabbouni, it is finished. Let us go."

Leading him away, Mary felt the circle of his friends close around them again, and she could only shake her head. "Where were *you*?" she wanted to ask, but kept the chastisement to herself. Time enough for that later.

CHAPTER 25

Leaving the Temple grounds, they were trailed by a crowd of people who had witnessed the events in the Court of the Gentiles and were whispering and nudging each other. Marcus Quintius maintained a protective grip on the nape of Demetria's tunic.

"Just keep moving," he ordered.

Mary glanced at Jesus' mother, who tightened her lips in resignation and said nothing. She could not be ready for her son to put himself at odds with the religious leaders, certainly not in the public way he had chosen. What a toll his cleansing of the Temple must have taken. *Just look at him,* Mary thought. *He is worn out.*

The following mob was begging for Jesus to speak to them. He stopped and turned, as though he might actually try to address them. The tide of people flowed onto a dusty mound just off the crowded road that led into the city. Those who were nearest sat down in front of Jesus, while others stood in a wide half circle—men, women, and children, some leading domestic donkeys or carrying small animals they had purchased for sacrifice. Diverse as their places of origin, from Galilee to Alexandria, from Jerusalem to Rome, some of obvious means, others quite poor, all had been stirred by an identical purpose—the Passover pilgrimage to the Temple—and all were now equally distracted by the holy man who spoke with authority. Mary had seen Jesus attract and fascinate crowds many times. This, however, was a group that had been engaged in the most sacred acts of the most sacred festival. Even they abandoned what they had come for in order to follow him from the Temple and out of the holy city.

"We must get him away from here," Mary told Peter.

"I agree," he replied, and then addressed the crowd. "Go back to the Temple now. The rabbi will return tomorrow."

When the companions encircled Jesus and escorted him away, the crowd slowly fell off. One determined man pursued doggedly and succeeded in getting close enough to be heard, even as the disciples tried to restrain him. "Rabbi, hear me, please!"

Over the objections of his companions, Jesus stopped and turned to listen.

"Have you a place to stay tonight?" the man asked. "Come to my home. I live not far from here. In Bethany."

"I thank you, brother, but we have come from Galilee and there are more than a few in our company," replied Jesus, indicating the knot of people around him.

"My house is spacious, sir. The upper room is large enough for everyone and there is food aplenty. It would honor me to be your host," said the man, placing his fist over his heart.

Mary watched Jesus as he considered the invitation. She had learned that when he gazed at another, as he was doing now, he was looking into the heart of that person as well as into the eyes. When she heard Jesus' reply, she knew there must be something special about this persistent man.

"Well, then, I accept, with gratitude, and my friends as well. What is your name, brother?"

"I am called Lazarus."

"Lazarus, 'Assistance of God.' A good name," said Jesus, clapping his new friend on the shoulder, both unaware of the extraordinary event that would come to pass between them in the future.

As they made introductions before setting out for Lazarus' house, Marcus Quintius drew Mary aside. "I have made arrangements with a friend," he said.

"Yes, of course," she replied.

"What about Demetria?"

"Oh, dear."

Mary was torn. It went without saying that Marcus could not accompany her into a Jewish home. But Demetria, a quiet girl, dressed as a Galilean, had become like her daughter. Mary could not remember when she had last thought of Demetria as a gentile who would be unwelcome among Jews. Yet she did not want to do anything to discomfit a family she did not know.

Marcus Quintius provided a solution. "I can take her with me. Dexius has daughters about her age. She will be quite safe there. We can meet you early tomorrow at the Temple. What do you say?"

Mary fell pensive. Before Jesus, there had always been Marcus Quintius to help shoulder her responsibilities, to sort out complex problems, and to be a loving companion. Recently, Mary had been so taken up with her new life that she had neglected him. Yet here he was, always faithful, always helpful. How could she have been so inconsiderate of the man who had championed her ever since her father died? And continued to do so, even as her own life was drawing her farther away from him?

"Marcus, I know this trip must be costing you dearly—to be so long absent from Rome and your responsibilities there. But see how much you are helping me. Thank you for taking care of my Demetria and forgive me for thinking only of myself."

"For you... I have wanted to..." he stumbled with his words, trying to communicate the welter of emotions that came up in him. That she would ask for his forgiveness—it was almost too much. He struggled to say more, but Mary turned to Demetria.

"Child, I hate to ask this of you. I can't see an alternative, at least for this one night. Do you mind?"

Cheerlessly, Demetria shook her head no.

"All right, then. What is the name of your friend, Marcus? In case I need to contact you."

"Aulus Dexius Clemens. His house is in the Upper City."

"Near the palace."

"Not too far from the palace, yes," he said.

Mary hugged Demetria and whispered "thank you" in her ear. Then Marcus Quintius gathered up the unenthusiastic girl and departed for the Roman section of the Upper City. Reconciled to the situation, Mary waved goodbye to them and turned to catch up with the group, which was already several paces ahead on the way to Bethany.

The town was a mile and a half from the eastern wall of Jerusalem, on a road that wound through the dry Kidron Valley, past the Garden of Gethsemane, up the western slope of the Mount of Olives to its peak at 2,643 feet above sea level and a short way down the eastern side. Though the walk to Bethany was not long, the evening weather was still warm, and all in the entourage were tired and very hungry when they arrived.

Lazarus' elder sister, Martha, reminded Mary of Shoshanna with her unblinking vigilance over household details. Like Shoshanna, she was short and stocky. Her hands and fingers were thick, useful for domestic work. Her looks were plain, made less attractive by dull brown hair and one weak eye. Even her smiles brought no loveliness to her face, because they seemed more to acknowledge her own work standards than the actual pleasure her hospitality gave to others.

Maryam, on the other hand, was anything but plain. Mary noted a certain family resemblance, but the two seemed more like mother and daughter than sisters. Maryam was thin and lithe. Her tunic was cut with a very wide neck, showing off her shoulders. Mary wondered if she had intended this to be provocative or whether she was one of those young, rare, innocent beauties who truly do not understand their effect on men.

Martha and Maryam greeted the guests eagerly, took their turbans, and sat them down to soothing footbaths provided by a servant, there being no children in the household to perform the traditional ritual of hospitality. They furnished clean robes to replace their soiled traveling clothes and ushered them to the upper room for the evening meal.

The smell of fresh baked bread alone would have set their mouths to watering, but it was only the beginning. Plates were piled with handmade cheeses. There were bowls of olives, dates, and pomegranates placed strategically all around. Skins of fresh goat milk hung from hooks on one wall.

Martha and Maryam bustled happily, serving their guests and pressing them to try everything, to eat more. In a time and place where hospitality was at the very foundation of society, these two sisters of Lazarus, without husbands or children to distract them, and with plenty of money to spend, were high priestesses of hospitality, lavishing their guests with every comfort. Mary did notice, however, that, while Martha did most of the work, Maryam served slowly, lingering close to Jesus when she could, to hear what he was saying.

Forbidden by the genial hostesses to lift a finger to help them, Mary sat at table watching others wolf down the meal, a welcome feast after days of virtual fasting on the road. She picked at her food, trying to be gracious, but she could not eat, so preoccupied was she with the scene in the Temple. She remembered pushing people around, giving instructions, even endorsing Jesus' whip-wielding by releasing her grip on him and standing out of his way. How had she summoned the audacity to do that? Her most vivid and appalling images were of the aftermath. Those priests and Pharisees glaring down on them. Jesus in some kind of a daze and needing her to lead him away. She had done what she had to do, and she wondered what the others thought of her now.

She was grateful when the supper was finished and the men settled onto the roof to take in the evening air and relax before bed. She, along with Amma Mary, insisted on helping to clean up. Like women everywhere, when they went into another woman's kitchen, they saw the familiar. Instinct told where the plates were stacked, where the leftovers were stored and how to dispose of waste. The four women settled into their work, washing and drying dishes, storing utensils according to the dietary requirements of the Law, tossing dirty towels into a basket for tomorrow's laundry. They performed these activities in such concert and camaraderie that, when their work was done and they went to join the men on the roof, they had become appreciative friends.

"Welcome, women," said Lazarus, motioning for them to take soft cushions in the circle and join their conversation.

As she sat down, Mary observed that the disciples were whispering among themselves with animation and strained, persistent voices. After a few moments they fell quiet, and Simon, the one Jesus called Peter, his "Rock," cleared his throat.

"Master," he said, "we have been wondering why you disrupted the sacrifices."

Jesus looked over to the other men sitting together. "Did they elect you to speak for them, Rock?"

Never quite sure how to interpret the playful nickname Jesus had given him, Simon looked ill at ease.

"The price of being leader, eh? Well, then, Leader, can *you* suggest the meaning of what I did in the Temple today?"

"We ourselves went there to make sacrifices, so no, Master, I cannot."

"Anyone?" he asked of the other five.

They shook their heads slightly, or said, "No," or looked down at the floor.

Mary's heart turned over when she looked at them, unable as they were to answer his question. She had been educated by an elite tutor and was, by any Jewish standard, worldly. She was, if not wildly rich, at least affluent. By comparison, they were ignorant, unrefined fishermen who could barely read and who labored hard for what they had. These men must be quite out of the ordinary, or Jesus would not have chosen them.

Mary's thoughts were interrupted when he turned the question to her. "Well, then, sister," he said, "what about you?"

She would not refuse to answer, but she wished he had not asked, because she knew too well what the men's reaction would be. Drawing strength from the three women seated near her, she retained her composure. "I saw that you were outraged, Rabbouni. At first I did not understand why. Selling sacrifices and exchanging coin have been carried out in the Temple for as long as anyone can remember. I think that driving out the money-changers was a way of establishing your authority in the Temple."

She heard the men sniggering. Nathaniel choked on some wine he was just swallowing and had to blot it from the front of his robe.

Jesus turned on them. "Why do you deride her? Have you no understanding? The Reign of God is not a passing fancy. It is a new order instituted by God."

"And so it means destroying the Temple?" asked Peter the Rock.

"Not destroying, Rock, but restoring, fulfilling the Law, as it was intended from the time it was handed down to Moses. Tell me this, why do the religious leaders put so much emphasis on obedience to the Law?"

John's answer was tentative as though he were feeling his way in a dimly lit room. "Do not despise the LORD's discipline, for the LORD reproves the one he loves."

"Blessed are you, John," whispered Jesus.

All in the room fell silent as the heavy history of their people was clamped onto them like a cattle yoke. The story of their nation taught that, through the fires of adversity, God was perfecting the chosen people, was subjecting them to constant and bitter punishment, to burn away their dross. And why? So they might be made fit for their glory.

But they were not fit. Because of their sin they had always fallen short. Through the centuries, they had been enslaved to a string of heathen overlords. They had been scattered over the face of the earth, far from the Land of Promise. As a result there were more Jews in Alexandria than in Jerusalem and far more in Syria than in Palestine. Even in territories that were nominally Jewish, even on the shores of the Sea of Galilee, they were a minority among their gentile neighbors.

And still, throughout their history of slavery and dispersion, one hope glowed in the heart of every Jew, like a lamp burning down to its last drop of oil and refusing to be extinguished. When Israel had truly repented of her sins, when all her sons and daughters were obediently and perfectly performing God's will, then, and only then, would the Golden Age of their restoration be accomplished.

Jesus explained, "This is why the leaders of Israel insist on following every jot and tittle of the Law. Where the Law is murky, they interpret it as literally as they can, hoping that God will be pleased."

Looking at the disciples now, Mary saw what she had never expected to see. Every man among them was weeping. The truth of what Jesus said had been so completely self-evident that they had ordered their entire lives around it, just as their parents and their parents' parents had done. How could every single Jew live in such a way? How long must they live in perfection to please God enough that he would judge the entire nation worthy?

Mary wondered what Jesus was thinking as he, too, scanned the faces around him. That which had begun as a genuine desire to please God had been corrupted into the present-day abominations in the Temple. She imagined Jesus' heartache when he looked on that scene, and the righteous anger when he leaned down and picked up that whip.

Then he said, "In the letter of the Law, the Spirit is lost."

"And you, Master, have come to restore the Spirit of the Law," said John.

"Twice blessed, John!" replied Jesus.

"What about the priests and scribes?" asked Peter.

"What about them?" scoffed Jesus, and even Mary was amazed to hear him chuckle when he said it.

"It is nothing to jest about," she warned.

Mary knew that to follow Jesus meant not just believing in *him*, but being part of his challenge to the establishment. The scene in the Temple today would put Jesus—and all of them—on a road of conflict with the religious power structure. Neither Jesus nor they would come out of this unscathed.

Finally Jesus signaled that he was tired and it was time for bed. The men moved up to the roof and settled down with blankets and pillows. The two women from Galilee followed their hostesses to the sleeping room they would share.

Martha patted a cozy-looking cot. "This bed is for you," she said to Jesus' mother. You are over here, sister," she added, leading Mary to the opposite corner of the room and placing a small oil lamp on a table nearby.

"Oh, please, do not let us take your beds," protested Jesus' mother, seeing that the sisters had made pallets for themselves on the floor.

Martha was resolute. "It is our joy to have you in our home and to share all that we have. We are greatly honored by your presence."

Maryam added, "Our home is your home. You are family now, dear lady."

Indeed, they were sisters. Like every Jew, their common ancestor was Father Abraham who, 2000 years before, had been called by God out of the land of Ur to be established as God's chosen people. What was unusual was that these four women had become fond friends, not just a segment of the obligatory sorority.

Jesus' mother, deeply touched by the loving welcome of the sisters, replied, "Then you must call me Amma."

In the way of women, the four of them set about preparing for bed, washing their hands and faces with water from a bowl on a stand and clean towels for each of them, sharing their various oils and ointments, and admiring one another as they unbound their hair and let their tresses loose.

Settling into bed, Martha stretched and yawned. "I am exhausted," she said.

"Not I," said Maryam. "I am too excited to sleep. I have never known anyone remotely like Jesus. Nor you either, Mary. How did a woman get to be a rabbi's closest disciple?"

"Closest and cleverest!" said Jesus' mother.

Mary was glad for the dim light cast by the three little lamps around the room, which she hoped would hide her crimson cheeks.

"I am not the closest, nor the cleverest, I assure you."

"Of course she is."

"Amma, don't," said Mary with a soft protest, secretly delighted to hear Jesus' mother praising her.

"It is obvious," said Martha, agreeing with the others. "Anyone with eyes and ears can tell that he favors you."

Jesus was right to accept Lazarus' invitation to the home of these new friends. They were generous and insightful, just the kind of followers they were hoping for, the kind they would need in Jerusalem. Mary decided to share her story.

"I am indebted to Jesus in ways that the men are not. He drove out demons that had tortured me for many years and would have killed me eventually, I am sure. There were times I *wanted* to die just to end my suffering. When Jesus restored me, I was so completely liberated that all I wanted was to be near him, to help him." Mary lowered her head, wishing that she could control the uninvited blushing that happened every time she thought of being near Jesus.

CHAPTER 26

Marcus Quintius was in no mood to entertain Demetria on their walk through the city. His mind was on the scene at the Temple. *Jupiter's eyes! What was Jesus thinking?* Rome did not allow disturbances in the Pax Romana. Jesus would be crushed like an insect if he continued on this path. Marcus was right to come to Jerusalem. Mary might very well need the protection of his friends, he thought, knocking at the door of the best among them.

A steward escorted them in, and Marcus Quintius saw three people approaching from across the foyer. Recognizing Julia Clemens, he searched his memory to identify the other two. Aulus Dexius Clemens' daughters were twins. It was three years at least since he had seen them, and he was surprised by how much they had grown. He disliked seeing children after long absences, his own aging marked by their changes as they advanced along the scale of maturity. Even as undistinguished twelve-year-olds, these two had the high-boned rosy cheeks, the straight teeth, and the prominent hook in their noses that marked them as classic beauties in Rome. Though physically more mature, they had lost none of the silliness that Marcus Quintius remembered from earlier visits. Children in soon-to-be women's bodies, an unappealing combination.

Their mother was a Roman matron of the Julian clan. Julias were renowned for their looks, but this woman was quite magnificent even by Julian standards. *Too bad*, thought Quintius, seeing how she kept her personal splendor under control, her hair in a bun pulled back at the nape of her neck, eschewing any curl to break up the severity. She wore a floor-length tunic layered over by a *stola*, the long, sleeveless dress suspended at the shoulders by short straps which marked her status as a married woman. Her clothing, though very fine, was completely unadorned by the abundance of elaborate jewelry normally used by Roman women to publicize their wealth.

Her only concession to extravagance was a golden ring set with a ruby the size of a robin's egg, glistening at the lighter end of the red scale, so that it could be seen straight through. The ring was said to have come down to this Julia from a distant cousin, Aurelia, the mother of Caesar. A myth had arisen that the Roman dictator Sulla had given the ring to that legendary woman in a fit of unrequited lust. When Julia Clemens held out her hand in greeting, Quintius almost lost his composure at the sight of its uncommon clarity.

"Julia," he said, bowing over her hand.

"Marcus Quintius Severus," she replied. "Welcome to Jerusalem, and our domus."

"My compliments on your home! And these excellent girls of yours." Marcus Quintius' practiced gallantry enabled him to say this without hesitation.

"Thank you, Quintius, but you have misjudged. They are imps. I am doing what I can to civilize them, but I fear they are quite beyond refinement. Aulus Dexius sends his deepest regrets that he is not here to receive you. He was unavoidably detained this afternoon, but promises to be here shortly. I can offer you the pleasures of our baths while you wait."

He nodded gratefully.

"And is this Demetria, then?" Julia asked.

"Yes," he said, gently bringing her to his side. "Demetria, let me introduce the Lady Julia Clemens."

Demetria bowed her head and greeted her hostess modestly. A short exchange ensued, after which Julia said to the girls, "See how courteous Demetria is. You can learn from her." Then Julia turned to her young guest. "You are a tribute to your foster mother, child. Please, give her my compliments. And, by Juno, do not allow these two to corrupt your manners."

Demetria responded with an unconscious, embarrassed fluttering of her long, thick lashes. Eyes as light as Demetria's were rarely seen. Julia seemed captivated.

"Girls, take our guest to her room and get her settled. Offer her some refreshment before she perishes. Off you go, now."

Each girl grabbed one of Demetria's hands, fairly dragging her from the atrium before she could take proper leave of the adults. The various rooms flashed by her in a stream of marble and murals and bouncing light brown curls. Before she knew it, she was seated on an intricately carved chair with a velvet cushion, the Roman elves holding trays and goblets in front of her face.

"I am Julia Junia," said an elf.

"I am Juliana," said the other.

They spoke so rapidly, talking over each another, that Demetria was unsure which was which. Perhaps it did not matter. She would not be here long.

Demetria ate from the array of dishes she was offered. In many ways this house reminded her of her shame in Tiberias, the same stunning mosaic floors, tall arches and secret gardens, quiet slaves appearing and disappearing, bearing every delight, desired and undesired. But the revulsion that Demetria had felt in Tiberias was absent here. The twins chose or did not choose, oblivious to what had produced the luxury around them. In spite of herself, she found there was something charming about the giggling girls. She began to relax.

The twins had two slaves, motherly beings who seemed to belong to them alone and addressed them as Lady Junie and Lady Julie. After frequent repetitions, Demetria was able to connect their names to the colors of their tunics, one magenta and one taupe. If the elves were to change clothes, she would have to begin again, because their faces were interchangeable.

"Dolores?" said the magenta tunic.

"Yes, Lady Junie?"

"What shall we do tomorrow?"

"I believe your *mater* has invited Salome to visit you," replied Dolores, whose announcement brought on squeals of delight.

"Oh, Demetria, you will *love* Salome!" declared the twins in unison.

"I won't be here tomorrow," said Demetria, imagining that Mary was even now making arrangements to join her in Bethany. *Just one night,* she thought, remembering Mary's promise. "Marcus Quintius Severus is returning me to my family in the morning."

"You do not have a family," said Junia.

A bewildering panic engulfed Demetria, choking her with embarrassed imaginings that intensified as she pictured them. Did they know about her impoverished childhood on Sicily? Her kidnapping from her father? The way she was ripped from her mother's arms in the Roman slave market? Did they know she had been forced to dance naked in a Roman villa in Tiberias? What if Aulus Dexius was friends with the vile master there?

Demetria wanted to disappear. Her initial impression was wrong. She should not have been charmed by these spoiled, selfish girls who had an abundance of everything, except any of the difficulties of life. Marcus Quintius had said that Dexius' children were about her age and therefore would have something in common with her. These frivolous, mewling babies were nothing like her. *Demeter, help me!* she prayed to the goddess. She owed the foolish children nothing. She would do what she must to survive until the morning, when she would be back with Mary. An evening meal, one night's sleep, and a quick breakfast. She had lived through far worse and began to count the hours.

Early the next morning, when they departed for the Temple to join Mary, Demetria was beyond relieved. She had managed, she thought, to keep her outward aspect courteous, not showing the sullenness and impatience she felt inside. She remembered only one awkward moment. Passing alone through a foyer she had spotted a basket of plums sitting on a table. She had never seen such fruits and wondered where they had come from. She lifted one from the top of the stack and was immediately captivated by its smooth purple skin, which faded to pink and lavender as she turned it round and round, admiring.

"What are you doing?" a voice demanded from behind, startling her and causing her to drop the ripe fruit onto the marble floor.

Demetria looked down in horror at the mess she had made and then up at Juliana, the one who had surprised her. Quickly stripping a bandana from around her neck, she got down on her knees and began to wipe up the pulpy spot.

"Just leave it," said Julie. "A slave will clean up."

It seemed to Demetria that all Romans lived in a kind of magical world inhabited by unknown fruits and exotic music and incessant pleasures—and slaves to clean up their messes. She didn't know what to do with the plum dripping pulp into her hand. She couldn't return it to the basket. She could smell its sweet juice. She wanted badly to taste it. Was it now forbidden?

Julie was already skipping away. Her back was turned. No one was watching. Just as Demetria lifted the plum close to her mouth, Julie looked back.

"Drop it on the floor," she said.

Demetria crouched to the floor and placed the plum on the dark spot it had made on the gleaming floor. She followed Julie into the courtyard licking nectar from her fingers.

Perhaps she had appeared somewhat aloof at dinner as she tried to differentiate herself from the juveniles, but Marcus Quintius seemed quite pleased as they walked the streets of Jerusalem. She guessed that he had not heard of the incident with the plum and that she had not done anything else to shame him. Well, all that was over now. Mary was waiting for them just inside the gate to the Court of the Gentiles.

"Oh, Mistress, how good to see you!" exclaimed Demetria, hanging onto Mary as though the twelve hours they were apart had been twelve months instead.

"Shalom, Demetria," she replied, looking at Marcus questioningly.

Marcus Quintius shrugged and shook his head.

"Did you enjoy the Clemens children?"

"It was nice," said Demetria, "but I missed you."

Demetria's "it" did not escape Mary's attention.

"What about the girls? What are their names?"

"Julia Junia and Juliana, but they are called Junie and Julie."

"Yes. And what are they like?" asked Mary, pressing.

Demetria erupted in a fit of crying. Alarmed, Mary looked again at Marcus, whose confusion was obviously deepening. Mary pulled the girl aside and sat her down on a bench by the wall of the court.

"What is it, dear? What has happened?"

"I do not like it there, Mistress. Those girls are spoiled brats."

Mary wiped Demetria's face with a handkerchief pulled from her sleeve. "What reason is that to cry? Were they unkind to you?"

"They know about me. They know I am an orphan. They know I do not belong anywhere," she said, fresh tears rolling down.

"How can they know such things, when they are not true?" Mary said, trying to comfort her. "You belong to me, darling,"

"Yes, yes, I do. And I am so glad that I can come to Bethany with you tonight, Mistress. I want to forget all about those Julias."

Mary bit her lower lip and pulled Demetria's head to her breast. How could she tell her that it was impossible for her to come to Lazarus' home just yet? She could not eat with them or help in the kitchen. And where would she sleep? Mary would not ask such a thing of Martha and Maryam at this time. They had declared that they were family, but it was a Jewish family nonetheless.

Mary kissed the top of Demetria's head. "Stay here. I'll be right back."

"You look angry," Marcus Quintius said as Mary approached him.

"What happened over there?"

Marcus Quintius gave what information he knew. He affirmed that the Roman girls were quite silly, but seemed to adore Demetria, even in their short time together.

"What did you tell them?"

"What do you mean?"

"I mean, what did you tell the Clemens family about Demetria's background?"

"I told them nothing. I introduced her as the adopted daughter of a Jewish woman of substance. The fact that she is traveling under my protection was enough for them. They are too gracious to inquire further. Julia praised Demetria repeatedly and sent her compliments to you. What is wrong with her? I do not understand this, Magdalena."

"I think I do, Marcus. Come," she said and led him back to the bench where Demetria waited.

Marcus Quintius stood over them, watching as Mary sat down beside the expectant girl.

"Demetria, I have never been so proud of you as I am today."

"Why, Mistress?"

"Because," she said slowly, "according to Marcus Quintius' report, your behavior as a guest was flawless. Your hostess remarked on your courtesy. You even impressed the young Julias with your maturity. They enjoyed having you in their home. I know, from what you have told me, that this was not easy for you. You were unhappy, but you did not let it show. I think you did this for my sake."

Demetria lowered her head, but her eyes looked up at the Roman, towering over her. "And for Marcus Quintius' sake," she confessed.

Marcus, caught unawares, almost gasped, but turned the breath into a throat-clearing maneuver.

Mary went on. "Demetria, do you remember when you first came to Magdala, how difficult it was for Shoshanna to accept you?"

Demetria nodded imperceptibly.

"Remember that she did not want you to touch our food? How she grumbled about having gentiles in the house?"

"She thought I was like Mummius," Demetria said, smiling at the unpleasant memory, made amusing by the passage of time.

"Think about how Shoshanna loves you now. How she relies on you."

Mary saw the sudden alarm in Demetria's face and heard it in her voice when she stiffened and asked, "Why are you talking about Shoshanna, Mistress?"

"Demetria, I cannot bring you to Bethany with me tonight."

"You mean," said Demetria panting, "that I must go back to that house?"

Mary was silent, allowing the truth to sink in.

"Mistress, no. Don't make me do that. I cannot. Please!"

Mary placed her hands on the girl's shoulders. "Demetria, we are in a serious situation. You saw what Jesus did in this very courtyard yesterday. You saw the crowds that mobbed him afterwards. There is a great deal of confusion in Lazarus' home as we try to sort out what danger we might be in. Aside from the problem of the religious laws, I do not think it is safe for you there."

Demetria did not respond. Mary wished she knew what she was thinking.

"We are, every one of us, being called upon to do things that we do not wish to do. We are all scared because we do not know what the priests might decide to do. Staying with Marcus Quintius is your contribution to managing these difficulties." Mary delivered her final stroke. "I need you to help me. This is the way you can help."

Will this make her hate me? Mary wondered, dreading the possibility, but willing to accept it, seeing no way out.

Demetria surprised her. If Mary could manage her fears, she could do the same. They were small by comparison. Taking a deep breath, she said, "Seven times seven," indicating that there was no limit to her willingness to sacrifice for Mary.

Later during the course of that morning, Demetria, being resigned to her pledge, looked with fresh eyes on Jesus. She saw that her mistress was completely focused on him as he dealt with the crowds, and he seemed to concentrate when she spoke to him, which was often. Demetria was trying to understand what Jesus was doing and why it was so dangerous. She was disappointed when Jesus decided to go back to Bethany early, which meant that she would be forced to leave the company and return with Marcus Quintius to the Clemens' house for the midday meal.

They walked in a strained silence until Marcus Quintius blurted out, "I did not tell them anything about you, child."

Silence.

"Do you not believe me?"

More silence. And then, with a sure voice, she answered, "I believe you, Marcus Quintius. My fear is within me."

Marcus Quintius was not one to feel admiration for girls, Roman or otherwise, but his respect for Demetria grew as he learned more about the kind of woman she was becoming. Unable to express himself in words, he rested his arm on her shoulders.

Demetria took in a determined breath as they approached the Clemens' domus. The grating crunch of the crushed rock path under her sandals felt like a fitting start to her impending ordeal. Then, the squealing imps were upon her.

"Demetria!"

"You're back!"

"Girls. Calm yourselves. I will not have this unseemly screeching," commanded their mother.

Demetria watched in dismay as the three of them streamed toward her. In her desire to please Mary, to help as she had been asked, she had almost forgotten the annoying silliness of the girls. Now she had to spend the entire afternoon with them, pretending. As they drew nearer, Demetria noticed something. Obedient to their mother, the twins stopped squealing, but they were still running toward her, arms open wide. When they squeezed her in their hugs, she was moved.

All morning she had watched people surge at Jesus, call his name, reach out to touch him, grab at his clothes. Dismay and resignation did not seem to be part of his reaction. Rather, he welcomed them, along with their endless demands. When Demetria saw the gladness shining in Lady Julia's face, she caught a glimpse of the unreserved generosity with which Jesus accepted everyone who came to him and how they loved him for it. *No wonder the priests fear him,* she thought.

"Come, Demetria, come!" said the elves in unison. "It is time for our meal. We are having fish cakes and olives and water with lemons. Right after lunch Salome is coming. You will love Salome! Come, come."

As they dragged her off, Demetria turned back to Marcus Quintius and winked.

"Who is Salome?" Demetria asked, taking the last bite of her fish cake and licking her lips contentedly, for it was indeed delicious.

"She is the niece of Chuza," said Junie.

"Who is Chuza?"

The girls' eyes grew big.

"You don't know who Chuza is? Well! You don't know anything."

Demetria fought the urge to feel insulted. *They don't intend to offend me. It is just their ignorance,* she thought, an idea that was confirmed when Junie carried on unabated.

"Well! Chuza is Herod's Chief Steward."

"*King* Herod?"

"He is not really a king, silly. Caesar won't let him be a king. He is only a tetrarch."

Demetria searched her mind. She visualized the maps Mary had used to instruct her and remembered that Herod Antipas ruled Galilee in the north, where Magdala was, and Perea, a separate piece of land that lay farther south, just east of the Jordan River.

"This is Judea. What is the *tetrarch* of Galilee and Perea doing here?" asked Demetria, jokingly emphasizing the title.

"Well!" began one of the elves.

Demetria cringed. These girls must be taught not to begin every one of their pronouncements with "Well!"

"Well! It is Passover. All the Jews in the world come to Jerusalem for Passover. It is their great feast, you know."

"That's why you are here, is it not?" asked the other elf.

"Yes, it is. But I am not a Jew, so I do not make the Temple sacrifices."

"Oh," they said flatly.

Then the Junie/Julie combination continued its explanation.

"When they are in Jerusalem, Joanna brings Salome to play with us."

"Joanna is Salome's aunt."

"Chuza's wife."

"Your mother and Joanna are friends?" asked Demetria.

"Yes. Very good friends."

"I see," said Demetria, trying to decipher the relationship between these Roman children and the ruler of the Jews.

At that moment one of the nursemaids arrived with an announcement. "Salome is here."

If Demetria had known anything about anthropology, she would have seen in Salome the Edomite blood of her ancestors. If she had been familiar with the political history of the region, she would have known that the royal line of the Herods, called Idumean, was an Edomite tribe, descended from Esau, the "ruddy and hairy" twin brother of Jacob. If she had learned her Torah a bit better, she would remember that Jacob had become the "chosen one" of God's promise to Israel by stealing his inheritance from Esau.

As it was, Demetria could plainly see that this eleven-year-old was a perfect example of the Edomite characteristic called "red." She had hair the color of copper, which her ancestors had pulled from their mines. It was long and silky, thick as the coat of a wild animal in winter. The hair around her eyes, lashes and brows, was a slightly lighter shade of red that contrasted with the dark brown, almost black, eyes they framed. Her nose was broad and flat, and her teeth, when she smiled, gleamed very white against her ruddy complexion. She was short and sturdily built, and Demetria, born running in the open fields of Sicily, recognized in her another girl who preferred to play outside, boys' games, like climbing trees. Still, she would have been surprised to learn that Salome's aunt had given permission for her to learn to ride a horse, but in private.

Young and vigorous as she was, Salome nevertheless had a regal demeanor that could have resulted only from life in the royal court. Demetria even heard what she thought might be a note of deference in Lady Julia's voice when she welcomed Salome, who accepted it as nothing unusual, like a birthright. When the twins screeched and ran to greet her, the unflustered Salome spoke to them quietly, which had a calming effect on the elves. Demetria could see why Julia regularly sought out the influence of this girl for her daughters.

"I have something new," said Salome, reaching for a linen purse held by her slave, an older girl who looked to Demetria to be Egyptian. "Let's go outside and I will show you."

Outside, of course, mused Demetria, *where else?*

Salome led the way to a dense privet hedge and, ducking her head, disappeared into it. The Julias followed. Demetria, being the tallest, had to duck to her knees through the opening.

"This is our secret world," explained Junie.

It appeared that the three of them had spent many hours creating little passageways and rooms within the giant hedge. They had swept the ground with branches to make it flat and hard. There were stashes of toys and dolls. Mostly they had to crawl from place to place, but in certain locations they had cut back the growth overhead enough to stand.

Salome found her spot and they all sat. She slowly untied the ribbon holding the neck of the purse together and slipped her hand in, enticing her audience. She pulled out a closed fist and rocked it back and forth.

"Can you guess?"

The elves reacted with their usual enthusiasm, but could not come up with the right answer. Salome opened her hand and sparkling, polished stones tumbled out onto the ground. A game of chance!

"*Mater* would never allow this," said Junie, glancing around.

"Don't be silly," said Salome. "It's fun."

Participating in games of chance was ubiquitous. Romans did it. Arabs did it. Jews did it. Not just for entertainment either. Casting lots was a method to decide matters of import, even determining the will of God, because God was said to have a hand on the outcome when the lots were prayed over.

Any way she looked at it, Demetria could not imagine that Mary would be pleased to see her rolling dice with Romans and Idumeans. On the other hand, she did not wish to make a scene. She decided to play along.

Salome taught them the rules of several games, and after a while Demetria understood what she was up to. Precocious little Salome had the key to keeping the twins engaged, concentrating on one thing, not flitting from this to that, bouncing and screaming. They had not budged from their seats, nor squirmed, since they sat down with the thrilling stones. After about an hour, Salome excused herself, said she'd be right back, and went into the house, to relieve herself, Demetria imagined. When she returned, Demetria saw that it was a different matter altogether.

Salome's eyes were as red as the rest of her, and swollen. She smiled, but the sparkle around her mouth was betrayed by the sadness in her eyes. Demetria could imagine her weeping in secret and then splashing her face with water to rinse away the tears and reduce the puffiness.

"Salome, what is wrong?" asked Demetria, causing the Julias to look up from their game.

"It is nothing. Excuse me…" Salome said, trying to hide her face under a lovely lavender veil she pulled up from her shoulders.

The elves spun into action. "Oh, Salome, don't cry, everything will be all right, let's play, it will take your mind off things," they said, petting her and kissing her face.

What could have knocked this self-assured royal so completely off her moorings? Whatever it was seemed no surprise to the twins. Demetria, being a stranger, wished she could leave them to handle their intimate problems privately, but by now the bereft child was sobbing and the twins' agitation was making the situation worse. Demetria sat down on her heels in front of Salome and, putting her finger to her lips, hushed the ruckus.

"Why are you crying, little one?"

Salome's breath came in quick gasps. When she took a handkerchief from her sleeve to blow her nose, Demetria stared at the luxurious square. *Silk!* she thought, amazed, forcing her attention back to Salome. The entire lower half of the girl's face was clenched and trembling.

Junie asked her, "Do you want me to tell?"

Salome nodded.

"Her Aunt Joanna has an evil spirit," Junie said with unexpected sensitivity. "Salome, did the spirit enter her this morning? No. Last night? Yes." Junie turned to Demetria. "When the spirit comes, it throws Joanna onto the floor and her eyes roll back into her head." Behind her hand she whispered and made a face, "Sometimes foam comes out of her mouth."

Demetria is swept through time and space to the streets of Magdala, alone and terrified. Howling wolves, glimmering in the light of an ominous moon, are bearing down on her. Turning a corner, she happens upon her wandering mistress, Mary, whom she seeks, in the distance, hands outstretched to the shining sky, arms raked with blood, her wails mingling with the sound of the night predators. She is a child like Salome, wondering how to aid the suffering woman who is a mother to her.

Demetria pulled the shuddering girl close to her. She understood now that Salome was mature not so much because she was raised in a court, but because her young shoulders carried an impossible burden of love. *How long have you lived like this?* Demetria wondered.

"Why did Salome come here today, when she is so unhappy and tired?" Demetria asked.

It was Julie who replied. "Her Aunt Joanna insists on it. She doesn't want her affliction to interfere with Salome's life. Isn't that right, Salome?"

When the child in her arms nodded, Demetria felt a new admiration for the twins, who seemed genuinely affected by their friend's plight. Perhaps they were not so shallow as she had thought.

Demetria whispered into the soft, fragrant copper on top of Salome's head, "It is not easy to carry on as though nothing has happened, is it?"

Salome shook her head.

What more was there to say? The four unhappy girls sat quietly within the privet hedge waiting for the flurry in their hearts to subside. But Demetria's impatience would not fade.

She thought the day and the night would never pass. She was eager to be on the way to the Temple again, but for a different reason from yesterday. She and Marcus Quintius had barely turned the corner from the walkway to the street when she asked, "Sir, do you know the Lady Joanna?"

"What, you mean Chuza's wife?"

"Yes."

"I know of her."

"Do you know of her affliction?"

"Do *you*?"

"Marcus Quintius, please, this is important. Joanna's niece Salome was at the Clemens' house yesterday. She was exhausted because her aunt had experienced a possession of demons the day before. Finally she broke down completely. It was pathetic to watch."

Marcus stopped and gave Demetria a worried look. "What does this have to do with you?"

"I want to help her."

"How?"

"Jesus can heal her."

He turned and started walking. "That will not happen."

Demetria had thought that Marcus Quintius would be her ready ally in this. She needed him. He was the connecting link between two worlds.

"Why not?"

"Demetria, there is much you do not understand, too many forces at work. It is not an easy thing for the Lady Julia, a Roman, to befriend Joanna. She is a Jew, well, a kind of Jew—Jews do not consider Idumeans to be pure Jews. She is attached to the royal court. Jesus is a roving rabbi with a questionable reputation. The Clemens family can have nothing to do with him."

"*You* have plenty to do with him," Demetria shot back.

"Watch your mouth, girl," he said, testily.

Demetria changed her tone, but she would not back down. "Salome is just like me, Marcus Quintius, and Joanna is just like Mary. We must help her."

The rest of their walk to the Temple was a silent one, two people at odds with each other and with their circumstances. Marcus Quintius was angrily wondering why he had allowed himself to get into this quagmire. His sole desire to watch over Mary had led to Demetria and Demetria had led to Salome, who had led to Joanna. And all of them led to Jesus.

Somewhere in the back of his mind, Marcus heard an echo of Mummius' attempt to warn him. "Severus, do you not see? Jesus has the lady under his control now. We have no idea how Jesus will use his power over her."

A plague on these women! Marcus Quintius grumbled to himself.

CHAPTER 27

All Jerusalem was gossiping about Jesus. Throughout the remainder of the festival week, he could be found in and around the city, speaking of the Reign of God and satisfying the desire of the crowds to see him work some miracle. Each evening he returned to the house in Bethany to partake of the limitless hospitality there and disclose to his friends the deeper meaning of his day's teaching and actions. Each night, as the others were settling down for sleep, he went to the garden. There, tucked into a secluded corner of the wall, he had found a mossy rock where he could escape to pray in solitude.

As evening turned to night and the household bustle faded with the waning light, Mary stayed alert. She would walk unobtrusively from room to room, picking up a used cup or a discarded towel that had been overlooked, or giving the kitchen a last minute tidying up. She filled small oil lamps that would burn through the night and provided extra pillows or blankets to anyone who needed them, though here in this house of high hospitality, little was ever left undone. Mary's simulated chores provided the pretense she needed while she waited for Jesus to slip out the back door to the garden. Only when she was sure he had quit the house unhindered did she finally retire.

One night, past the hour of midnight, Mary lay awake. All around her were the sounds of slumber, women turning softly in their beds, occasionally adjusting the covers just so or murmuring someone's name in a dream; on the roof, a man snoring loudly—probably the Rock, who had overeaten—and outside, crickets punctuating the night with chirping, playing their filelike wings as stringed instruments of music. Every night since they arrived here, she had lain thus, unable to sleep.

Mary would have been embarrassed for Jesus to know how much she thought about his every move, how full her mind was of his sights and sounds: Jesus wading through a crowd of people, touching their heads in blessing, unperturbed no matter how closely they pressed in on him; Jesus describing the Reign of God, illustrating his points with familiar examples from nature; Jesus making jokes about scribes and Pharisees and laughing with his audience while those very leaders of Israel stood at the edges of the throng, scowling; Jesus licking his fingers after a particularly delicious supper, hugging the blushing Martha and saying what a talented cook she was; Jesus poking his disciples with hard questions to draw out their understanding, alternately amused and peeved at their answers. Jesus, Jesus, Jesus.

Mary turned over and punched her pillow to make an indentation for her head. *I must get to sleep.* She remembered, when she was a child of four or five and could not fall asleep, that her mother would sit on the floor in the room where she and her brother had their pallets among the sheep and goats, stroking the hair away from her face to soothe her. Rebecca had the gift of song, and Mary requested lullabies. Her favorite was a psalm that told of God's love. "The LORD is gracious and merciful. The LORD is good to all, and the compassion of the LORD is over all that the LORD has made."

"Mother, does this mean that God loves everybody the same?" she would ask. "Oh, yes, everyone." "And animals, too?" "Yes, of course, animals, too," her mother would assure her, and then take up her singing again, repeating the psalm over, ever more quietly and slowly, until Mary could resist no more and fell fast asleep.

Now, Mary sang in her head. *The LORD is good to all and the compassion of the LORD is over all... The LORD is good to all, the compassion of the LORD is... The LORD is good... The LORD is good... The LORD is...* The welcome weight of slumber began to relax her limbs and evaporate her thoughts. She was sliding, sliding...

She had almost drifted off when a quiet, rhythmic sound began to call her back to consciousness. Knocking? She listened intently, holding her breath. The sound came again. Incredibly, someone was knocking at the front door.

Mary got up and wrapped a long shawl over her sleep shift. The other women had not stirred. She thought of waking Martha, or Peter, but decided against it. Certainly this would be no one intending harm, no nighttime intruder, knocking at the door. Best not to disturb anyone, just answer it on her own. If she needed help, she could call out an alarm and people would come running.

She tiptoed barefoot to the door and said quietly in Aramaic, "Who is there?"

"I am Nicodemus," was the reply. "I have come to see the rabbi."

From his voice Mary imagined a Jewish man of perhaps fifty years, and refined. "I am a member of the Council."

The Council! Why is a member of the high Council stealing around at night, seeking Jesus?

Mary did not hesitate. "Sir," she said urgently, "will you wait outside the door, please? I will bring him here immediately."

Mary ran through the house, her bare feet making no sound. She flew out into the garden, her eyes casting about for the figure of Jesus. Every shadow looked as though it might be he, and then was not. She began to call in a loud whisper, "Rabbouni! Where are you?" This way and that she dashed until finally, her eyes adjusting to the darkness, she caught the glow of his white robe upon the rock where he knelt. Even as she drew near, still calling, he did not move until she touched him on his shoulder and he jumped. She jumped back in response.

"I am so sorry, Rabbouni."

"No. No," he said, a little breathless and blinking rapidly as he recovered from being startled out of his meditation. "I was very deep in prayer..." He shook his head and seemed to become more aware of her. "But what is it, dear woman?"

"A man is at the door, seeking you."

"At this hour?"

"Yes, and, Jesus, he claims to be a member of the Council!"

"Strange," said Jesus, as though to himself. "Well, there is nothing to fear, I am sure." He stood and put a reassuring arm around her shoulder. "Let us go to see this midnight man."

"His name is Nicodemus," she said.

"Oh, my," said Jesus with a tone of such surprise that Mary looked over at him to see why. His raised eyebrows and that slight lifting of the edges of his mouth told her that he was amused. She hated it when he made light of grave matters.

At the door, Mary held back, but Jesus did not hesitate to open it wide and invite the visitor in. "Rabbi Nicodemus, peace be with you."

He already knows this Pharisee? wondered Mary.

"Peace be with you, Rabbi," responded Nicodemus, stepping into the house.

Nicodemus' physical form belied his stature among the religious leaders, for he was short and stocky. Even at this hour of the night, after a long day of working at Passover duties, he was immaculate, his turban and robe clean and unwrinkled. His nails were polished and his coarse, black beard, sprinkled with grey, was neatly trimmed.

Jesus made polite introductions. "This is Mary of Magdala, one of my disciples traveling in our company from Galilee. Mary, Nicodemus is well known as one of Jerusalem's most respected teachers."

"Shalom," she said, warily, but Nicodemus only nodded in her direction.

"What can I do for you, Rabbi?" Jesus asked.

"Please forgive my intrusion so late at night. We have been consumed with Passover duties—as you can imagine—and I have only just now been able to get away."

"And it is easier to move about in secret on a moonless night, eh?"

Nicodemus did not take the bait. "Rabbi, I am sure you know that all the leaders are talking about you."

"I imagine that they are."

"May we talk privately? There is much I want to discuss with you."

"We can go to the garden, if you like, but Mary will come with us."

With that statement Jesus handed Nicodemus his first tutorial. In the Pharisee's head must have been something like, *You would have us discourse about matters of the Law and the Prophets in the presence of a woman?* But he spoke none of that, only nodded again and said, "As you wish."

Each tingling with anticipation, the three of them walked to a corner of the garden and sat down by the wall. Jesus and Mary waited while the Pharisee organized his thoughts.

"Rabbi, it is clear to us that you are a teacher who comes from God."

"What makes that clear to you, Nicodemus?"

"It is well known and well documented that no one could do the God-revealing acts that you do if God were not the source."

"Indeed, Nicodemus, it is true that you have to be born from above to see what I am pointing to: the Reign of God."

Oh no, thought Mary. *This cryptic talk of his.*

"I do not understand what you mean. How can a man, already born of his mother and grown, be 'born from above,' as you say?"

"What I mean is, that in order to enter the Reign of God, a person must submit to being recreated in Spirit." Jesus paused, reaching for an analogy. "Think about a newborn baby. When you look at it, you see only a human body. Inside the tiny body is the person-to-be, the person who will take shape and is formed by what you *cannot* see—the Spirit—and over time the baby becomes a living Spirit."

"Let us say, for the sake of argument, that I accept what you are saying. I still do not understand how it can happen."

Jesus was quiet, looking long into the eyes of the Pharisee. It was Mary, her heart thudding with courage, who finally broke the silence.

"With respect, Rabbi Nicodemus, what is it you really want to know?"

This great teacher of Israel, unaccustomed to being addressed by any woman, much less interrogated by one, looked at Mary as though she had lost her senses. Nicodemus turned to Jesus, who shrugged and said, "I wonder that myself, sir."

Nicodemus' eyes narrowed as he stared at the traveler from Galilee—Nazareth, of all places, a backwater in every sense of the word. He had spent his life in the orderly pursuit of God through disciplined reading of the Law and faithful obedience to all its prescriptions and proscriptions. If the young Nazarene before him, an unpretentious man who clearly had the mantle of God on his shoulders, was telling him that his understanding of the Law was a mistake, that he had to begin afresh like a child, would it negate all he had valued and built his life upon? Again Mary and Jesus were silent, waiting for Nicodemus to frame his inquiry.

"I want to know who you are and why you have come."

"I am glad for that, Rabbi," said Jesus, his eyes moistening with gratitude, "because you will hear that it is very good news."

In Mary's heart was compassion for the man. Most of the people who listened to Jesus and followed him were simple folk. They adored him for his message that they were welcome in the Reign of God, equal in importance to—no, more important than—men like members of the Council who held the power to interpret God's mind for them. Here was one of those men, driven by his desire for God to put so much at risk. She thought of Nicodemus waiting through the hours to steal away from his colleagues. His two-mile walk from the Temple to this place, checking over his shoulder to see who might be watching. So what if he wanted anonymity? He had come, had he not?

They talked all night. Jesus proved to Nicodemus that he knew the scriptures thoroughly, so that the Pharisee listened to him more and more intently as the hours passed. And it was clear that this woman of his, this Mary of Magdala, grasped the Reign of God as well as Jesus did. Finally, Jesus confronted Nicodemus by asking, "You are a great leader of the people, Rabbi, and yet you do not really know the truth. How can this be?"

Nicodemus said, "Often I have felt remorse for the punitive nature of our pronouncements. I have spoken up in the Council, but now, with Caiaphas as high priest and his father-in-law, Hanan, pulling his strings, the few of us who offer a different opinion are generally silenced." In the grip of penitence came the truth. "In the letter of the Law, the Spirit is lost." Then, the light, "Rabbi, have you come to restore the Spirit of the Law?"

And Jesus said, "I have."

Always and everywhere in the soul of every Jew lived the Shema, the confession of faith: "Hear, O Israel; the LORD is our God, the LORD alone. You shall love the LORD your God with all your heart, and with all your soul, and with all your might." This was the true Spirit of the Law, the underpinning of every regulation, along with its companion piece, to love others as you love yourself. "Measure every act against these two standards," said Jesus, "and you will live in perfect harmony with the Law of God." This is what Nicodemus longed to hear. This is what filled the void in the midnight visitor's hungering heart.

What remained was for Nicodemus to determine what he would do with what they called the "good news" of the Reign of God. Embracing the good news would not be easy. Resistance would be strong. Nicodemus would have to be careful.

Just before sunrise, Mary nodded toward the east and said, "Rabbi Nicodemus, perhaps you should consider returning to Jerusalem."

"How right you are, dear woman. Thank you for keeping watch for me."

So, thought Mary, *he offers me thanks and calls me "dear woman." I wonder if he will see other women differently now.*

Jesus waited in the garden while Mary escorted Nicodemus to the door and the two bade each other shalom in an immeasurably different spirit from their greeting a few hours before, hours that might have been a millennium for all the change that had occurred between the two of them. Then she returned to the rock where Jesus sat.

They were alone for the first time since they had left Magdala. The strain of the road, the incessant activity filling their days in Jerusalem, Jesus' need to replenish himself through prayer at night, all this had kept them apart. He reached out and pulled her down to sit close to him.

Jesus' hands felt like glowing embers and caused the tiniest pearls of perspiration to form on her forehead and her nose. The longing she was constantly at pains to suppress welled up in her. She shut her eyes so he would not see it. But when Jesus placed a hand under her chin and lifted her face, she opened her eyes and saw the desire he had for her. Mary wanted to feel herself joined to Jesus, to be absorbed into him, to merge with him. She wanted to cease to exist as a person separate from him. She had heard a few women speak of desire like this for their husbands and had pitied them. Now she knew how fortunate such women were.

Who can know what would have happened next if they had not been in the garden of someone else's home, if there had not been ten people in the house nearby, if the sun were not already rising?

"We should go in," she whispered.

Jesus did not move. It was Mary who made the decision then. She stood up and, tugging gently on his arm, abandoned the moment to the rock on which they had sat.

CHAPTER 28

Clay pots in the courtyard were dark with a light sprinkling of rain which had fallen overnight in Magdala. Plants glistened. Any moment now, the morning sun would warm new leaves and call waiting buds to open with a riot of persimmon and chartreuse, goldenrod and periwinkle.

Mummius walked a circuit around the perimeter, inspecting the irrigation pipes for breaks and leaks. As he went, he looked among the plantings for signs of disease and made mental notes for the gardener on where and when to prune. When Mary returned, if she returned, Mummius wanted her prized garden to be immaculate, flourishing as though she herself had tended it.

Mary had always watered the plants by hand, pacing to and from the reservoir with her pitcher, filling and pouring, again and again. Shortly after his arrival from Rome, Mummius had made an offer. "Lady, a system of pipes would ease your burden." She had worried that an unsightly run of pipes would detract from the enjoyment of the garden, but he reassured her. "Allow me to install it," Mummius said. "If it is not to your liking, I will simply remove it." Being quite sure of himself, he was not surprised to hear her exclaim, "Why, Mummius, this is indeed a marvel!" What did surprise him, though, was the soft touch of her hand on his arm when she said, "Thank you."

How he longed for those early days in Magdala and—if he could have admitted it—the nights. Mummius was a man on a mission then, pursuing any course that would appease the suspicious cynic that had taken up residence in his soul the night that Maret—and his manhood—was stolen from him. Noted physician that he was, mental giant, master agriculturalist, gifted musician, none of that could satisfy his longing. But when Mary leaned on him, when he held her head and helped her sip the potions he prepared for her, when she lay in bed and he sat on the floor beside her, singing her to sleep, then, for a few moments, the deep hole inside him steadily filled and he was pacified.

During the years of caring for her, his need for her to need him had crept upon Mummius unawares. Then, when Jesus restored her life and she needed Mummius no more, he was back where he had started. The hole in him was empty again, leaving him permanently unsatiated. Mummius knew that Mary was lost to Severus, and had told him so, but what he could not fully accept was that she was lost to him as well.

Deep in his memories and his gardening, Mummius was provoked when an agitated servant interrupted him.

"Apologies, Chief Steward," he said. "Here is a courier from Tyre. He insists on seeing you personally."

"A message for Marcus Quintius Severus," said the courier unceremoniously.

Mummius, equally brusque, waved away the servant and held out his hand for the scroll. The courier was short of breath, having ridden a horse hard and fast from Tyre, but tired as he was, he knew his orders.

"No, sir. This is for Marcus Quintius alone. I am to deliver it personally. Where is he, please?"

In no mood for courtesy, Mummius glared. "I am Severus' Chief Steward in Palestine. The message is safe with me."

"But, sir…"

Mummius moved in close. He did not need to lay a hand on the ill-fated courier to hold him uncontested with his hard, narrowed eyes.

"Listen to me, you fool. Marcus Quintius is not in Magdala. Your only hope of delivering that message is to give it to me. Do that and you will be rewarded by sender and receiver. Fail, and you will die. Either way, I have the scroll."

By now the courier was no longer panting with fatigue, but trembling with fear. "It is of the utmost urgency," he whimpered, reluctantly handing over the scroll.

"Good boy," replied Mummius. "Now go to the kitchen. They will feed you. Wait there for my reply."

Turning his back on the frightened man, Mummius strode to his apartment and into the inner sanctum. He placed the scroll on his work table and examined the seal. Seeing the Severus stamp, possessed exclusively by Marcus Quintius' father, the patriarch of the family, he knew instinctively what must be inside. He popped off the circle of clay and unfurled the parchment.

"My dearest son," it began, "I am gravely ill. By the time you receive this I will be gone. I struggle to dictate this letter so that you may hear it from my own lips and know that my last breath was for you. May your grief be overcome by contentment, knowing that my life has been a joyous one, owing primarily to you. Receive this as my final blessing, noble and worthy Marcus Quintius. Farewell, beloved son, and remember, *dignitas*; above all, *dignitas*."

Although he had anticipated the message, Mummius could not harden himself against it. He put up no resistance against his tears that came for the living and the dead, two men who had befriended him, an Egyptian, a slave, a eunuch, as others would not. He wished now that it was not he who must ensure the delivery of this devastating news to his friend.

The letter went on.

"Marcus Quintius, it is with deep sadness that I send your revered father's last words. After what I have inscribed above, he spoke no more, only closed his eyes and slept. I know you are wondering how it happened. It is a mystery to all. Just a few days ago he began to complain of a fever. Within hours he could not remove himself from bed as the fever raged. He came in and out of consciousness. No physician could aid him. They only gave him drafts of henbane and other medicinals to relieve his pain. Though he did not write it, he spoke to me of his desire that you return to Rome as quickly as possible to register his will in the court. This I know you will do, whatever may be detaining you so long abroad. I have engaged the services of the best undertakers, and they have initiated funeral plans. There will be an ample number of mimes and musicians available, as well as mourning women, but you must come home to order the details. May your journey be swift and safe. Lucullus"

Mummius had seen Roman funeral processions, vast parades moving slowly through the streets of the city, a bizarre scene of players making music, dancers undulating in and out of the marchers, and professional mourners wailing, all in counterpoint to the cluster of family members advancing together in silence, their faces covered with *imagines*, the death masks of their ancestors, a custom reserved for the noblest citizens of Rome. He grieved to think of his friend, wearing the black toga of mourning, leading the sorrowful march.

Marcus Quintius Severus was *paterfamilias* now, with the power of life and death, as well as control of the family's fortune. The entire Severus clan, his sisters and brothers-in-law, their sons and daughters, would look to him as head of the family. Likewise would all of Rome know that his was the voice of the Severi. Mummius wondered if it would change him. He thought not. Marcus had been groomed for this from birth, and he had never made a single misstep as heir-in-waiting.

Mummius took down an ink pot and rolled out a short scroll of papyrus to write a postscript letter of his own.

"My dear Severus, I have received the enclosed letter but moments ago and am speeding it on its way to Jerusalem with the expectation that it will reach you at the home of Aulus Dexius. I imagine that you will want to proceed directly west to Joppa on the coast, there to obtain passage to Rome on the first available ship. I will also instruct the courier to watch for you on the road, on the chance that you are already on the way back to Magdala.

"Severus, you know I loved your father. He was good to me while I was in Rome, and I will never forget his kindnesses. May the gods bless you as you ascend to your place as *paterfamilias* with the honor and *dignitas* he taught you. Your friend in all things, Mummius"

Then he wrote to Lucullus, chief of scribes for the Severus family in Rome, explaining the situation and offering his condolences. He sped the Tyrian courier on his way with that letter and then set out for the town to find a man to race for Jerusalem.

Mary could not have been more taken by surprise when she saw Demetria arrive at the Court of the Gentiles accompanied, not by Marcus Quintius, but by a Roman she had never laid eyes on, fully dressed in a toga.

"Mistress, this is Aulus Dexius Clemens," Demetria said, solemnly.

This was something extremely serious. Warily Mary pulled Demetria close.

"Are you Mary of Magdala, friend of Marcus Quintius?" asked the Roman in polished Greek.

"I am," Mary answered.

"I regret making your acquaintance in this way, lady, but Marcus Quintius has received tragic news from Rome and asked me to come for you."

"What news, Aulus Dexius?"

"His father is dead."

Mary had never met the father, but she knew him in the son. Mummius had described them as mirror images of each other, the father only slightly taller and perhaps a bit more reserved, although, if anything, even more attractive to women, with the deep wave of thick brown hair that fell over his beguiling eyes when he laughed. But Mary knew that the legacy for which Marcus was most grateful was his pure joy of living, which he had learned from his father and which his father encouraged in him, the intense interest in everything new, the yearning to travel, the acceptance and appreciation of things beyond Rome. Already she could feel Marcus' heartbreak.

Mary and Demetria followed Aulus Dexius as quickly as they could through the streets, which were becoming crowded with merchants setting up their shops and pilgrims arriving. When they arrived at the Clemens house, Dexius ushered Mary to the door of Marcus' room. Looking in, she imagined what had occurred there in the early hours of the morning: Dexius waking Marcus Quintius to receive an urgent courier; Marcus immediately alert with that capacity of military men, perfected in the field of war and never forgotten; the scroll rolled out and held under the flickering flame of the night lamp; and the realization. Mary glanced at the abandoned bed, the covers thrown back, an untidy testament to the sorrowful scene.

By contrast, Marcus Quintius was already perfectly attired, every buckle and knot securely done, every hair in place, the picture of self-discipline. In one corner a slave was strapping down what little baggage he had brought with him to Jerusalem, preparing for the journey to Joppa, a detour that would turn thirty miles into a thousand, because he was in no way ready to forsake Mary in Jerusalem.

"Marcus," she whispered as she went to him.

When he embraced her, she felt the slight distance between their bodies, the rigid arms, the note of decorum when he said, "Thank you for coming."

Mary scanned the familiar eyes and face. What did she see there? Iron control over his emotions, or reserve, displayed for his friend Dexius? Their life together had been on her home ground, in the company of her companions. Among his own, was he, after all, embarrassed by her?

"I am sorry about your father," she said, pushing gently away.

His response was all business. "I am leaving immediately for Joppa and thence to Rome. Mummius has matters in the north well in hand. I have dispatched a courier with final instructions to him." Then he turned abruptly to Aulus Dexius and asked, "May we have a moment alone, please?"

"Of course," he responded, marshalling both the slave and Demetria from the room.

Marcus pulled Mary to the unkempt bed and sat down woodenly. She had to turn his face with her hands to get him to look at her. She searched his face, trying to read what she saw there, for never had he seemed so closed.

"I do not know when I will be able to return."

"You have much to do in Rome," she answered, still looking for an explanation for his odd and distant behavior.

The one he gave her was not what she was waiting for. "Magdalena," he said, his voice husky, "I want you to marry me."

It was as though she were in a small boat on the Sea of Galilee when the storms come up, rocked side to side, waves crashing over the edges, threatening to swamp and submerge her. She was holding her breath and did not notice that her hands had gone up to cover her heart as though to keep it in.

"I love you. I have loved you from the moment we first met in Tyre. I was young and bold. It was not long before I was begging your father for your hand in marriage."

He paused as the words sank in, but Mary was unable to reply. Over the years she had loved him variously as a brother, a father, a companion, a trusted partner. Sometimes she had flirted and teased him as a woman does a man, and she thought he had returned her favors innocently. Now, she wondered if she had unfairly used him. The unwelcome truth was that her intimate playfulness had an unintended result. It had enslaved him.

The words that had been locked inside him for twenty-five years poured out unchecked, insistent words that had waited long for this, their day.

"At the time, you had just broken your betrothal to ben Jahdo and vowed never to marry."

Hanani ben Jahdo. Mary saw him frequently in the market in Magdala, or with his wife and seven children at the synagogue. He seemed to be very happy, and she was glad for that. She had not wanted to hurt him, but she had meant to save him from a far worse fate. She would not marry and inflict a life of demon-induced suffering on a blameless husband and children. Charitably, Hanani and his father had made it easy for her to withdraw her pledge.

"Aaron made me promise that I would never speak to you of my love—because of your demons." Marcus Quintius looked on Mary with assurance and declared, "Now that you are released from their hold on you, I, too, am released from my sacred vow to your father."

Mary laid her head on Marcus' chest and wrapped an arm around him. She closed her eyes and breathed in his familiar scent—the fresh smell of a clean linen tunic, the masculine aroma of leather rising from his belt, and the fragrant oil of Lycian bergamot that he used to soothe his face after he shaved. When his arm went around her waist, she felt the protection and strength she had always associated with him. When his hand moved slightly upward toward her breast and then stopped, she was disappointed. She wanted him to continue.

She thought of the day she had waited for him to arrive, her shoulder broken and bound, insisting that Shoshanna dress her in her best silks and put on the amethyst earrings, commanding the reluctant Mummius to prop her up in a chair by the window so Marcus would find her in the best light. She had wanted to take his breath away. Was this what she had really wanted then, to feel his hands on her body, as she did now?

In her desire, Mary was at once both aroused and ashamed. Had she not just come from such a moment with Jesus? Is this what it meant to be healed? To be free? That she would yearn for men in ways she had taught herself to avoid at all costs? Mary had been very young when she made the commitment not to marry, to keep her affliction to herself. At the time, her choice had seemed a painful and necessary sacrifice. Most people, women particularly, pitied her life of celibacy and loneliness. According to their customs, the life of an unmarried and childless woman was hardly worth the living.

Mary had come to enjoy her life in many ways. She liked being independent. She loved her Pax Magdalena and all the people she helped. Now that she was released from her demons, the longing to be married rose in her with a zeal she thought was buried, and Marcus was offering her what Jesus would not.

What could she possibly add to the life of a man of such *gravitas* and *dignitas*? *Nothing,* she thought. Why, then, did he ask her? It must be love and love alone. What woman does not wish to be so desired? Marcus Quintius was not a man given to patience. In the face of his enduring and long-suffering wait for her, she was compelled to consider his proposal. What would it be like, she wondered, living in Rome as wife of a man like Marcus Quintius Severus?

Mary had never been to Rome, and yet she thought she knew it. Reports of the queen of the Great Sea had come to her from her father, from Mummius, as well as from Marcus. She knew she could not adapt to life there, the social pressures and the politics that would consume her husband and make demands on her. But she might be happy in the country. Mary imagined presiding over a great villa in the Italian countryside, raising sheep and vegetables. And she would have her weaving. Surely Marcus would allow her to continue her fabric business.

It was that word "allow" that troubled her. She remembered her conversation with Jesus—it seemed long ago now—when he first introduced her to the idea of a marriage of the spirit, a relationship of equality that would transcend social norms. And she understood, then, why it was essential to Jesus that he not marry. He did not want to have a woman to obey him, to be legally bound to him. He did not want a woman over whom the Law gave him control, even though he might choose not to exercise it. Mary had accepted the idea of what Jesus offered her, but now she felt it in her heart. She saw more clearly what she must relinquish in order to have the extraordinary life he had invited her into.

Mary wanted to say something encouraging to Marcus, something that would not add to his burden of grief, something like, "This is not the time. Take care of your father's funeral. Write to me." But anything short of the bare truth would only prolong his agony. She sat up straight and removed his arm from around her waist.

"Marcus, dearest, I cannot. Just as your obligations call you away, so do mine. After the Sabbath I am leaving with Jesus to take his message throughout the whole of Judea. I do not know when I shall even return to Magdala."

Marcus' eyes darted around her face as though trying to locate something encouraging, something believable, but there was only resolve.

"You are staying with him for good?"

"I am."

With his dream evaporating even as he grasped for it, Marcus said, "But, I have waited so long." Vainly he attempted to fight off the inevitable, the final loss. "I knew it was too soon," he stammered. "I planned to wait until… My father's death… Please…"

"Marcus, stop. You must know, surely, that I have to go with Jesus."

Marcus Quintius Severus, a man who had never known defeat, knew it now. What should he do in the face of his rejection—surrender? Retreat? Marcus stared at Mary with the loathing he felt when he had caught her and Jesus unawares in the upper room in Capernaum—loathing, mixed with desire and rage, ending in utter confusion.

Aulus Dexius rescued him. Barging suddenly into the room, he said, "Quintius, it is imperative that you depart immediately." He must have seen something of what was going on in Marcus Quintius as he strode over and took hold of his hand and shoulder, pulling him to his feet. "If you do not take advantage of every moment, you will miss the early passage from Joppa. You may have done so already. You *must* go."

Marcus Quintius stared blankly at Aulus Dexius, the picture of Roman manhood, his own kind, standing before him, calling him to his duty. It was the sight of the toga that finally brought Marcus back to himself, the toga and the man-to-man grip on his shoulder, and the deep, commanding voice that said, "*Dignitas*, Marcus."

Marcus Quintius felt himself pushed from a precarious perch on a high ledge onto the solid rock beneath, the enduring foundation, the fail-safe certainty of Rome.

"Thank you, brother," he said, tightening his belt and tilting up his chin. Turning to Mary, all he could manage was, "Farewell, Magdalena."

Aulus Dexius accompanied him to his waiting escort, and he was gone.

CHAPTER 29

"Mistress?"

Demetria had whispered from the doorway, but Mary did not hear. She was sitting on the bed, facing the place next to her where Marcus Quintius had sat, as if searching its emptiness. The vacant space beside her was still warm from his presence, throbbing, like a phantom limb that makes itself known even after it has been severed. Mary was remembering the afternoon of Marcus Quintius' arrival in Magdala, when she was weak and broken from the demons' assault, but still trying as best she could to make herself beautiful for him. How insignificant her efforts seemed now that he was gone, now that, unbelievably, she might never see him again.

"Mistress?" Demetria repeated.

When she looked up at the girl she loved moving timidly toward the bed and saw tears balancing on the thick, blonde lashes of Demetria's glistening, blue-grey eyes, Mary stood up and held her close.

"When is he coming back, Mistress?"

Unable to find even the semblance of reassurance, Mary replied, "It is hard to say."

"Excuse me," came another voice from the doorway.

Mary looked again and saw the lady of the house. Modestly dressed, as always, the magnificent Julia was nonetheless a woman in obvious command of her home.

"Mary," she said, "I am Julia Clemens. Please accept my condolences. Marcus Quintius holds you as one of his dearest friends. You must feel his loss as though it were your own."

"Thank you, Lady..."

"Call me Julia."

"Of course. Julia. What a terrible disruption this must be. Allow me to collect Demetria and her belongings, and we will leave you to restore tranquility to your home."

"Tch, tch. I will hear nothing of that. Come with me. I have a tea of mint and herbs, which I promise will soothe you. You need to recover yourself."

You have no idea, thought Mary, the image of Marcus' cold stare and his bleak "Farewell, Magdalena," floating on the air between them, a thread of smoke trailing him when he disappeared, as though conveying his shade to Sheol, out of reach forever, departed to that netherworld of the spirits.

Mary would welcome a few more moments here, where his memory still lived, before she would have to leave him behind. Julia's observation was correct. She did need to recover before she returned to the intense drama swirling around in the Temple—and Jesus.

Summoning a meager measure of a smile to offer in return, "I would very much appreciate some tea," she said.

As the lady of the domus led Mary to her personal apartment, Demetria followed, downcast, certain that she would be dismissed to her own room there to wait for the twins to rise and have breakfast, for it was still early morning. She was elated when Julia nodded to her, indicating that she should follow.

The three of them sat on cushioned chairs in a small vestibule just outside Julia's bedroom. A citron wood table, inlaid with an intricate pattern of ivory, sandalwood, and cedar, was spread with petite savories and ripe fruits on embossed metal trays. Seeing that Mary selected a few items and put them on her plate, Demetria followed her lead, taking exactly the same number and kinds of delicacies for herself. A slave poured cups of steaming tea. When Mary raised her drink and, momentarily closing her eyes, breathed in the vapors, Demetria did the same, breathing in, but she did not close her eyes. She must watch everything Mary did, to mimic her, so as not to make a wrong move. Having been included in women's activities, she did not want to make a child's mistake.

Demetria was thinking sadly of little Salome and her aunt Joanna, suffering with a demon. Marcus Quintius had departed and, with him, the hope of helping Joanna. Or had it? Sipping tea and eyeing the women, Demetria realized that Marcus Quintius was not the only bridge between worlds. What if she could be that link? Demetria waited alertly for a chance to plead her cause. It was not long before an opportunity presented itself.

Julia was saying to Mary, "It has been a pleasure to have Demetria with us this short time."

"I am gratified to hear it. She is the light of my life in Magdala," Mary replied with an approving glance in Demetria's direction.

"See how she blushes!" observed Julia. "Her modesty is a considerable part of her appeal. If only I could impart some of her attributes to those daughters of mine," she lamented as she picked up a tray of fruit and offered some to Mary.

Demetria seized the moment.

"Junie and Julie are really quite endearing, Lady Julia," she said, stepping into the breach and watching for responses from both the women.

Julia's eyebrows lifted ever so slightly in surprise. "Why do you say so, dear?" she asked, grasping for the slightest compliment to her girls.

"Well, they are high-spirited, of course, but that is preferable to a colorless, uninteresting character, is it not?" Sensing Julia's expanding interest, Demetria dared to proceed. "And amusement is not their only strong point." She took a drink of tea and placed her cup down carefully on the table. "When I saw them with Salome yesterday, I noticed something very kindhearted in them."

The reference to Salome brought a nervous flicker to Julia's eyes. Demetria knew that Mary saw it, too, because her mistress shot her an admonishing glance. She said nothing more, apprehensive about pressing the matter further unless invited.

After a tense, momentary intermission, during which Demetria stared into her lap and Mary stared at Demetria, Julia said casually, "I had forgotten that Salome came to call yesterday." Then, turning to a slave standing in the corner, "Freshen the tea," she ordered.

Demetria thought that it was quite impossible for the mistress of this house to have forgotten anything that had happened in her home yesterday, particularly something having to do with her children. Demetria had led them into thorny territory, and she knew that Mary would want to stop the awkward situation.

"Thank you, Julia," said Mary, taking a last sip from her cup. "The breakfast was delicious, but we do not have time to linger. My friends are waiting at the Temple. They will be concerned."

In spite of these protests, her hostess neither stood nor offered to escort them to the door.

Julia Clemens was in turmoil. Of course she knew that Joanna had been in the grip of her demon yesterday and that little Salome's distress was the result. How she longed to ease Joanna's suffering! She had heard of Jesus, the Galilean wonder-worker. Everyone in Jerusalem was talking about the man who could cure every malady by the laying on of his hands. At night, in bed, when she inquired, Aulus Dexius had told her that Jesus was nothing but an itinerant rabbi, unrefined in the extreme, and would soon be gone from Jerusalem. He had consulted the Jewish High Priest, he said, and was assured of it. He forbade her to speak of him further. Even here, in the protective company of women, Julia was reluctant to lay herself open to the displeasure of her husband.

She was unaware that Demetria could deduce what she was feeling, and so she was surprised when the girl rose from her chair, went to stand directly in front of Mary, and said, "Salome's aunt Joanna is possessed of a terrible demon. Salome loves her like a mother, so that the poor niece is suffering as much as the aunt. Mistress, please, let us ask Jesus to help the Lady Joanna."

Demetria appeared suddenly full-grown. Perhaps some Greek artisan had been at work upon her plump, rounded face, sculpting the hint of angularity beneath the cheekbones and along the jaw line down to the chin, when no one was watching. There was an assurance in her bearing. Her clothing did little to cover the maturing sense of self beneath the layers. Still, increasing maturity alone would not have entitled Demetria to make this request in the presence of such a personage as Julia Clemens.

"Demetria, it is not your place to make that suggestion," Mary said, surprising Demetria with her reprimand.

It was Mary's turn to be surprised when Julia interrupted. "Do not reproach her, Mary. It is my fondest wish to aid my friend Joanna. I fear that the demon that plagues her will kill her. Chuza has tried everything, of course..."

"Chuza?" said Mary. *Herod's steward! O LORD, deliver me.* What had appeared to be a week of harmless hospitality with aristocratic Romans had brought danger.

The idea of Rome's occupation as a cruel domination was ubiquitous, time-honored, and misguided. As a matter of fact, the policy of Rome regarding its provinces was very astute. Governors were instructed to allow as much freedom as possible within their domains, and they rarely interfered with local culture. As a result, in Judea, the actual government was vested in the Jewish Council, a native aristocracy at whose head stood the High Priest.

Rome's financial system was no less commendable. The governors received fixed salaries, and taxes were collected by salaried officials whose books were carefully audited. A large portion of the revenue was spent in improving the province. The one major weakness in this system was the one that grated on the population most. The collection of customs duties was farmed out to the highest bidder, thus making the process liable to abuse. The tax collectors, called publicans, were hated as the most visible and immediate agent of Rome with whom ordinary citizens came into contact. They were widely viewed as thieves robbing God, the true Lord of the land, of what properly belonged to God.

For the most part, things were quiet in Judea. The governor stayed in Caesarea and came to Jerusalem only at festival times, to make sure that the crowds did not become unruly. It was in the interest of the Jewish authorities to maintain the status quo, so that Pax Romana would be preserved, and the Romans would leave them alone to govern as they saw fit. As a result, the Jews were constantly vigilant against anything that might upset their cart, such as rebellious actions by home rule enthusiasts—or the occasional wilderness preacher with a dangerous message. Rome and the Temple cult were, therefore, locked in a mutually beneficial alliance to keep the populace under control.

Jesus had already drawn unfavorable attention from the Jewish authorities as a rabble-rouser. Now, Mary was confronted with a situation that threatened to bring him face to face with Rome as well. How could she steer a course around this peril?

Mary sat down and addressed Julia in a voice that came out faintly when she tried to speak. She cleared her throat and began again. "Julia, Jesus is just a humble rabbi from an inconsequential place called Nazareth, in Galilee."

Julia countered her resistance by saying, "He is a wonder-worker, is he not?"

"Well, yes, I suppose you could call him that."

"Then what does it matter where he comes from?"

"Julia, listen," Mary said, her voice gentler now with rising empathy for the desperate appeal she saw in the Roman's face. "Jesus is a prophet—a Jewish prophet—sent by God with a special message for the Jewish people." Then, struggling to come up with something to avoid Julia's request, she added, "He has nothing to do with gentiles."

In Demetria's unblinking gaze, Mary could almost hear the girl's silent reproach, *What about Chloe? She's a gentile!* and was immediately chagrined. Mary remembered her own audacity when she had pulled Chloe to the seashore and called back the boat filled with Jesus and his disciples. There in the cool waters of the Sea of Galilee, for all to hear, she had asked, insisted really, that Jesus heal Chloe. He had done it without hesitation. But Chloe was one of Mary's weavers, an innocent child, certainly not a member of the royal household.

A sudden image of Jesus' face came into Mary's mind and seemed to fill the room. Is this what he would want? For her to turn her back on a woman suffering for so long? It would be highly improper for a noblewoman such as Joanna to go to the Temple precincts to meet him—was it Mary's responsibility to bring him *here?*

Her mind racing, she barely heard Demetria trying to get her attention.

"What? What did you say, child?"

"I will ask him," she announced brightly.

Mary scoffed at the idea. "You want to do this yourself, ask Jesus to heal Chuza's wife?"

"He likes me. He wouldn't mind."

Mary didn't know whether to rebuke Demetria for insolence or to laugh out loud. If Jesus were here, she knew that he would be laughing. He was always amused by an unexpected turn of events, and consequences never seemed to matter to him when measured against the blossoming of a new perspective in someone. *All right,* she thought, *let it be.*

Moments later, they were walking through the city toward the Temple. Mary watched Demetria, head high with satisfaction and anticipation, and utterly ignorant of the potential peril into which she was leading them. Mary wondered how Jesus would respond to this girl's innocent request to walk directly into the lion's den. Would he allow a Roman matron to introduce him to the wife of Herod's Chief Steward? Would he lay his hands on her and give his substance to driving out her demon, thereby adding the powers of the palace and the Empire to those of the Temple cult already arrayed against him? It would be up to Jesus to decide if it was time for that.

At the Temple gate Mary led Demetria into the Court of the Gentiles and quickly located Jesus.

"What detained you?" he asked.

Pulling Demetria from behind her and pushing her toward Jesus, "Go on."

"Good morning, Jesus. How are you?" Demetria began, not realizing that she had slipped back to her native language.

"Are we speaking Greek, then?" he asked, creases of a smile appearing at the corners of his eyes.

"Oh. Excuse me," she said in Aramaic.

He answered, "I am well, Demetria. How are you?"

She did not intend to be abrupt, but Demetria was so eager to accomplish her mission that she could not maintain pleasantries, and she blurted out, "Will you please go this afternoon and heal Salome's aunt Joanna of a demon?"

As though on cue, Jesus laughed. "Hmm," he said. "I don't know about that. Who is Salome, and where is Aunt Joanna?"

"You are teasing me, I think," said Demetria, blushing.

"Yes, young Greek maid, I am teasing you a little." Then, adopting a more serious tone, he went on, "Tell me more about what you want me to do."

Demetria poured out the story of her little, red-haired friend Salome and the suffering she bore watching her beloved aunt in the grip of a demon. Even the palace physicians could not cure her, she reported, so would Jesus please come to the Clemens' house and drive out the demon? When she was finished, she stood before him, breathing fast, looking expectant.

Jesus was not laughing now. His face had become a pensive mask.

Mary was hoping beyond all hope that he would say no. His actions against the Temple were enough for now! Yet she knew that it was not in him to leave someone to suffer. His compassion, as always, would outstrip his personal needs for security.

Finally he said, "You don't know what you are asking, Demetria."

"I know that you love everyone," she answered back.

Jesus stared at Demetria, or rather through her, for a long time. Eventually, his eyes came into focus on her face.

"It is God who loves everyone, child."

"You are God's prophet, are you not? I have heard people say so," she argued, with the unvarnished clarity of the mind of a child, which Jesus must have found irresistible, because again he was silent for a while, never taking his eyes off her.

"If I agree to do this, Demetria, will you show me the way?" asked Jesus, his sudden smile ravishing.

She gave him back a smile like his own. "Of course I will!"

During the course of their conversation, the disciples, one by one, had gathered around Jesus and caught the gist of Demetria's request. When they heard him agree, they were scandalized.

"Master, you must not!" declared Peter.

Peter did not need to voice what was on all their minds: what Jesus was about to do had the potential to move them all directly into the heart of

Rome, where their conflict with the Jewish authorities would merge into a risky encounter with the Empire, like two rivers flowing together, swamping them in the confluence. Their beautiful Way of peace and love would be nothing more than an insignificant mud turtle stepping stupidly into the flood. This was not why they had followed him from Galilee.

But Jesus, placing his hand on the shoulder of brave Demetria, said, "You are wrong, Peter. This is exactly what I must do."

Thank God we are leaving soon for the safety of the countryside! thought Mary.

The rest of the day flashed by quickly. Much had happened, all of it so unpredictable, so astonishing, that by the time Mary found herself at last alone, in Martha's kitchen, her head was pounding. She remembered a Grecian urn she had once seen in Tyre picturing athletic games with runners engaged in a race. One runner was at the finish line, collapsing in the dust, exhausted.

At the time, she was shocked to learn that Greeks competed without clothing. She was only sixteen, and it was the first time she had seen even the representation of a naked man. Public nudity was not permitted among Jews. Even at home, nakedness was rare. Her instinct was to avert her eyes, but she did not want to seem an unsophisticated provincial to her Roman host, so she did not.

Forcing her mind past its initial aversion, she looked intently at the graceful lines of the urn, the inky blackness of the underlying ground, where the artist had applied a dark terracotta slip to the surface, and the contrasting figures in the natural color, terracotta buff, blushing here and there to coral. The clay burned black had been applied perfectly, thick enough to prevent the surface from misfiring to red, or to streak unevenly. Musculature had been incised with great precision and relief dots applied to create texture in hair and flora. Among Jews, representations of humans and animals were considered idolatrous, so Mary had never been permitted to see anything like this. As she stared, somewhere in her mesmerized consciousness Marcus Quintius' voice was offering a tutorial, explaining that the ideal citizen of Greece developed his body as the vessel for a similarly well developed and balanced mind and that a man's trained body was a requirement of war, the principal weapon of the citizen army.

The urn was pulling, pulling, siren-like, calling her to open her heart, to come to another time and place, to experience the unknown, and to imagine something in a way previously unexplored. Suddenly, she was in the dust. She could smell the sweat and feel the rod-like tendons straining in the runners' legs and the gasping for breath. In her own ears she had the roar of the crowd and, then, on her own face, the rush of victory.

Now, a quarter century later, Mary felt again like that runner at the finish line, utterly spent and ready to crumble. There was one last chore to accomplish before she could allow herself to lie down and sleep. Lighting a bright lamp and placing it on a short stand beside her, Mary sat on the floor and rolled out a piece of parchment. Having acquired writing equipment from Joanna, she dipped a pen in ink, and wrote.

"From Mary in Bethany, to Mummius, Chief Steward. What a remarkable day this has been, my friend! It started before daybreak with the startling arrival of your letter to Marcus Quintius. You can imagine how devastated he was to receive the news of his father's death. You were right; he made straight away for Joppa and Rome. I was so sad to see him go, Mummius, a changed man."

Mary thought that Mummius would assume that she referred to Marcus as "a changed man" because of the exigencies of fortune surrounding his father's demise. She would not tell him how cold he had been when he departed, nor why. She could still see the two Romans with their backs to her as they left the room, Dexius in his toga, Quintius in his traveling clothes. Most Jews despised Rome and its arrogant citizens and its legions, striding through their world, their masters. To her, Rome was and had always been primarily Marcus Quintius, his nobility of spirit, his intellect, his humor, his *dignitas*, and his warmth, generously shared. Now he had withdrawn, separating himself from her as certainly as if a great stone wall had been constructed between them, a wall impossible for her to scale. She wondered helplessly what he was thinking now, on the other side of that wall, making his way to Joppa.

She returned to her letter, determined not to expose her feelings to Mummius.

"I know that Marcus wrote to you of business matters, but he did not know, at the time, of my decision to go with Jesus on a tour of the south, where he will be teaching throughout the towns of Judea. I will not return to Magdala for some time, perhaps many weeks. This was not a difficult decision for me, Mummius, as I am now entirely dedicated to Jesus and his mission.

"There is only one problem, as you have already guessed, and that is Demetria. It goes without saying that she cannot accompany me further—the difficulties of travel, the dangerous conditions of the road—it is just not the place for her. But how to get her back home? Mummius, the answer to that question will be as utterly astonishing to you as it was to me.

"Upon our arrival in Jerusalem, we met and stayed at the home of one Lazarus and his sisters, Martha and Maryam. We had planned to sleep outdoors, where Demetria's presence would have presented no problem. But when we accepted Lazarus' hospitality, of course I could not take a gentile into an unfamiliar Jewish home. Marcus Quintius to the rescue! He had already written to Aulus Dexius and obtained an invitation for Demetria to be a guest in his home. There, Demetria became acquainted with the Clemens' children, two girls, twin Julias, a few years younger than she.

"'Of what possible interest is that?' I hear you asking. Prepare to be amazed. The children are friends with an eleven-year-old girl named Salome, who is, remarkably, a niece of Chuza, who is the chief steward to Herod, and his wife, Joanna. Another marvel: Joanna has for many years been possessed of a demon. You know far more about these matters than I do. All I can say is that it is—or it was—the kind of demon that enters the victim's body and throws it upon the ground. The body becomes rigid and trembling. The eyes roll back in the head, and there is often foaming at the mouth. I believe you may have cast out such demons, Mummius. Did you not tell me so?

"You can guess the rest without hearing it from me. Jesus drove out Joanna's demon and the exalted Chuza is now indebted to him. Which brings me back to Demetria. As soon as the Passover week is over, she will travel to Tiberias with Chuza and Joanna and a portion of the royal household. I want you to be there to meet her and escort her home to Magdala. You know how she fears Tiberias; who would not after what happened to her there? They will travel slowly. It may take a full five days or even more, so you can plan your trip accordingly. I know you enjoy visiting Tiberias, so this is a chance for a little vacation. Do not hesitate to present yourself at the palace; they will expect you.

"Thank you, faithful Mummius, for this service to me and my precious girl. You are my best ally in this and every matter. I have no doubt that in the coming weeks you will look after my home and my worldly goods as dependably as you always have. I will write to you from the road when I can. With an affectionate heart, Mary"

Done, she thought, yawning. Reading the letter over quickly, she was satisfied that she had struck all the right notes so that Mummius would know that he was her confidante, as ever, and would not be able to deduce the turmoil she felt inside.

She was rolling up the scroll when another thought came to Mary's mind. Could it be that Mummius knew of Marcus' love for her? They were the closest of friends with few secrets between them. If Marcus had so long withstood his desire to marry her, almost certainly he would have disclosed it to Mummius; or Mummius, in his cleverness, would have discerned it.

Suddenly she saw everything she had shared with Marcus through Mummius' eyes. She imagined them soaking in the baths at Magdala, lounging around with cups of strong wine, perhaps making men's jokes at her expense. She felt mortified thinking of the dozens of letters she had written to Marcus, dictated to Mummius and inscribed by him. Had he sometimes added furtive notes about her? What had he told Marcus in his own letters?

On the other hand, if Mummius was privy to Marcus' secret desires, he had held them close. What else could be expected from a friend? How difficult it must have been, treading lightly on such a path, remaining loyal to both of them. She did not know how she could face Mummius again. *Well,* she thought, *I do not have to face him. For a time anyway.*

CHAPTER 30

Demetria and Salome sat together upon a stout, reliable donkey, riding north as the royal train slowly wended its way from Jerusalem to Tiberias. The day was warm, and the rhythmic plodding of the furry beast lulled Demetria into a reverie of the past few days, a woeful litany of what-ifs. Among the possible futures that Demetria had anticipated, this particular path was not one. Never had she thought that Mary would just leave, abandon her on the road—to virtual strangers.

Salome's wild red locks were escaping her veil, thread-like tendrils of hammered copper, glinting in the high sun. First one, then two, then three curios counted out by Demetria as they burst their silken cover until at last the defeated veil slid off, revealing a living crown atop the head of the treasure child. Salome pulled her veil back on and, stuffing the hair in impatiently, exclaimed, "Oh, Demetria, I wish I were a man so I could wear a turban that would stay on!" Demetria's arms went around Salome's waist, clinging as though she were a shield, her only protection.

At the end of the trip from Jerusalem, Salome begged her to remain in Tiberias, and Demetria considered it. That in itself was a remarkable turn of events; the city she acutely despised, and once was relieved to see the end of, now seemed a possible refuge? Much as she might long to stay with Salome, however, she knew she had to go home to Rachel and Shoshanna. They had been astonished when she announced that she was going to Jerusalem with Mary. What would they think now that she was returning to Magdala alone? They, too, must be deeply disillusioned by Mary's continued absence on the road with Jesus.

When Joanna and Salome came to say good-bye, the little girl, her lower lip trembling, held out a chubby fist.

"What's this?" asked Demetria.

Salome opened her hand and disclosed a strand of hair. "Aunt Joanna said I could give you this and she has a gold locket to put it in."

Joanna added, "Demetria, my dear, you must promise to send word to me if ever you need anything. Anything, at all. Do you understand?"

"Yes, lady, I understand. I do not know how to thank you for your many kindnesses to me."

"It is I who am in your debt," she replied.

While Demetria held her hair up in back, Joanna tied the locket on with a silk ribbon. Demetria folded her fingers tightly around her golden charm, the soft, copper curl sleeping inside.

The next morning found Mummius waiting in a foyer. It would have been easy for him to walk the five miles from Magdala to Tiberias and go directly to the palace in one morning. Instead, he had stayed in the home of a colleague, a Greek physician, the night before, which gave him an opportunity to wake rested and prepare unhurriedly for his visit to the palace. He had attended carefully to his toilet, applying the kohl around his eyes with a restrained and steady hand. Every hair of his wig was in place, black wings flaring out in perfect symmetry on either side of his neck. His robes were new. He had wanted to make sure his clothing was perfectly clean and unfrayed. He wore his best jewelry, the wide collar of silver and lapis lazuli and the udjat eye bracelet with its multiple rows of small, colored glass beads strung into links. At moments such as this, and they were rare in the Galilean backwater, Mummius was aware of what a magnificent figure he made.

He stood tall and relaxed, long arms clasped together behind his back, admiring an elegant statue of some minor god. Mummius knew that this would be a Roman copy of something Greek. It was a very good copy in marble, whose beautiful, cold white surface had been liberally painted to achieve a lifelike appearance. The painter had done a commendable job. The eyes and hair of the god looked almost real from a distance.

This is where I belong, thought Mummius without rancor. Even here in the insignificant anteroom of a residential wing far from the living quarters of the tetrarch, everything exuded power. The halls carried it, the walls carried it, the impeccable, lowly servant who announced Demetria's arrival carried it.

"Sir, the young lady is here."

Mummius looked up from the sculpture and said affably, "Demetria. It is good to have you safely returned from Jerusalem."

"Thank you for coming, Mummius."

Demetria felt a bewildering rush of happiness to see him. Her surprise deepened into astonishment when he said, "Is this your bag? Here, let me take it," and slung it casually over his shoulder by its strap. On Demetria, the bag hung to her hip; on Mummius it seemed to be tucked into his armpit.

They stepped into the fresh morning air, and the road for home.

"We have a pleasant day for traveling," he said.

"Yes," she replied, unsure what to make of his geniality, but thankful for it nonetheless.

Mummius looked down at the top of Demetria's head as she glided along beside him. She was extremely lovely in a way found occasionally among Greeks, with her yellow mane, the color of a ripe quince, falling in deep, lustrous waves down her back, her fair skin and iridescent blue-grey eyes, not at all in conformance with the dark, smoky, long-limbed, Egyptian standard of beauty, but quite intriguing nonetheless.

He had noticed her growth spurt immediately. It happened that way with children—one day they were sucking their thumbs and mewling, and, before you knew it... He had not seen her for three weeks and the changes were subtle, but marked. The most noticeable was her demeanor, which spoke of a degree of self-confidence that he thought she had no justification to claim. How old was she now? *Fourteen, I think...*

He scrutinized her face, then down past her ears and chin where a glimpse of the small, uncovered, wedge-shaped section of skin at her throat told him that her neck had developed into a long and graceful curve. Now *that* was something an Egyptian could appreciate. He had observed that she was wearing a locket, but knew nothing of its significance. Suddenly Demetria's hand went to her throat and folded around the ornament there, as though to hide it. *Hmm,* he wondered, *what secrets lie within that gold?*

"Did you enjoy your trip?" he asked casually.

"You mean, except for not being able to stay with Mary, and Marcus Quintius' father dying, and having to come home by myself?"

Demetria was Mummius' only ready source of information about everything he wanted to know of the happenings in Jerusalem. He was determined to put her at ease. "Yes, except for those things," he said.

He maintained his sympathetic tone and, before long, she was chattering about the wonderful things she had seen. *Still an eager child,* he thought.

"Well! The first day that we went to the Temple, Jesus picked up a whip and snapped it with a loud crack over the heads of the—the men who sit on benches with coins piled up—what are they called?"

"Money-changers?"

"That's right, the money-changers. Coins were flying and rolling everywhere and the men were chasing them, trying to pick them up. The herders were having difficulty controlling their animals." Demetria's hands were sweeping overhead and punching the air, demonstrating how it was.

Mummius had been to the Temple at Passover. He had seen the crowds, the thousands of sacrificial animals, the exchange of coins to pay the Temple tax. He was imagining the near-stampede, the chaos. "Jesus must have been quite angry."

"Oh, yes, Mummius, you should have seen it! Jesus was in a frightful rage. It was Mary who finally led him away."

Mummius almost stumbled over his own feet. "The mistress led him away?"

"She did. Yes."

"Where were his disciples?"

"They were in the crowd somewhere, I guess. I didn't see them."

"What did she do?"

"She seized his arm and said, 'Rabbouni, it is finished. Let us go.'"

Mummius tried to imagine the soft-spoken Mary issuing a public command, tried to imagine Jesus so unchecked that he would need supervision. There was much about Jesus that Mummius would have emulated if he could, but this was something he would never be reduced to—to lose control, to be bodily guided away by a woman. He wondered why a master of Jesus' stature would permit such degradation to himself. Perhaps he was not the paragon Mummius had believed him to be. Perhaps there was an unexposed weakness.

"What else did Jesus do?"

Demetria seemed encouraged by his questioning. "Mary told you about the Lady Joanna, did she not?"

"Only just briefly."

"I was the one who introduced them!"

She had his full attention now. "That is quite astonishing, Demetria. How did you come to be acquainted with Lady Joanna?"

"Marcus Quintius took me to the home of Aulus Dexius Clemens."

"Yes, yes," he said impatiently, already aware of the arrangements.

"Aulus Dexius has two daughters, twin Julias. I passed my days with them—though they are younger than I—and one day they had a guest. Salome, younger than all of us, who, I was surprised to learn, is the niece of Lady Joanna."

"Ahh. Joanna, who is the wife of Chuza, who is Herod's steward."

"How do you know that?"

"I know lots of things," he said, trying to sound as though he might disclose some of his secrets to her.

"Salome told me that her Aunt Joanna suffered from a demon. Not as bad as Mary's demons; nothing is as awful as that. Anyway, I told the mistress and Lady Julia that we should bring Jesus to heal Joanna."

"By Bast! You didn't!"

"Oh, yes, I did, and Mary said I should be the one to ask him."

"Did you do that, too?"

"I did."

No wonder she seems more mature, he thought, unable to resist a measure of respect.

Mummius continued to press Demetria for details, which she was happy to furnish. The conversation made the walk pass quickly until at last they approached the environs of Mary's farm.

"Here we are," Mummius said. "I have some business in the flax fields. And you have your joyous homecoming to attend to," he added, smiling.

She took her bag from him. "Thank you," she replied, and watched, still amazed at the apparent change in him, as Mummius turned off the road to make his way to the fields behind the house.

Demetria walked the short path to the front door alone, glad to be home. She paused, remembering the first time she had entered here. Almost two years ago now. Long enough to turn from girl to young woman. Long enough to learn to read and write, to converse in Aramaic and Latin, to weave fabrics, to keep house. In Jerusalem, Julia Clemens had treated her as though she were an adult. Perhaps she *was* a woman grown. Demetria drew in a deep breath and stood a little taller as she stepped expectantly across the threshold into the loom room.

Chloe was the first to see her. "Demetria!" her voice rang out in a sweet-sounding lilt. For a moment Demetria, still not accustomed to the sound of Chloe's voice after her long silence, was surprised to hear it, and almost said, "You can talk."

Immediately the other weavers took up exclaiming—Sahadia and Sudi, Avireina and Jamileh, all rushing to her, hugging, smiling, and touching her face and hair. Demetria was laughing as she returned their embraces. Then she started to cry.

"Oh, poor thing!" "Come and sit down," they said, and "What is wrong?"

Demetria sniffled into her handkerchief, "I am just so happy to be home."

Hearing the commotion, Rachel appeared from the kitchen.

"Little Bit!" she cried, hurrying over.

Demetria saw that Rachel looked tired and thought that, even in her enthusiasm, she was holding something back.

"Where is Shoshanna?" Demetria inquired.

Rachel lowered her head and seemed to sink more deeply into her fatigue. Demetria glanced around at the weavers and lifted her shoulders in a silent question.

Her face a worried mask, Sahadia divulged the sad truth. "Shoshanna is in bed."

"At this hour! What has happened?"

Rachel spoke quietly. "She lay down soon after Mary left for Jerusalem, and has hardly gotten up since. She eats little and never goes out."

He could have told me! Demetria fumed, thinking of their long walk from Tiberias when Mummius had mentioned nothing of Shoshanna's condition. It was she, Demetria realized now, who had done all the talking, while he had asked all the questions.

She wasted no time extricating herself from the weavers and moving toward the bedroom. Rachel followed across the courtyard, trying to prepare her.

"I must warn you, Little Bit. She does not look like herself. She is wan and listless. She has grown quite thin."

Demetria did not hear the last caution because she was already at the bedroom door, rounding the corner. She walked past Rachel's cot and then her own, taking no notice, intent on reaching Shoshanna. The old woman's body was turned to the wall.

"Shoshanna?" she whispered. "It is Demetria."

The grey head turned, its thinning hair an ephemeral nimbus that seemed to float above the pillow where it lay. The dimpled cheeks and chin were flaccid, emptied of the padding and moisture that had made them plump. Her brown eyes were faded to a muddy blue and seemed to be set on other things, elsewhere, beyond the room, beyond the moment. Unexpectedly, a little light came into her face, and Shoshanna spoke.

"Girl, you have returned."

Relieved, Demetria said sweetly, "Of course, I have returned. What else would I do?"

"And Mary. She is with you."

Demetria looked for guidance to Rachel, who set her mouth in a thin line and shook her head. Demetria picked up Shoshanna's withered hand and, holding it to her face, felt the chill seep into her cheek. There was a smell, a musty odor, like a closet long closed up. The faint undertone of eucalyptus arose and hung in the still air around them and with it a forlorn thought: could it be that Shoshanna was emptying her mind and body to depart from this world? Were Rachel and Mummius just keeping her comfortable with their ministrations while she did it?

No, that could not be. Shoshanna only needed rest. Demetria would take care of her. She would get better.

Forcing a little cheer into her voice, Demetria said, "Mary is still traveling. She will be home before long, I am sure."

"Wake me when she comes," Shoshanna said in a rasping voice, and closed her eyes.

After a few moments, Rachel, needing to get to work, moved her lips, silently forming the word "supper."

Demetria whispered, "I'll stay for a while."

Nodding, Rachel went to the kitchen. Demetria rested on the floor beside the low cot, holding Shoshanna's hand and watching the erratic rise and fall of her chest beneath the covers.

It was not in Shoshanna's nature to accept gentiles. In the beginning she had resisted Demetria because she was young, because she was Greek, because her presence distracted Mary and disrupted the orderly household. But, like an irrepressible kitten, Demetria had persistently curled herself in Shoshanna's warm, abundant lap and, before long, Shoshanna had welcomed her. She laid her head down on the edge of Shoshanna's bed. "My mamee," she said to the withered hand of the only grandmother she had ever known.

Her next awareness was of Rachel gently shaking her by the shoulder. "Wake up, Little Bit." She lifted her head and slowly unfolded her hand from Shoshanna's so as not to disturb her. Still groggy, she followed Rachel into the kitchen where the delicious smells of roast lamb and bulgur, swirling with the fragrances of parsley and mint, woke her up and set her mouth to watering.

"Where is Mummius?" Demetria asked.

"Who knows? Sometimes he is here for the evening meal, sometimes not."

"Where does he go?"

"Again—who knows? He is well liked in the town. I can't imagine him condescending to carouse with those Greek fishermen, but it is possible, I suppose. I leave food out for him when I go to bed. It is usually eaten by morning. Like feeding an alley cat."

"You eat alone, then?" asked Demetria, imagining the sad, solitary scene of her friend, so used to cooking for a crowd, sitting at the long board, heavy with silence at the end of each day. "Well, good riddance to him," Demetria said, but she was thinking about the genial man who had walked with her this long day, who had carried her bag, who had talked to her like a companion.

Settling into her place at the table, she asked, "Tell me, then, what has happened to Shoshanna?"

"I don't know, Demetria. She has never trusted Jesus. Of course she was grateful when he drove out Mary's demons. But the other changes... The Mary that Shoshanna helped to raise from a baby would never have left her home and family the way she did! To go off with a man she barely knew, to live in Capernaum, to become his disciple, to discard all of us in the process, and to be so happy with him... I think that Mary has broken Shoshanna's heart."

"And yours, Rachel?"

"Yes, mine, too." she said, slapping a spoonful of bulgur onto her plate. A sour look descended upon Rachel's countenance. "Is it not so for you, Little Bit?"

Of course it was so. Demetria thought of her own wounded heart that first night in the house when Mary had left for Capernaum. She remembered the agony of being torn from the arms of her birth mother and shipped away to Galilee. That mother would never have *chosen* to leave her, as Mary had chosen.

Demetria and Rachel were alone here with the worn-out Shoshanna and the intimidating Mummius, who, without knowledge of Mary's whereabouts or when she might return, held complete power in the household as Chief Steward. The two women saw that only by mutual reliance did they have a hope of managing this crisis. Though neither spoke of it, they knew that they would have to learn to live without Mary.

Throughout their meal, they kept up a chatter, each soaking up the other like a dry sponge. Rachel demanded to know everything that had transpired in Jerusalem. "We had very little news," she said, and it became clear that Mummius had kept most of the information in the letters he received to himself. "He can be so…"

"…insufferable," said Demetria.

"I was going to say 'furtive,'" replied Rachel, and they both laughed, enjoying the moment at Mummius' expense.

Demetria regaled Rachel with her description of the Clemens house where she had stayed with Marcus Quintius. She shocked her with the account of Jesus breaking the banks of the money-changers in the Temple. Most astonishing of all was the telling of her acquaintance with members of the royal household and her friendship with Salome, which had resulted in the remarkable healing of Lady Joanna.

"It is as though you have traveled to a foreign country full of magic."

"There is still more to be told," responded Demetria. "And it is very bad."

"Whatever can it be?"

"It's about Marcus Quintius."

"What about him?"

"He is gone."

"Gone where?"

"To Rome."

"Little Bit, what is bad about that? Why should he *not* go to Rome?"

"Rachel, I don't think he will ever come back."

"Well, that cannot be."

"He was in a great temper when he left Mary in Jerusalem."

"Not in a temper at Mary!"

"I'm afraid so."

"For the love of heaven, Demetria, tell me what you are talking about."

Demetria reported what she knew about the letters informing Marcus Quintius of his father's death and how she had gone to fetch Mary from the Temple and bring her to the Clemens house to express condolences. From the hallway, Demetria had overheard snippets of Mary's conversation with Marcus Quintius, things like "Marcus, dearest, I cannot" and "You are staying with him for good?" then "I have waited so long" and "Please..."

"Rachel, it was awful. Aulus Dexius Clemens marched right into the room and told him he had to leave immediately in order to arrive in Joppa in time for the ship. Marcus Quintius replied, 'Thank you, brother,' and then he turned to Mary and said, 'Farewell, Magdalena.' Oh, his face was cruel stone when he uttered that."

Rachel said nothing in response, so Demetria asked, "Do you know anything about their feelings for each other?"

Rachel looked at the head of the table, Mary's place. Her head began a slow nod that quickened into a knowing perception.

"You do know something," urged Demetria.

"Well, as I think back on it, Mary has always delighted in his visits, making us turn the house upside down with cleaning and cooking. She wears her loveliest clothes and usually buys new jewelry in anticipation of his coming."

Indeed, Demetria had been part of the preparations for Marcus Quintius' last arrival, going with Mary on a shopping trip to buy new earrings to match her dress. But the jewelry had been completely forgotten in that night of wolves when Demetria experienced first-hand the ravaging of Mary's demons. Even now, the howling of the nighttime creatures that had threatened them in the streets of Magdala rang in her head. She could feel the weight of Mary's body as she struggled to get her home from the town, in the dead of night, barely able to stand by the time they reached the house. She covered her mouth with her napkin, gagging involuntarily as her nostrils burned again with the stench of Mary's blood drying on her skin.

Mummius had saved Mary from the demons that time, but the encounter had weakened her so badly that, in order to greet Marcus Quintius, she had to be propped up in a chair and drugged to endure the pain. Demetria had been frightened of him, as she was of all Roman men, when he swept into the courtyard like a conqueror of enemies who would put everything right. Observing that everyone else seemed in thrall to him, she watched, awed, as Marcus Quintius lifted Shoshanna's rotund body in his arms, calling her "Shushu," and turning the old woman into a giggling maiden. He had praised Rachel's culinary talents and caused her to blush. Everything about this Roman spoke of familiarity and intimacy. Even Mummius had become cheerful when he appeared.

Demetria had always accepted the version of the story that said he was an old friend of the family who had taken Mary under his wing when her father died, an avuncular figure who taught her how to conduct business and helped her make money in Rome. Now, after her travels with Marcus Quintius, she could see more clearly. Their stay with a Roman family, where he was in his own element, had done much to expose the complexities of the relationship between Mary and Marcus. Would an uncle follow a grown woman to Capernaum, find her a house, and then linger there?

Would a wealthy friend of the family waste time traveling to Jerusalem when clearly he was overdue to return home?

"He has loved her all this time?" Demetria ventured.

"Perhaps that is so," replied Rachel.

"But now he has lost her to Jesus?"

"We have all lost her to Jesus."

"No," said Demetria, resisting.

"She sent you home with strangers, did she not?"

"And now…," said Demetria, nodding toward the bedroom door.

There it was, the unspoken truth, steeped in a shared, simmering anger: they were left to take care of Shoshanna, when it should have been Mary.

Mummius stood at the entrance to Marcus Quintius' rooms in Magdala and hailed the custodian. "Rufus Gaius, to the door!"

He did not have to wait long before he was greeted enthusiastically by the jovial steward and invited in.

"Welcome, friend. Your refreshments await."

"You were expecting me?"

"Expecting? Perhaps. Hoping, yes. You are making it a regular event, Mummius. To my great pleasure, I might add."

Mummius carried no bag, for he had already left a cache of clothing and toiletries here. Following Rufus Gaius into the small, well-appointed atrium, he sank appreciatively into his favorite chair—the regal one with a tasseled cushion of red silk embroidered with lions worked in gold thread—and draped his wrists over its graceful, curved arms.

"Got the good silver out, have you? What's the occasion?" Mummius asked, reaching for a goblet of wine.

"Time for polishing. Thought I'd take advantage of the opportunity to see how well these cups are working," said Rufus with a hearty laugh.

Mummius liked Rufus Gaius. He was just the sort of man Marcus Quintius Severus would want handling his domus. And though Severus did not stay here often, it was important that he have a home base when he traveled to Galilee and not rely completely on Mary's hospitality. In the long interims, Rufus Gaius lived here and attended to everything. He was utterly reliable.

"Any word?"

"It is far too soon, Mummius. Besides, I am sure he would write to you first."

"He might send a letter to me here."

"Why would he do that?"

"Never mind. Just eager to hear from him, I suppose."

Mummius took a deep draft of his wine. Something was wrong. He could feel it in his bones, like a persistent chafe, warning him that Severus was weighed down in some unknown way, and not just by his father's death. He had no information to support the hunch, but he never doubted his intuition. He should have questioned Demetria about this. Maybe she knew something.

Mummius finished his wine and drank another, and another, relaxing, letting down his guard ever so slightly, knowing from experience that Rufus Gaius' lips were firmly sealed over anything and everything that took place in these quarters.

"So, physician, how would you like to be entertained this evening? Dancing girls? Those two Nubians?"

"No girls tonight, Gaius. I have had enough of women at present."

"I can't believe what you're saying, Mummius. You have the magic potions, eh?" he said with a lusty wink.

"It's not that. I am weary of living in a household buzzing with women. Their chattering and giggling and crying provoke me so."

"Perhaps it is the absence of the buzz of the queen bee that provokes you."

Mummius very nearly lashed out at the impertinent suggestion, but, recognizing that Gaius had sunk a little into his cups, he carried on with the banter. Pointing his index and middle fingers, making a sign against the evil eye, he protested, "I'll have no more women around me!"

"More wine then."

"Yes, more wine."

They drank into the night until they were slurring the words of their bawdy jokes and couldn't remember the verses of the raucous songs they sang and had to make them up as they went. When Gaius could sustain it no more and fell asleep where he sat, Mummius took hold of the nape of his tunic and dragged him to bed. "Sleep it off, comrade," he said. Meaning to toss him good-naturedly onto the mattress, Mummius lost his grip and Gaius fell, one leg dangling off. "Sorry," said Mummius, folding the errant limb up onto the bed.

Mummius staggered only slightly on the way to his sleeping cubicle. From a small chest of potions he took a vial of liquid, poured some into a cup and swallowed the remedy that ensured he would experience no after-effects of his drinking when he woke. He chuckled, knowing the suffering Rufus Gaius would, on the morrow, be holding his head and puking, if and when he ever did arise.

Mummius undressed slowly and smoothed out his tunic and robe over a rack placed in the corner for that purpose. He poured water from a pitcher into a bowl and splashed his face to clear his head. He shook his head to dry it and dabbed the remaining water with a towel. This he folded into a tidy square and placed on the table beside the bowl. Then, as he did every night before retiring, he took out a mirror, a round sheet of polished brass, and examined his face. Turning first one way and then another, he gently pressed on the skin on his cheekbones and under his eyes, looking in the lamplight for puffiness and padding. He was a eunuch, yes, but he would never, ever be fat and ungainly like those sagging, sycophantic geldings one found at court standing guard over harems of women. Whatever it took, he would be lean and taut and agile till he died.

Mummius was satisfied with his life. He had successfully mitigated any resistance to his management of Mary's affairs, ingratiating himself to everyone who might raise doubts, particularly the priests. He had assured them that the tithe they had come to expect would be paid promptly and in full. What did they care about Mary? As long as their palms were greased, they were appeased. How would they know if he made tithes to himself first?

The weavers had been somewhat sullen, but they had to earn a living. So far, they had continued to work industriously. Now that Demetria was back, he could use her to keep them singing. She was smart; he could teach her enough of the business to occupy her, but not so much as to cause suspicion. If only he knew what was going on with Severus...

His nightly inspection completed to his satisfaction, Mummius lay down and breathed in the clean fragrance of freshly laundered bedding—another refinement of the sophistication of the house. *I wish Severus were here,* he thought, drifting into sleep.

Poor Mummius. Even if he had been aware of it, which he was not, he would never have been able to admit the truth: it was not Severus whom he missed, but Mary.

CHAPTER 31

Mary and Jesus were time travelers now. Along with their friends, they traced unhurried paths through the ancient land of Judea, traversed the countryside where storied towns came alive, each with its own particular chronicle calling up the fabled deeds of their ancestors. Here the world of Spirit had become the common property of their people. This Judea, where the world of ordinary experience intersected with the world of Spirit, had bred a group of mystics—seers and wonder-workers, prophets and reformers—who bridged the two worlds, men and women who knew the world of Spirit firsthand.

The tradition of everyday persons being elevated by God to Spirit-filled, mystical experience was not unique to Jews, but it did dominate their nation's political life in a way unknown to others. God was their king, the very leader of the state. No other nation made such a claim. Human mediators, the greatest of whom was Moses, received the disclosures of God; then others wrote them down in sacred scriptures, which had come to be called "the Law and the Prophets." This is what they said: the Spirit of God is present everywhere, immanent and transcendent, not somewhere else; not "out there." God is all around us and within us. We are in God; everything is in God.

If contemporary dogma had come to emphasize the letter of the Law, rather than the underlying truth, well, that was part of why Jesus had brought them to Judea. The farther they moved away from Jerusalem, the more apparent his purpose became. He wanted to leave the frenetic power politics of the Temple cult behind and concentrate on bringing the message of God's love directly to the ordinary people of the provinces. Here, in Judea, he would follow in the footsteps of the Spirit-filled intermediaries, who, like Abraham, saw the doorway into the other world, which he called "the gate of heaven," and "knew God face to face" like Moses, or was carried into the other world by "chariots of fire," like Elijah. All those charismatics and more, like John the Baptizer in that present day, were known for their intimacy with God. Many had even been called "son of God" by heavenly voices. It was in this stream of Spirit-filled intermediaries between the worlds that Jesus stood, and now, through Judea, walked.

Mary had adapted easily to their journey through history, a four-month expedition during which they traveled the country in a slow southwest loop. At each stop they fell into a guessing game, trying to remember as many events as they could that venerated the location. Hebron was a fitting beginning to their tour, because it was there that Abraham—the first of their people to hear the voice of God—had entertained angels unaware when three strangers came to his tent. They recalled that Abraham offered them hospitality: water to wash their feet and a lavish preparation of veal, cheese, meal cakes and milk. After they had eaten, the guests gave Abraham and his wife a blessing from the LORD: Sarah would have a son, and from this son would spring a mighty nation.

After Hebron, they came to Beersheba, and Jesus asked his followers, "What has Queen Jezebel to do with this place?"

Everyone knew the story of Jezebel in the distant north, but no one could remember what connection she might have to Beersheba, so far to the south.

Suddenly, Mary said, "I know! Elijah fled here from Jezebel's wrath."

"Exactly," said Jesus. "Well done, Mary."

Even though she was the wife of the king of Israel, Jezebel had been a worshipper of Baal, the popular Canaanite storm-weather-god. Jezebel was intolerant of faiths other than her own, so she ordered all the prophets of Israel to be slain. But Elijah escaped the massacre and came to Beersheba, where the LORD spoke to him through an angel and sent him into the wilderness. There he stayed for forty days and forty nights and prayed and had visions from the other world.

They walked westward to Gaza, and no one had difficulty remembering the famous story associated with that town. Here it was that the mighty Samson, consorting with Delilah, a Philistine, had been vexed by her into revealing the source of his great strength. When she sold the secret to the Philistines, they cut off his hair and his strength was gone—and God was gone from him, too, because he had broken his promise to God not to divulge his secret.

"Women can be so wicked," said John, teasing.

"Men can be so weak," replied Mary, and they laughed.

From Gaza they made their way north along the Mediterranean coast to Joppa, the port of entry to Judea, and, for pilgrims, the beginning of the route inland to Jerusalem. All along the way, when they stopped, they did not go into the synagogues, but gathered at wells in or near the towns. There Jesus took the water for baptizing, and often the disciples baptized, too, for Jesus was not the only one on whom the Spirit of God descended. Mary would never forget the first time it happened to her.

Very soon after they started, so many people were coming to be baptized that Jesus could not do it all himself, so he asked Peter to help. By the end of the first week, all the men were baptizing the crowds until, finally, Jesus stepped aside and let them do it.

One day Jesus and Mary were standing a little way off from the well where many people were waiting their turn. A woman with two squirming children, far at the back of the swarm, became impatient and, stepping out, walked toward them. Mary turned slightly, inviting the woman to approach Jesus. But it was Mary she wanted. Holding her toddler by the hand and cradling a baby in the other arm, she stood directly in front of Mary, eye to eye, and waited. She would not move. Nor would Jesus, when Mary beckoned to him. Seeing no alternative, Mary nodded. Jesus held out his arms for the children, and their mother handed them over to him.

Mary and the woman walked toward the well surrounded by the crowd in the desert. The disciples glanced questioningly at Jesus, but John, ever her champion, stepped aside, taking a segment of the crowd with him, and made room. Silence fell over the scene as Mary rolled up her sleeves and plunged her arms into a basin that had been filled with water. As the water rose to her elbows, Mary's arms were strangely warmed where they were submerged. She felt the warmth flow up to her shoulders and swirl within her chest.

When she raised her dripping hands and placed them on the head bowed in front of her, the Spirit-warmed water mingled with the woman's hair and flowed down her neck and onto her breast, darkening the bodice of her dress. Time slowed. And stopped. There was nothing but the women and the water.

Mary spoke. "You are welcome, sister, into the Reign of God," she declared, and no one could distinguish the baptismal water from the tears that flooded the woman's face.

Neither could Mary distinguish the water from the warm stream of power that inundated her heart and very nearly took her breath away. It was like standing in the Sea of Galilee, with Jesus guiding her, healing Sudi's wounds and bruises. She had become a channel for a power greater than herself. Around her, women were lining up. Old ones leaning on walking sticks, mothers cradling suckling infants, women of means mingling with prostitutes, each one came to receive her initiation into the Reign of God, as equals. Mary baptized them all.

The other disciples who witnessed it looked at her differently after that. For a while, the divisions between men and women fell away. Awed and humbled, they became united, co-workers with Jesus.

For four cycles of the moon, from Passover until that day, Mary had felt the thrill of offering herself as a vessel in service to others. Now, she had a problem, something that made her wish it were over.

On an early September afternoon, Mary came to the shore and sat in solitude, staring out to sea, the brisk business of the port of Joppa swirling around her. She covered her knees with her skirt and hugged them to her chest, encircling her pain. The day before, when a gripping ache in her belly had caused her to wince, she moved a short distance away from the well and sat down. What had she eaten, she wondered, that would cause this sudden discomfort? Perhaps she should withdraw to the latrine pit, in case her bowels loosened unexpectedly. Then, another stab inside and the unmistakable surprise of warm menstrual blood dampening her inner thighs.

How long had it been since her last monthly cycle? A year at least, perhaps two. Occasionally her body would taunt her with an ache in the belly or some brief spotting, but, as time wore on, and the moon waxed and waned, she had come to accept that she had forever lost the sure mark of womanhood.

She was unprepared. At home she would have had a ready supply of soft wool batting, but, here on the road, she was now forced to tear strips of fabric from one of her veils to tuck into her loincloth. Even so, underclothes were by no means her most pressing problem. Under the Law, she would be unclean for the duration of her cycle and must not associate with men. Afterwards, she would need to perform the cleansing ritual before rejoining them and taking up her ordinary duties.

She tried to imagine asking Jesus to interrupt their journey, stay a while in Joppa, so she could separate herself. The words for such a request could not be found. Women did not mention these matters to men. At home, they removed themselves as necessary, and it was never spoken of.

Perhaps she should not speak of it now. No one would know she was unclean if she did not tell. Would it be so wrong to hide her condition and let them carry on, unaware? Was Jesus not forever speaking against being slaves to the Law and missing the underlying truth? She did not feel unclean. That onerous burden had been lifted when Jesus drove out the demons, saying that it was not her fault, assuring her that God was not punishing her. If possession by demons did not make her unclean, then surely her monthly cycle did not. Their business in Joppa was over, and it was time to move on. The unimpeded progress of their mission was more important than her bodily functions. Surely it was.

Mary studied the waters of the Great Sea, shimmering in a long line against the hot blue sky, casting about for a solution to her dilemma, when out of the western horizon came the thought that it would have been from this place that Marcus Quintius had departed for Rome, sailing away into that very horizon. Another stabbing pain, not of the belly but of the heart, ripped through her and caused tears to spring to her eyes, evidence of the undercurrent of sorrow attending the loss of Marcus. It was never far from her, try as she might to ignore it. Oddly, she found herself wondering how Roman women took care of their monthly hygiene.

"Jonah took ship for Tarshish from here," came a voice from overhead.

Shielding her eyes with her hand, she looked up and saw that it was John, whom Mary had grown to love for his humor and his generosity, come in search of her.

"And wound up in the belly of a great fish!" she answered, sweeping away the tears.

She turned up her palm above the sand, so he, too, sat down and looked at her, his brow suddenly furrowed. "Are you not well, sister?"

In the comfort of John's presence and with the gentle sound of the tide going out, Mary made her decision. Like Jonah, who had tried to escape God's intention for him, she was tempted to flee, to take the easy way out. It was no use. God had called her; she had made her commitment.

"Thank you, John. I am quite well," she said, "but I will miss the sea when we turn inland for Lydda."

"Tomorrow," he said.

"Yes," she replied, "tomorrow."

It was done. Mary would keep her own counsel. She would do nothing to delay their travels. Again she hugged her knees and offered a pained smile, which she intended for John to take as a sign of sadness at the prospect of leaving the fresh sea air behind.

They walked on, into the interior through Lydda, Accaron, and Emmaus. Another four months they traveled, southeasterly, and then circling back up again to the north. Autumn came and went, and it seemed that they had spoken to every living creature in the Judean countryside, spreading the good news of the Reign of God, until, at long last, all the towns of Judea were behind them, and they came, in December, to the northern border. Now, only Samaria lay between Judea on the south and Galilee in the north. As with horses nearing the stable at the end of the day, *Almost home!* strained in every heart.

Starting early that day, they had already walked many miles to the border, then another eight miles into Samarian territory to the place of Jacob's well, near the city of Sychar, arriving about noon. The rainy season had made the traveling heavy, and all were tired, so they rested at the proverbial well-seat of old, first established by the patriarch Jacob. Disappointed to find no rope to use for drawing from the well, they drank what was left from their depleted and flattened water skins.

"Tell us the story of Jacob, Master," said James.

"Leave him alone. Can't you see that he is too tired for storytelling?" said Andrew.

"No, we want to hear," said Philip. "The story, Master, please."

To quiet their peevishness with a tale, Jesus consented. "All right, then," he said. "In the days of the patriarchs, long ago, Isaac, son of Father Abraham, had twin sons by his wife, Rebecca. Esau was the elder by a few minutes, and Jacob the younger. Esau, being firstborn, was naturally Isaac's legitimate heir. Which was good, because Isaac preferred the rugged and ruddy outdoorsman Esau to the younger son, who was a homebody. But Rebecca loved her baby-boy Jacob.

"Now, Rebecca had received a prophecy that Jacob would become preeminent over his elder brother, but was she was content to leave the matter in God's hands? Oh, no, not she! When the boys grew to manhood, she conspired with Jacob to wrest his birthright, the rightful inheritance of the firstborn son, from Esau. Fearing that Esau would kill Jacob in revenge, Rebecca sent the younger son away to her relatives in the north, to Haran. There he stayed for twenty years, marrying first Leah and then her comely sister Rachel, all the while working like a slave for his father-in-law, Laban. During that time, God blessed him with twelve children—eleven sons and one daughter, called Dinah—by his two wives and his two concubines, the wives' maids.

"At long last Jacob grew weary of his unscrupulous father-in-law—who was every bit as deceitful as he himself had been to his own brother, I might add—so he decided to return home, hoping that, after so long a time, Esau would forgive him and welcome him back. On the way, he had a fierce wrestling contest with God. After the encounter, God said to him, 'Today I am giving you a new name. From now on you will no longer be called Jacob, but Israel,' which means 'let God rule.'

"After that, Jacob was a new man, no longer trusting to his own shrewdness for success, but relying on the Spirit of God alone. When he met up with his brother, Esau, he asked for, and obtained, forgiveness for the wrongs he had perpetrated against him. By then Esau was a prosperous man with his own large clan, so he could afford to be magnanimous.

"And so it was that Jacob came to Canaan with his wives and his children and all his vast flocks of sheep and goats and bought a large parcel of land, where he settled. Here, he established this very well where we sit and where all generations from that day have drawn water. All around this place are springs of living water, the kind which flows in streams and fountains, but the still water from this well is superior to all."

Sensing that the storytelling was about to end, James nudged Jesus on. "But amongst all his blessings, Jacob had a terrible misfortune."

"Indeed he did. The ten elder sons sold the youngest, Joseph, to traders passing through, and the traders took the boy as a slave to Egypt."

"Because he was Jacob's favorite."

"And their jealousy got the best of them," said Jesus, rubbing his eyes. "But that is for another time."

The story finished, all were quiet, immersed in their belonging. Everyone among them was descended from those eleven sons of Jacob—renamed "Israel" by God—and the twelfth that was later born to him in advanced old age. Ever after, Israelites would be brothers and sisters of one blood and one heritage, chosen to shine the light of God into the world.

Peter's empty stomach broke the silence with rumbling.

"Time to eat, is it, my Rock?" Jesus chuckled.

"Come on," said James, taking a last sip of water and standing up. "Let's go into the town and buy some food."

"Must we all go?" grumbled Andrew.

Nathanael, usually placid, snapped. "We need to stick together! You don't know when some of these vulgar Samaritans might turn hostile."

"He's right. Get on your feet, boy," added Philip.

"Brothers, let us not insult each other. There is safety in numbers," offered John. "The sooner we get going, the sooner we eat."

Simon Peter, ever the spokesman, turned to Jesus to explain. "Master, we are quarrelsome because we are tired of traveling. We have been gone too long from our families and our work."

It was true. Everything at home had been neglected. Peter's boats had dried up and were falling to pieces in the heat of the summer sun, and his large investment in nets was by now beginning to rot at the seashore, unattended for almost nine months. He had left his wife and his invalid mother to make do as best they could without him. Each man had his own reasons for being anxious.

"Soon we will have been absent for a year. We *must* be there for the next harvest. If we could be sure that we are going home soon..."

"I understand," replied Jesus. "All right, Peter. We will not stop again before Galilee."

Some of the men whooped with joy; others merely sighed with relief.

"Off you go, then," Jesus said.

Hearts made light by the knowledge that their journey was almost finished, they formed a protective circle with Mary at the center, for it was she who would make their purchases, and set out for Sychar, two miles distant, leaving Jesus alone at the well.

"We'll bring a rope!" Andrew shouted over his shoulder.

When they were just out of sight, Jesus slid down wearily and leaned against the stone wall surrounding the well. His eyes burned. Rubbing only made them worse, so he blinked rapidly, trying to moisten them. Taking up his water bottle, he sucked out the last drops and tossed it onto the ground. Peter was right. It was time to go home. He had dragged his friends through the countryside, sleeping under first the stars at night, and then in winter, the rain clouds, for eight long months. He, too, was tired.

What could be said of their journey now that it was nearly finished? What had he accomplished? Did anyone among the thousands who came out to see them really understand his message? He wanted them to know that there were two different ways of living: the way of Spirit—wise, free and enlightened—and the way of the world—foolish, enslaved and blind. His overriding goal was to inspire people to center their lives not in the material world, but in the Spirit.

He knew his message was radical. The entire social and religious structure of his culture was based on the quest for security through family, money, social position and religion. This idea was so deeply embedded that from it had emerged a politics of holiness, a rigid hierarchy that governed every aspect of individual and community life. Jesus insisted it was a bag of snares.

Spirit, on the other hand, is compassionate, he said. In Hebrew and Aramaic the word for "compassion" is the plural of "womb," precisely the image that Jesus wanted to convey: Spirit as a nourishing, life-giving womb. Jesus stressed that compassion was a more appropriate model than holiness for conceiving of God, and community as well. Everyone falls short of God's holiness. Love for the sinner was what Jesus wanted, not punishment. He wanted a foundation of mercy to eliminate social boundaries and divisions. He knew that for those secure within the conventional mores of their culture, such a transformation could be hard; but he also knew that for those burdened by the restrictions of the culture—the poor, the sick, and women—it could be a welcome relief. Jesus' thoughts wandered to Nicodemus, the courageous Pharisee, who had taken a few brave steps against the holiness code of which he was an integral part.

As Jesus sat thus pensive, there came to the well a woman with a grass rope coiled over one arm. She was tall for a Samaritan. Her face, by nature soft and round, had turned hard-looking because of its etched-in scowl. Her hair had been colored false with henna, and there was defiance in her posture that belied her lowly status.

The woman did not notice him until she leaned over the well, ready to lower her rope. Startled to see the top of his bowed head and his muddy sandals sticking out from under his robe, she almost dropped her water pot onto the stone pavement below.

If the disciples feared to walk unaccompanied among Samaritans, imagine what this friendless woman must have felt when she saw a Jew sitting beside her well, within inches of her. She glanced around hoping to see another person whose presence might protect her, anyone at all, though at the same time knowing that the area was entirely deserted. In fact, that was the reason she had come here at midday—to be by herself. Other women drew their water early in the morning, but she had learned to avoid them and their malicious verbal attacks by waiting till noon. She was a solitary woman because she was shunned.

When Jesus looked up at her, she closed her veil tightly around her face and stepped back.

"Will you give me a drink of water, please?" he asked quietly. "I am very thirsty."

The woman was so surprised by his request that she momentarily forgot her fear. Shielding her chest with her water pot, she shot back a question. "How is it that you, a Jew, are asking for a drink from me, as I am a Samaritan woman?"

He told her the most remarkable thing. "If you knew what a wonderful gift God has for you, you would be the one asking me for some water—living water."

"What are you talking about? First you ask for water, then you offer it? Where are your bucket and your water pot that you can get living water? Do you think, sir, that you're greater than our Father Jacob, who gave us this well?"

Seeing that the woman was brave enough to challenge him, Jesus felt a burst of encouragement.

"Even Jacob and his children and his flocks were thirsty again after drinking from this well. But anyone who drinks the water I have to give will never thirst again. It comes from an eternal spring that waters people with life, forever."

The woman looked Jesus up and down, squinting. She had lived a hard existence, and she had depended upon a string of men to support her. For this she was shunned by the community and reviled by the priests. Every day her errand for water was a cruel reminder of the rejection inflicted on her by the other women.

"I am sick and tired of coming here alone to draw from this well. Are you a prophet that you have living water that I can drink and not be thirsty again? Give me some of your water, then, prophet!"

The woman was mocking him, but he remained sincere. Her hard face and flinty look were relaxed by a tentative quiver of hope. All she really wanted was to be accepted. Many people had requested many things from Jesus, but he could not remember anyone ever coming to him for something as simple as acceptance.

"Why do you rely on men?"

"Ha! A prophet with his head in the clouds," she scoffed. "How do you think any woman lives?"

"No. I mean, why do you not rely on God?"

The bitterness in her face deepened. "It is God who condemns me."

"Why do you say this?"

"You know the Law. You can see! I have no family, no honor."

"People put too much store in honor."

"Are you saying that honor means nothing?"

"I am saying that neither honor nor wealth nor family is the path to God."

The suffering of the woman's life seemed to rise up and overtake her from within when she whispered, "I wouldn't know what the path to God is. It is certainly not the one I am on."

"What do you mean?"

"I am sorry for how I have lived, being hurt, hurting others in return. Look at the result. I am alone and unloved. I wish I could change my life, but I do not know how. It is too late."

Jesus looked into the longing eyes of this reviled and wounded Samaritan woman and saw mirrored there his own longing for acceptance. He drew a deep breath and whispered the words he was desperate to say, to the one who was desperate to hear.

"God cares for your suffering, dear woman. I promise you, there is abundant life in the Reign of God."

"Not for me."

"Yes, surely for you. The Reign of God, where all is forgiven, is here, now, right in front of you."

"I would like to believe it." Now she was no longer scoffing, but trying to understand. "So, the path to God is in that living water of yours?"

"You say you regret the things you have done. You say you want to change your life. The path to God is your own desiring heart."

They talked for a long time, Jesus and the woman at the well. In spite of her personal tragedies, she was a devout woman who knew her theology, and they debated back and forth the differences between Samaritans and Jews.

"I prefer to worship outdoors," she declared, "where we find God on the mountain, and not like you Jews inside a Temple building in Jerusalem!"

Jesus laughed at that. "I can't say that I blame you for it. Tell me, woman, what do you think of this? A time will come when all people will worship God together and it won't be on this mountain *or* in Jerusalem."

"I will believe that when I see it with my eyes," she replied, looking at him askance. "I do know this, though—that the Messiah will come and, when he does, he will tell us everything."

"Messiah—Anointed One." A title customarily applied to anyone anointed with holy oil, like the high priest or the king. Abraham and Isaac had been called Messiah, as had even the Persian king Cyrus, because they were chosen to be administrators of the kingdom of God on earth. But when God promised the legendary King David that the throne would remain in his family forever, the title came to denote the representative of David's royal line. When the prophets of Israel spoke of a king who would one day appear to save the people from their oppressors, the word naturally was attached to that future deliverer. By the time Jesus sat with the Samaritan woman at the well near Sychar, "Messiah" was commonly understood to be the one who would come, empowered by God's resident Spirit, to establish a kingdom of God on earth, and, specifically, to drive the Romans out of their land by military action.

Suddenly the woman at the well fell silent and looked with narrowed eyes at Jesus' face. He stared back quizzically, but did not interrupt the stirring in her mind. What was she thinking, this outcast Samaritan woman, that would cause her abruptly to demand of him, "Are *you* the Messiah?"

Jesus was caught off guard. His mouth opened slightly as though to speak, but he could not find voice. When he recovered himself, he laid his hand lightly on her shoulder and put forward his own question, "Who do you think that I am?"

The woman let out a little gasp, not because a Jew had touched her but because of the fire from his hand where it lay. Her dark, brown eyes were opened wide, held by his gaze. "Only the Messiah would see where we will worship God in the future. Only the Messiah could see into my heart and make it free," she said, her voice trailing off, as if following her train of thought.

Jesus' unwavering gaze, his fiery touch, and his silence, seemed to lift her desire into belief. She jumped from her seat on the ground. "You are the Messiah! I must tell them all!" she announced, and she fled, abandoning her water pot. Jesus was left sitting on the ground alone, the sound of her "Messiah" ringing in his head.

The Samaritan woman was declaring now that this Messiah was a man of peace, not war. A man of compassion, not regulations. A man who had talked with God and brought her the message that, in spite of all the deprecating, demeaning things she had done, her sins were forgiven: God loved her. The Law had been wrongly used to imprison her. Jesus said that the soul of the Law was to love God and love each other. The Reign of God was not for the powerful, but for the compassionate. All she needed to enter the Reign of God was her own contrite heart. And compassion. For others and for herself.

The disciples, returning from their errand, were startled to see from afar that Jesus was talking openly to a Samaritan woman. They were accustomed to his surprising behaviors and so said nothing about it, just let her pass as she ran away.

Andrew untied a cloth he was carrying and spread it out on the ground. His bad temper apparently dispelled by their success, he said triumphantly, "Look what we found to eat!"

Jesus was not interested in warm bread, tidbits of roasted meat and sweet, chewy dates. "I'm not hungry," he said and turned away from them. He walked a little way off, detached, otherworldly, seeming to float as though his feet hovered over the ground rather than making contact with it. A light glowed from him, concentrated around his head and shoulders.

Mary had seen him like that before. "Leave him alone a while. He will come back when he is ready."

They ate, but it was a very solemn midday meal. When it was over and they were resting, Jesus returned.

"Now will you eat, Master?" "Please." "It is delicious." "You need to have some food or you will faint from fatigue." They all urged him.

"No, no food. The only food I need is to do the work that God sent me to do. You think the harvest is in the future, Peter? Look over there," he said, nodding in the direction of Sychar. "The harvest is coming to us!"

A huge throng was moving toward them, led by, of all people, the woman they had seen with him at the well, the woman who had fled.

The headman of the town of Sychar approached Jesus. "This woman came and told us that she had met the Messiah at Jacob's well, and we came to see for ourselves."

"Why did you listen to someone who is reviled by you?"

"Look at the change in her!" he declared.

It was true. Her transformation was extraordinary. Smiling, covered in joy, she had rushed into town, with no hesitation and no doubt, to proclaim the wonderful news to her tormentors. Of course, they had to see for themselves, and when they did, the citizens of Sychar begged him to return and stay for a while. He walked there with them, listening contentedly to their amiable quarrelling over who should have the honor of hosting him and his friends.

It was a remarkable scene, eight wandering Jews embraced by a whole town of Samaritans, who drank their fill of Jesus and his message. It seemed that they, too, had been longing for acceptance, ever since they had asked permission—500 years ago—to participate in the erection of the Temple in Jerusalem. Their offer had been spurned by the Jews because Samaritans had a history of combining idolatries with the worship of the One God. Samaritans were neither of pure Hebrew blood nor of uncontaminated worship. The resulting repugnance on the part of most Jews for association with Samaritans had hardened as the centuries rolled on. Now Samaritans were calling Jesus the long-awaited Messiah.

At the end of that unlikely day, Mary drew Jesus aside.

"What happened out there at the well?" she asked.

"Oh, Mary," he said, "through these months of traveling and teaching, I have been longing for someone like her. She is the first, besides us, to understand what I am saying about the Reign of God and to announce it to others." His eyes closed; tears eased from beneath their lids.

Mary placed her hand over his and stroked it. "Now, at last, the recognition you are worthy of," she said, but she was thinking, *Why her? Why was that particular woman chosen to be first evangelist to declare him publicly—and to these Samaritans?*

CHAPTER 32

Demetria was busy at her loom. In her hands the shuttle was flying back and forth through the thick warp threads as though they were ethereal, offering no resistance. The loom was part of her now, an extension of her hands and arms. Often she had noticed a look of rapture on the faces of the accomplished weavers and envied them. Now she understood.

"This is quite lovely," said Sahadia. She knelt on the floor and put her face closer to the emerging fabric. "I did not realize you had become so skilled."

"Nor I, Sahadia. It feels wonderful!"

Demetria stole a fleeting look at the woman's dark face, deeply lined with sorrows, the most recent of which was her daughter Sudi's broken engagement; and in that brief glance Demetria saw what had happened. With Mary gone and Shoshanna not well, Sahadia had become leader in the loom room, someone to be liaison with Mummius, for he did not have the foggiest notion of how to deal with these weavers who were, ultimately, the source of Mary's financial success. They were the workers who produced the exquisite fabrics that channeled money from Rome into the household.

"What are you making, dear?" asked Sahadia.

"A shawl for Shoshanna," Demetria answered brightly. "Something new for spring. Lightweight and pretty."

The lines in Sahadia's face deepened. "Shoshanna has plenty of shawls."

Enchanted by the spellbinding work emerging under her fingers, Demetria exclaimed, "Not like this one!"

Sahadia placed her hand in the path of Demetria's shuttle, leaving a bungle in the near-perfect cloth. Demetria frowned, her work, and her euphoria, abruptly halted.

"Come with me," said Sahadia.

When they were seated face to face at the kitchen table, Demetria demanded, "Why did you do that?"

"Do you not realize that Shoshanna is very sick?"

"Of course I know that she is sick. That is why I am making the shawl, to help her get well. I talk to her about it. She likes it. She taught me to weave, you know." Demetria could hear the note of desperation in her own babbling.

"Child, listen to me. Shoshanna will not get well."

"How do you know? You don't live here! I see her night and day. She is better. I take care of her."

That much was true. Ever since she had returned from Jerusalem—nine months ago it was—Demetria had nursed Shoshanna, holding a bowl of water to her lips, feeding her mashed vegetables with a spoon, even reading to her from the Torah. Every two weeks, she bathed Shoshanna's entire body with warm water, which the patient protested as a ridiculous extravagance. Demetria persisted, for it was then that she could take note of the angry bed sores that never went away. She applied Mummius' salves to the wounds, which kept infection at bay and provided some relief, though they could not prevent them. But it was *not* true that Shoshanna was better.

Sahadia's dark, wrinkled eyes softened with compassion. "You must accept the truth, Demetria. It is only your looking after her that has kept her alive this long. Shoshanna is dying."

"No! You are wrong. Do not say this again!"

Demetria stormed from the room out to the courtyard. Pacing blindly around the pavement, she felt trapped. She wanted to get far away from Sahadia's terrifying words. Driven by fear, she took refuge in Mary's quiet room. She sat on the bed and looked over the personal belongings resting on a small table nearby: the comb she had used on the mistress' extraordinary, ebony-colored hair; a smooth stick wrapped tightly with a piece of sheepskin with which she buffed Mary's nails; and a box of inlaid wood containing several pairs of earrings. Mary's scent was all around, in her clothing and linens. Mary was here, even when she was not. She was here in Demetria, the daughter Mary had ever longed for. She was here in the women: Shoshanna; Rachel and the weavers, each of whom Mary had rescued and provided with the means to earn a living.

It was an uncommon situation, this assortment of unpretentious, industrious women made independent by another woman's patronage and encouragement. When she touched their lives, they were made free. Marcus

Quintius had named it Pax Magdalena, and indeed it was—the Peace of Mary of Magdala.

Disappointed as Demetria was now, confused as she must be, she could not believe the worst of Mary. The mistress had not abandoned them. They were without her physical presence, yes; but they had everything else—food, shelter, their livelihood, and their companionship. Everyone had picked up whatever task was at hand and all the gaps were filled. Demetria had to acknowledge that Mary was right to leave Mummius in charge. Without him, the structure of commerce that sustained them would have collapsed. So what if he went off in the evenings, living a separate life somewhere?

Demetria had no doubt that the mistress would return, and she, for one, wanted the household to be running smoothly. She wanted to show Mary that she was worthy of the trust that had been placed in her. She wanted the loom room to be singing. More than anything, she wanted Shoshanna to be up and about her normal business. If only Jesus were here; he would heal her in no time.

When Jesus laid his hands on sick people, often he would say, "Your sins are forgiven." Demetria thought that she must be a terrible sinner. That was the only explanation for what had happened to her, being kidnapped from her parents, pressed onto a boat headed for Galilee, a place she had never heard of, and handed over to Roman men for pleasure. She was just a little girl then. Some god must have been very angry, or very cruel. When Mary took her in and loved her, Demetria thought that whatever sins she had committed might have been forgiven.

Demetria had watched Jesus healing the old, the infirm, anyone who managed to struggle into proximity with him. While those around him gasped and moved away, he had put his fingers right onto the seeping wounds of lepers, and their sores disappeared. She had seen him do it many times.

Remembering these things, Demetria felt Jesus' big, warm hand wrapped around hers, enclosing it, when they walked out of the Temple on the way to heal Joanna. She felt the weight of Joanna's locket of gold at her throat and instantly was aware of a connective substance that bound her together with Joanna and Jesus, as though they were right there in the room with her, and not somewhere far away.

Demetria rose from Mary's bed and returned to the loom room. Oblivious to the questions of the bewildered weavers, she sat down at her loom. On the floor beside her were several skeins of soft, creamy white wool and one of pale green, like new leaves in spring, which she had chosen for a band around the border of the shawl. Picking up the shuttle, she finished the row where Sahadia had made the bungle and cut the strings that held the shawl in place on the frame. One by one she began to tie off the edges, making tight, uniform knots, as Shoshanna had taught her to do. She spread the soft wool of the shawl around her shoulders and floated from the room. Chloe stood to follow, but Sahadia sat her down with a silent motion of her hand.

Entering the room where Shoshanna lay, Demetria walked with sure steps to her bedside. The beloved, ancient face was marred with a look, not so much of pain as labor, reflecting the elemental work of breathing.

Demetria lifted the corners of the shawl and covered her own head, as she had seen Jesus do. Incomplete as it was, the shawl was short, falling just to her shoulders, and when she pulled it over her hair, an unfamiliar force came into Demetria's body, a pressure that pushed into her head through an opening that seemed to appear there. With both hands, she reached around her neck and untied the silk ribbon holding the golden locket. Demetria laid the amulet on Shoshanna's breast and said her name, "Shoshanna?"

The old woman opened her eyes and offered a slight smile. "Girl, you are here," she said.

"I am," replied Demetria. And to the empty space in front of her, she implored, "Jesus, help me now." Then, slowly, to Shoshanna she repeated the magical words that had healed so many others, "Your sins are forgiven."

Hearing this blasphemy, Shoshanna squeezed her eyes closed. "No!" she gasped and seemed to faint—or die?

Demetria was shocked out of her euphoria. Her face flooded with shame and then went white as the blood drained away. She reached out her hand to seize the locket, desperately hoping that no one had stolen a look at the mad scene she had created. What did she expect, that Shoshanna would rise up and ask for something to eat, get dressed and walk to town? Demetria was ready to flee, but when she grabbed the necklace, Shoshanna opened her eyes. She pushed up onto her elbows, looking around, as if trying to determine where she was, or where she had been.

"How long have I been sleeping?" she asked.

"Not long, Mamee, not long," answered Demetria, who, feeling the nameless energy surge back out through the crown of her head, was suddenly and inexplicably exhausted. She felt empty, used up, unable to function. There was nothing to do but lie down, and it was only moments till she fell into a deep sleep.

She woke to the sound of voices, Mummius' resonant tenor asking questions and Rachel's excited chatter, praising God. Shoshanna was no longer gasping for air, but breathing comfortably. Her voice was strong and steady. She was asking to get up, but Mummius commanded her to stay where she was.

Seeing that Demetria was stirring, he asked, "Can you stand?"

"I think so."

"Then come with me."

Demetria wobbled to Mummius' apartment in his swift wake.

"What did you do?"

"What do you mean?"

"Shoshanna is alert. She said it is because of you," he replied, holding Demetria with his glowing eyes.

This was a Mummius she did not know, neither imperious in the normal way, nor cordial in the manner he sometimes adopted when he wanted something from her. Nor was this the special attentiveness, generally reserved for his dealings with Mary, and not seen by Demetria since they had left for Jerusalem. This much she had learned of him, that he was like a changeling, skilled in adaptation to suit the moment.

The Mummius who stood before her now was real. It was as though he had removed his jewelry and washed the kohl from his eyes, eyes that were clear, unhooded, and inquisitive. This must be the Mummius of old: the handsome, bright-eyed Egyptian who played upon musical instruments to please his betrothed, the dazzling youth of Bubastis whose vast talents as scribe and physician were only beginning to be cultivated. This Mummius was no longer closed, but open, like a red spring tulip seeking the morning sun. When he asked again, "Demetria, please tell me, what did you do?" she heard the sheer desire to learn that which he did not know. She felt tenderness for him, which she had thought was beyond the scope of their uneasy affiliation. Even though she wanted to give him what he wanted, she hesitated. But who else was there to make sense of the mysterious happening?

"May we sit down?"

"Forgive me," he said. "You are still tired."

Demetria sat in the chair he offered her in this, his office, where she had never before been invited to sit.

"First I covered my head with a shawl," she began, trying to remember the events accurately. "This I have seen Jesus do often. I tell you, Mummius, when I did that, a power came in through the top of my head and filled me within. Then, I laid my locket on her chest."

"Have you seen Jesus do that, too?"

Demetria gave Mummius back his own clear, inquisitive gaze and said, "No, I have not. But I have seen you do it."

At this astonishing admission, Mummius cocked his head to one side, like a small boy looking at something new and very interesting.

"I spoke Shoshanna's name. She recognized me. Then I spoke Jesus' name and repeated what he almost always says, 'Your sins are forgiven.' When Shoshanna heard those words, she cried out, 'No!' and fell into a faint. I thought she might be dead."

Demetria swallowed hard to belay her tears, but they rose anyway, and she brushed them away from the corners of her eyes.

Mummius touched her arm. "I am sorry," he said.

"I think it was but a few moments, though it seemed an eternity, when Shoshanna opened her eyes and spoke to me in a voice that was clear and strong, as you heard it just now. Then the force that had come into me left as quickly as it appeared, and carried my energy out with it. I slept. That was all."

For the moment, all their weapons laid aside, Demetria and Mummius wondered what had transpired, at what was even now transpiring between them.

"You need more rest, child," he said at last. "I will give you a restorative potion. You will sleep and awake refreshed."

"Mummius, is Shoshanna healed?" she asked, barely daring to say the words and at the same time wide-eyed with hope.

"Just drink your medicine. We will speak again when you have recovered," he replied, disappearing behind the curtain to his workbench to mix her tonic.

Late that night, Mummius stalked around the inner sanctum of his bedroom, on quiet tiger feet, reading scrolls by lamplight. All afternoon and evening he had examined manuscripts, absorbed in a search for some documented evidence of an event like that which seemed to have occurred, but could not have. He had paused only briefly to take supper with Rachel and Demetria, and twice to check on Shoshanna, whose condition was still vastly improved, though he insisted she stay in bed for a while longer.

His quest had generated nothing, no record of an uninitiated girl—untrained in medicine and in possession of no known spiritual power—healing another living person. For what must be the hundredth time, he reviewed the scenario. Demetria had accidentally employed the elements of an ancient prescription: speak the name of the subject, place the amulet, implore the divinity, and give the command. Still, it was impossible that inadvertent compliance with a formula and mindless repetition of another's script were sufficient. The answer was surely to be found in the force that entered through her head and filled her body. Had some god chosen her as a vessel? And why? Or was Jesus so powerful that he could hear her supplication from afar and thus direct energy to her?

He had known one other man so endowed—Amenwahsu, the great magus of Alexandria, who had challenged the young Mummius to a near-fatal match of wills in the dungeon of the Asclepian. Mummius had excelled in his classes and had become a favorite of teachers. Just about the time his self-confidence had reached a peak, he was summoned to the dungeon for a test.

There a hooded figure waited, concealed in the shadows. Mummius stepped forward, trying to make out who or what it was, but before his foot landed its first step, he was on the floor, the breath knocked out of him. The test was to be a wrestling match. He came up to his hands and knees ready to retaliate, but his opponent was not within reach. Mummius had been thrown, untouched, from across the room. He stood, summoning his strength. He held out one arm and sent a violent blow. It was deflected.

"Try again," said his challenger with a deep-throated laugh.

The battle continued with offensive and defensive moves, but no physical contact, only what force the opponents could generate from a distance. Occasionally Mummius landed a blow, only to be met by a response of escalated ferocity. Again he found himself on the floor, writhing, or up against a wall, an arm pulled up painfully behind his back. And again he tried to catch the master on the other side of the room in a hold.

When the battle was over, Amenwahsu was, of course, the victor. He released the hold of his unseen hand and dropped Mummius to the floor in a gasping heap. "A worthy opponent," said Amenwahsu. That horrifying yet seductive tribute was an invitation to be apprenticed to the clan of the dark magi.

Now, Mummius' body shook with the shudder that always went through him when he remembered the moment of truth, the first time he stood at the line between good and evil, and resisted. It was a never-ending struggle. He wondered if Jesus had ever crossed it. Surely he, too, would be tempted often. *What is it that keeps Jesus so firmly on this side of the line?*

Just before daybreak Mummius abandoned his reading and lay down, greatly fatigued. He had just passed over the threshold into sleep when Rachel's piercing call from outside his door brought him back through the barrier.

"Mummius, come quickly!"

He was up, and out, and across the courtyard before she could explain.

The women's bedroom was heavy with alarm. Demetria was kneeling on the floor beside the cot on which Shoshanna now lay dying. She had been propped up on pillows to help her breathe. Looking small among the blankets piled over her, she was motionless except for the slight rise and fall created by her breathing.

Mummius made no move towards her, only inclined his ear to the cycle of shallow, rattling breath, which grew progressively louder, then ceased. After a moment of fearful quiet, during which no one else drew breath, the cycle started again, slowly, and, again, the crescendo. A fly buzzed around her head, like a vulture. Demetria swept it away, then dipped a towel into a basin of minted water and wiped the unresponsive face.

Pitying the dutiful girl, Mummius went to her and touched her shoulder. She looked up at him and begged with eyes that seemed to overtake her entire face, *Do something.* He shook his head. Even if there were some remedy, some potion to relieve her, Shoshanna was no longer able to swallow.

Demetria leaned over the pillowed head, her long, golden hair falling around it, and whispered something. Shoshanna's eyes opened briefly and just as soon were closed again. The devoted girl, having done one miracle she thought, wanted to believe in another.

Mummius knew better. He placed two sensitive fingertips lightly on the patient's wrist and laid his ear to the chest. It was over.

Demetria and Rachel flung themselves over the lifeless body and wailed as though their hearts were bound to tear apart. Soon they would start rending their clothes, in the way of Jews in mourning. Mummius wished the weavers were here to take care of this fuss of women, but it would be hours before they arrived. He lifted Demetria gently by the shoulders and pulled her up. When she got to her feet, she turned and threw her arms around his waist and sobbed on his chest. His first reaction was to push away in revulsion.

But he did not. Could not, because he was home in Bubastis, the willowy, adoring Maret folded in his lap, her nut-brown legs hung over his arm, and one foot swinging rhythmically up and down, its jeweled sandal dangling from her toes. He could feel the pulse in her left temple beating firmly on his bare chest where she had laid her head.

Mummius surrendered. Demetria was no heavier than a winter cloak when he picked her up, like that other girl with her legs folded over his arms, and carried her outside. *What now?* he wondered, looking around for some answer. The entrance to Mary's room was a few steps beyond. He decided to take her there.

"I need to go back to Rachel," she protested weakly.

"You need to rest," he said.

He tried to place her on the bed, but she would not release him.

"Don't leave."

"I will stay till you sleep," he said.

"Promise me."

"I promise." Mummius' throat constricted with emotions he did not recognize and could not master.

Her arms slipped from around his neck and came to rest over her waist. Within a few moments she seemed to have drifted off, but he did not want to chance a move until he was sure. He sat stiffly beside her and watched her face, crusty with its salt bath of tears. A frown was drawn in deep lines between her brows where sorrow had made its camp. He put the pad of his thumb close to the place, to rub it out, and then thought better of it. Best not to touch her.

When he thought it worth the risk, he rose gingerly. She did not wake. From the chest along the wall, he took a blanket and covered her and, for a few moments, continued to stare down at her. What if she did have some gift? It should be cultivated. What would it be like to train such a girl?

Mummius rubbed his eyes and yawned. He was tired, tired of having to know what to do, tired of being in charge, tired of being isolated. He needed to sleep. He pulled himself away from the sight of Demetria sleeping soundly now and walked the few lonely steps to his apartment.

When Rachel came looking for Demetria she was surprised to find her asleep in Mary's bed. She shook her lightly by the shoulder and, when she did not stir, more vigorously. It took a while for Demetria to wake up fully.

"What is the hour? How long have I been sleeping?"

"Just after first light," said Rachel. "What are you doing in Mary's bed?"

"Mummius brought me here," said Demetria.

"What do you mean, 'brought you here'? What did he do to you?"

"He picked me up and carried me here. When he put me on the bed, I asked him to stay. Don't think badly of me, Rachel. I did not want to be alone when Shoshanna died. I was scared."

"It's all right, Little Bit. Tell me what happened next."

"I don't remember anything else. When I fell asleep, he was just sitting there beside me."

"Did he give you anything to drink? A potion?"

"No. No, I don't think so."

Rachel took Demetria's hands and pulled her arms away from her body, looking for signs. "Are you sore anywhere?" And they both knew where she meant.

"No. I think I am all right. And I feel better for the sleep. He was nice to me, Rachel."

"Whatever he is, 'nice' is not part of it. You must be on guard."

"On guard for what?"

"You do not see how beautiful you are, Demetria. Mary is not here to protect you. You must learn to shield yourself, not be so open."

"I know what it is to be ravaged by men, Rachel. Mummius is not dangerous. Besides, I would never..."

"Of course *you* would never. Men are a different matter, and you are an irresistible prize. You should know this by now."

They were quiet for a while, each ruminating on the implications of what Rachel meant, until finally she said, "We have much to do, Little Bit. Let's go to the kitchen. I will make us some khat."

Shortly they were sipping their tea. Demetria swirled her cup, mesmerized by sadness, trying to rewrite the past few hours in her head, but there was no escaping it: Shoshanna was gone. She asked Rachel, "What are we supposed to do with Shoshanna's body?"

"Well," replied Rachel, thinking, "she will have to be cleaned and anointed. We must tell the priest. Then she will be buried."

"Buried where?"

"She will lie in the public grave for one year. After that, her bones will be moved to..." Rachel faltered in mid-sentence.

"What is it?"

"I was going to say 'to the family burial house,' but that will be Mary's decision."

At the thought of Mary's return, Rachel again gave in to wailing and put her head in her hands. Mary would be devastated, not only by Shoshanna's death, but also by not being here to say she loved her, to offer comfort, to tell her goodbye. Why, *why,* was Mary not here at such a time as this?

It was Demetria's turn to show the way. "We have to concentrate on what is before us. Let us prepare to clean her body now."

Rachel chewed on her lower lip. "I think I must do this alone."

"Why?"

"I do not think it is permitted for a gentile to touch her."

"Oh, Rachel, do not deny me this! We could get permission from a rabbi…"

Rachel grunted. "No rabbis. It is better not to ask. Still, I wonder what Shoshanna would want? She could be a stickler about the Law."

That made Demetria angry, and it showed in her eyes. "Shoshanna loved me. She was a grandmother to me! What is gentile or Jew compared to that?" she flared, burning Rachel with her temper and causing her to cry once more. "Forgive me. I did not mean to hurt you," Demetria said, patting her on the arm. "Think of this, Rachel. Mary brought us here to live as sisters. And so we have done. We must make our own rules. Together we took care of Shoshanna in life; we must take care of her together in death." Demetria put her hand under Rachel's chin and lifted her head. "Yes?"

Rachel nodded. Demetria went to the water pitcher and poured a palmful onto a towel and wiped Rachel's tears away. "Have you ever done this before?"

"I have seen it done. And I know where the linens and ointments are stored."

Demetria was surprised. "I was not aware that there were separate items for preparing dead bodies."

"There are separate items for everything, Little Bit," replied Rachel. Then, as an afterthought she asked, "What of Mummius?"

"We can't involve Mummius, can we? He would have Egyptian embalmers at her," replied Demetria.

"Shoshanna herself would rise up to prevent that!"

They shared a laugh, and the humor of the moment lifted their spirits.

Rachel said, "I will gather the things we need."

"I need to wash," said Demetria.

"Come to our bedroom when you are finished."

"I will." But first, Demetria needed Mummius.

The sound of voices and laughter ringing through the courtyard were enough to wake the Egyptian, who, until that moment, had slept. He turned over and covered his head, trying to block out the noise, but he was instantly alert when he heard Demetria at the curtain.

"Mummius, are you in there?"

He answered by pulling back the heavy drapery with a loud scrape and staring down at her, his eyes red with fatigue. She had come alone. Whether or not he intended to seem aloof, his very height and a lifetime of confident superiority naturally gave him that presence.

"I brought you some tea," she said and held out the khat, grazing his face with her smile.

He could barely find the "thank you" he knew was expected. He took the cup and went to the chair behind his desk. She sat opposite him.

"Are you feeling better?" he asked, and waited, cautious, wondering why she was here.

"Yes." After a short, uncomfortable silence that seemed endless, she ventured, "Why did she die?"

An astonishing relief. The subject was not the episode in the bedroom, but Shoshanna. He was comfortable with death.

"She was always dying."

"But, I thought she was healed."

"I, too, thought that for a while."

"Then what changed?"

Poor Demetria. She was young, inexperienced—and so earnest.

"Nothing changed, Demetria. A brief time of alertness before death is not uncommon. It is as though a person who is moving toward the screen that separates this life from the next wakes up to experience earthly consciousness, one final time, before surrendering it for all eternity."

"You mean that what I felt was not healing power, that it had nothing to do with what happened to Shoshanna?"

"I do not know what you felt, Demetria. It was unquestionably extraordinary. I do not doubt that it came from the divine. But, no, it did not heal Shoshanna."

An unseen vise reached into Demetria's chest, gripped her unprotected heart in its iron jaws, and squeezed. She was so sure that she had been the instrument of some healing for Shoshanna. Grasping for new hope in the wake of her failure, Demetria turned a yearning face to him.

"Mummius, do you believe there is another life? After this one?"

"Believe? I know it for a certainty. Life on earth is mere staging. We spend our whole lives preparing for what will come in the next life, the real one. We Egyptians, that is."

Demetria was looking for comfort, but instead, she was confused. She had never heard this before. Because of her Greek heritage, she was possessed of a very different notion. She had been brought up to believe that, when people died, their psyches left them in a little puff of wind, and their bodies traveled to the Underworld, where they were ruled by the god Hades, brother of Poseidon and great Zeus. There, deep beneath the earth, the dead lived on as shades, shadowy, drifting remnants of physical bodies. The Underworld was not a happy place, not at all a desired state. Mummius appeared to yearn for the afterlife. He did not seem to mind the idea that earthly life was nothing but a preparation for dying. Perhaps it was the Egyptian cult of death that rendered him so inscrutable.

From within a perplexing swirl of doubts, Demetria was able to draw one conclusion: most people did not want to think of their own extinction. They looked to their religions for hope that they would live on in some kind of eternity.

"What about Jews?" she asked.

"Jews do not know what they believe about the afterlife," he replied, a note of ridicule creeping into his voice.

"What do you mean?"

"Well, some of their teachers—the Pharisees I believe it is—say there is a resurrection of the body after death. Others maintain that there is no scriptural basis for such a belief. Those are the Sadducees."

Demetria had heard of Pharisees and Sadducees, but religious factions meant nothing to her.

"What do ordinary people believe? People like Shoshanna?"

"I don't think it matters to them." Mummius' eyes were burning. He was too tired for this conversation.

"I don't understand," she said.

"Neither do I. If Jesus ever returns, you can ask him. He seems to know all there is to know."

When Mummius took a sip of his tea, smirking into his cup, Demetria stood suddenly, as if to leave. Mummius was flooded with a curious desire for her to stay. Why had he baited her with that tactless comment about Jesus?

"I did not mean to offend you."

He stared at Demetria, who was staring back. She was no doubt trying to decipher him. Little wonder. He was a cipher to himself these days. His defenses had long been cracking with little fissures, like a ruined potter's glaze, beneath the gentle assault of this heavenly girl with her long lashes and fair eyes and the way she looked for the softer parts of him, hidden under his armor.

Demetria did not go, but she did not sit down again either.

"You frightened Rachel," she declared abruptly.

He was unprepared for this turn and, for the first time in living memory, Mummius blushed with insecurity.

"Yes, you did. You scared her. She thinks you might hurt me... Do you intend to hurt me, Mummius?"

She had him at a disadvantage, standing while he remained seated, forcing him to look up at her. The hard, masculine part of him wanted to regain his rank, to silence her probing. Suddenly, impulsively, in one continuous movement, he pushed back his stool and came around the desk. With two wide paces he was close enough to strike her, to smell her, but it was not the anticipated reek of fear. It was the scent of her hair and the mildly pungent aroma of khat on her breath. Demetria stood her ground.

Within the sleeve of his robe, Mummius' right arm was cocked, clenched from shoulder to fist. His other hand went to the hammered metal bracelet that encircled his right wrist, the weapon that would send Demetria to her knees. He fingered the wide bracelet, twisting it slightly back and forth, long enough to reconsider, long enough to relax his arm, but only slightly.

"Do you think I intend to hurt you?" His voice was gravelly with the mix of emotions that surged inside him.

Without pause, without a trace of doubt, she answered evenly, "No, Mummius, I do not."

Immediately it was as though he were melting inside, returning to some primeval state of being where everything was unformed and all things were possible. He wanted to wrap her in gratitude, but fear of relinquishing too much of himself overtook him.

"Get out," he said.

Demetria, backing away, obeyed.

CHAPTER 33

"What kept you?" asked Rachel.

"I'm sorry," Demetria answered, trying to shake off the sound of Mummius' last, inexplicable command. "How shall we start?"

If Rachel was speculating on the reason for Demetria's delay, she said no more about it, because she was intent on the important task ahead of them. Everything was ready.

At the foot of the bed Rachel had placed a low table and covered it with a cream-colored Damask cloth. Upon the cloth sat a large bowl of unglazed earthen pottery and beside it a matching pitcher filled with water. Next to the pitcher was a stack of small, bleached towels folded into squares. Among all the implements arranged on the table, and serving as its focal point, stood an alabaster jar. It was fine-grained and translucent, pure white but for two streaks of reddish brown at the carved handles on either side. Round shoulders flared out in a graceful arc beneath its slender neck and tapered down to form its body. The beautiful alabaster jar was fragile, like life.

"We should begin with a prayer," Rachel said.

They stood on either side of Shoshanna's body and closed their eyes. Rachel, unschooled in leading prayers, did her best.

"O LORD, our God, we ask you to hear us. You are compassionate and merciful to your people. We are but two insignificant women inclined to do your will. Bless us as we cleanse and anoint the body of this, your daughter, Shoshanna. May our actions be acceptable in your sight. Amen."

Rachel lifted the pitcher and poured a trickling stream into the waiting bowl. They pressed their towels beneath the surface of the water. They wrung them out over the basin. Then, they began to bathe her. With each stroke of the cloth came a memory: the way she rolled up her sleeves when she washed the dishes; the way she rubbed her aching feet at the end of a walk from town; the way, on occasion, when she was feeling just right, that she enfolded one of them in her stout arms and squeezed, to show how she loved them.

They lingered over her hands, the thick skin of her fingertips and thumbs, calloused by decades of weaving, hands whose legacy, now bequeathed to these women, was an exacting standard that would forever live in their hearts and inspire their looms.

When the bathing was finished, Rachel lifted the alabaster jar and held it up to the window's early morning light, observing the mixture within, swirling it delicately. From Mary's private cabinet, she had chosen rare and costly extracts, adding them to a base of fine olive oil from the first press, dark and golden green. When she tipped some out into Demetria's cupped palm, and then into her own, the pungent perfume of aloe and myrrh arose and filled the room, causing their eyes to water.

They applied the precious blend to Shoshanna's face and head and rubbed it in thoughtfully, making small circles with their fingers. They massaged it into her hands and feet and when that was finished, they wiped the oil from their hands and stood back, looking upon their labor.

"She would be pleased," said Rachel, and Demetria nodded.

The rest was a blur: her body wrapped in strips of linen; her face covered with a cloth; the synagogue where many had gathered to hear the rabbi say final prayers, the Mourner's Kaddish; men from the town carrying her to the graveyard where she was buried in a tomb and the stone wheel rolled across the opening; the heartache of the weavers and the condolences of the townspeople; the sad trek home. What Rachel and Demetria did not know was that, even as they walked the short distance from Magdala to the house, even as they prepared to face its barren emptiness, Mary, too, was on her way home by another way.

On the road just south of the house, where it forked off to the Sea of Galilee, Mary had said goodbye to her companions. She handed Jesus the keys to the domus in Capernaum. "I will come as soon as I can," she promised. When he embraced her, she very nearly changed her mind about inviting them home with her, for she hated to be separated from him.

But in her head she carried a precise image of the glad reunion, and this she wanted all for herself. She thought of going happily from room to room, embracing each family member, enjoying their surprise. With this image in mind, she came to the front door and stepped lightly under the doorway arch. She entered the loom room, expecting to be surrounded by weavers shrieking with delight.

But there were no weavers. Only a hushed forest of looms, each one holding in its branches a work-in-progress, interrupted at a stopping place, skeins of dyed wool curled alongside like fallen bird nests. When she called out, no one answered. *Where have they gone?*

She passed through the courtyard, where everything, even though it was winter, was in remarkably good order. She went to Mummius' apartment, wanting to commend and thank him. It was empty. She went to the women's bedroom and found only tidy cots. The house was immaculate—immaculate and lifeless. Something was terribly wrong.

Through nine long months of trekking around Judea, separated from her family, Mary had been buoyed by charming images of home: happy weavers singing at their looms, Rachel contentedly cooking up pots of mouthwatering lentil soup, Shoshanna clucking over the housework, Mummius poised over his flawless scrolls, and Demetria, her darling, dancing through life. The longer she was away, the more intense these fancies became. Now, other, disquieting images came to mind as Mary began to consider alternatives. Something had drawn them all away: perhaps there had been a fire in town; or some trouble with the Romans; someone was hurt—or dead! *Calm down,* she thought.

She went outside, around the house, and up the stairs to the roof, apprehension mounting with each step. Leaning on the low wall that surrounded the flat rooftop and hemmed it in, she scanned the countryside. There was nothing unusual, nothing to provide a clue as to what had happened, and she was about to turn and go when, in the distance, indistinctly, on the road from Magdala, she saw two women dressed head to foot in dark clothing, their veiled heads resting together at the temples—mourners returning home—and without knowing, she knew. She ran to meet them.

"What has happened?" she asked of the two astonished women.

"Oh, Mary" was all Rachel could say before grief took her voice.

Mary looked to Demetria to give her the news she needed, but did not want.

"Shoshanna is dead."

It was almost on Mary's lips to accuse them, *Why did you not send word to me?* but she promptly and properly redirected the blame to herself. How could they have sent word, having no idea where she was? She herself had not known on any given day where she would be on the next.

In the staccato manner of the shocked, Mary questioned them.

"When?"

"Late last night."

"You buried her?"

"Yes."

"Did she suffer?"

"No."

In creeping awareness of how it must have transpired, she said, "I am sorry you had to endure this on your own."

When Mary began to cry and seemed about to crumple down into the mud of the road, Demetria held her up. "Let's get you home," she said.

It was then that Mary caught a glimpse the self-assurance and calm of the new Demetria. How blithely she had handed this girl over to Joanna in Jerusalem. *She will be fine,* she had thought, even as she saw the look of disbelief on Demetria's stricken face. Mary had been shadowed by the memory of that terrified and wounded face, which would occasionally arise in her mind and which she speedily pushed away in favor of more pleasing images. Who had Demetria become in these months of separation?

Rachel brought water to wash Mary's feet and her road-stained face and hands. Demetria helped her change into fresh clothes. Then they sat on the bed with her, waiting for Mary to be ready, waiting till she could say, "Tell me about Shoshanna."

Rachel, being the one who had watched it from the start, told of the old woman's decline. "Mummius tried to help her, Mary; we all did."

"Where *is* Mummius?" Mary asked.

Demetria answered, "Probably with Rufus Gaius."

"You mean Marcus' steward?"

"Yes."

"How odd," said Mary. "But go on about Shoshanna."

Hearing the tale, beginning to end, Mary was distraught by the conclusion that was before her. "It was my absence that killed her?"

"I would not say that, Mistress," offered Demetria, though she knew that Rachel was thinking, *That is exactly what I would say.*

Mary had never intended to be cruel, but now, in the faces of women she loved, she could see what a trail of woe she had left behind. From Magdala to Capernaum and back. To Jerusalem, to Judea and, of all places, to Samaria. When she started, she had no idea it would take as long as nine months! Anything could happen in such a time. And indeed it had.

Mary was caught in a maelstrom of bereavement and guilt. She should have been here with Shoshanna, just as Shoshanna had been with Mary's parents when they died, and her grandparents before that, to ease their passage. She should have been here to bear the burden that belonged to her, not foist it upon others. Was injury to her family the price of following her call from God? She lay down on her bed and hugged her knees to her chest, desolation pushing her down.

"Mistress, please..." begged Demetria.

The hardships of traveling in winter weather, the dirt-caked sandals and never-dry clothing, the uncertainty of food and shelter, to say nothing of the demands of the crowds they met, piled upon Mary like a mudslide.

"Let me rest for a while," she said.

Demetria and Rachel could not move from her side. After their recent experience with Shoshanna, were they to be drawn so soon back into the demands of caretaking? Was this a temporary collapse, or something more? Perhaps her demons would return. When she said, "I will be all right, truly. I just need to sleep," they left the room. Fearing to withdraw too far, they took up a vigil just outside, curled up on the paved stones of the courtyard, heads covered with wool scarves, legs tucked under their skirts, waiting for they knew not what. It was hours later when Mummius found them there, in the dark, a light drizzle falling on them.

"She has returned?" he demanded, startling them.

Of course she had returned. Why else would Demetria and Rachel be sitting out here in the rain? Mummius drew in a deep breath, tainted with alcohol, and straightened to full height. He put his hands to his belt and pulled it tight, accentuating his hip bones and flat abdomen.

"Do not go in. She is resting."

Mummius ignored Demetria's warning and stepped through the curtain. He was once again in Mary's bedroom looking down at a sleeping woman, not knowing what to do. Not knowing exactly what he wanted.

Mary caught him off guard when she opened her big umber eyes and, without moving, whispered, "Mummius."

For a moment, he closed his eyes and soaked in the sound of her voice speaking his name, imploring him, as she used to do when she was plagued with demons, as she used to do when she needed him. Perhaps she needed him now.

"Lady," he whispered in return, stepping to her bedside.

She held out her hand a little to greet him, and his fingertips instinctively touched down on her pulse. It was strong. She was well, except for the ache in her heart. He dropped to one knee beside her and held her hand.

"I cannot bear her death," she said. "The three of you alone with the responsibility."

"Her last thought was for you." But he did not say what kind of thought.

"I loved her, Mummius."

"I know." Then, a sudden impulse. "I loved her, too," he said.

Mummius stayed with Mary while she lay still, occasionally speaking a word or phrase cast up from the landscape of her anguished internal wanderings. It was clear that she was in some kind of shock from which there was no immediate escape.

"Lady, let me give you something to help you sleep."

She did not reply.

"Mary, I am going to mix you a potion," he said, but when he tried to take his hand from hers, she tightened her hold on him.

"I shall return very shortly. Do you understand?"

She nodded twice, almost imperceptibly. One by one he unfolded her fingers from his hand.

With Mummius' help, Mary slept through that night and every night for a week. The days in between were a struggle. Led by the weavers, the whole town came to visit, bring food, and grieve as a community for their departed sister. To Mary, each expression of sympathy was marred by an underlying note of reproach—or was it her own self-censure that she heard in the condolences of others? She was glad when the first seven days of mourning were over and the house was no longer flooded with people coming and going.

Mary had to turn to her family then, seeking reconciliation. She went from person to person. First to Rachel.

"It must have been very difficult for you," she said.

"You cannot imagine."

"Tell me."

"The beginning was the worst. On the very day you left, Shoshanna started her decline. We kept thinking her despondency would pass, hoping she would recover herself. I have to say that Mummius did everything he could for her. He was very attentive, but he said that she had made a decision not to live and nothing could overcome it."

Rachel's eyes turned hard and accusing. She had always conducted herself in a quiet, steady manner, not submissive, but never impolite, so the swift rancor in her voice was unexpected and shocking.

"Could you not suppose what you were doing to her? She had barely withstood your move to Capernaum. When you went to Jerusalem and then did not return, well, we just settled in, waiting for her to die. All but Demetria."

"What about Demetria?"

"That girl was a treasure. She nursed Shoshanna every day, bathed her, read to her, told her stories. Every day Shoshanna looked to Demetria for assurance that you were coming home, and she gave it. Sometimes she mistook Demetria for you. They lived in mutual avoidance of the inevitable, and thus kept each other going."

"And while Demetria was nursing Shoshanna and Mummius was running the farm, you did the shopping, the cleaning, the cooking, and the winter storage by yourself."

"I did."

"I have taken you for granted, Rachel."

"I do not see it that way, Mary. Where would I be without the home you have given me?" Rachel's voice was gentler now, free of indictment.

"That is part of the difficulty. I know it is hard for you to think badly of me, but why would you not? I have brought grief to you which I did not intend." Mary put her arm around Rachel. "Can you forgive me?"

Rachel's answer was to lay her head on Mary's shoulder and sob.

The next day Mummius looked up from his scrolls to see Mary at the door of his quarters, peeking in, smiling.

"Lady," he said, standing to greet her and scanning her with his physician's eye. "It is good to see you up early this morning. You look quite well."

"I feel well, thank you."

He offered her a chair and drew another near to it. They sat stiffly, searching for each other across the chasm that had opened between them, each wondering how to start.

Mary cleared her throat. "The grounds are in very good order, Mummius. You have outdone yourself."

"Your pleasure is my recompense," he said, in the formal manner.

"It was the first thing I noticed on the day of my return—the impeccable courtyard."

"Nothing as good as your hand, Lady, but I did try to keep it up."

Mary relaxed a little. "This is awkward, Mummius," she said and took a deep breath, gathering courage. "I owe you much."

"You reward me well, Lady."

"I don't mean money. I mean that without you, I could not have been absent for such an extended period."

Mummius looked at her long and hard. Was he ready to open himself, to offer again the friendship they had once known? Only he knew the extent of his emptiness. When Jesus drew the demons out of Mary, her need for Mummius had been drawn out, too. That which had held them together—her dependence on him—had fled as surely as those evil spirits. What had he to complain about? He was responsible, for was it not he, himself, who had sought Jesus out? He knew well that Mary would have died without Jesus' intervention. Since her restoration, Mummius did not know how to relate to her. Without power to control her, were they to be equals now? he thought, half-scoffing, half-wondering. He was not sure if he wanted to close the gap that her healing had carved out between them. Still, it was obvious that Mary was grateful for his recent medical help. More importantly, Jesus was not here to meddle. Perhaps this was an opportunity to build a new bridge.

"Was being absent so long the right choice?" With his eyes, Mummius maintained a hold on her until she looked away.

"Yes. And no. I did not like being away from home." She looked up, and his gaze recaptured her. "Not that I was needed. I see how everyone took a part and things went smoothly. Rachel said that Sahadia provided assistance to you."

"Talking to the weavers is not native to me, Lady. I was glad for her help."

When next she spoke, he heard in Mary's voice a note of desperation as she leapt to the heart of what she wanted him to understand. "Mummius, I had to go. I would do it again. Even seeing the pain it caused, I would do it again."

Mummius hardened. His eyes took on the hooded look that meant he was protecting himself. "Because of Jesus," he said.

"Because of *God*."

Mummius labored to keep his surprise from showing.

"It is God who has called me." Mary gripped Mummius' hand. It was her turn, now, to hold his eyes. "Jesus is showing me the way to God. I feel so… I can't describe it, Mummius. He has taught me how to direct healing power to others. You above all can understand that, can you not?"

Understand? By all means. Mummius had his own fantasies about learning the secrets of Jesus' mastery of the body and the spirit. He would have given much to be in her place, Jesus' confidante. At their first meeting Jesus had acknowledged his talents with a secret look that no one else recognized. If only the circumstances were different…

"People came to me to be baptized, Mummius! Women in throngs, and then men, too. The first time it happened I thought that the force that flowed through me might engulf me, but I have learned to be large and open. If I close myself, or fight it, it threatens to sweep me away." She bit her lip and lowered her head. "I probably sound quite mad."

Her body was shifting around in the chair, as though unsettled. To another man, it might seem that she was once again at risk of demons, but Mummius could see the truth. It was not evil spirits who visited Mary now, but God. If Jesus offered her that gift, she was bound to follow him.

Mummius' mind turned to Demetria. He had not been able to stop thinking about her description of the energy that came into her when she invoked Jesus' name, trying to heal Shoshanna. Now it was clear. Jesus was a conduit of divine power to everyone around him. How extraordinary! Mummius was arrested by the notion that he, too, might be part of the inner circle of such a master. If Jesus accepted a mere Greek girl as a vessel, surely he would welcome an Egyptian disciple of Mummius' genius.

Mummius opened his mouth and was on the verge of telling Mary about Demetria, to say that she had channeled some healing to Shoshanna, which had provided a few hours of clarity and peace, before her final departure from this world. Then he changed his mind and closed his mouth. He was not ready.

From across the chasm, he heard her say, "Mummius, do I sound mad?"

"Not mad, Lady."

"What then?"

"The gods choose us, Lady. Not the other way around. When they do, to resist them is to die, as you have deduced."

"You think we have no choice, Mummius? Is that what you are saying?"

"I am saying that the gods call, and we answer or we do not. But the consequences of refusal are grave."

"The consequences of consent are grave as well."

"Shoshanna was old. It was her time. Your absence helped her on her way, but, believe me, her body would have failed whether you were here or not."

"But I could have said goodbye. Demetria and Rachel should not have been the ones to bury her."

"It would have been good for you to be here, that is true. They missed you."

Mary's voice was soft with the gathering tears. "And you, Mummius? Did you miss me?"

Even though she sat immobile, Mummius could almost see Mary's hand reaching out to him. A longing to reach back surged within, and Mummius very nearly poured out to Mary what he had been unwilling to admit to himself. Every time he passed the door to her room, he had missed her. Every time he held a watering pot over one of her precious exotic plants, or snipped a spent blossom, he missed her. Every time he opened a scroll addressed to her, he missed her. For all the time she was gone, he had filled his empty days with work. He had struggled not to know his longing. It was not so easy to give up that struggle now and release what control he had.

"I missed you, Lady, of course. But I knew what was required. I like to think that I oversaw all your affairs adequately. Which reminds me..."

Mummius walked to the other side of the desk, opened a small wooden chest, took out Mary's seal, and pushed it halfway across the desktop.

Mary had forgotten the seal, forgotten that she had loaned him her name and her worldly power, ignoring her father's instructions, and Marcus', as well. By leaving the seal in his sole custody, she had meant to show Mummius the extent of her trust. She would not take it back now.

"No," she said. "You keep it."

"Lady?" he responded, slipping the seal back into its box.

"The truth is, Mummius, that I am leaving again very soon. I promised Jesus I would meet him in Capernaum. We plan to continue our ministry throughout Galilee. I will be home often, but I want you to remain in charge here in Magdala."

So, he thought, *I am to be left behind again, am I? Has she no thought for my wishes?*

"And, Mummius, please, say nothing," she continued. "I have not yet told the others."

"I will do as you ask," he said. But what he thought was, *I will go to Capernaum as well.*

"I knew I could rely on you, faithful Mummius."

He watched as she rose to leave, her every step unknowingly pulling the cleft behind her more and more open. The chasm was becoming an abyss.

Out in the courtyard, Mary sat on the central bench, examining Marcus' mosaic, its vibrant colors failing to cheer her. She had hoped that Mummius would respond enthusiastically to her trust in him, but he did not seem to want anything from her. She wondered if she would ever know what he really wanted—from her or from anyone.

Suddenly, from within her brooding, Mary felt Demetria's hands over her eyes from behind.

"Guess who!"

Mary had to smile as she allowed herself to be drawn into their childish game of old. "Who can it be?"

"It's me, Demetria!" the girl exclaimed, releasing her hands and plopping down on the bench where they had passed many hours talking and reading. "Oh, Mistress, it is so very good to have you home where you belong. I am like a silly child—just as I was when I first came to you," she bubbled.

Drawn into the spreading joy, Mary hugged her, and, when she did, she felt Demetria's full, high breasts pressing against her. She pushed her away slightly to get a good look. During the week of mourning Mary had been blind to the details of Demetria.

"Is this a new tunic?" Mary inquired.

"Do you like it?"

Demetria jumped up and twirled to show it off. At the end of the spin, her hem continued to circle around in the direction of her motion and then reversed and came to rest around her ankles, not at her knees, where a child's would be. Demetria held out her arms to display the tunic, standing, for a moment, breathless and still, at the portal of womanhood, from which there was no turning back.

"It is lovely, dear." *With your tapered waist and long legs, your beautifully turned ankles, long, golden hair, and light Grecian eyes, you are indeed lovely,* Mary thought, taking her in. *You will need a husband before long!* "Come with me," she said, leading Demetria into her room.

Light fell upon the contents of Mary's jewelry box when she opened it, setting the treasures within to sparkling. Mary was not a woman to acquire and cast off baubles frivolously. These were priceless gifts of the heart, received from others, or lovingly chosen by her to mark special events in her own life. She picked through the collection till she came to what she was looking for, a pair of carnelian earrings. The stones were perfectly matched, ruby-red, like wet pomegranate seeds, glistening as they do when the ripe fruit is first cut open. Each was framed by a thin bronze braid, which dangled from a delicate wire loop.

On the day Mary's mother, Rebecca, had slipped the loops through the tiny holes in her ears, she was a girl of ten, home from Jerusalem and the nightmare of Mikmik's death in the street. Jerusalem, where her father had cut the poor old donkey's throat to end his suffering and then held out the reins of their family's strong donkey, Alazar, loaded for the trip home, and said to his little girl, "Can you handle him until I return?" Mary's mother was striving to restrain her brother, Reuben, and Mary knew what she must do. "Yes, Abba, I can," she replied, not really believing in herself.

Mary had been brave and strong on that journey, and when they arrived at home, Rebecca rewarded her with the earrings. "They belonged to my mother," Rebecca told Mary, "a gift from my father, the best he could afford on the day she gave birth to me." Mary had often wished for a daughter to pass them on to, as a mark of maturity and confidence and faith in the future. She thought, *This is what it is to be a mother, to give your best for the child, without remorse, without hesitation.* When she held out the cherished earrings, she wished Rebecca were here to witness it.

"These were my mother's and her mother's before her," she said. "I want you to have them."

"What have I done to merit such a gift?"

"You have suffered much tribulation, Demetria. Through it all you have grown strong and capable and yet have not given in to distrust and doubt. You have retained your sweet nature."

Demetria lowered her head, for she could not look Mary in the eye. "You are wrong, Mistress. I am not always sweet and trusting."

"Whatever you felt in my absence, Demetria, you were justified. I am sorry I sent you home through Tiberias with Joanna—so quickly and without adequate explanation. And Shoshanna's death, I can hardly bear to think of it. I am in your debt for easing her passage. Even Mummius says you were heroic in your care for her."

"He didn't tell you everything."

"What do you mean, dear?"

"I know it was silly, Mary, but I tried to heal her. I had watched Jesus with all those people in Jerusalem. Each time I saw him restore someone, I felt something strange inside, warm and swirling, like a wind connecting me to him and to the afflicted person. Sometimes I couldn't breathe; at other times it felt like I was soaring in the air. I guess it made me think that I could heal Shoshanna if I did what Jesus does. I just wanted her to get well."

Mary was stunned. Wind, breathlessness, soaring. She recognized the struggle to find the right language to speak of inspiration. What was happening? Demetria's exposure to Jesus had been brief. Apparently it was sufficient to cause her to dare to believe in herself. A fleeting moment of envy passed through Mary, as it always did when she saw a particular connection between Jesus and another. She pushed it away.

"Demetria, what happened when you tried to heal her?"

"A force came into me and then swept out again. Shoshanna was better for a while. She sat up and talked. She seemed happy. She said she felt peaceful. I thought it was because of what I had done. But she died anyway, so it was nothing."

"No, Demetria, no. Believe me when I tell you, you brought her that peace. That was your healing."

"Mummius said that people often do such things right before they die."

"Sometimes they do, yes. But what you did for Shoshanna was extraordinary."

Mary understood Demetria's relief when the girl whispered, "I knew it."

"Demetria, I, too, have felt that force you speak of. In my travels I was often close to being swept away by it."

"What kind of force is it, Mistress?"

"It is the love of God."

"Which god?"

"The only God there is, Demetria."

"You mean the one you call LORD?"

"Yes."

Demetria looked at the wall. "Well, your God does not love me."

"Why not?"

"I am Greek. I do not follow The Law," she said, as though Mary did not know it. Demetria lowered her head until her chin almost rested on her breastbone. "I used an amulet," she said into her tunic.

What sweet innocence! As if using an amulet or not using an amulet had anything to do with the power of God. Mary laughed out loud.

Demetria looked up, abashed. "Mummius does it. I was trying everything I could think of."

By now Mary was laughing so hard that tears were forming and she had to wipe them away. "Child, what are you worried about?"

Demetria whimpered. "The LORD would not approve of something like that."

"Dear, dear girl. How do you know he would not approve?"

CHAPTER 34

The spring after Mary's return was warm and dry in Galilee. The streets of Capernaum, habitually full, were clogged with visitors mustered from all over the world to this crossroads of commerce, eager to make some sort of fortune by whatever means they could, legitimate or otherwise.

Arabs arrived in caravans with so many men and camels as to resemble an army. Both men and women were wrapped, as Arabs had been for centuries, head to toe in voluminous robes and capes, with patterned kuffiyyahs on their heads, indicating their various tribes and status by style, color, and opulence. They brought from their homeland assorted exotica: frankincense, myrrh, cassia, cinnamon, and laudanum—Arabia's prizes for her many trading partners.

Syrian Arabs, being great breeders of camels, brought doubled-humped animals, called ditulio, as well as a variety of single-humped beasts. Some were for milk and others for meat; some hairless, some shaggy. Some could carry on their backs up to 900 pounds of trade goods or five men, lying outstretched upon a couch. The short-legged and slender dromedaries could go for a long day's journey at full stretch, and were especially useful in trips through the waterless desert regions. In war, those same animals carried into battle two bowmen, riding back to back, one of them keeping off enemies in front, the other those who pursued from the rear.

Also along the streets of Capernaum were seen, frequently, togate Romans. Wearing togas was never a casual affair. It was difficult to drape them properly without assistance, and, once on, it could be problematic to keep them in place. When a Roman donned his toga, a transformation occurred. That toga, upon the shoulder of the wearer, said to all comers, "Treat me as you would treat Rome herself—consider yourself warned." In Capernaum, as everywhere in the world that was their Empire, the toga was seen when Romans were conducting official business.

Jews of every kind milled around in the ordered chaos of the city: turbaned and bare-chested fishermen, ebbing and flowing at the docks like a tide when the fish were biting; the wealthy who earned their money honestly and those who didn't, tax collectors the worst of them; priests with their special garments of white linen—short breeches, reaching from the hips to the thighs, a long, close-fitting tunic woven in one piece without seam, along with a symbolically ornamented white linen girdle, and a cap shaped like a cup. Women shopped or sold produce or plied their trade as prostitutes.

So, too, within the human stew that stirred in Capernaum, did a certain Egyptian walk with notable poise along the swarming streets, making his way unerringly to a dim and hidden amulet shop. At the doorway, he paused to glance around and take note of his surroundings. Seeing that no one was watching him, he ducked his head and stepped in. The owner was concluding a transaction and bidding farewell to his customer, so the Egyptian hid his face within the hood of his cloak. Only when the man left with his purchases did he reveal himself.

"Mentuhotep!" exclaimed the owner. "Where have you been, you mangy dog?"

"Why, Siamun, I was unaware you had missed me so keenly," replied Mummius, grateful for the sight of his friend and the cadence of his native tongue. For once, he was even glad for the sound of his Egyptian birth name, which long ago he had discarded. "Mentuhotep"—it might be useful for his mission.

Siamun limped his way around the counter. The two of them embraced, the bent and face-scarred Siamun, the elegant and polished Mummius, bound together in the brotherhood that came with being Egyptians in a foreign land.

"Are you here for potions, my friend, or will you be staying this time?"

"Thank you, Siamun. I wish to stay."

"I thought as much," he said, grinning. "Well, then, brother, let me show you to your room." Siamun led the way through a portal covered with a heavy drape, into the recesses of the shop.

Mummius was amazed. It was quite remarkable, the renovation of this corner of Siamun's clandestine world. Everywhere else in the shop were shelves heavy with bags and vials, and stacks of boxes on the floor, the contents of which were known to Siamun alone. The layer of dust that covered all was interrupted here and there where particular contents had been brought out to show or sell. But here, behind a drape hung for this purpose, was a private area cleaned and furnished and waiting. Mummius could see that Siamun had taken great pains on his behalf. He had asked for help, but he had not expected so grand a gesture.

"You have put yourself out, friend," said Mummius.

"Nothing, nothing at all," said Siamun, whisking away a spider that had started her tiny web between a chest and the wall. "I had begun to give you up. It has been many months since your last letter."

"My mistress was abroad much longer than expected and only recently returned to Magdala."

"Now she is back in Capernaum," said Siamun with a sly look. His unerring knowledge of all that transpired in this, his city, was one of the many reasons Mummius needed him.

"But it is your Jesus that interests you most," Siamun went on.

"He is not 'my' Jesus."

"Do not be coy with me, Egyptian! Jesus is a lodestone and you a tiny iron filing in the grip of his irresistible draw."

"Do not annoy me, *Egyptian*, or I will put a spell upon you," said Mummius, trying to cover his irritation.

"We both know you'd regret that," replied Siamun, harking back to an encounter years ago when they had indeed cast spells upon each other in a fit of rivalry, leaving one barking like a dog and the other speechless for half a day. They had agreed never to do it again.

"Just tell me what has been happening," said Mummius.

"All right, then. He arrived in the city two months ago, he and his six disciples, from their long journey through Judea. News of his coming preceded him, and people from all over the countryside gathered, waiting. Many had seen him in Jerusalem performing what they call 'mighty acts,' and they wanted more."

"That was a full nine months before," mused Mummius.

"Yes, and the 'mighty acts' no doubt had been exaggerated in the telling."

"Don't be so sure, Siamun. Is he performing any miracles now?"

"He does. But mostly he stands on the seashore shouting his sermons to great multitudes of restless and noisy pilgrims. He goes out there in the morning and they are waiting. When he leaves in the evening, they lie down to wait again. It is senseless. He keeps saying the same things over and over, and they keep listening."

Mummius squinted, thinking, then said in a low voice, more to himself than to his friend, "So, he has at last abandoned the synagogues and the intellectuals. No more reading and talking, just preaching in the streets."

"What?"

"Never mind. I want to see for myself. What do you have for me?"

Siamun gleamed. "Get up," he said. Slowly he lifted open the chest where Mummius had been sitting and mimicked a Roman trumpet call.

At the sight of the wonderful contents within, Mummius lost his composure. "Fabulous!" he cried, drawing in a breath.

One by one, Siamun took out folded garments and spread them upon the bed and the floor: common tunics and embroidered capes, sashes and belts, sandals old and new, a pair of boots, headdresses of every variety, eye patches, even a crutch. "How would you look as a whore?" he asked, roaring with laughter as he covered his face with a tired silk scarf decorated with tiny golden bangles. He spun around slowly, his one good hip undulating weirdly.

Siamun had promised to help Mummius, and he was better than his word. He had delivered beyond all expectation: a private place to stay in the hidden amulet shop and a plethora of disguises he could use to secrete himself in any crowd. Mummius would be a convincing Arab, a Jew, even a Roman if it came to that. He spoke their languages. All he needed was the appearance, which Siamun had provided abundantly.

And still there was more.

"I know you are here to write it all down, everything he says." Another trumpet call, and Siamun produced a basket of blank scrolls and a large box of ink.

"I bow before you, Great Siamun, Prince in Galilee!" Mummius gushed.

"I'll drink to that," Siamun replied, gleefully accepting the praise. "Wine!" he ordered, clapping his hands to summon a slave. They raised their cups in a toast.

Soon the masquerading Mummius was standing at the edge of the crowd beside the Sea of Galilee. He had removed his stylized wig, and his free-flowing tresses tickled his neck where they lay. He had to remember not to be constantly scratching. He felt almost naked with his eyes washed of the kohl that marked him as an Egyptian. What seemed most alien to his fastidious nature were his hands, grimy with the dirt he had applied to the nails and joints. Overall, Mummius was pleased, amused really, with his choice. He just needed to get comfortable with playing his part—an incense merchant from Nabatean territory to the east—for it was a perfect disguise.

Rome was a voracious consumer of incense. Wherever they went, Romans were quick to build temples to their pantheon. Each of these temples routinely burned ceremonial incense. In addition, incense was used at funerals to mask the odor of death. All of this had led to a massive demand, which the Nabateans were striving not only to fill, but also to monopolize. Years ago, the trade deficit got so bad that Caesar Augustus had sent an army to discover and seize the source of frankincense. He was unsuccessful. As a result, great amounts of money continued to flow directly from Roman coffers into the purses of Nabatean spice traders.

Mummius patted his hidden bag of coins. This was going to be entertaining. Easy, too, because, in addition to their native Arabic, many Nabateans spoke accented Aramaic. Communication would be no problem for the multilingual Egyptian.

Standing next to a man he took to be a local by his white turban, the national headdress of Galilee, Mummius tried out his charade. "Sir, what think you of this rabbi, Jesus?"

"Never heard anyone like him," replied the man, chewing on a straw. "The people love him. See how they laugh when he pokes fun at the religious leaders."

"Do you come often to hear him?"

"Had to. My wife wouldn't stop prattling about him," said the man, indicating with a nod of his head a group of women sitting near the front of the crowd, in rapt attention. "I wanted to see what was making my supper late every day."

"Women!"

"You have said it."

"And what have you learned, sir?"

"Well, he does have some unusual ideas. Yesterday I understood him to say that poor people will one day inherit great riches because God wants to reward them for their suffering." The man looked Mummius up and down. "You are an Arab merchant. You would not understand *that* notion."

"No," said Mummius, "in truth, I would not. A man makes his own way in the world, eh?"

"I've always believed that if you had money it was because God had chosen you for reward. But maybe I like this new idea. Cease struggling to make a living, be poor, and let the God of Israel pay my debts."

The man roared with laughter. People nearby turned and gawked. For a moment Mummius saw many eyes on him. Not the kind of attention he wanted. No one seemed to notice him particularly, so he stepped away, taking up another position.

He was nearer to Jesus, now, close enough to look him in the eye, but he did not. He studied the men standing around Jesus and recognized them as the disciples whom he had met in Magdala. Mummius was appalled at the way Jesus behaved toward his disciples, to say nothing of the unwashed hordes. Mummius had learned that one of the rewards of greatness was to be set apart. He would never get used to the idea of an exalted master being so open to others.

Mary was sitting in profile beside Jesus. It was the first time Mummius had seen them together in public. She was obviously attached to him, casual and familiar. Not surprising. They were teacher and devotee now.

Suddenly Mary was looking, not at Jesus, but at Mummius. He had intended to prepare for this inevitable moment by turning his head and taking up a stance she would not identify with him. *What if she recognizes me?* Surely his unconcealed concentration on her would betray him. *No, she does not expect me. She will not see me,* he thought, heart pounding. Mary glanced away. She had only been surveying the crowd, and apparently, he had seemed but one of many unfamiliar faces. *I must get used to this,* he thought, tearing his gaze away from her and turning to his own business, leaving behind a mysterious, unidentified wish that she would have, indeed, seen him for who he was.

Several thousand people were gathered there by the sea—and *on* the sea, as it were, for many had put out in their boats just offshore and sat bobbing, contentedly listening. Most of them were Jews to whom Jesus felt familiar, one of their own, a native Galilean who spoke their language, not only Aramaic, though that was what he used, but the language of their Law. This he knew better than any other teacher they had heard, ever, in the synagogue, at home or in school. No one had bested him in a theological argument, though many had tried.

He shared their daily lives. He had been a carpenter, apprenticed to his father, working on Roman construction projects in the area, just as many of them had done. He knew their farms and their struggles to earn their living. His friends were fishermen, and he spent time on their boats, pulling in the nets. He knew their trouble when the nets came up empty. Jesus was emphatically a man of the Jews and for the Jews.

From his new vantage point Mummius surveyed the crowd and noticed that it was dotted with gentiles. He thought their numbers represented most of the diverse elements that had collected in Capernaum that spring, many Arabs, the occasional Roman, Egyptians, others. He wondered what those non-Jews thought of Jesus. He was startled by an uninvited Demetria, coming into his mind, and he heard her say, "Well, you are not a Jew, Mummius. What do *you* think of him?" He shook his head to banish her, but Demetria's question remained.

Mummius had tracked Jesus to Capernaum to create an accurate record of his teachings. What he did not expect was to find himself drawn in along with the rest of the hearers. He would have to resist that. He remembered what Siamun had said of Jesus, calling him a lodestone. *"And you a tiny iron filing..."*

It was almost dusk when the weary Nabatean incense trader returned to the amulet shop.

"You are just in time for the evening meal, Mentuhotep. Sit down, brother," said the eager Siamun.

"Thank you, my friend, but not just yet. I have work to do. Please, do not wait for me."

"What are you talking about? You look utterly spent. Have you eaten anything today?"

"Now that you mention it, no, I have not. Still, I am not hungry. Could you just have some wine sent to my room?" Seeing Siamun's look of dismay, Mummius added, "This is discourteous in the extreme, I know, but I must attend to some business while it is fresh in me. It is not a reflection on you, my friend. It is just that I..."

"Say no more. I understand. Go. Your wine is waiting," said Siamun, having commanded a slave with a glance.

"I will make it up to you," promised Mummius, for it was indeed a serious breach of etiquette to decline Siamun's hospitality and deprive him of Mummius' report, which he longed to hear. He was relieved when his host departed with a friendly wave of his hand.

Mummius stripped down to his loincloth. A slave poured water from a pitcher into a large bowl and stood by with a towel while Mummius washed the grime of the long day from his face and hands. When he was finished, he handed back the towel.

"Shall I fill your wine cup, sir?" asked the slave in smooth Greek.

To the surprise of both of them, the imperious, untouchable Mummius heard himself say to the irrelevant servant, "Thank you."

The slave poured out a cup and left, blinking his eyes at the unexpected acknowledgement.

Mummius draped a shawl over his bare shoulders. He sat down cross-legged on the floor and pulled a writing board onto his lap. With a sigh of gratitude for his friend's endless consideration, Mummius mixed some water into Siamun's cake of ink. He opened the linen cloth in which his pens and stylus were wrapped and unrolled a blank scroll over the lap board. Long ago, in the aftermath of Mary's healing, he had said the obvious to Marcus Quintius Severus, "They will make him a god." That he could not prevent, but at least he could inscribe the facts as he witnessed them. Mummius was determined to write down the truth about Jesus, before the spellbound hordes distorted it.

He dipped his pen into a bowl of ink and held it poised over the papyrus. Mummius closed his eyes and sank into his soul, the dwelling place of the ancient, sacred name: scribe. Honored and revered. The one who hears, the one who interprets, the one who records. When he opened his eyes and pressed the nib of the pen down, out flowed, from right to left across the scroll, in Aramaic letters, this:

"These are the sayings of Jesus of Nazareth, witnessed and inscribed personally by me, Mummius of..."

He hesitated. He could not even say for sure where he was from. He had become a chameleon, adapting to whatever circumstances were presented, wherever he found them, in Alexandria, Rome, Magdala. Here, in Capernaum, he would be disguising his identity—changing his colors—perhaps every day. He longed to shed his temporary skins once and for all, to be who he really was, but who was that? If he were to make one final start in his life, where would he go? Mummius dipped his pen to refresh the ink that had dried while he mused. He laid the tip where he had suspended the introduction.

"...Alexandria," he wrote with a flourish.

CHAPTER 35

Mary was glad to be back in Capernaum. She had missed the men—James, Peter, Philip, Nathanael, Andrew, and particularly John. They had been a family for many months, sharing the hardships of the road and developing common bonds of allegiance to Jesus. They were familiar, but Jesus had added others to his circle now, and it seemed he could go nowhere without many of them in tow. In addition to the six who were always tucked in close around him, he attracted extras that, on any given evening, he would invite to supper. At the end of each day, they arrived as a group, famished.

Hungry for Jesus' words and my hospitality! Mary thought.

She had enjoyed her return to cooking, which her mother had taught her so well, but now the dinner crowd often exceeded her ability to prepare the meal herself. It was enough of a task just to oversee the culinary activities and ensure the comfort of her guests, so she had reluctantly given over more responsibilities to Joachim. In fact, Joachim frequently hired additional servants, for dear little Zimzi, his disastrously shy daughter, though she tried her best, could not be trusted even to serve without some embarrassing trip or spill. Then the men would tease her.

Why am I thinking of the meal? Mary was completely distracted from her morning prayers. Once her mind had wandered to the day's upcoming activities, there was no recouping the concentration required for meditation. She sighed, and before the sigh was finished Zimzi had appeared with tea. This task, at least, the girl had mastered. As long as Mary did not praise her too eagerly, Zimzi performed it well.

"Shalom, Zimzi," she said quietly.

"Peace to you, Mary," replied Zimzi, setting down the tray.

"Thank you, dear."

"You are welcome, Mary." And the girl hurried away.

Mary sipped her warm khat, thinking how to use this unfilled hour. *Just enough time for a letter!* "Joachim," she called, "will you bring my writing materials, please."

"My dearest Demetria," she wrote. "How I miss you! I see you sitting on our bench in the courtyard, reading some interesting book, yet unable to keep your eyes from wandering to the flowers that are opening in the warm spring weather. I know how you love to collect red tulips for the dinner table.

"A magnificent hoopoe pair has produced a nestful of babies in my garden this morning. I have never been so close to a hoopoe and am amazed by the way the muscles of their heads raise and lower their cinnamon and black topknot feathers, like a fan opening and closing. I wish you were here to see them.

"What else can I tell you about my life in Capernaum? Well, you remember the crowds that followed Jesus in Jerusalem. It is like that here. Each day many people come from the surrounding area and beyond. As a matter of fact, Jesus wants to take his message to people in different towns, people who cannot come here to Capernaum, so we will soon be traveling again. 'Oh, no, not another long journey' I hear you say, but do not fear. It is as I explained to you before. We will not venture far from home, and you will always know where I am and how to direct letters to me."

Mary had no intention to deceive when she told Demetria that their travels would not take them far away. She had every expectation that they would be visiting mostly towns around the sea, such as Chorazin and Bethsaida. How could she possibly know that they would eventually travel as far as sixty miles from Capernaum through four political subdivisions: Galilee on the west, Trachonitis to the northeast, Decapolis to the southeast and Perea, directly south? She would *never* have considered the prospect that they would walk this circuit many times in the upcoming year. Staying in touch with Demetria would prove a far more difficult task than she had imagined. For now, Mary was thinking only of a seaside tour of pleasant coastal towns.

"A friend of Peter has put a boat at Jesus' disposal. This will make it easy to ferry from place to place. With the weather warm now, we will be able to sleep under the stars and not have to impose upon people. Silly me! What am I saying? There is no dearth of invitations. 'Jesus, come, have dinner with me.' 'Rabbi, stay in my home tonight, please,' they all cry. He prefers to keep to his close circle of friends at night. That is when he talks to us privately, teaching us. Our barrage of questions never ends, and his patience is never exhausted. Well, that is not quite so. He does sometimes get exasperated when he has made a point, which to him is obvious, but is not understood by some of us. Often we talk so late into the night that everyone falls asleep here in my house. Sometimes they go home with Peter and Andrew, or stay with other friends."

Mary paused again in her writing. Their days were indeed very long. Jesus insisted on continuing their nighttime sessions even after they had spent all morning and all afternoon with the crowds. Then he was up before dawn every day, lost for hours in prayer. "Not lost," he said when they asked him about it, "listening."

When Mary considered the ferocious schedule Jesus set for himself, she could see that something was pressing on him, as though he had a great deal of work to accomplish in very little time, like a farmer laboring to get the crop in before the rains come. She did not understand this. It seemed to her that they were just getting started, that there would be no end to Jesus' thrilling work and her part in it.

Suddenly noticing the brightness of the sun shining into the garden, creating a dewy chiaroscuro, Mary went back to her letter.

"My dear, it is time for me to get to work. I look forward to a letter from you very soon. Perhaps yours will pass mine in transit. If not, sit down this very minute and write to me. Tell me everything you are doing, and it will be as though we are right next door to each other. Mummius will see that your letter is sent by the fastest courier. My love to you, Mary."

She rolled and tied and sealed her scroll, and sat back, imagining Mummius selecting it from among the day's mail and handing it over to the joyous Demetria. But when Mary's letter arrived in Magdala the next day, Mummius was not there to sort the mail. He was standing beside the sea in Capernaum, again playing the part of a Nabatean spice trader.

Observing an unusual commotion, Mummius turned to a man in the crowd and asked, "What's going on over there?"

"It will be a poor day for poor men. The fishing fleet has been out for five hours this morning, and nothing to show for it. All the boats have returned empty. The fishermen are cleaning their nets to put them away." The man shook his head, commiserating. "And the Sabbath begins this evening, so no fishing tomorrow."

"Too bad," said Mummius with a downward pull of his mouth. "But why all the commotion?"

"This rabbi called Jesus is trying to get some of them to put back out and try again. They are arguing that they know more about runs of fish than he does, but he keeps insisting. Wait. Look, the brothers Simon and Andrew are pushing off."

Mummius saw that the other fishermen remained on the shore securing their boats. Many were laughing and rolling their eyes. They had fished these waters their whole lives, and their fathers and grandfathers before them. They knew there would be no fish today. They knew that Simon and Andrew knew it, too.

As the lone boat rowed out a bit from shore, Jesus was heard to shout above the crowd, "Just a little farther, Peter!"

"Look where he's pointing," said Mummius' acquaintance. "There are never any fish in that spot. He is making sport of his friends."

"Who needs friends such as that, eh?" offered Mummius.

"You have said it," replied the man.

Mummius was not scoffing inside. He was waiting to see what Jesus had in mind as the brothers inattentively lowered their drag-net into the empty waters. It happened so fast that he almost didn't see it.

The net had just submerged when Andrew was nearly dragged over the boat rail by the weight of the catch. Had it not been for Simon Peter's mighty right arm pulling against the haul, his brother would surely have flipped into the lake. Even together they were unable to pull in the net and frantically beckoned to John and James to come quickly to help them. John and James were not alone in jumping into their boat. Every man who had not secured his nets was already racing out to the unexpected strike. This would be a good day after all—fish to sell and food for their families.

Mummius scowled, knowing that the crowd, eager to exalt the wonder-worker in their midst, would make of this a miracle, as though Jesus had created the fish himself. What Mummius wanted to know was how Jesus had discerned the location of the school of fish at that very moment. Perhaps some subtle pattern on the surface of the water. Or had he called them there when he wanted to demonstrate his powers? That was not outside the range of possibility for a master like Jesus.

Mummius wanted to cry out in frustration. He knew how to manipulate animals, snakes in particular. He had often seen rainmakers call clouds into the sky to end a drought. But Jesus did things that Mummius had never witnessed. He did not know it was possible for a man's power to extend so deeply into the forces of nature. He gritted his teeth and turned for home. Perhaps in writing down the story, some insight would come.

It was an auspicious prelude to the Sabbath, that remarkable catch of fish. It took the rest of the day for the fish to be cleaned and loaded into baskets for market. Even after hungry locals and caravan visitors had swept up a large share, there was plenty left for families at home. All the dinners had been cooked when the first trumpet blast sounded, half an hour before sunset, calling the peasants from their labors in distant fields and vineyards. A few minutes later, when the second trumpet warned merchants to close their shops, Mary was scrutinizing her housework, satisfied that everything was ready.

She had been cleaning all afternoon, each sweep of the broom preparing, not only her house, but her heart as well. When the work was finished, she took time with the ritual bathing of her hands and feet and face and, now, mind, body and soul were fit to welcome in the Sabbath, which she loved.

Just before sunset, Mary's guests arrived, dressed in their best clothes. She was grateful that Jesus had brought no strangers tonight, only John and James. She led the way into the triclinium and indicated where they should stand around the table, Jesus at the head opposite her, John on the right side and James across from John on the left. She looked over the table she had prepared and felt the stirring in her heart that always accompanied this moment. Stretched out before her was the treasured white cloth set with special-occasion dishes. The wine goblet stood next to two warm loaves of sweet challah, which were covered with a fresh linen napkin reserved for them alone.

Mary covered her head with her grandmother's pale blue silk veil, waiting, in the silent moment of slowed breathing and knowing smiles. The third trumpet sounded, telling all to kindle the Sabbath lights, which would burn till tomorrow at the close of the holy day. At the moment that the woman of every Jewish household did the same, Mary lifted a taper and lit the lamps. Their flames flickering in front of her, she covered her eyes with her hands and pronounced the blessing:

"Blessed are You, our God, King of the Universe, Who Has Commanded us to kindle the Light of Shabbat."

Mary prayed for her family in Magdala, Demetria, Rachel, Mummius and the weavers. She prayed for her friends who were joined as family in common devotion to Jesus and his teaching. When she had spoken everyone's name, she opened her eyes. "Rabbouni," she said, inviting him to recite prayers over the wine and the challah. She breathed in the sound as he spoke. "Blessed are You, our God, Creator of time and space, Who Enriches our lives with Holiness, Commanding us to wrap ourselves in the Tallit."

Another sacred moment: the invocation, yes, and the deep resonance that Jesus' voice took on when he pronounced it. But it was the tallit that stopped time when Jesus bent his head slightly and draped himself in it. The one whose fringe had been knotted by her own young-girl fingers. Her mother had told her that, according to tradition, each knot, as she tied it, would bind her forever to all others who were part of the fabric of her life.

It was still extraordinary, when she thought of it, the story of how the matchless prayer shawl had made its way, years before they met, from her loom onto Jesus' shoulders. Nonetheless, here it was. This was the tallit, and this was the man.

After the Sabbath dinner, they rested, John and James and Mary and Jesus, talking, as friends do, in the comfort of each other's affection. Tonight there would be no instruction in the Law or inspired teaching about the Reign of God. Jesus did not seem inclined even to discuss their imminent journey. Instead, they talked about the weather, the fishing and the spring crops, savoring the rare moment of respite from their taxing schedule. They told stories of childhood, laughing about good times in the past. Mary was amused, imagining them as boys, playing pranks and avoiding schoolwork. And they were amazed to hear of her precocious weaving talent and the vast education her father had given her. Finally, they recalled the events of the day.

"Did you see Andrew's face when those fish came in?" asked John.

"It was a wild look, all right! He is always so sure of himself, but that brought him down to size," said James, starting to laugh.

"You shouldn't tease him," Mary interjected, as a smile broke onto her face, too.

"Big brother Simon Peter saved him from going overboard!" roared John, causing James and Jesus to collapse in thigh-slapping laughter.

They were holding their stomachs and wiping the tears from the corners of their eyes, when James caught his breath enough to ask, "How did you do that, Master?"

They all looked to Jesus for his answer.

"Signs," he said.

Here it is, thought Mary, disappointed by this turn. *Time for instruction.*

"Everyone knows how to read the signs of wind and water. Anyone could have seen it."

"*We* did not see it," said John.

"That's because you know the sea too well, brother."

"There are never any fish in that hole!" protested James.

"There were today."

"Because you made it so," said John.

"Look, you rely too much on what you already know. Your minds are closed to different ways of seeing things. I'm telling you, sometimes there are fish where you do not expect them."

Mary watched the reactions of John and James. They must be trying to determine whether Jesus had called in the fish or had been able to sense where they were. To her that was unimportant. Jesus had told them that they would be "fishers of men," but they still did not seem to know what he meant. She understood that their mission was to call people into freedom and joy, and that they should look everywhere, even in unexpected places, for hungry souls to receive the good news of the Reign of God.

After a few moments of silence and furrowed brows, John spoke. "Well," he said, "that is enough to ponder for a while."

"Indeed it is," replied James, suppressing a yawn. "Time to go home, brother." And to Jesus, "Shabbat shalom, Master."

Mary accompanied them to the door, where they embraced her and thanked her for her hospitality and the Sabbath meal. She closed the door behind them and returned to the dining room where Jesus was clearing the last of their dishes.

"I am going out to pray," he said. "Sleep well."

She nodded silently, watching him leave. Ordinarily, those in their company fell asleep quickly at the end of their demanding days, especially since most continued to earn their living in the usual way, primarily the hard work of early morning fishing. Jesus seemed to sleep less and less, and all wondered at his never-ending supply of energy. Mary knew that it was in his hours of meditation that he found renewal.

She walked alone around the house, extinguishing lamps. She thought of Jesus making his solitary trek to the outskirts of Capernaum. By now he would be climbing the hill that overlooked the town to a little olive grove where he liked to be alone. She thought of him kneeling there, radiated by that force of God which she had experienced only once, in the burial house in Magdala. The force had frightened her out of her wits. At the time, she had believed that it would surely engulf and kill her, because she was too small to hold it.

She remembered the earth shifting and groaning and a voice emanating from the box containing the bones of her brother, Reuben, calling her by name. She remembered being separated from her body, observing it from a distance. She remembered the earth-shaking whisper calling her "beloved" and telling her to "go to your brother and live!" It was then that she realized it was God who had spoken to her and sent her to Jesus, her brother. Liberating as that moment was, it was still terrifying, that unexpected presence of God, and she too uncertain. She supposed that her fear of repeating the experience had kept God away since that time. The truth was, if she were ever to be in full partnership with Jesus, she would have to be wholeheartedly open to the presence of God, as he was.

Mary went to bed, but she did not sleep. She lay awake, thinking about the Sabbath meal and the quiet time with John and James. It was unusual for them to relax and make light conversation. She did not know why there had been so little serious instruction that evening, but she appreciated that her mind was unencumbered by any bottomless question of the Law, free to wander where it would. It wandered to thoughts of Jesus, still out there somewhere, deep in his God-listening. If he could stay like that all night long, she could surely do the same for a few hours. Mary had always been conscientious about her prayer life. Recently, though, she had become aware that if she were to keep up the pace that Jesus set for their ministry, she needed to develop his kind of proficiency. *Perhaps this is the time to try...*

Mary rose from her bed and, wrapping up in a woolen cloak against the pre-dawn chill, went out into the garden and sat down, leaning on a wall. Instinctively, she began with the holy words of Judaism. "*Shema Yisrael Adonai eloheinu Adonai echad.*" Hear, Israel, the LORD is our God, the LORD is One. She pronounced the Shema over and over. It wasn't long before her voice began to deepen and the words came out more slowly, with pauses that lengthened between each repetition. She was drifting off.

Mary shook her head to refocus her attention. She noticed that even the small physical comforts she had allowed herself opposed her efforts. She pulled the cloak off her shoulders and, moving away from the wall, sat unsupported on the stone floor. Soon, all she could think of was the discomfort in her legs and the weight of her eyelids. She forced her eyes to stay open as she moved from the Shema to other prayers and passages from the scriptures, hoping that variety would aid her. But she became alternately angry and discouraged as she heard the sacred words leaving her mouth through gritted teeth. This was not the serenity she had seen on Jesus' face when he was in deep meditation.

Thoughts of her warm bed brought Mary close to abandoning her endeavor. She yawned. She felt the skin at the corners of her lips stretch open with a painful little crack. She had not noticed how dry her mouth was. If she could only have a drink of water... She became aware of the fountain in the center of the courtyard, just a few feet away. There was no water bubbling up from its central pipe to fill the small top basin and then overflowing into the larger basin below. Joachim had closed the cistern valve for the night. The fountain was dry.

Mary could think of nothing but water. Every nook in her mind was filled with the idea of water, and she could find no other word or yearning within. She thought she heard a gurgling sound from inside the fountain. Wondering, she watched a stream of water emerge from the center pipe, slowly at first, then more fully, filling the basins and sparkling in the moonlight. The more the thirst-quenching fountain danced and sang, the more she wanted it, for it was beautiful, and sweet. As though in response to her longing, the flow of water increased and surged. It shot high into the night and became spangled with stars in the sky above. Then the water started to fall back to earth, raining down on her as though from a sudden burst of clouds. Mary stood up to scramble away, expecting to be drenched, but her night shift remained dry. The swelling fountain continued its gushing, but did not flood the floor or anything around her.

She was ready to run from the scene, but her body was still, like a statue, and, try as she might, she could not will her legs to move. As she stood thus, fixed in place, a voice, clear and sweet as the flowing water, issued from the fountain, a voice she had heard before, calling her name.

"Mary."

"Here I am," she answered.

At once, within the streaming water, there glistened the form of a woman, a spirit, high as the water sprayed up and wide as the water spilled down.

The spirit voice said, "I come to you as evidence of abundant life in the Reign of God. You, Mary, will be my witness."

Fearing to look upon the face of God, Mary covered her eyes with her hands. "What is it you want me to do?"

"The Spirit of God is upon you. You will know what to do."

Mary argued. "The Spirit of God is upon Jesus. I am but his servant."

"You are the servant of the LORD alone! You will show the way into the Reign of God."

"How can I, a woman, do this thing?"

When Mary said that, the fountain exploded with a sound like the blow of a mighty hammer on an iron anvil, sending out water high and wide enough to engulf the entire house.

"Why do you doubt? Have you delivered people from their suffering by the laying on of your hands? Have you baptized them in the name of God? Who do you think is the source of this authority? Open your heart, Mary, and know who I am."

Mary uncovered her face to look upon the wondrous water.

"*Hakmah*," she said. Wisdom.

"Go, and be my witness. Carry water to those who thirst, so that they will believe."

Instantly, the Spirit was gone. The fountain was gurgling softly again, its smooth stream of water flowing up the center pipe and cascading down slowly from basin to basin. And the flow ceased, and the fountain was dry.

What dream was this? No, never had there been a dream so real. It was a true visitation by God. Mary remembered what she had read in the scriptures about *hakmah. She emanates from the glory of the Almighty; she fashions all things; she was present at the creation of the world; she lives with God; to love her is to love God.*

Mary was consumed with desire to tell Jesus of her vision. She considered the idea of walking out to find him, but it was foolish for her to go out alone at night and venture so far. The city gate would be closed and locked and the olive grove was on the other side. He may as well have been in the southern desert, so impossible was it for her to reach him.

Just then, Mary thought she heard the voice of Hakmah whispering, "Go then."

I cannot.

"Do you still doubt?"

Then, filled with the certainty that came from all she had experienced and all she hoped, Mary answered, "LORD, I believe."

She began to feel light. She looked down at her feet and saw that they were still firmly on the floor. Vaguely she remembered the desire of her body to lie down and sleep, but that need was no longer part of her. It belonged to someone else who was like her, but was not her, for now she was hovering above the garden looking down at her physical self, standing barefoot, still fixed on the paving stones, clothed only in a sleep shift.

She heard nothing, for the world and all that was in it was utterly without sound. As she floated within that vast silence, the sound of a single word arose. "*Hakmah*." The word became a whispered repetition, "*hakmah—hakmah—hakmah.*" The word swelled into a fluid crescendo, stretching out, "*haaaakmaaaaah.*" The word intensified, causing Mary's body, still standing on the floor, and her spirit, floating in the air, to vibrate. The source of the sound entered her, body and soul, and she was the sound.

The word lifted her out of the garden and carried her on a warm wind beyond the house, over the sleeping city just outside the city wall to the olive grove where Jesus knelt among the trees, his head and shoulders awash in the light of God that lay on him. Mary was unaware that her face, too, was radiant, but Jesus must have seen it, for when she came to rest beside him and he looked at her, all his attention centered there.

Under half-closed lids, Mary's eyes glistened with tears. "*Hakmah.*"

Jesus seemed surprised by the word, and her voice was so quiet, that he leaned in close to make sure he had heard accurately. "What did you say?"

"The word. It was *hakmah.*"

His own eyes were brimming now, because he had waited long for this moment. "Mary, you are truly blessed."

They sat in the presence of God, made manifest within them and between them and around them. And the knowledge of God that they shared that night became their covenant.

Mary could not say how long she stayed with Jesus. Nor could she say when she returned to her own garden. All she knew was that she was once again hovering in the space above where her body still stood near the fountain, pulsing timelessly with the sound of *hakmah.* When the sun began to sparkle on the dew-lapped leaves of the trees and Zimzi tip-toed out to ask her what was wrong, she did not want to rejoin her body. She wanted to stay as she was, filled with the Spirit that had drawn her out. She wished Zimzi gone. Then Zimzi was gone, only to return with an agitated Joachim.

"Mary!" he exclaimed, blushing at the sight of her and leaning down to pick up the discarded cloak and cover her.

It was his touch on her shoulders that impelled Mary back into her body, passing through what felt like a wet, form-fitting linen shroud. She landed with a jolt on the floor, heavy again with substance. She felt the cold stones under her feet and the morning air and began to shiver.

"Are you all right?"

"Do not be troubled, Joachim," she murmured, as though her own voice were foreign to her.

Next, Zimzi held out a cup to Mary. "Oh, yes, water!" she said and put it to her mouth, but the reality of the water was less strong, less clear, less *all*, than the miraculous flow of water had been.

In spite of her disappointment, she said, "Thank you, Zimzi."

"You are welcome, Mary," offered the quivering Zimzi.

Mary was puzzled when she noticed that Joachim was staring at her hand. She looked and saw that she was holding an olive branch. It was a small, supple stem, with the tender, paired leaves of spring, dull green above and silvery beneath. The branch was in bloom, its delicate, creamy white flowers clustered at the leaf axils, holding the promise of profuse black orbs to come. Gently she pressed the olive branch to her face and, stroking the soft, silvery underside of one leaf, breathed in its fragrance.

Joachim asked, "Where have you been?"

"Among the olives," she replied.

CHAPTER 36

Mummius was the first to see her. She had dressed carelessly, leaving off her jewelry and…what? She was wearing mismatched sandals! Mummius turned quickly to watch Jesus, who was already stepping through the mass of people to the place where she was waiting for him. All eyes were on them when Jesus came near to Mary and greeted her—with a kiss.

Many in the crowd were shocked, for it was scandalous for men and women to show affection by kissing in public. But Mummius knew that it was not at all unusual for philosophers and teachers to kiss their students on the mouth as a sign of the transmission of special knowledge to their chosen ones, as a breath that calls something into being. This was that holy kiss, all the more shocking for Jesus' bestowing it on a woman.

So, thought Mummius, *she has progressed from grateful-recipient-of-healing to worshipful follower to Chosen One. He has received her as a counterpart.*

Jesus was lowering himself to encompass a lesser person—and a woman—yet would not be diminished by it. But why Mary? Why a woman who had lived plagued by demons in a prison of fear, often unable merely to function, while Jesus had devoted his life to the pursuit of spiritual power? Why Mary? Because the very gateway that opened her to demons would open her to beneficial spirits as well. Remove the evil blockage, and the divine could enter in equal measure. Why Mary? Because she was by nature compassionate, not seeking to put herself above another, and courageous in the face of injustice. Jesus loved her for the same reasons Mummius had allowed himself to love her. The difference was that Jesus could give Mary what he could not.

After he witnessed the effect of Mary's transformation, Mummius' daily life in Capernaum was anything but routine. He was consumed with desire to find out all that transpired between Jesus and Mary. The role of

Nabatean spice merchant had become too comfortable. Not wanting to risk the laxity that comes with familiarity, he began each day with the choosing of an identity, varying his disguise often. Besides, he craved access to places not generally frequented by Arabs. The synagogue, for example. He was tempted to try to pass for one of their scribes, but it would be too risky. He had some knowledge of the scriptures, but he was certainly no Hebrew scholar, and would soon find himself in the trap of a theological debate. He settled on representing himself as a Jew from Alexandria. It was perfect.

In the six centuries that had passed since the diaspora, Egypt's great city had grown a Jewish population that exceeded that of Jerusalem. Such was the Jews' assimilation into Hellenistic culture that it was common for Greek to be spoken in prayer services in local synagogues. Hebrew was reserved for the most ancient, most sacred liturgy—*Shema Yisrael Adonai eloheinu Adonai echad*—and it was understood by virtue of repetition. It would be easy for Mummius to become an Alexandrian Jew who spoke fluent Greek and struggled with Hebrew.

Mummius tested his disguise as he sat down to breakfast with Siamun, who squinted with his good eye and declared, "By Horus, Egyptian, you're a Jew!"

"Mmm."

"Let me guess," said Siamun, cracking open a cooked egg and beginning to peel, "A Jew of Alexandria, lately returned to his ancient homeland in search of spiritual renewal."

"Excellent," replied Mummius. "I confess it was a bit of a challenge to strike the right notes with the costume. Do you think the ring is overdone?"

"I do. Take it off. It would draw attention."

"Too bad." Mummius reluctantly removed the lapis lazuli oval and put it in the sleeve of his robe, a good quality garment with wide stripes of pale rust and beige, top to bottom.

"Do you realize that you are scratching your head?"

"It's this infernal turban."

"Well, get used to it, friend. Why are you playing the Jew anyway?"

"I'm going to the synagogue."

Siamun choked on a bite of his egg. "You can't be serious."

"Never more so."

"Your disguise could work in a crowd, Mentuhotep, but at the synagogue you'll stand out like a stork among doves. Everyone will want to talk to the new man in town: what's happening in Alexandria; who's your father; where are you staying; all that sheep's dung. Just go as an Arab, or an Egyptian for that matter."

"I have it covered, Siamun. Fear not."

"Well, I'll be waiting here to protect your hide when you are exposed and must flee. Pah!"

It was not so much that Mummius wanted to listen to the chatter of rabbis and Pharisees concerning Jesus, though that was part of it. His primary objective in going to the synagogue as a Jew was to increase his facility with disguises and identities, to be confident in whatever role he might choose, however alien it was to his nature, however dangerous. He wanted to be disciplined, to practice the tight control that would be needed when he entered the ultimate destination he had in mind—Mary's own home in Capernaum.

Mummius was greeted by an anxious Siamun when he returned from his morning at the synagogue. He was already stripping off the turban and rubbing his scalp with both hands.

"How did it go?" asked Siamun, genuine concern showing on his face.

"Tell you the truth, I could have gone in there naked and not been noticed. They are so consumed with gossip and speculation about Jesus that they neither see nor hear anything else."

"What do they say?"

"They say things I did not expect to hear."

"Sit down at once and tell all, for I am chewed up with interest."

"Well enough, brother, for I see you have spread the midday meal. Let us eat and talk," said Mummius, genially clapping Siamun on the shoulder. They sat down on tooled camel skin cushions around an engraved brass table and drank Egyptian beer. "What surprised me most was the talk of the Pharisees. You know these men, the Pharisees?"

"Yes, of course. Who doesn't? They have been a political force for hundreds of years."

"They are teachers, too. Jesus throws jabs at them, and the crowds howl with laughter. But I misunderstood his intention until I listened to the Pharisees themselves discussing his ideas. They were actually *discussing*, not condemning. The burning question of the day concerned healing on the Sabbath."

"I have heard a report that Jesus healed someone in the house of a Pharisee just two days ago—and on the Sabbath, too!"

"It is precisely that event that provoked their discussion."

Now Mummius and Siamun knew that the daily life of Jews was governed by the Law of Moses. They knew, too, that Torah was silent on many details, leaving confusing gaps. It was into these gaps that political parties joined the fray of interpretation. The Law stated that, on the Sabbath, the people "shall do no work." What did it mean, to "do no work"? Scholars were clear about not lighting fires, even for cooking. They were clear about the exact distance a man must not travel beyond the city wall. Hundreds of other particulars had been hammered out, but the question of whether "healing" constituted "work," though it was hotly debated, had not been settled.

"It appears that Jesus settled it for them," Mummius explained to Siamun. "The argument ensued right there in the house of the Pharisee, with a poor, suffering man practically sitting in Jesus' lap, begging for help."

"What sort of ailment was it?"

"A swelling of the legs and feet. I tell you, Siamun, I have seen such swelling till a man's legs looked more like tree trunks than human limbs. Beyond a certain point the standard treatment of diuretic herbs can do nothing to impede the progress of the disease. It isn't long after that till the heart fails. "

"Some among them wanted such a man to continue to suffer till the sun went down, ending the Sabbath," scoffed Siamun.

"Exactly. Jesus, holding one of the man's feet in his hands, apparently looked at the company gathered there and challenged them, 'So, is it lawful to heal on the Sabbath or not?'"

"Ah ha ha. Ha ha!" roared Siamun. "What could they say to that?"

"Nothing. They just watched, amazed, as Jesus stroked and rubbed the man's extremities till the legs and feet had returned to normal size."

"And then the Pharisees were livid."

"That is what is so surprising. From what I gathered, many accepted it. The main concern of the Pharisees, generally, is to guide people—I am speaking of individuals, now—into taking more responsibility for their own lives and the lives of the community. This is what Jesus teaches. He encourages people to know God within, not put their spiritual lives outside themselves into the hands of religious leaders, or anyone else."

"Mmm," mused Siamun, "a much more difficult task."

"Indeed. By the way, this lamb is delicious. Who is your cook?"

"Why do you ask?" inquired Siamun, baiting Mummius, because he knew the answer already.

The woman employed as Siamun's cook, as expected, did indeed provide Mummius with what he was after—useful information about Mary's household. She knew Joachim, she said, well enough to know where he shopped for food, and when. She reported that, since Mary's return to Capernaum, large evening meals were served. She had heard Joachim complain to merchants about the unpredictable number of guests, and she knew that additional servants were often hired to take care of the increase in work.

Mummius sat on the cot in his small quarters, behind the drawn curtain, considering how best to disguise himself in Mary's house, where he would be under her very nose. The biggest challenge was his height. He needed to be shorter. Hmmm. He would have to be bent over. Yes, a disorder of the spine, bent and slightly crooked. This would reduce his height and give him another advantage as well. His head would be down, forcing him to look at people sideways. No one would see his face straight on. It was a good thing he was fit; maintaining such a posture would require strength and stamina and breath control.

Late that evening, Siamun had not yet been able to close his shop, because several customers still milled around. He turned to hiss into the ear of his assistant, "They will buy nothing, and they want to finger everything. I must leave for a few moments. When I return, I want them gone."

"I know what to do, master."

Siamun departed. One by one, the stragglers were ushered out of the shop. "We do not have what you are looking for, sir," said the assistant to one. To another, "Come back later. We are expecting a shipment within the month." A third was only a beggar. That one the slave shoved into the street with his foot. "This is a business. Get out and don't come back!"

When Siamun returned, the shop was empty but for one remaining customer. He grabbed the slave by the neck and squeezed, pushing him through the curtain behind the counter.

"Why is he still here?"

"I, I, I think he is going to buy, master."

"He's a Jew; why would he buy potions?"

"I think he is looking for incense, master. Perhaps we should offer him something."

"I detest Jews coming in here. Get rid of him!"

Siamun watched from behind the curtain as his assistant, rubbing his bruised neck, approached the customer.

"We are closing the shop, sir. You will have to go now."

"A few more moments, only."

"I'm sorry, sir, the owner is quite adamant to close."

"The owner, you say? I am sure the owner would not turn out his compatriot, his respected colleague."

Hearing the switch from Greek to Egyptian and seeing the customer stand up straight from his bent-over stance, Siamun burst from his spying behind the curtain.

"Mentuhotep, you dog! You did it."

"Where is your faith in me, brother?" replied Mummius, his black eyes sparkling.

"Nevertheless..."

"If I can fool your sharp eye, Siamun, do you not believe that I can manage Mary's household?"

"Perhaps. Perhaps, yes. Still, I wish you would not go so far," urged Siamun, trying to persuade his friend to abandon his ruse.

"It is done, Siamun," said Mummius, bending over again and starting to shuffle toward the back of the shop.

Siamun laid a hand on Mummius' shoulder.

"Why do you not make yourself known? Go to see them. Ask Mary to invite you to dinner. From what you say of her, she would be happy to have you. Would she not, Mentuhotep?"

A deep black frown settled around Mummius' clenched jaw and into his eyes. Siamun was interfering in matters that were beyond his comprehension.

Siamun continued. "I have accepted the wounds that life has brought to me, friend. You have tried, but still something eludes you. What is it that keeps you obsessed? Ahh—you desire to be as close to the godhead as Jesus is. You want to be known for who you are, and yet you fear to be known. That's it, isn't it?"

The chord of truth had been struck too perfectly. Before he knew what he was doing, Mummius had raised his arm and pointed his hand at Siamun's face.

"Would you silence me with a spell, Magus? Go ahead. It will not stop the raging in your heart."

With that, Siamun turned his back on Mummius and disappeared behind the curtain leading to the back of the shop. Mummius stood motionless, his outstretched arm still at the ready. But there was no enemy in sight.

CHAPTER 37

After the night of the olive branch, Joachim knew not to disturb Mary when she prayed in the courtyard, silent and rapt. She would stir in her own time; then, he would serve her quietly.

"Peace be to you, Joachim," said Mary, as he delivered her breakfast one morning.

"Peace to you, Mary."

Then, as he turned to leave, she stopped him with a question. "Who is the man I saw in the atrium yesterday?"

"The new gardener," he replied.

"Have we hired a gardener?"

"It has been difficult for me to care adequately for the plants. With the increased work in the kitchen... I hope you do not mind."

"Forgive me, Joachim. I know you and Zimzi are burdened. I am glad you found someone."

"We are fortunate to have him, Mary. His fee is low, and he comes highly recommended. He has already rearranged some of the failing plants to suit their needs for light."

"And I notice some expert pruning here in the courtyard," she said. "But he is bent over. It is hard to see how he can do this kind of work. I wonder, is he in pain?"

"He says he can manage."

"What is his name?"

"He is called Reuben."

"Oh..."

"Is something wrong?"

"No. It's just that my brother's name was Reuben. He is dead now."

"May he rest in peace."

"Thank you." Again she stopped his departure. "Oh, and, Joachim..."

"Yes, Mary?"

"There will be, let me see," she said, counting on her fingers, "six, twelve, Peter's mother makes thirteen, Jesus and I—fifteen for dinner this evening. Can you manage?"

"Of course. Is it a special occasion?"

"Actually, yes. Jesus will be announcing plans for our upcoming journey. It is a celebration of sorts."

"Then I will take particular care of the arrangements." And off he went to do the shopping.

Not much later that morning, Mary was on her way out through the atrium when she noticed a man kneeling among the potted date palms. This must be the gardener.

"Reuben?" she said.

He turned his head slightly in her direction, but stayed on the floor with his hands in the soil of one of the pots.

"Mistress."

Seeing that he was shuffling as though trying to rise, she halted him. "Do not interrupt what you are doing, please."

"Thank you," he replied.

"You have done very nice work here already, Reuben. Joachim is grateful for your help. As am I."

"You are too kind, mistress."

"I have wondered, why do these palms not bloom?"

"They are young, about four years by my estimation. They will bloom this year, mistress. I promise."

"I am called Mary."

"Peace be upon you, Mary."

"Peace to you, Reuben," she said as she left the atrium.

Mummius' pulse was hammering. He had passed the first test, but it was not a difficult one. When he heard her coming, he had arranged himself on the floor, among the short palm trees, knowing she would insist he not get up. Even so, he wondered if she had noticed anything familiar about him, something to give her a clue to his identity. Or had the recent change in her blinded her to ordinary things that she would otherwise have noticed?

He had not detected anything extraordinary about her, no divine light wafting out behind her as she walked, no other-worldliness in her step. Today she looked like herself, in a simple dress with a long skirt and plain bodice. She wore no cloak, for it was warm, and he could see that she had chosen one of her favorite sashes, the color of dark red wine, which cinched in her tidy waist. Her earrings and necklace were in place—and her sandals matched. She looked like any other woman, but he knew that it was not so.

Mummius put his fist on his still-pounding chest until his pulse returned to normal. Then, he went back to work. Only he had noticed the tiny swellings along the stems of the date palms, evidence of buds-to-be. Now, he must tend them carefully to make sure they bloomed—because of his promise.

All day Mummius was there, and, amid the scurrying around, preparing for the important dinner, no one noticed. Many strangers were in and out, making deliveries. Others were in the kitchen, peeling and cutting vegetables, kneading bread, stoking fires. Joachim presided over the activity like a circus master.

In the bustle Mummius was free to wander where he would, memorizing details. Extra benches were moved into the crowded triclinium where the guests would dine. There was a path the servers took from the kitchen to the dining area. It would be a well-orchestrated flow back and forth to keep the diners supplied with food and drink.

One servant, emerging from the kitchen, suddenly disappeared on his way into the triclinium. Then, just as suddenly, the man reappeared, and Mummius saw what he had not noticed before. There was a small nook tucked into the wall between kitchen and dining room, for storage, perhaps, or a service staging area. In his eagerness to investigate, Mummius forgot his disguise and stood up straight to move swiftly toward the nook. Thankfully, no one observed his lapse. He bent over again and shuffled across the courtyard. He stuck his head around the corner and then stepped into the empty nook.

It was larger than it had seemed. There were shelves stacked with plates and cups, vessels of wine lined up on the floor along the wall, and, in the corner, one large basket. Mummius lifted the top and saw that it was empty. It smelled only of its own weave of reeds, and it was too large for anything but laundry. *Large enough to hold a bent over man,* he thought, *if that should be necessary.* Mummius listened. He could hear nothing from the kitchen. The voices of men walking from the kitchen, past the nook and through the courtyard, were quite clear, even as they entered the dining room.

Everything was ready. Soon the guests would arrive. Joachim stood in the courtyard, reviewing the preparations.

"Reuben!" he exclaimed, seeing the gardener. "Have you not gone home?"

"Just sweeping up a few stray clippings, Joachim. I want everything to be in perfect order."

"It is immaculate, Reuben. You must be weary."

"Well..."

"Listen, after the guests have been served, we will have our meal in the kitchen. Please, stay and eat with us. It is only Zimzi and I, and two others."

"I do not want to inconvenience you."

"Say no more. We would enjoy your company. Go to the kitchen and rest now."

My plan exactly, thought Mummius. "Thank you, brother," he said.

He had been in the kitchen only a few moments when the sound of laughter announced the arrival of guests at the door.

"Bring the towels, Zimzi," said Joachim, lifting a shallow bowl in one hand and a pitcher of water in the other.

"But, Father..."

"Come on, now, you can do it. They are only towels. Nothing to spill or break."

Zimzi was shaking, riveted to her spot, eyes wide with panic. It seemed she might never move. Oddly, it was the bent over gardener who took pity on her.

"Here, let me help you," said Mummius, as though gentling a nervous foal. "Hold out your hands."

When he placed the towels on her outstretched forearms, she looked like a page holding a pillow for a king's crown. Mummius was so charmed that he had to clamp down on the inside of his cheek to keep from grinning.

"All is well. Just walk slowly," Mummius told her.

Bearing their foot-washing implements, Joachim and Zimzi went to the atrium and were greeted by the waiting dinner party. Mummius could not resist stepping out to watch, to see how Zimzi would do.

"Set them there," said Mary, indicating a place next to Jesus.

Joachim put the bowl and pitcher on the floor and then relieved Zimzi of her stack of towels and placed them on the floor, too. He waited for Mary's signal to begin. But she did not give the signal. It was not to be Joachim, but Jesus, who knelt on the floor and tucked a towel into his belt.

"You first, my Rock," he said, motioning to Peter to sit on a short bench in front of him.

The jovial company fell silent in amazement. Of course they expected to have their feet washed upon entering the house, but it was the custom for this humble task to be performed by the lowliest person in the household, a servant, or the youngest child of the host, but, by no means, ever, an honored guest. They looked to Mary for an explanation of this travesty, but she did nothing to stop it.

"I cannot allow you to wash my feet," declared Peter.

"Sit down, brother, and remove your sandals," Jesus said kindly.

"I entreat you, Master, do not ask me to do this."

"Peter, you must understand. To humble yourself as a servant is to be righteous in the sight of God. If I am not your servant, then call me not Master."

In the hush that followed, only Mary remembered the words of the LORD spoken through the prophet Isaiah: "Here is my servant, whom I uphold, my chosen, in whom my soul delights; I have put my spirit upon him."

Jesus waited. It was clear that nothing would happen until Peter submitted. So Peter, the rock, this giant, loyal man, sat down before his master, who was kneeling on the floor in front of him. He slowly untied each sandal and set it aside. He lifted one knee, as though with a great effort, and placed his foot into the open hand of Jesus who lowered it into the bowl. Then Jesus picked up the pitcher and poured out some water.

Peter was a man of many strong emotions. Mary was accustomed to the sound of his heart-warming, deep-belly laugh, the reverberation of anger in the face of injustice, and his comforting, brotherly arm on others' shoulders when they were discouraged. But she had never seen him cry. Now, when Jesus began to bathe his feet and she saw that Peter's face was being washed with his own tears, she held her breath for love of him.

As each one of them, men and women alike, took a turn on the bench, Mummius, observing from the archway, felt his stomach clench with disgust. Why would Jesus suffer this humiliation? Did God demand such a price from his devotees? What could being a servant possibly have to do with divine power?

At last, when Jesus had washed all their feet, Mary gestured for him to sit on the bench. She knelt in his place, and she never took her eyes from his as she held first one foot, then the other, washing and drying, until the cleansing ritual was finished.

The atmosphere at dinner could not be called somber. Sacred would be a better word to describe it, for the humble, sacramental act in which they had participated caused all of them to reflect on who Jesus was and who they were when they were with him. He was calling them into servanthood. He was showing them the way, never asking them to do what he was unwilling to do.

When the last of the dishes were cleared and they were finishing their wine, Jesus began to speak of their upcoming journey. In the kitchen, Mummius and the others were eating their late dinner, except for Zimzi, who had rolled up the sleeves of her tunic and was washing dishes with her back turned. Mummius found himself wishing she would sit down so he could talk to her. Clearly, she was too shy to join in. When the meal was finished, they turned to the clean-up work and Zimzi withdrew to a corner to eat by herself.

"Go home now, Reuben," said Joachim.

Mummius scraped a dirty plate into the scrap pile. "The work will go faster with another pair of hands," he replied. "Truly, I want to help." And in his mind he heard Siamun guffawing at the sight of him debasing himself with kitchen work. *At least I am not washing the filth off other people's feet,* he thought.

As the last of the pots were being dried and the leftovers stored, Mummius heard the guests taking their leave. He supposed that he had learned all he was going to learn this night and was ready to depart. But then he heard something that told him otherwise.

"Are you coming, Master?" asked John.

"No. I am going to stay."

"Very well. Until tomorrow, then."

So the echoes of shalom made the rounds of the company until all had departed. The two hired helpers put on their cloaks and left as well. When Mummius saw that Joachim and Zimzi, too, were preparing to go, his heart started to race. This was his moment.

"Ready to go?" asked Joachim.

Seizing a small stack of plates that had been overlooked, he replied, "I am right behind you. I'll just put these away."

Joachim seemed to hesitate. Mummius knew it would not be his way to leave before the house was completely secured. Certainly, in Magdala, Mummius would not have done so. He knew what was going through Joachim's mind: Zimzi was exhausted; Jesus was here, so Mary was not alone; the gardener had demonstrated his goodwill in many ways; it was safe.

"Peace be to you, Reuben."

"And to you, Joachim, Zimzi."

Clutching the plates like a royal travel permit which would protect him in case he was found out, Mummius shuffled into the nook. He put the dishes down silently on a shelf and then was still, straining to hear. Their voices were clear, coming from the triclinium, Mary and Jesus talking.

"I believe I will write to Joanna to tell her we are coming," she said. "It will be so very good to see her again."

Jesus said nothing. Mummius wondered what was passing between them, an embrace perhaps.

"What is it, Rabbouni?" she asked.

A pause, and then the mole in the nook heard this: "Do they understand, Mary?"

Was there to be no end to surprises this night? Mummius, though he could not see the look on Jesus' face, could hear longing in his voice. Why did he care that mere followers understood him? He gave them his truth; it was up to them what to do with it. What was it, exactly, that he wanted them to understand?

Mary answered, "They understand that the Law of Mercy is imposed not from without, but from the heart within. They understand that compassion means to suffer with not just this one or that one, but each one. Unfortunately, understanding is not the same as doing, Rabbouni. We all struggle with that."

Mummius imagined that Jesus took Mary's hand when he said, "Not you, dear lady," but he did not imagine how intensely she blushed at the tribute Jesus paid to her.

She went on. "What they do not fully understand is that mercy and compassion are but consequences of Love, and that it is Love which liberates life from the tyranny of self-exaltation."

Another surprise for Mummius: "The tyranny of self-exaltation"?

Mary continued. "You yourself said that some are arguing over who will sit at your right hand in the Reign of God. It is human nature to desire adulation. We have learned to judge ourselves by how much higher we are than others. How can we unlearn an impulse so deeply rooted? Only in you, Rabbouni, has Love established complete sovereignty."

Mummius was puzzled. *Could it be that, of all the possibilities available to him, Jesus had chosen to become a sudden appearance of divine Love in the world?* If that were so, Jesus would not be the messiah the Jews expected—as some had begun to proclaim—not the one to drive Rome from their land and restore the nation to greatness. It would explain why he took fishermen and tax collectors and women as disciples. It would explain why he washed their feet.

It was hard to comprehend why someone would make such a choice, so oriented is the human psyche toward its own purposes. Mummius thought of the great men of the past, men like Julius Caesar and, before him, Alexander the Great, and before him, any number of Greeks, Persians, Assyrians, and Egyptians, who had sought to make their ambitions—what Mary had called self-exaltation—the rule of nations. All had proclaimed their special brand of morality to be the right one, the divinely inspired one.

Now it dawned on Mummius what Jesus wanted them to understand. No religion or philosophy or mysticism had been able to free mankind from the self-defeating desire for mastery over others. Only mercy could do that; only compassion for the very "others" whom they seek to dominate; only Love. Mummius saw further what Jesus' disciples—even Mary—did not yet understand. The earthly powers-that-be, the Roman in his palace and the High Priest in the Temple, would not tolerate Jesus in their midst.

Mummius had stayed too long in his moment of illumination, for by the time he heard voices, they were nearing the nook. He bolted for the basket.

"Did you hear something?" asked Mary. "A noise from in there?"

"I'm sure it was nothing, but I will look, to ease your mind."

Mummius thought the basket must be throbbing with the hammer of his heartbeat. He needed to gasp for air, but forced himself to take small, quiet breaths. Through the loose weave of the reeds, he could see Jesus' form, made huge by the lamplight behind him.

Turning away, Jesus said to Mary, "Nothing to worry about."

The moment was past, but the crisis was not over. Drawing a long, controlled breath in the darkness, Mummius thought, *He knows.*

It seemed an eternity till the house was quiet enough for Mummius to risk his exit. At last physical discomforts overtook him, and he pushed the basket top off over his head. But his cramped arms had grown numb, so it slipped and fell to the stone floor in what sounded to him like the clatter of a bundle of firewood. He held his breath and waited. No one stirred. Indeed he did not know if anyone was still in the house, sleeping, or if Jesus had gone outside to pray and Mary with him.

Slowly, he stood up and eased one leg over the edge of the basket and then the other. Shaking his arms to restore a flow of blood, he picked up the errant cover and replaced it snugly. Then, moving into the courtyard and using his plants as cover, he made his way to the foyer and out the door, into the deserted, moonless night. Relieved of his bent over persona, he walked briskly through the crooked streets of Capernaum toward his safe-haven, Siamun's amulet shop.

Mummius had been perspiring heavily during his long, cramped vigil, and the cool night air was evaporating the sweat, chilling his face. He reached up to wipe his forehead and run his fingers through his loosened hair. A surprising sense of pleasure turned to alarm when he realized why he felt so free. Wildly, he touched his head all over, vainly denying the inescapable truth. His turban was gone! He tried to remember where he had lost it. It must have come off when he climbed out of the basket and was distracted by the noise of the falling top. He wheeled around, ready to run back to the house—but that was folly. Perhaps he could arrive in the morning in time to retrieve it before anyone else found it. Chagrined at his lapse, but nevertheless resigned, Mummius turned for home.

Alone in his room behind the curtain, Mummius sat with a blank scroll on his lap board. Tense as the string of a drawn bow, he let out a curse to relieve the pressure. Siamun had provided him a bright, double-bowled lamp to protect his eyes from the strain of their late-night toiling. In the flames of the burning wicks, bronze beetles and papery moths fluttered and fell to oily deaths. Watching the tiny cataclysm around the lamp, Mummius' mind groped for some way to soothe the commotion inside.

Memory guided him to the days of glory in Alexandria when Asclepius, the Greek god of healing, had appeared to him and called him by name at his blessing ceremony and the entire class of initiates had knelt in homage to him. Then memory took him further back, to his youth and its delight, when Maret and he, in the bliss of their betrothal, had made offerings to Bast. Together they stood before the sleek statue of the cat goddess and lit a fire on the sacred table-hearth. Together they threw pinches of incense onto the fire and called out, "Give us your blessing, divine Bast!"

He had worshipped these gods, and all the pantheon of Egypt, made offerings to them, and tried to please them. But did they take pity on him when vile strangers made him a eunuch without explanation? Did they suffer with him when he moved from place to place, searching for peace? Did they *love* him? Mummius' adoration of the cat goddess of his youth, and Asclepius, who had guided his adult life, seemed sour now, like wine turned to vinegar.

Mummius sat before a blank scroll. How many like it, during his weeks in Capernaum, had Mummius inscribed with Jesus teachings? Yet how little he understood. He had recorded that Jesus called God "Abba," as children address their papas at home. Did Jesus imagine that God feels concern for each person, as a father does for the beloved child of his heart? Is God the One who desires, above all things, our freedom and joy, like a mother?

Then, in the course of his reverie, Mummius' hand, as though guided by another, picked up a pen, dipped it in ink and pressed it down onto the scroll. He watched, amazed, the Aramaic flowing smoothly from right to left, his hand writing what his mind did not dictate. Next, wonder upon wonder, a voice emanated from the page, the words seeming to speak themselves as they appeared.

> Why do you turn your heart away? You are heavily laden. Come to me, Mummius, and be free.

His hand was the only part of Mummius that was not shaking with fear when he asked, "Who are you?"

And the voice on the page wrote:

> Who do you say that I am?

Before he could frame a coherent response, the words he had written burst into flame, and the scroll was, in the instant, reduced to ash by an apparition, a column of smoke arising from the floor of his small room to the ceiling. Within it glowed two embers, the eyes of a spirit. Mummius averted his face in time not to be blinded by the fire, but his fingertips were blistered where they had held the pen and he dropped it with a yelp.

"Are you the voice on the page?"

A mocking laugh sprang from the smoky specter. "What has love to do with you? I have told you long ago, Mummius, that the way to satisfaction is fear. Love is a snare that traps the feeble lives of the simple-minded. You were born for greater things. You can know what it is to have men fall in fear before you. Now is the time to follow me."

"Amenwahsu!" exclaimed Mummius, discerning the identity of his teacher of old, many years dead and yet, alive, here, now.

A brilliant student in Alexandria, Mummius had been singled out by Amenwahsu for evil initiation, but he had resisted. The good in Mummius ultimately prevailed, but he had, nevertheless, waged a lifelong war against the lure of magic. Now, seeing that this spirit's power was eternal, that it could overcome death and appear in the present, and speak to him, Mummius felt himself being drawn in.

"What has it gained you to resist? Turn away from your unrest and come to me!"

What indeed had he gained by choosing the life of physician and scribe over magus? A boorish life in a grubby, provincial town at the edge of civilization, secretly whining after an itinerant Jew who consorted with the dregs of society. He should be in palaces in Rome!

Mummius laid aside his singed writing board and started to kneel in obeisance before Amenwahsu. "Great Lord..." he began. But before he could complete the act, Mummius was lifted by the neck in a vise-like grip, as Amenwahsu had once held him before releasing him to crumple on the floor. The force that clutched him now thrust him forward across the room, the vision of smoke and Amenwahsu's fiery eyes evaporating in his wake.

Mummius tried to summon enough magic power to fight whatever or whoever was controlling him, to no avail. The massive force could easily have choked or killed him, but that, apparently, was not its purpose. It seemed to be commanding him to focus his attention upon the wall. It was all he could to do to resist the impulse of what he knew would be a futile struggle to get away. He drew in a strained breath and stared at the wall.

A human hand appeared out of thin air and, as Mummius marveled, its finger of fire began to write upon the expanse of unadorned plaster:

I AM THAT I AM

He tried to back away, but the power that gripped him held him fast and his eyes stayed locked on the words. Mummius struggled to maintain control of his mind, so he could think. The phrase was familiar, something renowned from the Hebrew scriptures. Yes, one of their great prophets—it could only have been Moses—when he asked what God's name was. And God said, "I am that which I am."

Mummius regarded the name of God on the wall. He read the name again and again, forming each syllable slowly, more feeling than hearing the sound emerging from his mouth. He continued to repeat it, and the name grew in volume and intensity. As the vibration from within increased, Mummius felt the vise on his neck loosen until he was aware that it had released him completely. But, held fast by the awesome sound of I AM, still he could not flee.

Mummius no longer desired escape, for, in this moment, it was revealed to him that I AM, the Holy One of Israel, the One whom Jesus called Abba, was the voice that had spoken from his scroll before Amenwahsu burned the page. I AM was the One in whose presence evil had evaporated before his eyes.

Now, he was face to face with the name of God on the wall, and the name of God spoke to him, saying, "Beloved son, I wait for you."

And Mummius wept.

CHAPTER 38

Mummius liked solitary walks like this, under fair blue skies when the air was fresh, to clear his mind. The donkey's rhythmic clip-clop helped to focus his thoughts. Even after several days, he had not been able to decipher the meaning of God's visitation, for this was no ordinary theophany. God had called him by name. He had wept in the presence of the Holy One of Israel and had not been ashamed. Now he must determine what it all meant and what he must do.

He had not returned to Mary's house to retrieve his turban or to collect his wages. All that seemed insignificant now, for he was a changed man. Dressed once again as the tall, confident Egyptian, he had loaded a donkey cart in front of the amulet shop, where Siamun approached him, slowly, for they had not spoken in three days.

"You are preparing to leave."

"I am returning to Magdala."

"What has happened?"

Pained and confused, Mummius slowly touched the scrolls on which, for weeks, he had inscribed the words of Jesus. "I can no longer write."

"What do you mean, you can't write?"

"God has turned my hand to marble."

"What—the God of the Jews?"

"God came to me in a vision, Siamun, and spoke to me, and called me 'son.' God is waiting for me. After that my hand will be restored."

"After what?"

Mummius recounted the story of I AM writing on the wall, and the more he talked, the deeper the furrows etched themselves in Siamun's brow. "Each day, when I try to record Jesus' sayings, my hand turns to stone and will not obey my will. There must be a thread connecting this incapacity and God's appearance to me. I myself do not understand it, but I know I must return home—to Magdala—to search for the answer."

"The answer to what, Mentuhotep?"

"The answer to God's call."

"That which you have longed for..."

"Perhaps," replied Mummius. Then he went to his friend and laid both hands on his shoulders. "Siamun, you have been the soul of friendship these many years. In the last weeks, I have dipped far too deeply into the well of your generosity. Then, to treat you with resentment—to raise my hand to you... Forgive me, brother, for my offense."

"No, Mentuhotep, it was I who went too far."

"You only spoke the truth, Siamun."

"Your companionship has been a balm to me. I will miss you."

"Keep a light burning for me, Siamun!" Mummius declared, raising his hand in farewell. He hoped Siamun had forgiven him.

On the road to Magdala, he was absorbed in his purpose. An elusive memory tumbled around in his head, the story of a mysterious hand, which had written some message to a foreign king upon a wall. He was determined to find that tale within the Hebrew scriptures, even if he had to peruse the entire canon. Mary's library in Magdala was the place to find it.

Demetria had already sought refuge in Mary's library that day, choosing a volume of Greek poetry to lighten her mood. All around her, Magdala was in the full flourish of spring. Rowdy birds dashed and sang, announcing the triumphs of their nesting sites. The weavers blossomed with the darling gossip that comes in the season of flowers. Yet Demetria was sullen. She had not had a letter from Mary in two weeks—longer, if the truth be known. Mummius was nowhere to be found; he had said he was going to Tyre to purchase dye, but who knew when it came to that one? Worst of all, Rachel was being courted, incessantly blushing and preening her feathers, like one of the silly birds in the courtyard. Everything was Daniel, Daniel, Daniel. If she heard his name again, she would surely scream!

Demetria tossed aside the scroll she had been reading—she remembered nothing of it from the last half hour anyway—and headed for the sea. Through the garden and into the environs of Mary's farm, the earth was warm. The heady splendor of flower and field almost loosened Demetria's hold on her gloom, but she was determined to cling to it. Her feet glumly paced the path that would take her across the Roman road and thence to the lakeshore.

When she came to the paved road, she had to stop for a small contingent of soldiers, Romans in leather cuirasses and thick, laced sandals, beating out a precise tattoo upon the stones, heads held high, their eyes straight ahead. Marching from Tiberias to Capernaum, she guessed. She folded her arms and waited impatiently to cross. As the final rank was passing, she leaned into the road, ready to take a step forward, anticipating her dash. In that brief moment, the last man swept by, close in front of her, an ordinary soldier with the power of Rome on his shoulders and the assurance of youth in his step. She could smell the leather on his chest, the oil on his sword, and the just-sprung sweat which glistened on his bicep. Briefly, she caught his eye, and, when she did, he winked at her. Demetria stumbled into the middle of the road, going down on one knee, but quickly regaining her balance. She stood, absentmindedly brushing the dust from her skirt, staring after the soldier, longing for another look. But he was gone.

She was nothing to him, the soldier just-passed. She was nothing to anyone, she whined to herself, wiping her brimming eyes and making a muddy streak on her face. They were all gone. Mary to Capernaum. Mummius to Tyre. Rachel to Daniel. What could she possibly do to brighten her dismal situation? It was the road under her feet that answered her. Lady Joanna!

On such a road she had traveled with Joanna from Jerusalem to Tiberias. She had been her guest in the palace till Mummius came to escort her home. Wrapping her hand around the golden locket at her throat, Demetria remembered what Joanna had said as they parted. "My dear, you must promise to send word to me if ever you need anything. Anything, at all. Do you understand?"

Demetria had almost forgotten that she was standing in the middle of the road sniffling when, a short distance ahead, she heard the rattle of oncoming traffic. Looking, she was able to make out a lone donkey, pulling a medium-sized cart, led by a tall man who had a familiar air about him. If he were not in Tyre, far away on the coast of the Middle Sea, she would have sworn it was—Mummius? She strained and squinted and stared until there was no doubt. It was he.

"Mummius!" she exclaimed, her loneliness a wilting plant, eagerly drinking in an unexpected shower.

Picking up her skirt to free her feet, Demetria dashed to meet him.

"I thought you were in Tyre! Come to the house. I will make you some khat." She stopped short of embracing him, but the relief on her face was plain. "It is good to see you," she said quietly.

Mummius was as he had always been, elegant and poised, the strength of his arm easily holding the heavy donkey in check. He did not respond to her giddy welcome, only glanced at her briefly before he cocked his head and then with secretive, kohl-rimmed black eyes, began to examine his own attire. She watched inquisitively as he looked down at the distinctively Egyptian tunic of pleated white cotton. He lifted one foot so he could see his sandal, and then he held out his hand and turned his wrist right and left, inspecting the wide, hammered bracelet. *What is wrong with him?*

They returned silently to the house, Demetria keeping a close watch on her companion. Twice he had come to fetch her from Tiberias and take her to Magdala. The first time was her introduction to Galilee, years ago. Mummius had been imperious, walking ahead, as if she were a following puppy, which, by paying no heed to, he hoped to lose. She was forced to carry her own bag, though he could plainly see the strap was cutting into her bony little shoulder—if he had cared to look. When she first arrived at Mary's house and made some comment about how unremarkable everything was, he had cuffed her on the head. Well, maybe she had earned that, but she was lost and scared then.

The second time was just last spring, when Mary had left her in Jerusalem, turning her over to Joanna for the trip to Tiberias. Again, Mummius had been dispatched to escort her home. He had been friendly, asking many questions: Did she enjoy her travels? How had she become acquainted with Joanna, the wife of Herod's steward, Chuza? What did Jesus do in Jerusalem? She was surprised and grateful that he had listened attentively to her, as he would any other companion. What a fool she had been: he was interested in her information only, and not in her; but at least he was less distant after that, and she was no longer frightened of him. She thought she had come to know him.

This Mummius, however, the one who was at Demetria's side now, was different from all the Mummiuses of the past, for he had felt the touch of celestial fire. And of that, Demetria knew nothing.

Arriving at the garden behind the house, they were met by a servant, who held the reins of the donkey while Mummius began unloading the cart. Demetria remarked upon his curious load of scrolls.

"What is all this, Mummius?"

His voice was a quiet rumble that came from deep within his diaphragm, and he did not seem to be admonishing her, just speaking to the air around him, or to the scrolls, or to himself, when he said, "Nothing. Scrolls."

Demetria reached out to lift a scroll, to help. Immediately, she felt his hand land firmly on her wrist.

"No."

There was no particular force in his grip or his voice, just a compelling certainty that she was not permitted to touch them. Demetria withdrew her hand. Mummius must have noticed her, finally, and her disappointment.

"Did you offer to brew some khat?" he asked, and she was startled to see that he was smiling at her.

"Would you like me to?"

"That would be good. Oh, and Demetria, you have dirt on your face," he said, kindly, as she turned to leave.

Rachel had left the kitchen tidy, and, as usual these days, she was not there. *Daniel,* thought Demetria, her resentment temporarily mitigated by Mummius' return. Demetria poured water from a pitcher onto a clean towel to wash her face. She rubbed the cloth slowly over every part of it, thinking how astonishing it was that Mummius had remarked on her appearance. There was a time when he would have taken no notice, or, worse, would have let her go about with a streaked face.

Demetria hummed a tune while she waited for the water to boil. All her life, she had watched women performing little unrequested domestic deeds for the men in their lives. They seemed content to cook a favorite dish, or present a surprise gift, or make an unexpected visit. She had not understood the simple joy a woman could feel in such a moment. It would not have occurred to her to connect the wink of the Roman soldier with the pleasure of brewing tea for Mummius. All she knew was that she was happy to have him home.

She had finished preparing a tray with the tea and a piece of the morning's bread, when Mummius stuck his head through the doorway.

"Ready?"

"I was just bringing it out."

"Never mind. I'll take it here," he said, sitting down at his accustomed second place at the table.

Demetria took the food from the tray and set it down in front of him. She hesitated, not knowing whether to go or stay.

"Are those figs I see?" he asked, nodding at the side board.

"Yes. Very delicious."

"Let's have them. Sit. Pour yourself some tea."

Like a kitten with a ball of yarn, she pounced on his invitation. "There's honey, too."

"Perfect," he said.

After some moments of watching him drink his khat, occasionally swirling the liquid, closing his eyes, and bringing it to his nose to breathe it in, Demetria grew impatient. "Mummius?"

"Demetria?" he responded, again catching her off guard with a smile that showed straight white teeth against the dark bronze of his unblemished skin.

"I have been thinking about something."

"You wish to tell me?"

"Well, yes…"

But before Demetria could complete her thought, Rachel appeared, short of breath and flushed, at the door.

"Mummius!" she exclaimed, unloading market baskets on the table. "Where did you come from?"

"I am pleased to see you, too, Rachel," he replied, playfully mocking her curt greeting. "Demetria has provided these delightful refreshments. Won't you join us?"

Rachel had just lifted a bag of lentils from her basket. Her hand stopped, mid-arc, holding the bag in her palm, as though weighing its heft. Obviously bewildered, she looked from Mummius to Demetria and back to Mummius.

Enjoying Rachel's confusion, Demetria laughed. "Are you going to throw those beans?" she asked.

Rachel placed the lentils very, very gently on the table. "Of course not," she said.

"Come, sister," soothed Demetria. "Have some tea. Tell Mummius about Daniel." Then she looked at Mummius and raised her eyebrows, as though to say, *Watch this.*

Rachel succumbed to Demetria's irresistible opening, and before long she was raving about her suitor. She could not stop saying his name, blathering about his attributes, and her hopes for their future.

Mummius, having listened patiently as long as he could, was on the verge of saying, "Enough of Daniel, please," when the name itself came to rest on his lips. Daniel. Daniel. "I have to go," he said and rushed from the room.

"Rude as ever, I see."

"Perhaps you should have thrown the lentils at him," Demetria chuckled.

Mummius did not intend to offend Rachel, but she had inadvertently given him a key to the Hebrew scriptures. Now he was sure; it was the

Book of the prophet Daniel that contained the story of the hand, writing on the wall. Mummius thumbed through the pile of scrolls. Jeremiah. Ezekiel. Hosea. There it was—the Book of Daniel. He pulled it out and starting scanning.

Daniel this; Daniel that; exile to the royal court in Babylon; a fiery furnace... *Here it is!* The story he had been searching for.

Five hundred years earlier, from his capital of Babylonia, King Belshazzar of Chaldea ruled a sizeable empire, stretching from Egypt on the Great Sea to the Persian Gulf in the east. Among his people in Babylon were many exiles from the land of Judah, including young Daniel, who was widely known for his gift of the interpretation of dreams.

Now there came a time when King Belshazzar held a festival for a thousand of his lords, and they were all having a fine time getting drunk, including the king. "Bring in the vessels of gold from the temple in Jerusalem!" he commanded. The vessels that had been stolen from the house of God in the Holy City were brought in and filled with wine. The king and his lords and his wives and his concubines drank from the consecrated vessels and praised the gods of gold and silver while they did it.

At once, the fingers of a human hand appeared and began to write on the plaster of the wall of the palace, next to the lamp stand where the light shone brightly on it for all to see:

MENE MENE TEKEL PARSIN

The king was terrified. The blood drained from his face, and the royal knees knocked one against the other. Belshazzar cried out for the wise men of Babylon. He summoned diviners, magicians and Chaldean enchanters. He promised to promote anyone who could tell him what the inscription meant. That man would rank third in his kingdom. But no one could.

The queen had a suggestion. "O King, live forever! Do not worry. I know of a man of great enlightenment who can interpret dreams, explain riddles and solve problems. Your father, may he rest in eternal bliss, King Nebuchadnezzar, found in this man the wisdom of the gods. He will surely interpret the writing on the wall. Call Daniel."

"Call Daniel!" ordered the king.

When Daniel was brought before the king, Belshazzar said, "I have heard that my father the king brought you from Judah. Are you one of the exiles from Judah, Daniel?"

"I am."

"I have heard, too, that a divine spirit is in you, and extraordinary wisdom. None of my enchanters and wise men has been able to tell me the interpretation of that writing, over there, on the wall," said the king, pointing. "If you are able to tell me its interpretation, I will clothe you in purple and put a golden chain on you and give you third rank in the kingdom."

Daniel replied, "I will not accept your gifts. Keep them, or give them to another! But I will read what has been written to the king, since you ask. O King, let me remind you that the Most High God gave your father, Nebuchadnezzar, a great realm with glory and majesty, so that all nations trembled before him. But he forgot the source of his power and so he was deposed and made to wander in the wilderness and live like an animal until he remembered that the Most High God has sovereignty over the kingdoms of mortal men.

"You, Belshazzar, even though you knew all this, have exalted yourself above the Lord of Heaven. You and your lords and your wives and your concubines have polluted the vessels of the temple and have praised other gods while doing it. You have failed to honor the God who holds power over your very breath. So it is, that from the presence of God, this hand has been sent to inscribe this writing. You want to know what it means? Here it is: your kingdom is at an end; you have been weighed on the scales and been found wanting; your throne is given to Medes and Persians."

That night Belshazzar, the Chaldean king, died, and so ended the story of the handwriting on the wall. Except that Daniel did indeed accept the purple robe and the golden chain as a symbol of his rank of third in the kingdom.

What has this to do with me? wondered Mummius. *Is I AM telling me that I will lose everything? That I have been measured and found wanting? That I will not reap the fruits of my labors? If the Most High God is the source of my gifts—my very breath—and I have failed God, am I to die?*

Mummius laid his forehead on the scroll of the Book of Daniel and closed his eyes. Long had he lived in that world-between-worlds where those who are strong enough can be touched by the fire from heaven and live. But this scorching flame from the divine threatened to burn too hot for him to withstand. Would a sentence of death be imposed upon the one whom I AM had called "beloved son"?

Alone and in fear for his life, Mummius called out, "What do you require of me?"

In that very moment, Mummius admitted the long resisted truth—the answer to his question lay with Jesus.

CHAPTER 39

For the next few days Mummius kept to himself. He was not so much supercilious, as pensive, pleasant enough but in no way forthcoming. With Rachel continuing to moon over Daniel, Demetria passed her time in the loom room, weaving lackadaisically. Chloe endeavored to cheer her, but, although Demetria loved the weavers as sisters and Chloe in particular, she was beyond boredom. The others, after all, had lives that awaited them when their work was finished, homes, responsibilities, people who cared about them. At the end of each day, when evening approached and the darkness descended, Demetria was disconsolate.

She thought more and more about escaping Magdala. She had vacated the idea of writing to Joanna, because she was reluctant to approach Mummius. She had been close to discussing it with him that first day, but Rachel had interrupted them. After that, Mummius had retreated into his own world. When her craving for relief snuffed out the smoldering ember of her resistance, she knocked on his door.

"Enter, Demetria," he said routinely, glancing up from his charts of account. Then more amenably, "What can I do for you?"

Demetria had planned to soften him up, set the stage a bit for what she knew would catch him unawares, but when the moment lay before her, she blurted it out. "I want to write a letter to the Lady Joanna. I was hoping to visit her in Tiberias." Demetria saw Mummius' left eyebrow lift perceptibly and, seeking to fend off an argument, plunged on. "I do so long to see Salome again. Joanna told me to write anytime I wanted."

Mummius laid aside his scroll. She had his attention.

"So, Greek maid, your feet are itchy for the road, eh?" Mummius seemed to be making fun of her, but she thought otherwise when he continued. "I believe that Mary will be traveling soon, also in hopes of renewing her acquaintance with the Lady Joanna."

"Oh, Mummius, is it so? Has she written to tell you? What a surprise it would be—for Mary to find me with Joanna! I'm sure that the lady would send someone to fetch me..."

He interrupted her, wonder of wonders, with this: "I would be pleased to accompany you to Tiberias. Would that suit you?"

Had Demetria lost her hearing, or Mummius his mind? Her astonishment reached maximum proportions with his next offer.

"Fetch your writing materials. I will help you compose your letter."

Demetria jumped from the bench and rushed to her room. She stood before the shelf where she kept the precious box, her cheeks aching with the great grin that had broken out over her face. She slid her hand through the stack of clothing that concealed her prize and pulled it from its hiding place.

She was ready for the thrill that always came when she opened it—Mary's parting gift: ink, two pens, a wax wand and a small brass seal, engraved with the image of the mother-goddess, Demeter. Again as always, she felt Mary's presence in the room and whispered her prayer, "Mistress, thank you."

As Demetria walked back to the kitchen, the lingering image of Mummius' kind, attentive face slowed her down and then stopped her in her tracks. Why was he doing this? When she encountered him on the road a few days ago, he had examined his clothing as though it belonged to someone else. At the house, he had smiled at her repeatedly and used a soft tone when he spoke to her. Now the inimitable, exalted scribe of Egypt was going to help her write a letter? What was the great change in him that caused these unfamiliar behaviors?

Demetria knew better than to trust him completely. She knew, also, that she needed his help to get to Tiberias. She tightened her hold on the cherished writing box and stepped forward, on guard, to his office, where Mummius was waiting.

"Here, sit on the floor with this lap board, the proper posture of a scribe," he instructed.

Caught between excitement and suspicion, Demetria sat. Then, when she was settled and Mummius actually sat down beside her, she was nothing less than amazed.

"How do you want to begin?"

"Well, what about 'To the Lady Joanna in Tiberias, from Demetria of Magdala, Greeting'?"

Demetria saw the slight lift at the right corner of Mummius' mouth and, taking it for approval, was pleased. How could she know that he was simply amused at her determination to sound mature by addressing the noble Roman lady in the most formal language? How could she know that he had secretly read every letter she had ever written?

"Excellent," he said. "Write it down."

Demetria went on to tell Joanna of her desire to travel to Tiberias and visit Salome, and to ask permission to stay at the royal palace. It took almost an hour to compose the letter, with Mummius guiding her. At the end, her hand was cramped, and she was tired, but satisfied.

"There!" she said and began to roll up the papyrus scroll.

"Oh, no, girl, you are not finished."

"What more is there to say, Mummius?"

"Nothing. But you must read your letter over, aloud, to ensure that you have made no mistakes and no omissions."

Demetria sighed. "You have been keeping watch every moment. What mistake can there be?"

"Does your letter deserve less attention to detail than the scarf you are weaving? What impression do you want to make on the Lady Joanna? Think of that."

Now he was sounding like Shoshanna when she used to instruct Demetria at her loom. "Be careful," she would say. "If you make a mistake, pull out the thread and do it over; you must be proud of your work, child." Demetria did not even try to understand why Mummius had chosen to be a teacher to her. She just did as she was told and, rubbing her sore right hand, began to read her painstakingly written Greek.

"To the Lady Joanna in Tiberias, from Demetria of Magdala, Greeting. I hope this letter finds you well. I remember with gratitude our meeting in Jerusalem and the remarkable event of your restoration to health. I have not seen Jesus since that time, but I hear reports that he continues to teach in Capernaum, healing the afflicted by the hundreds. Mary is staying in Capernaum, too, in a house she has there. I saw her briefly when she stopped here in Magdala after their long trip through Judea and Samaria.

"Which brings me to the primery reason for this letter..."

Demetria stopped reading and looked at Mummius, dismayed. "I misspelled it, didn't I?"

"You did."

"Why did you not stop me?"

"Well, Greek miss, will you ever make that mistake again, now that you have discovered it on your own?"

"What should I do?"

"The best way to correct it now is to draw a line through the word and write it correctly in the space above."

Demetria laid her pen at the beginning of the word to make her strike-through.

"Stop. Get a straight edge so your line will be perfect."

Demetria could no longer contain her bewilderment.

"Mummius, why are you helping me like this?"

"Do you not want my assistance?"

"Of course I do, but I do not understand it." A veil of sadness settled over Demetria's face. Her mouth became a tense line, and she tucked her chin down, forcing her eyes to look up at him from under the overhang of her brows. "You have never been nice to me."

Mummius' body tightened. His cheeks were flat planes, evidence of clenched teeth within. Demetria wished she could take back her words.

"I'm sorry," she said.

In Mummius' core, a dagger twisted as the sound of her voice hung in the air between them—the same blade of truth that Siamun had wielded against him. And, as with his friend, Mummius wanted to strike Demetria with a curse. He could not tolerate these mirrors being hung up all around him, showing unwelcome images of himself. Mummius felt like a wild horse, suddenly shackled, struggling in his great, proud heart, to escape.

"Get out!" he commanded.

Slowly, Demetria replaced her writing utensils into their box and rolled up her scroll. She laid the lap board aside and, tucking her letter under one arm, stood to go.

Mummius wanted to stop her, but was slow to master his emotions. At the last minute, just as she was at the doorway to the courtyard, he called to her, "Wait. Come back. Please."

When she returned to where he sat on the floor and stood over him, gazing down on him, he was humiliated by the indignity of it. Was she aware of his disgrace? Would she use it to shame him? Every instinct in Mummius commanded him to stand up, look her in the eye, be a man.

But his instincts had a powerful foe now. He had been measured by the Most High God and had fallen short. He had seen Jesus kneeling on the floor before lesser men—and women. He knew that the fire from heaven was waiting to see what he would do. Mummius did not know what God required of him, but he knew surely that he must not now rise up and tyrannize this girl. So he said, "I regret the suffering I have caused you."

Mummius reined himself in tightly, waiting for Demetria's response. Would she smirk, furthering his humiliation, a moment he knew she had often dreamed of? Worse, would she sit down and, offering consolation, pity him?

She did neither. When Mummius saw her diminutive hand reach down to him, the surge of relief in his heart very nearly burst out through his eyes, but he managed to alter it into a smile of gratitude. He gave her his hand, and, when she pulled him up, he was surprised by her strength. Even now, in his head, the alarm bells rang, calling him to flee. But he rose from the floor and stood before her, steadfast in this moment of truth.

Mummius was reminded of Marcus Quintius Severus. Severus had rescued Demetria from a life of debasement from which, by now, she would have been discarded like trash, no longer a kitten but a marriageable maid. He thought of the vast sums of money Severus had made available, secretly, so that the child's every wish would be instantly granted, money Mummius could easily embezzle for himself without anyone's knowledge. He thought of Mary's devotion to this girl, how she had welcomed her to hearth and heart, bestowing on her the unearned privileges of a favored daughter, and a depth of love that Mummius could only envy from afar.

What had she done to be thus honored and celebrated? What was she but one insignificant runt among a litter of slaves? Compared to his talents and achievements, Demetria had nothing. And yet, they adored her. Her!

Mummius and Demetria held each other with their eyes, taking stock, each measuring the risk. It was she who took the first gamble.

"I have always wanted to be your friend," she said.

Mummius caught a glimpse of his image in the mirror that Demetria held up for him, and he knew that it was not Demetria, but others' love of her, that he had despised. He decided to take a small step.

"I know," he replied.

"...but you would not accept anything from me."

And taking a very long step, he admitted, "That was wrong."

Demetria looked down at her skirt and began to pick at a loose thread. They had gone as far as they could for now. Mummius lifted her chin with his hand.

"Shall we finish proofreading your letter?"

She nodded, and they took their seats on the floor. Demetria found two more small errors, which were easy to rectify.

"*Kudos!*" said Mummius when she was finished, and they both relaxed into the moment created by his praise. Then he said, "Perhaps it would be appropriate for me to add a post script."

Demetria watched Mummius ink his pen and lay it upon the scroll. Elegant Greek flowed out effortlessly.

"Lady Joanna, I add my greeting here, and wish to assure you that, if you choose to offer Demetria an invitation to visit you, I will accompany her safely into your care. All you need do is let us know when it is convenient for her to arrive. I am completely at your service."

He turned to Demetria and raised an eyebrow for approval, "Mmm?"

When she nodded enthusiastically, he signed his name with a bravura flourish.

"Mummius, Chief Steward and Scribe to Mary of Magdala."

Demetria stared with big eyes at Mummius' work, comparing his script to hers. She reached out her small hand and touched his signature.

"It is so beautiful," she said.

And Mummius, accepting her admiration, said simply, "Thank you."

Soon, letters were flying up and down the Sea of Galilee, over the water, around the coast, wherever a convenient courier could be found, all constructing a surprise for Mary. None created more delight than the one from Joanna to Demetria.

"Darling Demetria, you cannot imagine my pleasure upon opening your letter. Of course, you must come to visit me! My happiness is exceeded only by that of Salome, who is beside herself with glee. The poor little thing can hardly sit still for her lessons, now that she is expecting you. 'When will she arrive, Aunt Joanna?' is her constant refrain.

"When indeed? Well, Mary has written to tell me that she and Jesus expect to be traveling through the vicinity of the Decapolis before the month is out, and I have written back to say that I would like to meet her there. Handily, Lord Chuza owns a vacation home on the southern shore, at Sennabris, a lovely place for a rest from their travels. I have put it at Mary's convenience.

"Mummius can accompany you to Tiberias, and we will all travel to Sennabris together. I will write the arrangements to him in a separate letter.

"Thank you, dear, for your good wishes concerning my health. I will be ever grateful for your role in my healing and complete restoration.

"With great eagerness to see you, Joanna."

And to Mummius:

"My very good Mummius, how excellent of you to offer to accompany Demetria. I know Mary would welcome an opportunity to see you and conduct whatever business you might have with her. We will all sneak up on Mary with our surprise!"

Demetria was ecstatic, packing for their trip.

"Why did Mummius offer to escort you, Demetria?" asked Rachel, helping to fold Demetria's clothes.

"He said he always has business in Tiberias, and that it is a pleasant time to travel. I did not want to press him too far."

"I still do not trust him. Must you go?"

"Rachel, you worry too much. Mary delegates to Mummius all her worldly goods, the farm and the weaving business—and us. As for me, I need a change of scene. I am so restless! This spring weather makes me want to fly the coop," she said, holding a veil above her head for wings and swooping like a bird.

"You are such a traveler, Little Bit. I am a homebody, never wanting to stray far from what is familiar."

"Nor far from Prince Daniel!"

Rachel lowered her head. "I know I am acting the silly girl," she said. "It is just that I thought this kind of happiness had passed me by. Oh, Demetria, I had almost given up hope that there would ever be anyone for me to love."

Demetria sat down on the bed beside Rachel, the one who had been her friend from the start. Wrapping her veil wings around Rachel's shoulders, Demetria pulled her close. "I am happy for you, sister," she said.

Mummius, too, was packing. He pushed a final folded tunic into his bag. Then, placing a roll of pens reverently on top, he paused. He knew he was walking toward his destiny, where God would embrace him as a son. He was approaching the most significant crossroads of his life and the possibility of union with the godhead—the driving force of his life—that underlay all he had done and all he had desired. He was walking toward the truth of what God required of him, answering the voice of God that had called him beloved son—the imperative connection between Jesus and the writing on the wall.

As he closed his bag and secured it, Mummius remembered the astonishment turned to elation when he told Demetria he would aid her in her plan to go to Tiberias. It would advance his own means, yes; but he could not ignore the satisfaction he found in making her happy. He might not be ready to wash feet, but he could serve another by small gestures such as this. As for his feelings for her, it was a relief to be less rigid, less ready to defend, less—cautious. She was young and irrelevant to his aims; he could safely relax a little.

But a nagging voice in the back of his mind murmured, *Demetria irrelevant? Is it not she who is taking you on the road to meet Jesus?*

CHAPTER 40

The vacation villa occupied by Lord Chuza and his wife Joanna was rustic by Roman standards. Having grown one wing at a time to fit the irregular contours of the surrounding topography, the house lacked even a modicum of architectural orderliness. There was no proper central atrium, but an inelegant foyer that served as both entryway and reception area. Off the foyer stretched an extended corridor leading to the large triclinium, where crowded dining couches gave the impression that many diners were often crowded in at a single sitting. Sleeping cubicles were not laid out in contiguous, even rows, but tucked in here and there, wherever space could be found.

Everywhere the floors were paved in rough, mismatched sandstone tiles, inexpertly laid, resulting in a slightly uneven surface, nothing like the smooth expanses of polished marble artistry the residents were accustomed to in the palace at Tiberias. The unfrescoed walls were crudely dressed with plaster and whitewashed over. The furniture of local cedar was anything but elaborate.

Despite its shortcomings, however, the house did have one adornment so notable that no other was needed to commend it. On the north side of the villa, set upon a slight rise up from the water's edge, a colonnaded portico looked out on a splendidly unembellished stripe of white sand beach sweeping down to the bowl of glittering jewels that was the Sea of Galilee. Invariably, guests gravitated to this portico with its stunning vista, and remained there as long as courtesy would permit. Having once visited the portico and been spellbound by the view, they were not bothered about where they slept or with whom they took their meals.

It was within this colonnade that Mummius sat on a couch, playing a double-piped arghul of reed. His long, dark fingers moved with grace over the five stops of the woodwind, producing a haunting melody of old

Egypt. Breezes off the sea breathed in and out through white linen draperies, brushing their hems over the floor, transporting him home, to the shore of the Great Sea, to Alexandria. A woman's voice drifted in on the scent of oleander.

"I love the lake in spring."

Mummius stopped his song mid-phrase and prepared to rise. "Lady Joanna."

"Do not disturb yourself, Mummius," she said, laying her fingertips on his shoulder to prevent him from standing. "You are not only scribe and physician, but gifted musician as well? Please, play on."

"I am out of practice, Lady. Later perhaps," he said, placing the instrument upon a table.

Mummius was surprised by Joanna's appearance. She was dressed in country clothes, an unbelted tunic of drab, lightweight wool, which enabled her to move more freely, less deliberately than was possible under the constrained and formal obligations of Tiberias. On her feet she wore thick local sandals, made shabby, he imagined, by long walks along the shore where it became a pebble beach further on. Except for her meticulously pedicured toes, she could have been, not the wife of Lord Chuza, Chief Steward to Herod Antipas, but a simple Galilean woman, carrying a branch of oleander in her hand, for love of its scent.

By contrast, Mummius' best Egyptian attire seemed unsuitable. He had dressed in a long linen skirt, almost transparent through the fine pleats, which clung to his hips and legs as he moved. His torso was uncovered save for the jeweled collar he wore on special occasions. Mummius was well aware of the effect his bare chest had on women, and he was suddenly embarrassed that his extraordinary fitness was on display.

He watched Joanna arrange her skirt to fall just so over her outstretched legs as she took another couch, reclining on her left side in the conventional Roman manner, propped up on her left elbow. Following her lead, he reclined on his couch, on his left side, using his right hand to sip wine from a golden chalice and looking out over the water.

"It is easy to relax here," she said softly.

"Indeed it is, my lady. I had not realized how much needed this was for me. And for Demetria."

"Look at them running on the sand like boys. They will need baths before dinner."

Mummius turned to the beach. The first thing to catch his eye was the dazzle of Salome's thick mop of copper-red hair. Then the flash of both girls' legs, blurred like turning chariot wheels, carrying them in circles, down to the water and back, running first this way, then pivoting quickly that way, and ducking, as they tried to dodge the other's tag. *Yearling gazelles,* thought Mummius.

"I hope Mary will not disapprove."

"Of what, my lady?"

"That I permit Demetria's immoderate behavior."

Mummius chuckled. "No, Lady, she will not disapprove."

"You are certain?"

"Mary has a fondness for the freedoms of childhood. It is said that she was quite the unruly colt in her own youth. Her father encouraged it."

"Demetria is no longer a child," said Joanna, making her case.

"Then let her romp while she can," answered Mummius, making his.

Acquiescing, Joanna changed the subject. "I had a letter from Mary yesterday."

Too quickly, Mummius said, "Is Jesus...?" Regretting that he had blurted out what he did not intend, he corrected himself. "Will she be here soon?"

Joanna had already detected the eagerness in his voice that distinguished his desire to see the rabbi from all other enthusiasms. She rose up further on her elbow and peered at Mummius on the next couch. "Has he healed you, too?"

Caught unawares, Mummius cleared his throat. "An odd question, Lady."

"Not at all. I know what it is to be changed by him. Ever after, it shows on the face when his name is mentioned."

Mummius wondered what showed on his face just now. He took a moment to make sure that his voice would not betray him further when he opened his mouth to speak. He wanted to be truthful, but not completely. He knew that God had stopped his inscription of Jesus' words. But he had no clear idea what role Jesus had played—would continue to play—in the important events on which his life now turned. He did not want to try to explain any of that to Joanna.

He answered honestly when he said, "I have witnessed many of his miracles, but, no, I have not been healed by Jesus."

Then Joanna did a strange thing. She got up from her couch and came and sat close beside Mummius, still lying on his side. The color rose to his face when she took his right hand in both of hers. He wanted to sit up, but she held him firmly, and he was unwilling to struggle against her.

Joanna's eyes were sparkling, but not with tears, and she said, "I lived in a prison cell where my wrists and ankles and even my neck were bound with long tethers. Not a real prison, but it may as well have been. I could move about within the walls of that room, but I could not escape it. The greatest horror was never to know when the force that held my ropes would yank them tight and fling me to the floor. My body would jerk powerfully against my bonds till I was bruised and choking on my own spittle. That was my life, Mummius, a nightmare. Then Jesus came and laid his hands on me. It was as though I'd stepped out of my torture cell into a smooth and tranquil place, beyond harm, no longer fearing the unpredictable cruelty of unseen tormentors."

Unnerved by Joanna's intimate disclosure, Mummius stole an awkward glance at the beach and noticed that the girls were no longer there. He did not want them to walk in and see Lady Joanna sitting on the couch with him. What might they think of her gripping his hand, looking at him with her enchanted and glowing eyes? And what of him, reclining under her gaze, his naked chest polished with the oil he had regrettably applied?

Mummius was innocent—this time. In Rome he had developed a coterie of lovers, women whom he had seduced and kept in thrall with the magic of his love-making. But his activities with women in Rome had led to no good. Livia Valeria had become jealous and possessive and threatened to ruin him if he did not comply with her insatiable demands. Marcus Quintius Severus had rescued him by offering him the position of Chief Steward to his friend in Galilee, a woman of sound character who needed someone to oversee her business. In Magdala, he had left his reputation with women behind, in deference to Mary and to his own desire to start over.

Against all his intentions, here was still another rich and beautiful woman sitting next to him, whose mind, floating in some kind of dream, would provide easy prey. For a moment he was tempted to make a sexual advance—to feel that consummate prowess. But Mummius would not turn his back on God's call and all that had brought him here.

"Joanna," he said in the measured command of a physician calling a patient out of a trance.

She cocked her head and blinked. The unnatural light faded from her eyes, and she offered him a crooked smile. "My goodness..."

Mummius scanned Joanna's face and body for clues. If she were this susceptible to flights of fancy, if the mere thought of Jesus induced a state of rapture, perhaps her healing was not as complete as everyone believed.

Had Jesus substituted some of his own power for that of the demon he had driven from her? Did the people Jesus healed remain spellbound by him once the evil spirit had departed, thereby exchanging one possession for another? That might explain Mary's uncommon devotion.

"Aunt Joanna!" came Salome's call from the archway behind them.

By all the gods, no! thought Mummius.

Demetria's voice was added to the flurry. "Look who is here!"

He pushed up on his elbow as far as he could without knocking Joanna to the floor and turned to look. It was far worse than he had imagined. Demetria and Salome were skipping onto the portico, and, between them, each swinging her by the hand, they led a woman. Mary.

Mary stopped abruptly. Mummius turned his head away and closed his eyes and took a deep breath. Apparently unconcerned, Joanna rose to greet her.

"Mary, my dear, shalom. Welcome to Sennabris."

The life had gone out of Mary's wide smile, but it remained frozen in place as she responded to Joanna with a perfunctory embrace, all the while staring uncertainly at Mummius. Finally he rose and turned to her. Why had he allowed himself to be caught in a compromising position with no less a personage than the wife of Herod's steward? He had lived so long behind a protective barrier. Why had he let down his guard?

Trying to resurrect a shield of indifference, he nodded to Mary. "Lady," he said.

Among the girls' infectious bouncing, Joanna herded the new arrivals to the couches and bade them sit. With a slight rise of one hand she ordered refreshments from a slave who had been attending them. She sat next to Mary and, with puckish eyes, said, "Are you surprised?"

"Surprised cannot begin to describe it."

"I confess that it required all the constraint I could muster not to drop a hint in my letters," Joanna explained. "On the one hand, I was sworn to secrecy. On the other, I wanted badly to tell you that Demetria would be here."

"And Mummius..."

"Yes, Mummius! You are fortunate to have such a friend in authority over your affairs, Mary. He is the soul of integrity, and he is kind, as well." Then to Demetria, "Was Mummius not generous to aid you in our secret plan, Demetria?"

Resolved to distinguish herself as a young woman capable of fitting into the circle of adults, Demetria lost her giddiness and said politely, "He was very helpful."

After a moment of silence, Joanna, the good hostess, went on. "Tell me, Mary, is Jesus nearby? I do so desire to see him."

"Yes. He and his—what shall I say?—his entourage, for surely that is what it has grown into, are in Sennabris even now. It is like a stone rolling down a steep slope, gaining speed. Exhausting, really."

"He has always had a following," said Mummius, maintaining restraint when the talk turned to Jesus.

"Not like this. We took to traveling so as to reach more people with his message, but the people do not stay put. At every stop, more and more leave their homes to walk with us. It is a burgeoning flock. There is no solitude. We sleep outdoors, vulnerable to visitors at all hours. Jesus' close friends try to cordon him off at times, for rest, but he will have none of that. It is wearying."

Joanna clapped the palms of her hands in rapid succession, lightly. "Bring them here, Mary, do! We have plenty of room, and it is quite informal. Everyone can come and go at will. Please, do not deny me the pleasure of offering some respite."

"I would not dream of subjecting your home to such a press of people."

"Jesus can bring whomever he chooses and no others. There will be no press of people."

"What, Joanna, would you station a royal guard around the house?"

"No need for guards, Mary. They know who the owner is."

What a declaration! Was it only Mummius who understood the import of it? Jesus, an itinerant wonder-worker, wading around within masses of the vulgar rabble was, at the same time, an invited guest of the household of Rome's elect, Herod Antipas, Tetrarch of Galilee and Perea. Once again, Mummius was at the edge of incredulity. How could such a man move freely at both extremes of the social order, and among everyone in between?

Mummius thought of the light in Joanna's eyes when she spoke of her healing—the same radiance that lit the eyes of the common people who gathered around each day to hear the good news Jesus brought to them. They all wanted the same thing from him, and they all received, equally.

"Well, then, yes," he heard Mary say. "I will persuade Jesus to agree. How good it will be to have some peace and quiet at the end of these arduous days!"

"I will see to dinner. Come, girls, give me a hand," said Joanna. Taking a good look at them, she changed her mind. "No, you two monkeys, go to the bath."

Mary said to Mummius, "Will you accompany me to the town, Chief Steward?"

"As you wish."

If only he could undo the past hour, erase the complication of Mary finding him with Joanna. Well, he would find a way to explain...

They set out walking to Sennabris along the beach. Not wanting to begin a conversation that he did not want to have, Mummius waited for Mary to speak first.

"I was quite surprised to find Demetria at the villa."

"She was eager to visit Joanna."

"And you encouraged her."

"I did. Are you angry?"

"Not angry, puzzled. How is it that *you* are a guest in Chuza's house, Mummius?"

That might have stung him, but he knew she meant no disrespect. What could he say to her—that he was in the grip of a call from the Most High God? That Jesus held the answer to his future, and his life? Mummius found himself in a moment of intense desire, wanting to trust her. Why not let go of the complicated charade he was living, as Siamun had suggested? A crevasse of truth-telling yawned before him. One step forward and he would be flung, flightless, into the rift below. He backed away from the precipice.

"There was no such plan, Lady, but circumstance alone. Demetria was set on getting away from Magdala for a while. She wrote to Joanna, who insisted that she visit Salome in Tiberias. I wanted to write to you, but they were committed to their surprise."

"So you chaperoned Demetria to Tiberias..."

"As you would have wanted."

"As I would have wanted, yes... Go on."

"It was the Lady Joanna who suggested I accompany them to Sennabris. I resisted, of course, but once she had the thought, there was no arguing with her. I did not wish to come, but she was adamant."

"Why adamant?"

Mummius answered with the simple truth. "I do not know," he said. Before anything more could pass between them, their conversation was interrupted by the hum of an excited crowd rising up from the shore beyond.

There, just outside the city of Sennabris, at the effluence of the Sea of Galilee into the River Jordan at the southern end, was the site of a good harbor that could accommodate as many as 250 naval vessels. In this particular tranquil springtime, however, there were no military headquarters, but, rather, a prosperous business center. Many small creeks spread out between the river and the town, like crooked fingers, where boats could ride in safely. As if by design to supply seats, the shore on both sides of the narrow inlets was piled up with smooth boulders of basalt. Here the multitude, which had gathered to see Jesus, sat around the boat in which he stood.

As Mary waded through the crowd to get near the boat, Mummius wanted to hold back. In Capernaum he had made an art of secreting himself within the crowd, or hiding out at the edges. Now, pushing forward, steered by Mary to a prominent location where he would be on exhibit in her company, Mummius felt his chest tighten. Jesus had not yet come into view, but there was no mistaking the joy on Mary's face, anticipating the sight of him. Seeing her that way, Mummius was reminded that it was God who had called him to this moment. What, then, should he fear? Surely God had brought him here to be welcomed by Jesus into the fold of the chosen.

The crowd parted in front of them to let Mary pass. She raised an arm in greeting, which momentarily blocked his view of Jesus, standing in the boat, just offshore. Mummius knew that at last he was prepared to greet the rabbi, and be greeted, as a beloved son of the Most High God. Anticipating the long-desired scene of mutual recognition, Mummius beamed. But when Mary's arm came down and Jesus looked him directly in the eye, Mummius came to a sudden halt, his eyes riveted on the turban Jesus wore.

Mary must have sensed the tension in Mummius' body, now standing like granite behind her. She turned to him and asked, "Mummius? What is wrong?"

Mummius could not advance; he could not flee. All he could manage was a choked question from a throat garroted by a simmering storm. "Where is the tallit?"

"The tallit...?"

During the weeks when Mummius had kept him under surveillance in Capernaum, Jesus' head was always covered with his tallit, marking him as a holy man. The mystical prayer shawl, which Mary had made for him, was part of his daily attire, and he was rarely seen without it. Today, there was no tallit. Instead, as in earlier times in Nazareth, Jesus was wearing the national headdress of Galilee, a white turban wrapped so that a tail hung down on one side just short of the shoulder.

A turban like every other unremarkable turban, and yet, remarkably unlike all the rest. For this was the very turban that Mummius had lost the night he hid himself in the basket at Mary's house, the night he eavesdropped on them, the night he knew Jesus had discovered his disguise. He recognized the frayed tail, which had fallen into the path of Mummius' knife and been notched by the slice of the blade as he worked in the garden. There was the smudge on the side where Mummius had, with a muddy hand, tucked the tail in, out of his way. There was the unmistakable red-brown stain on the front where a branch had fallen too quickly, grazing Mummius' forehead, leaving blood.

Mummius could have returned to Mary's house to retrieve the turban. But in the aftermath of the staggering theophany when God entered his room and spoke directly to him, of what consequence was a turban? Now, Mummius thought that Jesus had found the evidence of his subterfuge and had taken it to trap him in his spying. Mummius imagined Jesus sending his own spies to track his comings and goings, lying in wait for an occasion to humiliate him.

The truth was much simpler than all that, if only Mummius could have seen it. Jesus understood Mummius' need to protect himself, to hide behind disguises in his pursuit of God. Jesus loved Mummius as he was, not as he aspired to be. He wore the turban as a sign of empathy. But Mummius did not want to be loved for his weaknesses. He wanted to be great, as Jesus was great.

Mummius had come here expecting Jesus to receive him as an equal, a son whom God had called beloved. Instead, Jesus was mocking him, or so he thought. Mummius wanted to punish Jesus for his part in this fiasco. If he had believed that there was even a distant chance of seriously wounding Jesus with a curse, Mummius would gladly have died thrusting it on him. But he knew it would not be like sparring with Siamun. Jesus would deflect his strongest hex with a mere glance, and Mummius' disgrace would be complete. In the next moment-turned-a-thousand-hours, Mummius recouped his will. He turned abruptly and, climbing over the boulders of basalt, fled, stumbling through the crowd, ignoring the grumbling of those he pushed aside and not responding to Mary's voice calling to him from behind.

He reached the pebble beach in a few moments' time, just enough to collect himself and enough to rebuke his own folly—again. His objective now was to return to the villa as quickly as possible, pack his things, and be gone. Like a sudden squall over the sea in summer, he stormed up the deserted white sand beach and onto the portico, oblivious to its splendors. He raced through the corridors, noticing the occasional inconspicuous servant, who let him pass unchallenged. *Just keep your mouths shut!* he commanded silently.

He spun through the entry of his secluded sleeping cubicle and leaned against the wall. His disappointment and rage at the scene at the seaside, contrasted with the expectation that had fermented in Mummius over the past weeks, swelled and burst. He let out a loud wail, which would have been mistaken for the panicked cry of a stricken animal to anyone who heard it. And the walls went up. Every protective instinct that Mummius had allowed to weaken locked in place again. It had been madness to follow a fake call from a fake god. How glad he was that he had not confided in Mary!

Mummius seized a goblet of wine left upon a small table for him and drained it. Then he sent the empty cup flying over the bed and crashing against the wall, marking the white surface with an angry red stain before it came to rest on the bed. He glared at it for a moment, unseeing. As his vision cleared and his furor was dissipating, Mummius noticed that the cup had landed on a scroll left lying on his bed. He did not remember being told of the arrival of a message. It must have been delivered during the short interval of his walk from the villa to the town and back. What was so urgent that a letter would be forwarded here from Magdala? He had left everything in order; nothing could go wrong in his absence.

Mummius picked up the scroll and, turning it, saw the identifying seal. *Severus!* He flicked off the circle of clay, unfurled the papyrus, and read:

"Good Mummius, Greeting! I know how much you must have longed for some word from me since my departure from Jerusalem. I regret my sudden leave-taking, necessitated by the unexpected death of my father. You can imagine the demands which have been placed upon me, first by the funeral and, since then, by taking up the reins of the Severi. I confess, though my father prepared me throughout my life for this role, I had not fully comprehended what it is to assume the title of *paterfamilias* of such a clan as ours. No more games and pleasures! At least not for a while. Which brings me to my point.

"I need you in Rome, my friend."

Ah, Severus, man of few words, how I have missed your blunt candor, thought Mummius. He sat down on the bed, picked up the goblet, slightly dented from its crash, and poured himself another draft.

"I remind you that your stay in Galilee was always to be temporary. You have done wonders with Mary's farm, far more than I expected. Your remarkable achievements can continue with the fine staff you have assembled there. As for your life in Rome, have no fear. The lady you so unfortunately offended is happily remarried and spends most of her time vacationing on the seashore in Cumae. When I mentioned you recently, she said, quite imperiously, 'Mummius? Who is Mummius?' So, you see, Livia Valeria will cause you no problem. Best news of all, I have found a way to bestow the citizenship on you. You need no longer rely on your connection to me as slave. You can finally accept my offer of manumission. My uncle will formally adopt you as his son, and you will become a member of our family. You will be in complete charge of all my property. You may hire the chief steward of your choosing.

"Think, Mummius, what a life we will have together in Rome! I await your immediate reply, confirming, I am sure, that which I desire. Severus."

The letter lay in Mummius' lap as he sipped his wine, considering the possibilities. Here was the door to new life, in which his mad pursuit of the godhead could be forgotten, and he could wrap himself in the mantel of Roman greatness. Once again, Marcus Quintius Severus had offered salvation. No longer someone else's steward; no longer scribe-for-hire; no longer physician to the undeserving. He rolled the name and title around in his mind. Then he dared to say aloud, "Mummius Severus, citizen of Rome."

CHAPTER 41

The goddess Fortuna had at last smiled upon Mummius, and his decision to follow her into Severus' lucky circle was quick and sure. He penned a short note to his hostess, Joanna. Then he took the time to change his clothes into something more suitable for traveling before he slung his bag over his shoulder and gingerly paced down a secluded corridor in an effort to escape the house without notice. He was nearing the front entrance when he heard her voice calling from behind. Joanna had been gracious to him. He had no wish to offend her, so he lied.

"I beg your pardon, Lady. I searched, but not finding you, I left a letter of explanation on the colonnade. Thank you for your unmatched hospitality, but events call me to Magdala. Will you be so kind as to inform Mary? She will understand."

His excuse was preposterous, for any of the villa's many servants would have been able to locate their mistress within a matter of moments. Joanna did not point out the fault, but said only, "It is late in the day. Surely you can delay your departure until morning."

Much as he regretted the longing face before him, Mummius replied, "Lady Joanna, I will treasure the memory of your company these past few weeks. It is not often I am fully accepted by others."

"I might say the same, Mummius. My responsibilities in Tiberias, of necessity, place a certain distance between me and other people. You are a rare and gifted man. I will remember your visit with gladness."

This is why she was adamant to have me come here, he thought. *She is isolated and lonely for intelligent companionship.*

"I hope we will see each other again," she added.

"If the gods will it..." replied Mummius, bowing deeply.

"Safe journey," she sighed.

Mummius took what he believed to be a safe path, well south of the swarming shoreline. It felt good to be in the open air, despite the hazard of being caught a second time in a too-hasty departure. Once he got into Sennabris, it would be easy to lose himself in the anonymity of the town. At least he had escaped the villa without encountering Demetria. The thought of her gave him a moment's pause. Who would accompany her home to Magdala? *Well,* he thought, rancor creeping in, *I am not the only servant available to them.*

He shifted his heavy bag to a better position on his shoulder and picked up his pace. The adjustments did not alleviate his discomfort, for it was not his body that was aching, but his spirit. He forced himself to think of the future, of Rome.

Mummius was reasonably sure that Severus and Mary had not communicated since he left for Rome and she set out on her tour of Judea with Jesus. He had broached the subject once, but Mary deflected his question, too agitated to discuss it. Mummius guessed that Severus, suddenly imprudent, had made some declaration of his love and been rejected. *I tried to tell you!* he thought, recollecting his failed efforts to persuade Severus that Mary's devotion to Jesus was complete, and that she was beyond his reach. Had Severus finally given her up, then? And from that question there arose a fresh suspicion: *What if he is recalling me to Rome to punish Mary?*

By now Mummius was passing south of where the crowd had been gathered earlier at the river. He was vaguely disquieted, hearing nothing of them from the shore, but the sight of rooftops on the horizon invigorated him. Soon he was nearing the city wall and sounds of the town met his ear. *Almost there.*

But not quite. An olive grove lay before him, obscuring one last bend in the road. As he took the turn, skirting the trees, he saw a man sitting on a rock outcropping, with his back to Mummius and his head bowed, fingering something he held in his lap.

The man looked up at Mummius. "I believe you dropped this," he said, holding out a turban. "Reuben, is it?"

Mummius' heart was hard as a cool stone when he scoffed, "I pity you, Jesus. You are a disgrace to the gods—to your God."

"What do you know of God, Egyptian?"

"You would be surprised by what I know."

"Why don't you enlighten me?"

Mummius detected no ridicule in Jesus' voice, but he was in no mood to revise his reading of events at the lakeshore. "I want no more to do with you," he said.

Jesus changed the subject. "I see by your bag that you are traveling."

"My business here is finished," Mummius replied, yet not departing.

"What business is that?"

"None of yours," he said, still unable to pull himself away, noting once again Jesus' tranquility and his own inner turmoil.

"Perhaps. But let us see. I want to show you something. Come with me."

"You expect me to follow you?"

"Not follow, just come."

Mummius fought his urge to go with Jesus, but when the rabbi stood up and started to walk away, he did not resist. Perhaps here was one last chance to learn some secret. And so they walked together, the din of city sounds overhanging the silence between them, until they arrived at the entrance to Sennabris on the eastern side.

Among the varied activities at city gates was often found a bench of prostitutes where hapless women, having exhausted what few economic choices they might have, sat, waiting for customers. Here men could walk by, evaluate the wares, and make their selections, frequently dragging the women around some corner to do their business. The bench of prostitutes and the pathetic creatures who earned their meager living sitting there were shrouded in a thick veil of contempt, cast over them by decent women. Even men, whether they were customers or not, flaunted their scorn, as though they were not party to it. No matter how young and beautiful, no matter how well-wrapped in showy silks, not one among them treasured this life, nor would have chosen it if there were any other possibility.

Mummius stepped far around the odious bench, but Jesus walked directly toward it.

"What? Are you going with a harlot?" exclaimed Mummius, revolted.

Like a buyer making a selection from the bench, Jesus went to the woman on the end. She was turned sideways, whispering to another woman. "Dear lady," he said.

When the woman looked up at Jesus, Mummius saw with his eyes what his mind could not imagine. The woman who sat among the prostitutes was Mary. Mummius was sickened by the look of adoration on her upturned face. *This is how you honor her—sending her to a bench of whores?* Was Jesus so engulfed by personal authority that he would inflict this degradation on a devotee just to demonstrate it? How could Mummius ever have yearned to be associated with him?

Mummius watched Mary turn to kiss the woman beside her, bidding farewell, then watched her stand and walk in his direction. Seeing that she was about to embrace him, he backed away.

"You think I am unclean, Mummius?"

"In truth, yes," he replied.

Mary withdrew her outstretched hand. "Oh, Mummius, it is not what is outside that contaminates a person. If I accepted that notion, Demetria would not be under my roof, neither Demetria nor half the weavers. Nor you, I might add."

He knew that was true, and, though she said it with kindness, Mummius heard the judgment that, as a gentile, he was unclean according to Jewish law, and that it was only through a massive act of condescension that she had taken him in.

"We must be about our business," Jesus reminded Mary.

"Yes, I am coming," she replied.

"And you, Mummius?" Jesus asked as they turned to walk, not into the city, but away from Sennabris.

The city gate—and freedom—was at hand. Mummius shifted his bag. The wooden bar around which Severus' letter was rolled pressed against his hip bone. And, once again, he could not tear himself away. *No rush,* he thought. *Rome is not going anywhere.*

Mummius went with them, but he brooded, walking between Mary and Jesus, who talked around him, chatting about their travels and minor events that had happened. There was nothing to give him a clue as to the horrors that lay ahead.

In those days it was imperative that lepers be separated from other human beings, to prevent physical contagion, certainly. It was even more important to avoid spiritual contamination. For lepers were those who bore, in their bodies, the punishment dispensed by God for their extreme impurity. And because association with them would transmit that impurity to the unafflicted, lepers lived their lives isolated by ignorance and fear from the rest of human society.

They were not permitted to reside within the confines of a walled town, but their camps were close to towns, often in caves, where the physical needs of the sufferers could be supplied, usually by family and friends who would bring food and clothing out to them. What a grievous excursion for a mother or a brother or a cousin to make! Having packed some old, expendable basket with bread and dates, a supply of salted fish, and perhaps a bit of fresh fruit, or simply tied them up in a towel, the loved one would trek to the colony, calling out a name to make sure the offering was received by the designated one and not some other poor soul for whom no one had come.

There was an unmarked barrier where lepers, while they still could, might walk out to exchange information and expressions of love shouted across a wide swath of ground dividing the living from the living dead. The visitor would set the basket down and, moving away to a safe distance, watch the beloved one fetch the delivery and then slip back to the protection of the camp. Inevitably a day would come when mother or sister or son emerged no more from the shadows, and the food would be picked up by an anonymous person who had won the pathetic race to the unclaimed basket.

When Mummius and his guides approached Sennabris' leper colony, he was slow to recognize it for what it was. They had come to a shallow defile on the opposite side of which was a series of small caves. The scene was, in fact, quite pleasing, for the nearby waters of the Jordan River sweetened the land and made it lush with early summertime foliage. The sun, now lowering in the western sky, flooded the area with golden light.

Mummius' heart was flooded, too, as he was transported back home to Egypt to stand once more upon the banks of the Nile, to speak the sacred name of Amun-Re, the Egyptian one-god Ra, who had called the other Egyptian deities into existence by the power of his spoken word. Uninvited, a hymn to the deity, of which all other gods and goddesses were but aspects, arose in Mummius' heart, and he sang secretly:

"Honor to thee, O Ra, who rises in the horizon,
from day to day unchangeable,
who passes over the sky,
and every face watches thee and thy course.
Thy sacred barge goes forth with light;
its red and yellow rays are without number,
and its beams shine upon all faces."

Looking down into the valley of caves, Mummius' face indeed shone with the reflection of Amun-Re's red and yellow beams. His spirits soared to the sky as the glow of the god's passing solar barge poured over him like anointing oil, filling his heart with the glory of god.

He stood thus until Mary moved in front of him, pulling her shadow across his face. She had stepped around him to take hold of Jesus' hand. *Is she afraid?* he wondered. Jesus turned to him and nodded in the direction of the caves, and did not need to say, *This way.* When a few weeping women passed by, headed dolefully in the opposite direction, Mummius' caution went up.

"Where are we going?"

Neither Mary nor Jesus answered. Mummius wanted to turn back, but could not. He was unable even to pause, to wait, to see what would happen. The same unseen force that had driven him at critical moments over these last weeks drew him forward now.

From the mouth of one of the caves an awful cry: "Unclean, unclean!"

But they kept going.

Another cry: "We are lepers here. Stay away!"

Still they walked on.

Mummius gripped Jesus' shoulder from behind and dug his heels into the dirt. "Rabbi, what are you doing? Do not go in there."

Jesus was silent.

"At least do not take Mary with you. Lady, I beg you, do not go!"

"This is the way I have chosen," she replied. "Will you come?"

Mummius looked from Mary to the yawning mouth of the cave beyond. And, in his mind, he was once again face to face with the name of God on the wall. Again the name of God spoke to him, saying, "Beloved son, I wait for you." Could it be that God was waiting for him in that den of lepers?

Mummius felt himself pulled off a cliff into a chasm of longing. Suddenly the self-assurance that Jesus wore like a mantle when he drove a legion of demons from Mary, when he knelt to wash his disciples' feet, when he put himself in the company of harlots, suddenly that steady self-assurance, that all-encompassing certainty, was within Mummius' grasp.

Jesus' voice broke in on him like a clap of thunder, "Mummius, are you coming?"

His fear outstripped his longing. "I cannot."

Jesus and Mary turned away and resumed their trek, hand-in-hand. Mummius squatted on the ground, watching them go, the sounds of "unclean, unclean!" echoing ever stronger from within the darkness ahead, and finally stopping when the two of them disappeared into the maw of the cave.

How long did Mummius wait, squatting there in the declining light, unable to move? He thought he had seen disappointment on Mary's face when he refused to proceed. What did she expect? That he would expose himself to a ghastly disease for which there was no cure? Mummius saw his reflection in a polished bronze mirror, admiring his body. Then he saw the tiny specks beginning on his eyelids and on his palms, which gradually spread over his body, making patches of scales layered, one above the other, wherever they appeared. He saw the bright silvery luster of the crusty scales progressing into terrible, swollen sores. He saw the final assault, as the disease ate inward to his bones, rotting his body one piece at a time, forever destroying any hope of ordinary life.

Looking away from his image in the mirror, he saw another vision: Mary, lying on her bed in Magdala where he had lovingly attended her as physician. He knew her body, and every inch of it, for he had struggled with the evil spirits that inhabited and stripped her naked. That battle had very nearly killed him. Now he saw her gorgeous frame slowly perishing under the attack of leprous sores and scales. This could not be!

Two figures appeared from within the darkness of the cave. *Praise to all the gods,* thought Mummius, thinking Mary and Jesus had regained their senses and were abandoning their mission. He was about to hail them when the indistinct shadows sharpened into the clear outlines of two women. Their skirts were in tatters. Their hair was matted and as filthy as their clothing.

They did not cry out "unclean!" as lepers were required to do when they approached. Mummius scampered backward, crablike. The strap of his bag tripped him and he fell, splayed out, onto the ground. The women were close enough now for Mummius to see the light in their eyes. The exposed skin of their forearms was unblemished, and their faces, too.

"Hold!" commanded Mummius. "Are you not lepers?"

"Not any longer!" answered the taller of the two, with a laugh. "Now we are going to the priest to get certified." That set her shorter sister to laughing, too. "As if we need *his* proof." More people emerged from the cave, touching each other's faces and their own arms, throwing off veils and turbans and cloaks to allow the air to bless their newborn skin.

Mummius was seized with an impulse to act. He stood and walked to the yawning mouth, which seemed ready to swallow him. He paused, drew a deep breath, and was very nearly knocked back by the stench emanating from within. In the waning rays of Amun-Re's solar light, Mummius stepped into the cave, where the light of Ra was extinguished from his face. A little way off, he saw indistinct images of Mary and Jesus sitting on flat rocks against one wall of the cave. There was a glow of light surrounding them, which he had come to expect from Jesus whenever he was in the grip of his healing power. But he had never seen this light around Mary. Mummius was surprised when she broke her concentration to smile at him.

"Here is your place, Mummius," she said, indicating a smooth rock next to her, every trace of disappointment gone now from her expression.

He went forward and lowered himself onto the seat next to her. Extending out from where they sat, a hushed line of people stood, waiting their turn. The pathetic lepers approached solemnly to receive a blessing from Mary or Jesus, as individuals were healed and departed and the next in line moved up. One by one, inhabitants of the colony in various stages of infirmity stepped forward, or were carried on litters by others, waiting to be touched by the wonderful hands that would cleanse them and make them whole.

And then, it happened. A girl, a lithe and beautiful maiden, with copper-colored skin and ebony-black hair, stepped from the end of Jesus' line and came to stand in front of Mummius. She held her veil across her face, as modest maidens do, so that only her brown eyes were showing. The sight of her took Mummius' breath for a moment. *Maret!* His beloved, his betrothed.

It could not be. Maret was far away in Bubastis, by now a matron, married, and a mother. Then, who was this vision? How did such an innocent come to be cast off into the human wreckage of this stinking cave? With the movement of her arm, the girl gave him his answer. She withdrew her veil, letting it fall to her shoulders, exposing her ravaged nose and mouth.

Unable to fight down his violently rising gorge, Mummius turned his head to vomit. The girl pulled on her veil to hide her ugliness, and Mummius was filled with regret.

"Please help me," she said.

Mummius wiped his mouth on his sleeve. He wanted to reach out to her, to pull her onto his lap, as he used to do, crazy in love, with Maret. He wanted to lay his hand on her face and restore her. But it was beyond his capability. Accomplished physician though he was, he could not do this.

Mummius looked to Mary, begging for help, but she was deep in her efforts with others. He turned back to the girl. "Go," he said. "Stand in the line."

The Maret twin, her dark eyes boring into Mummius' self-doubt, whispered, "I want you to do it."

When his tears came, Mummius did not fight them. "I wish I could," he whispered back. Never had he meant anything so devoutly.

Mummius looked to Mary, again, and to Jesus, but they could not help him now. They had shown him the way. They had trusted his deepest desires. The rest was up to him.

Calling on all his training, Mummius the physician reached out to the girl and removed her veil. She was otherwise fully clothed, and yet it was as though she were standing naked before him, exposed and trusting. Perhaps if Mummius could restore her, just do this one compassionate thing, then all the torment of his own life might be redeemed as well. Forcing himself to study the girl's ravaged face, Mummius saw that it was not only her mouth and nose that had succumbed to the disease, but her chin and her jaw, and it was beginning to eat away at her small, sweet ears. His heart cried out within, *O God, the suffering!*

With those words, a key turned, opening a rusted lock, and the voice of God that had spoken from the writing on the wall spoke again, and the cave reverberated with the sound: BELOVED SON! Mummius glanced at other people, none of whom seemed to have heard it. Neither did they hear the cry of his heart in response. "Here I am."

He began to examine her, unflinching. As he did so, he realized that in his mind he was seeing, not wounds, but firm, healthy flesh and soft, clear skin. He pulled her closer, and when he laid a hand on her shoulder, he felt underneath his palm a fire so hot that he had to constrain himself from pulling away. He raised his other hand and laid two fingertips at the opening to her mouth where lips should have been. When he drew hot fingers across that opening, new flesh appeared. Painting her portrait, he traced first the top lip, then the bottom. He stroked the tip of her nose, circles on either side, and her nostrils were restored.

Bolder now, Mummius took her face in his hands and sent the heat from his palms into her jaws and her ears. He rubbed his hands over her shoulders and down her arms. She held up her bare feet, and he spread healing fire over them and up her legs to the knees, and beyond, following the course of the disease where it was manifest and where it was going. And neither of them was shamed by his touch. Then it was finished. Mummius held up his hands in front of his own face, expecting to see hot coals. But they had cooled, whatever bellows had fanned the flames, now stilled. The restored face of the lovely girl was the last thing Mummius saw before he slumped, unconscious, to the floor of the cave of lepers.

When Mummius opened his eyes, there was darkness all around him, relieved only by hazy, flickering shadows. He was lying on a clean bed, odors of aloe and camphor hanging in the air. He tried to turn his head, but his muscles, except for his eyes, seemed paralyzed, and Mummius wondered if he had crossed over from life through death to eternal life. He heard a low moan from across the room. He listened for the source. When the second moan came, he realized that it had emanated from his own throat. The moans must have summoned a woman—a goddess—because she appeared to him and called him by name.

The face looking down at him was very beautiful, with long golden hair and pale eyes. This was no Egyptian goddess. Greek, he thought, dimly aware of his own confusion.

"You're awake," she said, picking up his hand and pressing it to her cheek. Mummius felt her hair flowing over his arm. "Speak to me, please," she implored.

He blinked, moistening his stinging eyes and focused again. "Demetria?" The sound of his voice was alien to him, cracked and dry.

"It is I," she said, tears spilling onto Mummius' hand.

"Where…?" he started to ask, but his throat would not respond.

"Here, drink some water." She rubbed a bit of balm on his lips and gave him sips from a cup.

"Where am I?"

"At Lady Joanna's house."

Mummius began to remember: he had received a letter from Severus; he was on his way to Rome. Why was he back at the villa?

"How?"

"Jesus and another man brought you on a litter. You went to the leper colony with Mary and Jesus, and you healed a girl there. When it was over, you fell in a faint. Jesus said it was a great miracle that depleted you, and it would just take some time to recover yourself. I wanted to believe him, but I was very worried, so I stayed here to keep watch over you."

"You kept watch?"

"Three days," she murmured.

Mummius was only partially lucid, but there was no mistaking what she said next.

"They told me you were going to Magdala without me," she said, voice trembling.

The agonizing betrayal in her eyes awakened Mummius to the central, heart-breaking fact of Demetria's life. From the first moment she was snatched from her father's arms, she had been shuttled from place to place and person to person, vainly seeking permanent sanctuary. When Mary left Magdala to be with Jesus, Mummius had become Demetria's last hope. She was clinging to him as though to a raft in open waters. Now, he, too, had decided to abandon her.

And this was the central fact of *his* life—he had traveled from crossroads to crossroads, propelled by the insatiable desire to be compensated for what had been taken from him. Deprived of his manhood, he would use his vast talents to become greater than other men. He would be so far exalted that his defect could not diminish his eminence. When the gods failed to satisfy his desire, he had put his trust in Marcus Quintius Severus. Was he like Demetria, then, stumbling from hope to hope? Would Rome fail him just as he had failed Demetria?

"Is it true, Mummius? Were you going without me?"

With a great effort, Mummius turned his head and squeezed his eyes shut, pushing out from the corners a flood of tears that streamed down into his ears and onto the pillow where he lay. Demetria continued to clutch his hand in a feverish attempt to block out this latest uncertainty.

That was how Jesus found them when he came to look after Mummius. He went first to Demetria, distracting her from her frozen vigil by saying, "Child, go and fetch your mistress. Tell her Mummius has awakened." Then he sat down softly on the bed. "Physician?"

Mummius opened his eyes, slowly, and offered Jesus the hint of a smile.

"You did a great deed," Jesus said.

"It was not a dream?" Mummius asked, pushing up on his elbows. Jesus tucked a pillow under him for support. "It felt like a fire that did not consume."

"It was no dream. The power of the Living God—in you."

"I believe that, Jesus; I do. But why is the power given for the likes of lepers and prostitutes?" Even after what he had done for the dark, lovely girl in the cave, that was what Mummius did not understand.

"I know it is not easy for you to hear, but this is what it means. If you desire to be a son of God, you must love indiscriminately, as God loves, not choose whom you will love and whom you will not. Loving others is the way to God. It is the only way. The truth is, Mummius, very few can do it."

"To have access to God's power, I must spend my life up to my elbows in filth, living with the stench of that cave in my nostrils forever?"

"That is not how I would describe it, but, yes, it is partly that. The greater truth is this: an act of compassion for the outcast does not bring down the one who does it; rather it lifts up and restores the outcast one."

"I knew a man who had been cured of leprosy and ever after, before lying down to sleep, he was compelled to conduct a fearful, minute inspection of his body, searching for the tell-tale spot that would show what he dreaded—a return of the disease. Now I will have to live like that."

In the look that passed between them, Mummius saw Jesus' unflagging self-assurance, and marveled. Surely Jesus, who exposed himself daily to all manner of disease, did not examine himself each night for symptoms.

Before Jesus could speak again, the sound of Mary's eager arrival at the door caused them both to look up. She hurried to the bedside, flush with worry. She stared at Mummius, but she addressed her question to Jesus. "Will he be all right?"

"You look like a mother hen who has found her lost chick," Jesus observed.

"Do not tease, Rabbouni. Move over," she commanded, sitting down on the bed. "Mummius, how do you feel?"

"Never better, Lady."

"You men and your jests!"

Demetria appeared at the other side of the bed, observing the lighthearted banter from which she felt excluded.

"Come, Greek maid," Jesus said, ushering Demetria from the room. "You are weary. Let us have something to drink."

Alone with Mary, Mummius was ill at ease. He tried to sit up.

"Be still," she ordered. "Would you like some water?"

"Indeed I am very thirsty."

Mary brought the cup to his lips and put her hand behind his neck to help him. He drank appreciatively. Rested. Drank again.

"Thank you, Lady." After a few moments, during which she continued to inspect his face, he added, "Is this not an awkward turn of events—I, the patient; you, the care giver?"

"It is my joy to serve you, Mummius."

She was his servant now? What kind of love was this? Mummius was compelled to make a confession. "Lady, did Joanna tell you about...?"

"Speak not of it, Mummius."

"I must. Go to my bag and withdraw the scroll you will find there."

Mary was puzzled. No one was invited to go through Mummius' things, ever. Her face darkened when she saw the seal. She glanced at Mummius as though for reassurance, then unrolled the letter and read.

"This is where you were going? To Rome? Without so much as a word?"

"Lady, forgive me."

"Did you imagine that I would fail to endorse your decision, however much it might pain me? Do you have so little faith in me, Mummius?"

Abandoning the scroll, Mary stood and turned her back to him, a heavy yoke of sadness weighing down on her shoulders. Mummius pushed his body up off the bed and put his hand on the wall to keep from crumpling. He took a few shallow breaths and spread his feet wide apart to gain his balance. When he was sure he was stable, he released his grip on the wall and brought his hand to her shoulder. She met his gaze.

In her look, Mummius understood something else that had escaped him before. When God called him "Beloved son" and said, "I wait for you," it meant that God was waiting for him to receive love without reservation, and to give it in return. During the years in which Mummius was Mary's physician, he had mistaken her dependence on him for love. Then, when Jesus took Mary from him by healing her, Mummius had been jealous and possessive.

Now, he saw that Mary had always loved him, not as a dependent, but as an equal, a brother. Dependence and exclusivity had nothing to do with Love. In fact, they are its opposite. Mummius had known this kind of Love one other time. He remembered his sacrificial act for Maret, when he disappeared so that she would be free to make a new life for herself, find another man to love, one who could give her children. He realized that Mary would sacrifice her own needs in that same way, in the service of his freedom.

"Go if you will, Mummius. But surely by now you must know what you will be giving up and that you cannot leave your wounds behind."

Mummius could not restrain his grief. Grief for who he might have been. Grief for who he was. Grief for betraying everyone who loved him, and for closing his ears to God. Like a huge bird of prey, regret sank its claws into Mummius' heart, and he could no longer bear Mary's decency. He dropped down onto the bed. "Please, Lady, leave me alone now."

He lay there for a long time, in the darkness, alone with his thoughts. At last he gathered the energy to remove a small lap board and writing utensils from his bag. He unrolled a piece of papyrus and picked up his pen and wrote. "Listen to me, all of you, and try to understand. God loves the one whose heart is filled with faith." It was an ordinary moment, that writing in his familiar script and, yet, when he saw it, Mummius was jubilant. He continued to write, quickly now: "You think you know what is pleasing to God? Go, make prayers and sacrifices. But when you do, look into your own heart. Are you filled..."

Mummius refreshed the ink on his pen as the words of Jesus flowed out onto the page.

"…with Love? Or are you just going through the motions? God sees what is hidden within you, not the outward acts displayed for others."

Mummius laughed and wrote, and wrote and laughed, until there were no more thoughts in his head. Everything he had stored up in his mind from the pen-stilled days in Capernaum were captured and written down. Reading over what he had inscribed, he laughed till he cried. Then he cried till the tears of joy turned to tears of sadness and the shaking laughter became shaking sobs.

Mummius did not want to look into the black hole of self-adulation that was his heart, fearing that there was no Love there. Not the kind of Love that Mary had, not the kind that God wanted. And yet, he had laid his hands on that girl in the cave, put his fingers into her sores, and restored her flesh. He had been willing to risk almost certain contagion. Mummius held out the long, graceful hands that made music and papyrus and healing potions. He turned them over slowly, looking for red bumps, the commencement of the disease. *Too soon.*

What would that act of righteousness cost him? Mummius laid his head against the wall and closed his eyes. *Entry into the Reign of God comes at the price of all other desires.*

What did Mummius know about his own desires? Not the outward, self-aggrandizing wants, but the deep longing of his heart? He had always wanted to be empowered by God, fearless and revered. But to gain that lofty state required relinquishing his lifelong idea of greatness and turning to humility and compassion. Like Jesus. Like Mary.

Mummius could no longer think. He fell into a worn out sleep, and, as he slept, he dreamed.

Mummius is standing at a crossroads in the desert. To his left, the road to Rome; to the right, Jerusalem. *Why Jerusalem?* But in the way of dreams, the dreamer lets the question pass unanswered. On the left, he sees a pile of his possessions—a bag of clothing and prized jewelry, a case of sacred scribal implements, the locked potion chest—everything he will need for life in Rome.

Turning to the right, he sees only an empty road, stretching out into a thick fog in the distance. Mummius strains to see. Nothing there. Wait. The fog lightens into a mist and two figures emerge. The mist is not a fog, but a blanket of light, within which he can see the forms of Jesus and Mary, walking away. A voice emanates from the light, "Are you coming?" Mummius must choose: all—or nothing?

Mummius woke up at midday, stiff from many hours of sleeping on the floor. He stood and stretched his sore back and legs. Something wonderful had happened to him, a dream.

He washed his hands and face and changed his clothes and went to the portico, where he imagined everyone would be gathered, waiting for him to appear, recovered. But when he arrived at the portal, the porch was empty. No talk, no music. No breeze off the Sea of Galilee bringing the draperies to life. Just a soft voice from behind.

"Friend, are you well?"

Mummius turned to see Joanna, obviously weighed down by concern.

"I am very well, Lady," he said, shining a rare, breathtaking smile on her. "Where is everyone?"

"Gone."

In an instant his smile was erased, returned to the hidden place from which it had momentarily emerged. "Gone? Gone where?"

"To Magdala."

"But—why?"

"Mary said she was homesick, that she wanted to see Rachel, to return with Demetria and visit her weavers. She has sacrificed much to follow Jesus, would you not agree, Mummius?"

Mummius ignored Joanna's explanation, and her question. "When did they leave?"

"Hours ago, at dawn."

"Half a day's journey."

"Perhaps you can catch them," Joanna said. "If you want to."

The crowd would be moving like a swarm of bees north on the road to Magdala. Jesus would be encircled by his close friends, those fishermen from around Capernaum. Demetria would be tucked closely under Mary's protective wing, leaning into her side. Above all, they would be happy. Mummius slipped his hand into his pocket, feeling for Mary's seal, and thought of Rome.

Was his desire for acceptance stronger than his fear of rejection? Was his compassion for the beautiful young leper sufficient to redeem him? *If I go to them, what if they no longer want me?*

"Do you want to catch up to them?" he heard Joanna ask.

"I do," he replied.

"Well, you must hurry, then."

"Do you mind if I leave my bag with you, Lady Joanna? It would only slow me down."

"Your belongings are safe with me, Mummius."

He took her hands and brought them to his face and kissed them fervently. He departed with Joanna watching his march along the sandy beach, aimed for the Sennabris road.

The vast human train bound for Magdala had stopped for the midday meal. A little way off from the crowd, Mary and Demetria found a tranquil spot near the water's edge where soft moss grew. Demetria took off her sandals and sank her feet into the velvety green carpet. Amused, Mary did the same.

"Tell me, Demetria, what has been happening in Magdala?"

"Rachel has an admirer."

"That is indeed happy news!"

"She spends every waking moment with him."

"Oh, my dear, that does not leave much time for you, does it?"

Demetria's fear, desperate for expression, pushed up from its hiding place. "Is Mummius coming home, Mistress?"

"Is he important to you?"

Color rose on Demetria's cheeks and her eyes lit up, more blue than ever.

"I like him," she said. "Most of the time."

The sound of the lapping sea blew into shore on an eastern breeze sending Mary's thoughts to the road before her, a road that would take her away from Magdala, leaving Demetria behind again. She studied the girl's eager, earnest face.

"Well then, daughter of mine," she said, "we must convince him to come home. Indeed we need Mummius to come home."

EPILOGUE

It happened in a garden—an event a mortal being does not forget—the heavy sweep of angel wings at close range. That one time, and no other, the angel came to the garden, and Mary was the only one to see him.

The garden is a burial ground like any other: round stones, massive wheels, rolled across the entrance to the graves and, within each one, its corpse. Human remains in various stages of decay, swathed in linen, large white shrouds for the bodies, smaller ones to wrap the heads in. Everything dead and unclean.

In the early morning hours, solemnly on the path, comes a woman with an alabaster jar. Silent and determined, she leads three others who cannot keep their tears at bay.

After two sleepless nights, they have walked several miles to get here and are tired. They sit down on a stone wall to rest. The woman in the lead kicks her heels softly against the wall. She pities her companions who cry and sob, so she tells them to stay awhile. She will search for the tomb they seek. The garden is unfamiliar to them and, in the confusion of tombs, they cannot make sense of where to go.

She goes on alone. And then, all at once, she isn't. Before the opening of a tomb just beyond, a white light shines. Within the light a man, or what seems to be a man, and is not. Too tall, too insubstantial, too bright. She sees why. Wild, enormous wings spread out from behind him and then fold back down into place with a quiver. Like a massive swan drying his feathers in the sun.

He speaks. "Whom do you seek?" And the sound of his voice rolls through the garden, pulsing even the rocks.

She, too, vibrates with the earth and almost loses her footing. She is here to anoint the body of Jesus of Nazareth, buried three days ago; she is looking in the wrong place; she will not find the living among the dead.

She takes up a vigil near the empty tomb, helpless, for where else can she go now, deserted by Jesus?

The gardener appears. "Why are you weeping?" he asks. She begs to be told where Jesus' body has been taken. And then a miracle—the beloved voice. "Mary!" Her relief is so profound that she thinks she might die of it when at last she breathes out, "Rabbouni."

"Mary," he says, "will you go and tell them? Will you be my witness?"

Mary knew what he wanted her to do. She would be the first to proclaim it: he lives!

She proclaimed it to the disciples. He lives!

She proclaimed it to Mummius who wrote it in a gospel, which he buried in the sands of Egypt.

She proclaimed it to Demetria, who wove it into the mystical instruction that Mummius passed on to her.

She proclaimed it to the faithful in homes where they gathered for prayer.

She proclaimed it to Marcus Quintius who brought her, finally, to Rome.

She proclaimed it to Tiberius and gave him an egg, a symbol of new life, saying: 'Christ is risen!' The emperor responded that no one could rise from the dead, any more than the egg she held could turn from white to red. A rumor spread through gossip-hungry Rome that the egg immediately began to turn bright red in testimony of her declaration. He lives!

She proclaimed it to everyone she met, in every time and place; she proclaimed it till the day she died. He lives!

FINIS

3280303R00269

Made in the USA
San Bernardino, CA
22 July 2013